# I-STATE LINES

## CHARLES HUGH SMITH

THE PERMANENT PRESS
Sag Harbor, NY 11963

Copyright © 2006 by Charles Hugh Smith.

*Library of Congress Cataloging-in-Publication Data*

Smith, Charles Hugh, 1953–
    I-state lines / Charles Hugh Smith.
        p.    cm.
    ISBN 1-57962-127-9 (alk. paper)
    I. Title..

PS3619.M559I18 2006
813'.6–dc22                                                    2005056494

Printed in The United States of America.

For:

*Arrol Gellner*
who read it first

and my friends from youth:

*Jim Erler*
(since Huntington Intermediate)


*Gary Baker*
(since Punahou School)


*Steve Toma*
(since University of Hawaii)

# Acknowledgements

The book could not have been written without the unknowing contributions of all my friends:

Mike Dakota
Vic Pataca
Krishna Addagiri
Bamrung Khamhaengwong
Fred Roster
Gayland Baker

my brother Craig (*naturellement*)
Colbert Matsumoto, my co-editor of the *Cop-Out* underground newspaper and our advisor, Burk Bagley
The 1969–70 Lanai High School Pine Lads Basketball Team and coach Matsui

The A.F.S.C. gang:
Jeff, Ian, Dexter, Colin, and all the other dedicated souls

The Island Trends gang:
Denny, Bill, Edaniel, Frank, Craig, Dave,
Bruce, Mike, Sam, and the rest of the crew

The People's Party Triumvirate:
Jeff Blair, Dexter Cate, and Ken Ellingwood

The Maka'ainana gang:
Mike T., Don and his Dad, Brad, Billy, Frank (again),
Thumbs McGregor, The Hobbit, Tony, Paul, et al.

The Kipahele Street Garage / Bunker Band
Gayland, Kirk, Wade, Steve, and Richard and Joe

The O.B.C. / Building Education Center gang:
Syd, Michael, Skip, Glen, Barry, Chuck, Tony, Jim, and all
the teachers

in Berkeley:
Joe, Bob, Steve, Koichi, Hisao, Kazu, Yasu, Taka, Carlos, Facundo,
Zubin, Atsushi, Wade, Roland, Gary, Andy, J.B., Ken, Juan, and
all the guys who have shared the corner of Channing and Milvia

And Misato, for the photo of herself

# CHAPTER ONE

Alex says it's me, but it's him. It's got to be him, because this kind of weird griff never happens when I'm alone.

Take our bus ride from Kansas City. It should have been the snooziest cruise in the universe to get to Alex's uncle's farm in Liberty. But no, everybody else on the bus makes it to Iowa except us. Why? Alex.

He blames me because I'm the one who bought Old Man Ching's Dodge, but the Lancer only died because it got sick of Alex bitching about it. It had been running ragged ever since the New Mexico border, and on this melt-lead morning in K.C. it coughs like an old man who's just sucked his last cig and goes four paws to the sky.

Alex swears and pumps the gas but it's adiosed, and he barely gets us off the I-State. We coast down the off-ramp, make it through the intersection just as the light turns red, and roll to a stop in front of a boarded-up supermarket.

Alex turns off the ignition and stares straight ahead. Then he sits back and closes his eyes, and I can see he's making an effort, but he can't quite damp it down.

He slams his big fist on the dash and flames up on me, the usual about what a nuclear-waste catfish the Lancer is, the ugliest car ever, what a piece of crap, and now we're stuck, bruddah, really stuck.

When Alex gets bent he slips into his Hawaiian pidgin. That usually makes me forget his bad mood, but I've heard this speech so many times it takes all my willpower not to launch a major loco-moco myself.

It's bake-brain city, not a puff of breeze, and we just sit there sweating because we both know this could be the end. We're only heading to New York because his cousin Tita just got married and he hadn't seen her in years. Even so, it was damn depressing to end it in K.C., after all the work we've put in the Lancer and all the big plans we'd made.

I let Alex click down and after a while we get out, pop the hood and try the easy fixes—wiggle the spark plug wires, clean the distributor, tap on the carb, chant the humba-humba—but nothing helps. There isn't much to say; we both know the engine needs major surgery, and that we don't have the gitas to pay for it.

We're breathing the hot-oil smell of the engine, listening to it creak as it cools, when Alex comes up with a plan. One of his father's uncles runs a farm in Iowa; Alex is obligated to visit at some point during our cross-country gig, so we might as well do it now. We can call L.A. and borrow enough money from our parents to fix the Lancer. Alex figures we can probably get close to the farm by bus.

By some miracle the dangling pay phone in front of the dead market works—our cell phone never made it out of Las Vegas alive, thanks to Alex accidentally crunching it under the Lancer— and I get the bus info and directions to the station. I'm worried about leaving our Cruiser in this hollowed-out block, but we've got no choice. I leave a note on the windshield that says, "Car dead, be back soon to fix, please don't tow," and hope that helps. Then we grab our day packs and the presents for his cousin Tita, lock the car, and head for the bus station.

It takes a half-hour to walk there, and my T-shirt is soaked and sticking to my back in the first two minutes. Alex peels off his tanktop, the holey white one with the green Hawaiian elf sleeping under a rainbow, and lopes along like la-di-da. The heat doesn't bother him, but I'm dying. I can't complain, of course, because it's all my fault we bought the Lancer.

SoCal is plenty hot, I mean it's all womp-rat desert, but this is the first time I've felt a sidewalk putting out invisible steam, and seen the slices of sky between old bars and closed-up shops filled with a bright, light-hot blue like in a dream. They either forgot to plant any trees, or chopped them all down, because there's nothing to shade the liquor store steps or the alleyways. In this heat, the only smells are piss and Pine-Sol.

The station hasn't been painted since I was born, and it's in the part of downtown that hit its last three-pointer forty years ago.

8

We push through the glass doors into the cool air inside and look around.

It's big and old and almost empty, like a set for some black-and-white movie about small-time grifters who drink gin. It smells like Ms. Minny's classroom back in the third grade after Tony Nguyen rorked up his tuna surprise, and it looks like the circus is leaving town because everybody's got that tired look of old crumpled newspapers.

We walk up to the grubby window, buy our tickets from a sweaty fat woman, and then go over to the greasy pay phones so Alex can tell his relatives we're coming in.

He hangs up, nods once to let me know everything is set, and we take a seat against the back wall. The only other people waiting in the rows of cracked pink plastic chairs are a shaved-head grunt who looks like he just got out of boot camp and an old man who isn't sweating, even though he's wearing a black suit and one of those hats with fishing flies stuck in the band. I try to shift my feet, but the floor is so sticky from spilled sodas I can barely peel my shoes off the old linoleum.

Alex is like a pressure cooker with the heat turned off. He's got this just-sucked-kumquat face, and even though he's just sitting there with his hundred-pushups-a-day arms folded, his eyes have this metal-sparky look that I try to stay away from. He told me he hated having to ride the bus in Honolulu, but the main reason he's torqued is the Lancer. He always thought my obsession with getting it from Old Man Ching was loopy; he wanted a Mustang or a Malibu. But he went along with me, and now we're stuck, bruddah, really stuck.

Just to get away from his mood I go over to the drinking fountain, but the dribble coming out is warm and tastes almost as bad as L.A. water. While I'm avoiding Alex, an old lady with her hair tied up in a tight little grey bun sits down next to a cute Af-Am mother with a sleepy baby and starts talking with the mom.

I'm starting to think about everything in the Lancer that I wish I'd stuffed into my pack when our bus finally comes in. After spocking the station I'm surprised the bus is clean and air-conditioned and smells better than the inside of a cattle-car 737 at the L.A. airport. You know what I mean, that air coming out of those nozzles feels cool, but it's already been breathed ten times that day.

These I-State buses are pretty much King Tut; Alex lets me have the window seat, and I figure we're as high as an eighteen-wheeler cab. The seats are big, not like those crappy ones on airplanes, so you can actually stretch out. You get a real window, too, not some little plexiglass salad plate that's so scratched you can't even see outside.

Once we sit down I figure I'm safe, Alex can stew all he wants, but we're on our way again whether he likes it or not.

I should know better, but then Alex looks so damned innocent that he fools even me. Grandmas see his easy white-teeth grin and they can't resist saying, "What a nice young man!" Then he slouches a little so he doesn't seem too cocky and looks down with this aw-shucks expression. It's enough to make you puke, and it happens all the time. Sometimes you want to punch him, but then getting turned into a pretzel just isn't worth it.

The old lady with the gray-hair bun boards and sure enough, she takes one look at Alex and smiles. He's got this serious look, but he beams back at her with his patented beachboy grin and even though I feel like gagging I'm relieved his mood is more beach and less volcano.

The real freeze is that these same ladies take one look at me and figure I'm some kind of bargain-rack hoodlum. Me, who's actually the nice one. It's not that I got my father's skin; Alex gets even darker than me once he's been in the sun a few days. Sure, I got stuck with the wimpy body while he got the athletic-god bod, but not everyone who's short and skinny looks like a grifter. I guess it's my face, but I don't know why. My father's no movie star, but everyone thinks he's a nice guy, so why me, Lord? Alex says I have this wise-ass expression even when I'm asleep, but that's a hack. I'm probably smiling because I'm having a good dream.

Meanwhile, Alex drops chaos wherever he goes, and in between explosions grandmas smile at him and give me the glare-dagger. But don't get me wrong, I'm not complaining. It could be a lot worse. Alex could be an enemy instead of my friend.

An overweight blind woman in a bright orange muu-muu gets on board after the grandma. She's holding a white cane and towing a scarecrow boy about nine with hair like old hay and a stained T-shirt that's two sizes too small. The woman pauses and seems to scan the bus with her looking-at-you-but-not-looking-at-you eyes.

She says, "Driver, can you help me to a seat?" The driver's watery-blue bug-eyes worry me a little because he looks like he's living on No-Doz, but he guides her to one of the first rows of seats and the kid jumps in by the window.

We pull out of the station and I start to relax. Maybe this detour will work out okay. We'll be in Iowa by early evening, maybe it won't be hellhole hot anymore, and at least we'll be staying on a real farm.

We get on I-State 35 North, and after a while we've left the city behind and it's open country again. I lean my seat back and watch the hot, faded blue-jeans sky outside creep past the deep blue seat cover in front of me, and my eyes start sagging closed. I've almost dozed off when the blind lady's raspy voice jerks me awake. "Joseph, you got your butt planted on a seat?"

The thatch-haired kid is wandering up the aisle, staring at people, and he doesn't answer. I turn around and see the brat make a weird face at the old man in the black suit and fishing hat. Then he leans over the young mother in the next row and pokes her baby in the cheek. The baby starts crying its guts out and the brat makes another gargoyle face. Meanwhile, the blind lady goes right on jawjacking with some woman across from her. I hear the woman ask the blind lady something, who answers, "How'd I get a kid? Just like you did—in the dark," and then she cackles this wheezy laugh that's right out of a bad horror movie.

The kid sprints down the aisle from the back of the bus to where we're sitting. He doesn't say anything to Alex, but he asks the old lady behind us if he can have some gum. The lady says, "I'm sorry, dear, I don't have any gum." The kid brays like a hyena on laughing gas and I'm starting to get a little irritated.

People are muttering about the brat and I glance over at Alex. His arms are still folded, but there's this metallic shine in his eyes that makes me knot up inside.

The blind hag finally notices her kid's still M.I.A. because she interrupts her motormouthing long enough to call out, "Joseph, get your butt down here," and then goes right on cackling and jawing.

11

The brat ignores her and asks the young Army grunt in front of us if he can play his radio. The guy says it's not allowed and the kid swears at him and starts jumping up and down, making ickabod grunts and hoots.

The brat is running past us when Alex's hand whips out like a bolt of thick brown lightning and grabs his arm. "Hey, you hear your mawdah?" he says to the brat, holding him. Alex is toggled to pidgin, a bad sign. He nods toward the front of the bus and tells the kid, "Go sit down."

The kid struggles to free himself and says, "Let go, asshole."

This is just about the most unwise word selection possible and Alex squeezes the brat's upper arm really tight. The kid squawks and the mother finally pays some attention to him. She spins around and shouts, "Joseph? What's wrong?"

The kid cranks up some fake whimpering and cries, "This asshole's hurting me!"

Alex didn't really hurt the brat, but he lets go and says, "I was only trying to help you with your brat, lady!"

The blind hag hefts herself out of her seat and starts creeping back toward us, bracing herself on the seat backs. In a voice mean enough to melt lead she screams, "Which son-of-a-bitch said that?"

The kid runs to his mom and shoves his crying up to full RPM. She's looking around with her cat's-eye marble eyes, everyone's quiet, and I feel the bottom fall out of my stomach.

"Somebody should control the boy," the old lady behind us says angrily. I see the driver's black Ray-Ban shades in the rearview mirror and the bus nearly swerves off the road.

"Driver, call the cops," she yells. "Some son-of-a-bitch hurt my Joseph."

"Alright, everybody back to your seats," the driver shouts, and he romps so hard on the brakes the blind hag is almost tossed on her face.

The driver yanks the bus onto the gravel shoulder, and everyone is staring and talking. The driver takes off his shades and says, "Lady, go back to your seat." His voice is as tired as his bulging eyes, but he's not taking any griff on his bus.

"Some son-of-a-bitch hurt my boy," the hag says in a blowtorch wheeze.

12

"Lady, get back to your seat or I'll put you off the bus," the driver says, and the hag and her brat grudgingly shuffle to their seats.

The driver walks back to us and his eyes are almost out of his skull. "Okay, guys, off my bus."

"The kid was—" I say, but he cuts me off and says, "You want me to call the cops?"

I shake my head and stand up. Alex is sitting like a statue, staring a hole in the seat back in front of him.

"The young man is right," the old lady behind us tells the driver. "That child should have been controlled." In a voice loud enough for everyone to hear, she snaps out, "Some people aren't fit to be parents."

The blind hag hears this and jerks to her feet. "You saying a blind woman shouldn't be a parent? Some people!"

The old woman stands up and her gray bun is quivering in a full meltdown. "I didn't say a blind person shouldn't be a parent. I said *you* aren't a fit parent. Letting your child run wild like that! You ought to be ashamed of yourself!"

"Lady—" the blind hag is breathing heavily from the effort of standing up, and tugging at the front of her orange muu-muu—"Fuck off." Then she says to the rest of the bus, "Does anybody else think blind people shouldn't have kids?"

"Being blind's got nothing to do with it," yells the old man in the black suit. "You shouldn't let your kid run all over the place."

Right away, both the young mother and the grunt on leave say something in favor of the old man.

The blind lady listens to this in disbelief and then shouts, "Joseph, stay away from these assholes. They think they're better than blind people."

"Lady, give it a break," the old guy in the back shouts in disgust. The brat is silent and keeps his eyes on the floor.

"Okay, folks, that's enough," the driver yells. "Lady," he says to the blind woman, "sit down or you can get off, too."

She sits down with a grunt and mumbles like a sailor on a Tequila drunk about getting off just to get away from these assholes.

Alex finally stands up and we follow the driver to the front.

"It's not right, putting them off the bus," the old woman behind us says, and her voice is vibrating with old-time-religion outrage. The driver just puts on his Ray-Bans and follows us through the doors and down onto the asphalt edge of the parking lot.

He opens the luggage compartment, we pull out our bags and he locks the steel door again. "Sorry boys," he says. "It's the rules." He tears two coupons off a book and hands them to us. "You can get a refund with these."

He climbs back on the bus and the door whooshes closed. The passengers give us thumbs-up signs through the windows and then the bus rumbles off, leaving us alongside the corn fields, our hair whipping in the tailwind of the cars and big-rigs blasting by.

I want to say something booga-booga to Alex, but it's not worth the effort. We stand there in the hot blue afternoon sun, watching the young corn tassels swaying in the I-State breezes, and eventually Alex says, almost to himself, "If only we had a normal car."

I want to say, Alex, we're not normal, so just forget it, but then he already knows that.

Instead I sprint across the lanes of hot I-State pavement and start trying to hitch a ride back to Kansas City.

# CHAPTER TWO

But griff isn't unusual for Alex. It's normal. One day we went up to Venice, to check the pulse and girl-watch, and a water balloon hits Alex in the back. He spins around, ready to cast a victim for a "ten fingers of death" kung fu classic, but there's no sign of anybody with water balloons. Where did the balloon come from? Who knows? Why did they pick out Alex? See what I mean? It's him. He swears it's me, but it's him. It's got to be him.

Alex hates riding buses. It's for old people, he says, and school kids and poor people. That's who ride buses in Honolulu. Nobody who owns a car rides the bus. Mambo old men who were born old ride the bus. I think it's a triple seven; every once in a while I like to ride the bus. You've just got to be in the mood.

Riding the city buses is definitely fricative. You wonder, Where did they dig up all these mambo people? One time we're on a bus in San Francisco, the Cruiser's over in Berkeley, and there's this white guy talking to himself about injunctions and plaintiffs, stuff like that. Is this what happens when you fail law school? You ride the buses and talk to yourself about torts? Maybe the guy went gravitational on *Perry Mason* reruns, who knows.

I look at the city bus drivers, lots of them women, and I feel sorry for them. Every day they haul around people with some major burr up their butt, poor people whose lives are so loaded with problems that you wonder why they don't just jump off the bridge. You look in their eyes and it's the eyes of the hunted. Tired eyes, like they just drove across country without stopping.

Of course nothing's as good as having your own transpo, hearing a good tune on the dial and blowing past all the bunk boxes around you. And nothing's as spiked as when your transpo's feet are in the air.

There's no worse feeling than trying to fix a car that won't let itself be fixed, that's fighting you every step of the way. Your

15

knuckles are bleeding through the old grease, you've checked everything possible, you've talked nice to it the whole time, and it still won't turn over. You just want to kill it, drive it off a cliff and laugh when it explodes.

It's not always the transpo's fault. We're chugging up a hill in Iowa in our replacement car, a light-blue Falcon, a virtually indestructible vehicle, you understand, but it starts gagging like a fat guy on a big piece of steak. Stutter-stepping like some wizard roundball guard. Now grip this. This is the Midwest, right? It's flatter than a K-Mart parking lot for hundreds of miles. And we're going up a hill! Just a rise, really, but now the car is really acting up, missing, wheezing, catching, sidestepping, dying, then catching again.

I'm driving, and I'm jumping up and down in the torn driver's seat—it's torn because some old fat guy must have driven it three hundred thousand miles doing a Willy Loman number because there's a big crater in the middle. The springs are sticking out of the straw or whatever they used in those days to pad the springs, there is a big-butt rip in the seat cover that we filled with one of Alex's old T-shirts and I'm jumping up and down, praying and banging the steering wheel, "Oh please God, don't let this dog-meat piece of crap die, come on baby, you can do it, come on, keep it alive," and the Falcon staggers on, we're almost to the top of this rise, the only one in four states, and then it gasps and we lose pulse.

"NO!" I shout. And Alex is laughing, but not too much because he can see that I'm bent, and he says, "Daz, it can't hear you. Talk to it all you want, but you can't talk it up this hill. We've got to push it."

"Push it?" I scream. "This isn't a Toyota, this is a real machine! This thing weighs! It'll roll right over us like we're jackrabbits!"

We get out, look under the hood, can't see anything wrong, but it's terminal. Alex starts doing his kung fu stretching exercises which I always feel is just for show, so I say, "Cut the griff, there's no girls around," and he says back, "Hey, if you strain your groin pushing this car up this hill"—although I can't say it with his Hawaiian lilt, his little sing-song way of saying something when he wants to talk to you like you're three years old and stupid even for a three-year-old—"then you're going to think there's a red-hot stake in your balls." His imagery is pretty graphic, so I bend over

16

and swing my arms around, doing the same half-assed warmup routine I used to do in gym class.

We grunt it up the hill, a few yards at a time, stop, rest, the car starts rolling back, with Alex yelling, "Daz, get your brown ass in gear!," and push again. Then when we get it to the top, it starts right up.

Condensation in the carb, Alex says. Yah. I know the car is torqueing us, because it's been so good to us until now. It burns about a quart of oil for every one hundred miles. We'd have been busted for smog in L.A. in four seconds—but what the hell, it runs solid.

We got it for $200 in Kansas City. We knew the Cruiser needed an overhaul and we didn't have the gitas for that. We'd tried the bus and been fragged off so we decided to buy a beater vehicle, get to Iowa, borrow some money, come back and get the Cruiser fixed. We'd have been better off just getting a job and making a few hun to get it over with, but we didn't feel like working at that point.

You know how many hollowed-out blocks there are in Kansas City? Old wrecks with guys hanging around, decaying just like the houses. We look in the paper, but you know nobody spends money on an ad to sell an old beater, so we take a bus downtown and just start wandering, it's the John Muir Trail of the Damned, until we find this old junkyard.

There's so much old rubbish in this empty lot, we can't believe it's a business. Who would want any of these broken-down desks, radiators, sagging shelves, ancient radios, and old rusted chunks of iron? There are cars all over, cars in the street, cars back in the lot, most of them with grass growing out the doors already. A tinny radio is tuned to some oldies station, Nat King Cole, that kind of mambo sound, so I know there's an old guy around somewhere. My legs are tired, we're lost, I'm depressed by the neighborhood and our go-nowhere bus ride, and here we are in a bottomed-out junkyard looking for a car.

This old Af-Am guy comes out of the piles of junk and asks us what we're looking for. He's polite but suspicious. "A cheap car," I tell him. "We got two hundred dollars and we need a car." He thinks on that for a while and finally says that he don't have too many cars that are in running shape. I feel like saying, so does the bear make poo in the woods, Jack? These cars are sad, I'm telling you. But he's still thinking about something, so we just stand there waiting for the thought to come out like a slug out of an old tin can.

"There's a car up the street," he finally says. "Runs good. The owner might let it go for two hundred." I'm so naive I think, oh, good. Alex is like the inside of a church on Thursday, he lets me do the talking most of the time, and then criticizes me after the deal goes vertical. "How come you didn't say this or that?" he says. "Hey, you do the talking next time," I tell him, and he always says, "Okay, I will," and then he never does. I don't push him. Not worth it.

So the old guy tells us to wait here and he strolls up the street. We wander around looking at all the stuff, we're talking major katakana, like a set of cards from some Las Vegas hotel in a plastic case on top of the seat of a broken plastic riding toy, with a 50's-looking lamp that's ugly enough to melt wax plunked down by the front wheel. Alex holds up an old set of bongos with no skins and says, "Hey bruddah, this is great." I pick up a Buick hubcap and say, "We should start a hubcap collection—no, a hubcap museum. In Vegas. Definitely Vegas."

So the old guy comes back, the wheeler-dealer in him in high gear now, and he says the guy wants 250. I say, "We gotta look at the vehicle." So we motate up the hot pavement, past the kids crying and the kids playing, past the weeds and the Colt .45 bottles sticking their necks out of little crumpled paper bags, and turn into a driveway.

There it is, an old light-blue Ford Falcon, maybe a '63 or '64. My heart starts pumping. A Falcon! I mean, this is a classic! This guy comes out of a broken screen door, and he's hard, maybe six feet but solid, smoking a no-filter Camel nicsplif, with a what-the-hell-do-you-want expression on his face. He looks us over with a quick glance and waits for the old man to start his part of the scene. "These young men are looking for a car," the old man says. I hate to even meet the hard guy's eyes, but they're softer than I expect.

I get the feeling he wants to know what we're doing here, so I tell him the whole story: we're from California going to points east, our car broke down, it needs an overhaul, but we can't afford one, so we need a cheap car that will get us at least to Iowa. The mean-looking guy drinks this in like it was liquid and then turns away to exhale the Camel smoke. I start telling him how we're going to borrow some money from relatives and come back and fix our car when I realize I'm babbling. I just trail off in mid-sentence and nobody says anything. The hard guy crushes the life out of the butt on the cracked asphalt and then he walks back into his leaning, peeling old garage. I look over at Alex and he just shrugs.

The hard guy comes out again with a battery. He props open the hood with a stick and puts the battery in. It sparks a little when he's putting on the cables so I know it's good. He yanks open the driver's door and sits down, making himself comfortable like it's a sofa. The key is already in the ignition, so he turns it over and the engine grinds some as huge black and blue clouds of smoke pour out of the tailpipe, and then it catches. It sounds like it's running on three cylinders, but he revs it, chokes it, plays with it, and eventually it evens out. The muffler's shot, the tick-tick-ticking of the tappets is louder than it should be, but I like the old piece of junk.

Mr. Hard-Ass is sitting in the car very comfortably, holding the wheel with one hand, and I get the feeling that he likes this car, maybe had good times in it, and I feel kind of sad.

I'll tell you why the Falcon spiked us that day in Iowa. It was annoyed, and rightly so, because Alex had drag-raced it. Stupid, right? I can't put all the blame on him; I was sitting there laughing my ass off the whole time.

We had a six-pack of brewkowskis in the cooler. We don't drink and drive—we aren't stupid—but that afternoon was hot and we felt like having a beer with lunch.

So we stop in at a local choke-and-puke, grind down some burgers, and we're ready to vector when we notice these guys next to us in an old small-window VW Bug. It's basically down the road already, but somebody was trying to fix it up a little. The driver is revving up the engine, like he's trying to clear the plugs. So Alex gets a wild hair up his ass and revs up the Falcon. Not just once, like a warm-up, but repeatedly, like a challenge. I think it started out as a joke, like yah, check out our piece of scrap, but the other guy revs back and Alex can't refuse.

I should have seen heavy jank on the horizon. Once Alex moves, look out. If he's asleep, you're safe. Otherwise, forget it. So Alex rolls down the window and exchanges a few words with the guy: "Hey, wanna show us what you got?" "You kidding?" "No, show us." "Okay."

So we follow them out to a paved farm road that's straight as an elephant's dick. I'm slightly warped, two BKs down and a third one open between my knees, and I'm saying, "Alex, I don't know about this." I've never been in a drag race before and I'm worried about dying on this godforsaken piece of road, James Dean style.

What a nominal memorial Dean has, I'm telling you. Some Japanese guy paid for it. It's up in nowheresville, between Hellay and the Bay. It's this strat chrome sculpture that looks like it ran away from a museum and somehow made it to the hot dusty wide spot in the road where the Dean-Man finally connected the dots.

Anyway, I've got the h.j.'s because Alex isn't the most cautious driver and our Falcon might not hold up so well past fifty-five. But Alex has made up his mind; he's saying, "Bruddah, is this a machine or what? Is some piece of Kraut crap going to run us down?" Then I know he's at least seven-eighths to the pink because I know he loves old Vee-Dubs. When he's not looking I make a sign of the cross. It would make my mom happier if she knew I died clean.

So the guy revs his engine and suddenly drops his arm to start the race. He gets a jump on us; it's cheating but nobody gives a damn at this point. Our Falcon is automatic-systematic all the way, so Alex has his huge paw on the thin little "drive one, drive two" auto-shift lever. He crams his size twelve to the floor and the Falcon is giving us its best shot. We're gaining on the guy in the bug just as he shifts into third.

That puts him out ahead because third is the Bug's best gear, but the Falcon is a tank; it's gaining momentum like a 747 taking off. The road is dog meat, our soft springs are sloshing up and down, and then Alex gets us into "drive two." I think the tranny has just gone vertical because there's this pause where nothing happens and then it suddenly catches. Both vehicles are at full wind-out, but because the Falcon has the weight it's still accelerating. The bug hits fourth, but that isn't do-wa-diddly in a bug for acceleration and we are definitely gaining on it.

I'm pushing against the cracked dash, ("Come on, you dog, keep going."), and Alex looks like he's trying to push the gas pedal through the firewall onto the pavement. What a glorious moment when we steam past the bug!

I look at the speedo and the poor thing is between ninety and a clean hun. Does Alex ease off? No, he wants complete and total victory, so he keeps his foot on the gas until I feel the lug nuts vibrating off the hubs and the pistons straining to jerk through the hood and the whole vehicle is shaking itself into parts. I finally have to yell at him. He eases off and the fields are in slow motion again and death gives us another reprieve. Fricking Alex. He attracts it like flies on fertilizer.

So we pull over and the other guys come alongside. I'm afraid Alex will lord it over them, but he's beach to my relief, praises their machine, admits they beat us in the quarter mile, and we offer to buy them some brewkowskis. Naturally, we end up warped and lost. Total and complete misery.

And the car was torqued, too. You laugh, but cars do have souls. Some will hang in for you long after they should have bought the yard. This one was willing to be good to us, but what do we do? We drive it a hundred miles an hour! Who wouldn't be annoyed? So that's why it died on that Iowa hill. It was paying us back for hacking it. Once we'd suffered a little, it forgave us and started right up again.

That car did all right by us. I'm not spinning you. It never really broke down, I mean ass-kicking broke down. Here's the really weird thing—we drove it back to Kansas City and sold it back to the same hard-ass for only twenty less than we paid for it! And he was happy to see it again, too. Who says life isn't strange?

The guy was so pleased with the deal that he gave us a King Tut splif. Alex has this superior attitude about herb; it's always Hawaiian is "da best" and everything else is dried horsepoo. So he takes a puff of this and I expect the usual skag, but instead he kind of concentrates, like hey, wait a minute here, and he takes a short second toke before passing it over and swirls it around his mouth like it was fine wine.

Alex says, "This is Hawaiian weed, bruddah," and Mr. Hard-ass says, "So right." Alex is getting a little excited, saying, "I think this is Puna Butter, from the Big Island," and the man is grudgingly respectful, saying, "Right again, that's what they call it." So

21

I say, "Oh wow, man, you win a free subscription to *High Times*."
But Alex ignores me and pretends to savor this wonderful weed.
Alex. Sometimes he's so frustrating you'd like to punch him out
except that then he might shred you.

The great thing about both the Lancer and the Falcon is the
full front seat. All these German and Japanese transpos have
bucket seats. You can't sleep on them. I read somewhere that Volkswagen was trying to track down the four hundred people who
had been born in Vee-Dubs in the past thirty years, and I thought,
man, I hope the mother gets lifetime chiropractic care. They must
mean the microbuses because having a baby in a bug would be
totally loopy.

The article also said that VW regretted not being able to track
down everyone conceived in a VW. Now that could be a hell of a
lot of people in the buses, but I think somebody should give an
award to everyone conceived in a bug. Or maybe an award to the
parents. You'd have to be midgets, contortionists, or mighty quick
on the draw to do it in a bug.

So the good thing about these old American vehicles is the full
front seat. When you've both got to sleep in the car, and you have
to rotate between the back and front seats, you come to appreciate
that nice roomy seat and the column shift. Sure, your legs still
cramp up and the windows get foggy and the earthquakes from big
rigs rumbling by wake you up, but at least you won't impale yourself on the stick shift. How'd he die? Oh, he turned over in his
sleep and it got him right through the heart, poor bastard. Or be
awake in the middle of the night trying to stuff a T-shirt into the
crack between the seats so you can finally, finally get to sleep.
Meanwhile, you want to kill the clown snoring comfortably in the
back. Jerk! Why should he get to sleep when I get this torture rack?

# CHAPTER THREE

After awhile, you run out of conversation on those long stretches in the open states. You just stare off into the distance and start thinking things, maybe a bad memory or how something should have gone. You say something and the other guy just says, "Yeah," like, sorry pal, I'm bored out of my mind and too tired to talk. Other times, you want to talk but there's nothing to talk about. You try to make something up, like "Remember the time we got ozoned and. . . ?" or "Hey, what're we gonna do when we get to. . . ?"

But all the good stories and all the good plans have already been talked about by New Mexico, so you talk about things you see. "Hey, look at that tumbleweed." "Sure is lonely looking out there." "Six big-rigs in a row—a new record." "Look, a rig with Vermont plates. Didn't know they had any up there." It's not much of a conversation, the other guy just nods or mumbles, "Yeah."

We developed a few things to ease the boredom, but even they didn't always work. One was trying to cross the lane dividers without hitting any. You know the lines of little white bumps that separate the lanes? It looks pretty duck-soup to just ease over into the next lane and not hit any, but it's harder than you think. One time I slipped through by accident and then bragged about it. Of course Alex figured that anything I could do, he could do better, but it turned out to be harder than he thought, so it became a game. After a while we got pretty good, so the challenge became to make a smooth four-wheel transition.

At first, we did one wheel and then the other, but that was too easy. So it got to be like the Olympics. Was it a smooth and nectar 10, or was it flawed? Correcting in the middle lowers your score. Sometimes we got pretty bent, like, "That was a ten." "No way, bruddah, you jerked." "Hey, spin it, it was perfect." You have to be careful, because there's no escape in a car. If you're torqued at the other guy, it totally stones the whole day.

One time we stopped for gas in a small town. Alex is driving; we'd gotten mad over some minor hack, and I go to the head to take a leak. When I come out the car is gone. I ask the pump jockey what happened to my car, and the guy says, "Your buddy drove off." For a second I'm really torqued. I want to kill that Hawaiian, but then I know he's just jerking me.

Now I could mess with him and disappear, but then he might really get fried and leave me, so I decide to play it beach. I dig some quarters out of my pocket, buy a juice from the usual grimy machine, and just sit on the curb waiting. At first, I'm thinking of some funny lines to say when he drives up, but after a half-hour I'm really smoking.

He finally pulls up with a kind of hidden smirk on his face. I open the door, get in, and say, "Don't pull that griff on me ever again. It isn't amusing. Remember the movie where the guy can't fall asleep because the other guy will kill him and run off with the gold? Just remember, slick, I sleep very lightly. A Mack truck can drive through the room and you just roll over. So don't frag me, okay?" He didn't know what to say and we dropped it.

It's a scary thing, how a bad joke could have blown up the whole trip. Some things you just can't forget. Now I know why people end up clawing each other's faces off—you know, men and women. A few things you can't forget and that's all you remember.

I did get back at Alex for that drive-away stunt, but you have to swear on the holiest of holies not to ever tell him because if you do, then he'll grind me into fertilizer. I'm not spinning you. You've got to swear a blood oath to never tell this story to anyone, okay?

I read that if you take someone who's asleep and you put their hand in warm water, then they piss in their pants, and I wanted to know if it was true. I get into these experimental moods. One time I pressed my own carotid artery until I passed out because I read you could do that. Sounds dangerous, but I'm completely normal. Yah!

Anyway, one night we're in a fleabag motel and I can't sleep. I think it's because we were drinking brewkowskis, and that puts me to sleep right away and then I wake up later in the middle of the night. So I'm laying there thinking about this experiment and I decide, Well, what the hell; let's give it a try on my old snoring buddy. I get up—no problem because Alex sleeps like a mummy, a Hawaiian Rip Van Winkle—and I run the sink water until it's nice and hot and then I take that little plastic ice container they always leave in the room and I fill it with nice warm water. It's the three bears—not too hot, not too cold, just right.

Then I creep over to his bed and start pulling the sheet a little, just slow and easy. I have to get the sheet off of him enough to free his arm. This takes time, because even though I know World War Three wouldn't wake him up, I've still got the heebie-jeebies. If he knew what I was planning, it *would* be World War Three and I'd be the first casualty.

So I ease the sheet off and then I get him to roll over so his arm flops free. I know from experience how to do this, because every so often, maybe every week or so, Alex starts snoring and it sounds like cats screwing. It's awful, so I pinch his nostrils shut and he shifts positions and stops snoring. I was dropping bricks the first time I did this, but I was nearly out of my mind after listening to him for an hour, just hoping and praying he would die in his sleep or whatever it took to stop the snoring.

He claims he doesn't snore, that I was making it up, even though one night I taped it all on our little boom box. I stuck the mike right up against his nose for about five minutes. But when I play it back he insists that I did the snoring myself because it sounds so fake.

By the time I get his hand free, the water's cooled off, so I have to go get hotter water. When I get back he's rolled over again, which really spins me. This time I get hot water and then start to work. I finally free up his arm and gently dip his hand in the water. Damned if it doesn't work! He must have emptied a whole brewkowski into that bed. I got up really quick and made it outside before I started laughing. I knew I had to laugh my ass off now, because if I laughed later and gave away the experiment, I'd die a dog's death.

The next morning he must have got up before I did so I missed the discovery, which is just as well because I doubt if I could have stifled a laugh at that point. He was looking perplexed, throwing the covers over his bed with a totally uncharacteristic show of neatness. "What's up?" I ask him, and he says, "Nothing."

"Do you feel alright?" he asks me, and I say, "Well, I got a splitting headache from that cheap beer. Why?"

He just shakes his head and says something about that beer jerking his body around. From that day forward he never drank that brand of beer again, and warned anybody who did that it was jank and would do weird things to your body. Meanwhile, I have to keep a straight face the whole time and say, "Hey, no kidding, it's horse piss."

Now remember, this is a nominal secret. Even if you spill it I've got total deniability or plausible deniability or whatever the government calls it because I can lie and smile the entire time if my life depends on it. I tell the truth but I'm talking my life here, slick. This is no joke.

You know, this crossing the lines without hitting any of those little bumps is not easy. Try it and you'll find out. It takes real concentration. In New Mexico I'm practicing on an empty stretch of I-state, just weaving back and forth trying to find the right rhythm while Alex is dozing.

I'm really in a groove, hitting three clean four-wheel transitions in a row when all of a sudden I'm jerked right out of my body by this loudspeaker voice saying, "Pull over." I look in the rearview mirror and nearly drop a brick because there's a state trooper right on my bumper in a big Dodge, the kind with a 460 for high-speed chases. I start saying, "Oh man, oh man," and Alex wakes up.

I take my wallet out and put it in my lap and put both my hands on the top of the steering wheel. I learned this from an older cousin of mine who's a cop up north of L.A. He told us one time about walking up to a car he'd just pulled over. He looks through the rear window and sees the guy leaning over like he's pulling something out from under the seat.

So my cousin gets a little nervous because the guy could be going for a roscoe—you know how many fools carry guns under their seats—so he bends way over and sneaks up on the guy and then just whips his .38 against the guy's skull and says, "Drop it, asshole, or you're history." The guy pisses in his pants, I mean really pisses in his pants, because he's holding a beer can, not a gun. He was trying to hide his half-empty beer.

So I do what my cousin told me: no fast moves, stay in the car, hands up high on the steering wheel.

The cop comes up to the window and asks to see my driver's license and registration. It's a blast furnace outside, but this guy is beach; he's moving very deliberately. His shades are telling me he's a badass, but his voice is in neutral, just idling. My heart is racing, but I'm thinking, hey, it's just a warning, don't worry. He spocks that my transpo's from California and I could feel his suspicion. He says, "Just sit tight," and then he goes back to his vehicle. But I'm gripping the scene, Jack, because I know from my cousin that he's checking the computer to see if we have any arrest warrants or tickets. So I relax, because I'm Mr. Clean; I've never gotten a ticket.

So when the cop comes back and says, "Okay son, step out of the car," I nearly piss on my Converses. What's going on? I get out, and now the scene has Alex's full attention. I have a napkin in my shirt pocket from some lard-faced drive-in we'd stopped at, and the cop asks to see what's in my pocket. I take out the folded napkin and give it to him, saying, "It's my napkin from lunch." Maybe he thinks I'm keeping a few spliffs wrapped up in the napkin, who knows.

"You know you were weaving quite a bit," he says. I say, "Yeah, I know, officer, I'm sorry. I was doing it on purpose." I figure I better tell the truth because any lie is going to sound defective. He's looking at me like I just said I was the President of the United States in disguise, and he says, "And what purpose would that be?"

So I say, "I was bored. It was a little game to keep me alert."

"There's better ways to keep awake than weaving all over the road," he says, and I feel like saying hey, no, really? Then he says to Alex, "I'd like you to step outside the car here with your friend, son," and when Alex does, he says, "Now I want you both to place your hands on the hood of your vehicle and just stay put until I tell you otherwise."

It's about a hundred-and-ten in the shade and the hood of the Cruiser is frying pan city. The green paint picks up the heat real good, it's gee Mr. Wizzy, my science project is solar heating of steel out in the New Mexico desert. My hands are really starting to cook, but the cop leisurely frisks us and then goes around to the other side of the car and makes a little search, rummaging through all the junk behind the passenger side.

27

Then he says, "Would you mind showing me the contents of the trunk?" I'm spinning out, my vehicle is being searched like I'm a dealer! I say "No," and Alex gives me his what-the-hell-did-you-get-us-into-this-time-asshole? look.

I vector over and open up the trunk, and I feel ashamed everything's such a mess; our sleeping bags and boxes of food and the ice chest are all covered with Big Mac containers, magazines, old soda and beer cans, a lot of trash. I'm standing there and he says, "Just put your hands back on the hood, son," and he pokes through this traveling garbage dump for a while.

Then he says to me, "Okay, your partner can get back inside. Why don't you slip off your shades?" I realize I can't see his eyes, but he wants to see mine. So I take off my Ray-Bans and he puts his shades real close to my face and stares into my eyes. In that sun my pupils would be tiny anyway, so I don't know what he's looking for.

He asks me to stand on one foot and I get the h.j.'s, thinking oh please don't fall over now! I have this image of me having to ask my dad to bail us out of some hellhole jail. Alex's dad was less than pleased that the cell phone he'd given us was already pancaked, but that was nothing compared to having to post bond to get your kid out of jail. I'm thinking he'll kill me; he'll fricking kill me. But I manage the one-legged flamingo act okay and the cop says I can get back inside.

What's funny is that he doesn't say jank about the drug search. He just leans on the door, with his face and hat and shades inside the Cruiser, and tells me to get out and do a few push-ups to get my oxygen going the next time I feel bored. It's one-oh-nine in the shade, they're performing experiments on melting asphalt, and I'm supposed to jump out and do a dozen. Yeah, my oxygen will really get going, along with my heat prostration. "Yes sir, Officer," I say, "Thank you, thank you," because I'm so grateful that he didn't find Alex's spliffs and I didn't have to go to a hellhole jail with mother rapers and father rapers and God knows what other scumsuckers.

But here's the good part. While we're standing there, trying to just touch the frying pan hood of the Lancer with our fingertips, then our palms, then the side of our palms, and then back to the fingertips, I see a vehicle blow by. This is one scene I will never

28

forget. It's a new minivan filled with the old-style family: Mom, Pop, and the brats. And for one split second, just a flash, I see these brats staring in awe—in awe—of our deep desert bust scene. Here are two guys getting smoked right in front of their eyes; this wasn't some phony bust on TV, this was real life. They couldn't change the channels, and their eyes were wet and wide.

It gives me some satisfaction that my brief moment of infamy had a little moral lesson for passing brats. It can happen to you anywhere, kids, so don't even start. Even the desert isn't safe.

Needless to say, Alex demanded the steering position, and I got to lay down in the back seat and cool off from what almost went vertical.

# CHAPTER FOUR

A couple of big, ugly, white jock types had somehow picked me to spike in junior year. They called me "Haagen Dazs" and whipped towels at my bare butt in the locker room. I didn't have protection from the homeboys because I wasn't in any gang, didn't live in their neighborhood, and hell, don't even know Spanish worth a damn.

I went out a couple of times with some of the wimpy shy ones who were like me, but the older guys were in another location. Their women looked about thirty, the type who would suck you off in the front seat while you're driving, spit it out the window, and then kill the taste with a swig of tequila. They looked, how you Americans say, experienced. And all this jank about guns and drugs and who screwed who and was gonna die a dog's death and cars and cheap beer, sitting around looking tough waiting for something bad to happen—it's not me. These guys see me as white, so they don't feel comfortable with me either. Never mind my dad is old-line *Californio,* a padre here and there but mostly Indian; I speak only English, I'm wimpy, no tattoos, I don't smoke, or listen to their music, I got no girlfriend, never shot anyone—just not a whole hell of a lot in common. Plus my mom is white, the pale Scots-Irish type, and I live in a white neighborhood, so I'm a stranger even if I had looked exactly like them.

So they ignored me and the white jocks called me "Haagen Dazs," as in "ice cream butt," har-de-har. One day I said something back, something wise, and it went unappreciated. They pantsed me on the far end of the field during P.E., and I had to slump over so my gym shirt would cover my dick and kind of shuffle off like a hunchback to the showers.

You get the idea. I was their chosen plaything. After the pantsing I was a total laughingstock. Even my friends were ashamed to be seen with me for a few weeks. And they, I mean the big white guys, kept referring to it in the locker room after that. I tried to ignore it; I mean what else could I do? I knew all my friends were just glad it had happened to me instead of them.

Alex was the new kid in senior year, some guy from Hawaii who kept to himself. He was on the football team, but only the other guys on the team knew who he was, and I guess he never said much to them. I'd spocked him the first day, maybe because I had a feeling about him. He was about the same color as me, bigger of course, because his dad is a tall *haole* guy and his mom is Hawaiian-Chinese. The Hawaiians are not small people, but Alex wasn't big enough to play lineman.

So we're out on the field in between games, the kind of situation I dread. With nothing better to do, these assbites would start jerking somebody around.

Sure enough, these guys start their usual line: "Hey, let's pants the ice cream cone again, see if his dick got any longer." This is still early in the semester, right? Alex is standing there with his arms folded while these numbnuts taunt me.

I put on a grin and try to go along, yeah, ha ha, it won't be much fun, you've already done it before. But that doesn't stop them, even though some of the scholar-jocks are starting to look uncomfortable. One even says, "Why don't you lay off," and the biggest scumbag challenges him to, quote, "Shut up or do something about it," unquote.

I turn to my tall skinny friend, but he's getting scared and puts some space between us. He knows if the conditions are ripe, it will be him that's hobbling off the field trying to cover his nuts instead of me.

This asshole feels a little cocky so he pushes me, maybe to aggravate me, or maybe just to lord over me a little. Alex steps over with his arms still folded and says, "Stop fucking with him."

The scumbag turns to him with a stupid grin and says, "Who the hell are you and why should I care?" Alex says, "If you mess with him then you're messing with me."

This big assbite must weigh at least two hundred because he's six-four or close to it and beefy—he's a shot putter on the track team. He has about thirty pounds and four inches on Alex. He says, "Am I supposed to be scared now?"

31

I turn to Alex and say, "Hey, it's okay," but he's staring intently at this big scumbag.

Nobody's ever seen this assholina get close to a real fight. Alex makes it easy on him. He tells the guy, "You mess with him again and I'll break your ass." Some of the other jock jerks start hooting, because now their friend has his nuts in a wringer. He can forget the macho posturing if he doesn't take Alex right now.

But the big Gorgon isn't totally stupid; he tries to buy some time. He says, "Okay, moke, after school behind the auto body shop." He knows the cops or the principal will stop it, and if not, he'll have all his friends there to make sure he wins. But Alex says, "Not later. Right now." And he walks up to this guy, about three feet away, his arms still folded.

I figure Alex is going to get punched out and humiliated, and all because of me. Now the other guys are really quiet, looking around for the coach, but he's jacking off or talking to the girl's coach or some other slackmaster action.

So the buttwipe is in a real quandary. Finally one of his friends, one of the guys who's always right with him when they're in my face, says, "What Tod, too much for you?"

Now the guy has to do something because of the audience. Thirty guys are watching him melt down. So he acts like he's starting to turn away and then throws a punch at Alex's head, a real wicked punch that would have taken my head off.

But Alex is human lightning. He dodges the fist and then grabs the guy, spins him around, buckles his leg from behind and pushes him down. Then he twists the jerk's arm up behind his back and shoves his face deep into the grass and shouts, "Eat!" The guy is struggling, he keeps turning his head and trying to free his big legs that could press two hundred fifty pounds, but Alex has him pinned like an insect in biology class, Alex is a demon, and he tells the guy he's going to break his arm. Then he jerks it up so hard I figure it broke right then.

The asshole is kind of whimpering, and he finally turns his head into the turf and takes a big bite, just like it was spumoni ice cream instead of grass. Alex twists his arm one more time with a powerful jerk, and I see his muscles rippling under his smooth brown skin like steel cables. Then Alex looks up and spots the big drib's friend, the one who egged him on, and he points to him and says, "You!"

The guy freezes like a big dumb animal who just spocked a cheetah, and then he starts running toward the locker room. Alex is after him in a flash and the scene looks just like "The Wild Kingdom" because Alex is running low and smooth and this other guy is running like a scared ox. Alex catches the big numbnuts, drags him down, and after a brief struggle, the second asshole is tasting his first big bite of grass.

Now here is Alex's genius. I don't know how the guy thought this up. He could have broken their arms, or made their faces look like gargoyles or whatever, but they would still have had some pride. It was a fight, and they lost. But there was no fight. Alex put them down and made them eat dirt. Made them eat dirt, can you grip that? The news spread like wildfire that this crazy moke had stood up for the little half-breed greaser and made the two big proud jocks eat dirt. Eat dirt! You have no pride left, assbites; you have just suffered total and nominal humiliation.

Now the coach comes running up the steps as Alex is crouching on this second jerk's back. The coach is swearing, "Jesus Christ, I was only gone a few minutes," and Alex gets off the guy's back, and slaps, just slaps the back of this guy's head as if to say, remember this well, asshole. You egg your friend on, you suffer the same fate.

The coach grabs Alex by the arm and Alex shakes free. The coach wants to know what the hell is going on and I'm afraid that Alex will make him eat dirt too, so I jump in and say that it's my fault.

The coach seems relieved that there's a simple answer to the who-is-guilty question, and he grabs me by the arm and says, "Okay, what happened?" So I say that these two guys were razzing me, so I flipped them off, and they grabbed me, so Alex stepped in to help. By this time the first big asshole is up and ambling over, with dirt all over his jaw and a look of pain on his face, which doesn't look so intimidating to me or anybody else now.

"Looks like you bit off more than you could chew this time, boys," the coach says to the two size extra-large assbites, and the line follows the rest of the story through the whole school. The Coach knew these guys had pantsed me before, and I think he was pleased they got taken down a notch.

I tried to thank Alex but he brushed it off, saying something about hating big talkers.

All four of us were suspended for a week, which was a blessing to those guys. Not that they were suddenly pussycats. One of their buddies made a joking reference to the action the following week, and he visited the infirmary and met with the school cop as a result. Both of them were suspended for a week, too. I heard the principal called up the biggest asshole's parents and read them the riot act.

I was thinking, "Gee, Mr. Wizzy, I thought miracles only happened in the movies," when I saw that big jerk struggling, twisting and turning, grunting and swearing, all to no avail. See how it feels, asswipe! And the way that Alex just tapped the other jerk-off's head, with that, you know, haughty flip, like, hey kitten, don't try it again. I am your master.

Of course they wanted revenge. I found a note in my locker when I got back to school that said, "Someday we'll find you without your moke bodyguard and then you will eat shit." Shit was underlined, just in case I missed the importance of the word. They wanted even more extreme humiliation than their own and I was scared.

I asked Alex for some advice. "Should I buy a gun?"

"No, man," he says, "guns are for cowards. I'll teach you some moves." That's the first time I go over to his house. He shows me his room and garage. The garage has punching bags, one hanging down and one up by the rafters. "Why up so high?" I asked, and to answer he did this kung fu kick that nearly reaches the bag. He looks chagrined and says, "Usually I make it." In his room he has Bruce Lee posters and pages from magazines that show Asian guys doing stick-fighting and other kung fu stuff.

He shows me his weights, and then we go out to the garage again where he unrolls this mat. He shows me some moves from Filipino and Hawaiian martial arts. That's when I find out how much work it is to get good at kung fu. I'm too lazy to crank it out like Alex does every day. Weights, jump rope, meditation, katas. That's why he got the Summer Phys Ed job with the city after we graduated.

Needless to say, Alex's stock went through the roof as a result of this takedown. Everybody gave him wide berth in the hallways and the football guys were afraid to tackle or hit him too hard. He played defensive guard and linebacker. When the season started, everybody found out that he was a demon on the field, too. He turns into a single-minded machine, I'm telling you. One day I walk over to his house and he is messing with his helmet. I ask what he was doing and he explains that he's adjusting it so that if anyone ever face-masked him he could just jerk the helmet off and kill the guy.

He also started getting dates with the lapis lazuli women. One time I admitted to him that I admired this girl who was on the volleyball team. She was nice and had tits from Planet X. So later on he tells me, "Yeah, you know so-and-so's tits? They feel even better than they look." And he gives me this superior grin. "You dog," I told him; "you probably boned her too."

"Hey bruddah," he says, all innocent sounding, "You have to respect them. I wouldn't tell you if I had," and then he punches me in the shoulder, a play punch. It hurt for a week.

Alex just doesn't like arrogant, inconsiderate, obnoxious loudmouths. Did I tell you how we came up with our nickname for BMW's? Big Moronic Wimps? We're at a post office in Fort Worth. Alex has some post cards he's mailing home—you know, the really great ones with the corny jokes like the jackalope, furry trout, and giant grasshoppers, that kind of hokey stuff—and there's a red zone in front of the curbside mail boxes.

We want to pull up next to the curb and dump the cards, but there's a red BMW parked there. Parked, grip; no one's around. It's not like the guy is just a little bit in the red zone; he's taking up the whole curb.

"Who is this guy," I say, "King Tut? Nobody else has any letters to mail? He thinks his Beemer gets a free ride in red zones? We ought to jink his snotty little Kraut box."

I'm just spouting off, but Alex gets mad too. He edges up along the asshole's vehicle, just sizing things up. I don't know what he's doing; I'm still motormouthing. He backs up, spins the wheel, and slides right alongside the red Beemer until there's about one inch between the two cars. Now the Lancer's bumpers are these big old heavy chrome numbers, with big bulges like young tits on them. There's no way the BMW owner is going to slide past the Lancer without tearing off the gimpy plastic bumpers of his own vehicle.

Now that my door is one inch away from the Beemer's, I blurt out, "What are you doing?" because while I talk big I hate confrontations.

"No worry, brah," says Alex. "Just watch."

Alex opens his door, gets out and hikes up his jeans like he means business. While I'm sitting there wishing with all my might I'd kept my mouth shut, Alex saunters over to a sidewalk trash can and pulls out a can of Coke, a crumpled newspaper, a Taco Hell bag, and a half-eaten hot dog. After considering his haul for a minute, he drizzles the Coke over the guy's hood vents, lays some newspaper on the sticky mess and then casually smears a leftover bean burrito over the guy's windshield.

I'm saying, "Oh man," when this chunky white guy with short dark hair comes running out of the post office. "What the hell is this?" he screams.

"You're in a red zone, asshole," says Alex. The guy goes over to push Alex away from his car but Alex's eyes make him think twice. "You like to join your car, pal?" says Alex, and we're talking menacing because when Alex is toggled to full pidgin it's a red flag to approach him with an "I'm gonna kick your ass" look unless you're ready, willing and able.

"I'm calling the cops," the guy says, like it's a big threat. Alex says, "You better hurry," and then squishes some taco sauce right in the side mirror.

This spins the guy out. He's feeling massive alienation, looking around for someone to come to his rescue. But no one's around, Daddy's not here to protect you, buttwipe, and Alex just waves his hand like you do to kids, like go on, get out of here. The guy finally makes a dash for the driver's side, rolls down the window and says something like, "I'll see you hang for this." Alex tosses the catsupy hotdog toward the open window, a beautiful underhand which just clears the glass and lands in the guy's lap. The jerk rolls his window up, starts the engine, and squeals onto the curb in full panic mode. Once he's around us he bounces back onto the road and screeches off with a scared look on his face.

That's how we came up with Big Moronic Wimps. We considered Big Monkey Wimp, because the guy was pretty ugly, and some BMW drivers look so spun out we also thought of Big Martian Wimps, but in general Big Moronic Wimps locks it down pretty tight.

It's a pretty good name. Its only flaw is that sometimes it's a woman driving or a small wimp. The women we call Bitch Morose Witches because they never look happy. Spike BMWs, Mercedes, Audis, Saabs, Volvos, Peugeots, Lexuses, and Infinitis. Spike 'em all. Their owners always act like they own the road because they spent too much gitas on a damn car. When they're speeding up to pass us we swerve in front of them. When they honk at us we just give them the double bird and shout, "Go get spiked, asshole!" They take one look at our car and another look at us and then they get scared, because they can see we've got nothing to lose.

# CHAPTER FIVE

All these snotty sophisticates on the coasts like to make fun of the Heartland. But let's face it, the Northeast is the large intestine of the country, and SoCal is the gall bladder. But then I also get tired of hearing cornballs talk about the California crazies. I want to whip out a roscoe and say, "Yeah, you're right, boom boom boom, you're right and you're history."

What I'm saying is that I like the Midwest countryside. Things are growing, things to eat. How can that be boring? Everybody complains about I-5 in the Central Valley, what a gimp it is, but they're alienated. It's great. I never get tired of it. There's stuff growing out there and people busting their tushes helping it grow. Plus there's always mysterious mountains somewhere in the haze, somewhere just beyond the dust, either desert mountains in the west or the Sierra on the east or both.

Now grip this. I love the desert, but that stretch from Hellay to the Bacon Strip in Vegas is, how you Americans say, not all that fascinating. It's pretty interesting from the air, but that's because you only have to look at it for twenty minutes. After twenty minutes it's definitely tired.

It's okay at night, with Hendrix and *Electric Ladyland* up in the air, with a nice cool wet towel wrapped around your neck, a cold Coke between your legs, the Lancer humming along, and the hot wind whipping through the chrome teeth of your machine. You're burning up dinosaurs and the engine is just pumping, very smooth, very big, reassuring, and comforting in the way it just floats along. The night outside looks like there could still be dinosaurs out there. It's dark but the moon is out enough to light up the ghosts. You can really feel the mystery, all the weird unknown stuff that spun down over the centuries.

You stick your head out the window and you can smell the juice of the cactii, and it feels really good to have your hair whipped around. You close your eyes; it's a black desert highway, hot wind blowing, sagebrush smell, the Hotel California's lights on the horizon. You can't hear anything but the wind in your ears and the tires moaning on the asphalt.

The stars are out like we never see in the city, making you feel small, small but special anyway, and you're thinking about this girl, about kissing her, about her liking you, and your foot is tapping out the beat. The Lancer is vibrating like a stone woofer, arcing up into your spine, and you get chills even though it's still hotter than a toaster oven. It's like Hendrix wrote it for this desert on this night: princess kept the view, while all the women came and went, barefoot servants too. You can see her, she is so beautiful and she lets you touch her, and it's fine, Santa Cruz beach sand.

This was our very first night on the road, heading for Las Vegas. It's tropo, man, truly King Tut City, to finally be away. After all those months of saving money, fixing up the Cruiser, looking at maps, daydreaming about where we're going to go, we're out. What's funny is I didn't expect much joy off that first leg, but it's one of my happiest memories. It's the unplanned stuff that just spirals in.

Take our visit to Alex's relatives in Iowa. Our plan was to get some money from home, go back to Kansas City and get the Cruiser fixed, and then head East again. There was also this family obligation for Alex to visit any relatives on the way, so it was a two-birds-with-one-stone gig. That was the plan. Instead, well, lots of other stuff happened.

Just like the night drive into Vegas, I expect Iowa to be cripped, a zero. But it's great. The weather's hot beach; we get to see all these giant farm machines, sit in cafés with farmers, and get off the I-states onto little two-lane roads that run past abandoned farms and through these little time-warp towns.

Then his uncle's farm is tropo, a full–rev scene because it's working. They have all these animals—rabbits, dogs, cats, cows, goats—and all this other farm stuff like dead combines and old kerplunkety Ford tractors. Plus everything is green. From a distance, all the fields look like giant lawns. And I met Leslie there.

But not all unexpected stuff is tasty. Some of it is played by Griffin Spike and the Funktones. One scene on the farm went down to the ground for Alex, but I have to tell you another story before I unroll it.

This was when the Funktones played my song. It sounds so cornball when I tell it. It happened at the Senior Prom. Yeah, stratocaster hokey, but the football guys were all going and my Mom told me, "Daz, you'll regret it later if you don't go. There's only one Senior Prom."

Uh huh. It's like the movie: you may not regret today or tomorrow, but you will, and soon, and for the rest of your life. My life is ruined, Doc. I didn't go to the Senior Prom. So I ask this girl Lyn. Nectar cute. I'd liked her for a long time and always tried to get into her study groups and go to parties where I knew she'd be, just to talk to her, but I'd never had the guts to ask her out for a real date.

So I figure this is it; she's probably going away to college, might as well take a number. So Alex coaches me. It's so ridiculous. You know I'm not shy, I'm always the one who makes the first contact, somehow I don't mind that, but asking for a date, whew. Couldn't I just go crawl around the Vatican on my knees a few times? I pick up the phone and feel my hand turn to Jello. "Nah, Alex, I can't do it, she'll just laugh me off the line."

"No way, brah," he says, "I checked around, no one else has asked her. She wants to go."

So I pick up the phone again. I start to dial, and lose my nerve. "Nah, she'd rather go with someone else. Let them ask her."

"Brah, you know you want to go with her. I just told you she wants to go."

"I think I do better in person. I'll ask her tomorrow."

Alex puts the phone in my hand and gives me the evil eye.

Okay. Here goes. Sweat is dripping off my palms. I feel flushed like I'm on stage in the crappy junior play again but I've forgotten my lines. I'm twelve years old again. I just can't do it.

So finally he gets bent. "Okay, Daz, I'll ask for you. Give me the phone." So, out of shame—he's so sly—I just steel myself and punch in the numbers. Oh man, I told myself, just die right now and get it over with. Her Mom answers, she gets Lyn, who accepts immediately. I arrange the timing and hang up. I punch Alex on the shoulder and scream, "She said yes!" I was King Tut, king of the sands of time.

So we go. It's at a fancy hotel ballroom; somehow all those stupid events raised enough money for this downtown yank, and we're all jinked up in these rented tuxes.

"Alex," I say, "you look like a spiked penguin," and he says, "Yeah, but the toughest penguin on this block of ice." He's a cocky bastard sometimes. He drove his old man's Buick. We pick up his date, a lapis lazuli girl he's not really close to, and then we pick up Lyn. God, she's beautiful, just really really pretty. I'm blown down that this is my date. I'm thinking, hey, maybe this will be okay after all.

It's hokey, warpomatic, but sort of fun. The guys are all there, dressed up like you've never seen them, people are dancing and hanging around like they're actually adults. I'm with Lyn, and she seems to be having an alright time. We're with other people, it's too scary to be alone, and she says she wants to see a few other friends. She drifts off and I go over to a group of the football guys. I don't see Lyn around for a long time and I start feeling kind of torqued, like where is she, am I just the chauffeur or what?

So I vector to the patio, feeling kind of low, like what am I even doing here, when I glance over at the parking lot and I see some guy kissing some girl. They're all wrapped up and then I feel this electric shock because I realize it's Lyn.

It's not like I thought she was in love with me or anything sappy like that, it was just a dumb dance, but still I feel a hot flush, like when you see a gun pointed at you, or when something big and fragile is about to hit the ground. I feel blown into pieces that couldn't breathe any more.

I couldn't quite make out the guy, but it didn't matter. If you'd have shot me right then I would have thanked you. I mean, I'd never felt that kind of massive alienation before. It gives me the h.j.'s to remember it. It's like getting gutted, swish swish swish, oh, those are my guts on the floor. My heart's racing, my hands start vibrating, and I'm trying to take big deep breaths, but it's like all the oxygen has disappeared.

I wander back into the room, floating on ice, really cold, and I find Alex. "She's making out with some other guy," I say like a zombie.

"Who?" he asks.

41

"Lyn." His face gets serious and he pulls me aside. "I'll go kick his ass," he said.

"Nah, forget it," I say. "I'm just acting stupid, man, it's no big deal. It's not even a date." Even though it was just some stupid fantasy of mine dying, I couldn't help thinking, couldn't she even wait until tomorrow? Why let me see them? Why did she do this to me?

"She wasn't that great anyway," he says. "Wait here for me."

I ask, "Where you going?"

"To take a leak," he says, and I stand there, cold and blind and dumb.

After a while he comes back. I'm still standing there, dog turd city, and then this cheerleader comes up to us. She's nice, not phony like I thought when I first met her, and she starts talking to us.

Then one of the football guys comes over with his date and they start talking to us. After a few minutes she asks me to dance. I say, "No, I'm no good," and she laughs and says, "Well, neither am I," and she forces me so I try it and it's okay, not as bad as I thought.

After the song ends some other football guys come over and start joking around, telling stories about some of the fricative stuff I've pulled in the locker room, witty things I said that really smoked somebody. So after awhile I can actually see again, see people's faces. By the time the thought enters my mind that all this is just a bit too perfect, I'm already over the worst of it.

Yeah, it was Alex. Afterward, outside my house, I tell him, "Alex, you should be in the movies." We just look at each other, he's smiling a little, I punch him on the shoulder and he grips mine, hard. I feel like crying.

When I tell this story to Benny, Tita's hubby, he says, "You're damned lucky to have Alex for a friend." Well, you sure as hell don't want him for an enemy.

Okay, so Griffin Spike and the Funktones play Alex's number in Iowa. Here's what happens: Alex falls in love with one of his cousin's friends, but she dusts him off.

Looking back, I can see that Alex was blown down because he never got dumped before. He was always careful to not get too committed until he knew the girl liked him. This time love snuck up, cuffed him, read him his rights, and hauled his ass off before he could say ditti-wom-ditti. You know, love doesn't allow any phone calls or L.A. lawyers. There's no Perry Mason to bail you out. You're dragged in, convicted, and your ass is hauled off immediately.

Alex is already acting pretty katakana, alien zone here, ma'am, when something went gravitational one night. We're sitting around like usual in the basement, listening to tunes, the cousins and their friends, including this girl I liked, Leslie. No big deal. Alex is sitting across from Meg, just hanging on her every word and look.

After a while they go off alone, and I think, fricking Alex, he's off for some action. The rest of us do the social oobla-dee a while longer and then I vector to my crib and fall asleep.

Alex shakes me awake the next morning and says, "Let's go." He looks like total dog poo. Fantasy Island has turned into Devil's Island. He's serving hard time. His face looks like he'd crammed it in a dead fire and shaken it back and forth a few hundred times, like one of his kung fu heroes got his ass whipped. He's shrunk up and inward like there's a vacuum cleaner on in his soul.

He's completely spun in so I start joking around, but he's silent as a street at 3 AM. We go to the main house to say goodbye, but everyone except the mom is already out working. I'm thinking about coming back to see Leslie on our way home, but I don't mention it.

It only takes a few minutes to pack up our stuff, cram it in the Falcon's trunk, and haul derriere. I'm driving, still trying to cheer him up with my usual booga-booga. I'm saying stuff like, "Man, wake up and smell the dog crap, hey brah, how about some tunes? God, don't you love the smell of leaking gas in the morning? Let's get some breakfast. I want some grits," and I say it stretched out, "guuuurrreeets," and he still looks like morgue slab city.

I'm thinking, man, nothing is working this AM, what is wrong with him? So I say, "What happened, your dick fall off last night?"

He just stares straight ahead and says, "Fricking haole." Now he sometimes says this as a joke, kind of a warning to back off, but now he means it and I get the h.j.'s. Haysoos Cristo, an alien ate his brain last night.

"Hey Meestair, what de freeg?"

This phony accent of mine—my sister says all my accents sound the same, French, Indian, Russian, you name it—usually pries him open, but it pancakes this time. He tells me, "Nothing, Just drive."

"Okay, sure." So I'm driving, its a beautiful fresh-sky morning, the road is open, I feel great except for the Rue Morgue next to me, the igloo in a box that blew in from the Yukon and landed in the Falcon.

Okay, think, what was he doing last night? Mooning over Meg. So that's it, heartbreak hotel: they check in, but they don't check out. "It's Meg, isn't it?" I ask him. He's silent but just ripped with pain.

Now here's where I make my first mistake. I say, "Griff, Alex, she wasn't that great."

He just looks out the window, but I can see that he's blinded, just like I was on prom night. Uh oh, wrong approach, delete, delete, backspace, backspace. "Well, there's other girls," I say.

"Fricking Daz, you're so stupid! There's no one like her!"

Man, how can I be so stupid? I don't know booga-booga about this love mambo. I think oh, to hell with it, I can't do a damn thing for him. We'll just have to weather the storm, what a spiky nightmare, a hurricane-stomped, zombied-out, alien-stole-his-brain, broken-hearted Hawaiian stuck next to me in this tiny little box. I look out the window and I see the sun shining on the wheat fields, the air is warm, the Falcon's cruising fine—but it's all wasted. But then I remember how he helped me and I think, I've got to try again.

"Hey look, I know she likes you, she was just in a bad mood," I say.

He's silent. I guess she made it clear that she didn't like him. Dead end. Okay, I'm desperate, it's like final exam time and I've got to figure out what I can riff off of to get the mojo cranked up. Come on Daz, kick in with your best shot, I tell myself, find the volume and let it rip.

I'm thinking, keep trying, you might get credit for trying, you might get lucky. How did he help me? By pegging the girl down? No, then I felt even more ickabod. That's why I felt bulldozed—I liked her. He helped me by making me feel like I wasn't on training wheels.

"Look, Alex. How many girls have you ever liked?"

He's silent, we're in a Charlie Chaplin movie.

"Yeah, well, it's probably been a dozen or so, right?" I say. "And how many of them have liked you?"

Silence.

So I say, "Every one of them, slick, except for Meg. She likes you too, but she's scared of liking you. You're older, and she's too young to know how to handle it. She just got scared."

Come on, I'm thinking, kick in! "Take a guy like me," I tell him. "I'd die happy if I had a dozen girls like me."

There's still no sound, and I'm getting worried that Griffin Spike and the Funktones have drilled him to the core.

"You know," I say, "Meg is really nice, but she needs to grow up some before she can handle her feelings. Give it time, brah, give it time."

And finally I see some life in the coals. There's still heat in there, just blow on them a little and they'll flame up again, and I feel good because I can see he's lifting off the bottom; there's some air back under him.

He was still busted up for a while, but hey, I'm no miracle worker.

# CHAPTER SIX

One of the best guys we met was this retired Marine, Rich. He used to be a colonel. Now on the face of it we ought to hate this guy, a rigid jerk with a steel rod up his butt, right? But Rich and his wife treated us like we were worth knowing, which clamped my surprise down tight.

We're camping out in the Colorado Rockies, trying to conserve gitas for food and gas, but we don't have much equipment: a couple of plastic bottles for water, sleeping bags, air mattresses, and a camp stove. We're low on grinds, just some cans of beans and applesauce.

So these people next to us have a real I-state boat, a big motor home, and I'm afraid they're going to chase us off because we're young and maybe look a little weird. I mean, some of these places are one hundred and three percent white. Maybe there's a few Indians around, but that's it. Sometimes it makes me a little self-conscious.

Anyway, I'm feeling like I don't belong in this campground when this guy comes out of the RV and vectors over while we're trying to light our camp stove. We've been sitting in the car nursing a beer, worrying about the way the Lancer's been running ragged since we left New Mexico, when we decide we might as well heat up some beans and get it over with. The wind keeps blowing out the stove, and it's cold because we're up in the Rockies, and I'm starting to feel to hell with it, I'll eat the beans cold, when this guy comes over to our table.

"You guys traveling alone?"

He seems friendly enough, so I say, "Yeah."

He says, "Why don't you join us for dinner? My wife cooked too damn much again."

Alex is quiet but he looks at me and I'm thinking hey, I know Alex is needing more than these fricking beans for dinner, so I say, "Yeah sure, thanks." But I'm actually thinking, copacetic, Jack.

So the guy asks us where we're from, and Alex says, "Hawaii."
The guy says, "Sure, I know Hawaii, I was stationed at Kaneohe." Alex gets a little animated because that isn't far from where he used to live. They trade a few stories about Hawaii and then Rich says, "I wish I'd done something like you're doing when I was younger."

I'm blown down that this guy actually admires us for taking this trip. Most of the time I feel like a scumbag for just driving around having a good time while everyone else has this serious life, you know, frowning artists wearing black and people with screaming brats and lousy jobs and some losers so desperate that they have to drive a Mercedes to survive. All those moments of loud desperation. Here we are in our Lancer just listening to tunes. And finding trouble, of course. Thanks to the expert, Alex. Like a cat and sand.

So this guy Rich and his old lady Pauline kind of adopt us. We'd already decided to riff off the mountains for a few days, and it turns out they're staying a while, too. We end up eating a lot of meals in their I-state battleship. I think Pauline liked cooking for us because we ate everything she laid out. No leftovers. Her cooking was strat, especially after a couple of days of beans and applesauce.

Rich and Pauline are cruising around the country, just stopping where they please and camping out, sort of like us.

Pauline loads up our plates with seconds and Rich asks, "You guys heading somewhere in particular?"

I was hoping Alex would answer, but he's concentrating on stuffing his mouth with mashed potatoes, not the kind from a box but homemade, still a little chunky, just the way my Mom makes them.

I almost say, "Well, sir. . . ." but catch myself. Rich doesn't look big—medium height, kind of slight build, short brown hair—but there's something about him that makes me want to call him "sir" even before I knew he used to be a colonel.

I clear my throat and give him the clean-shaven version about visiting cousin Tita in New York.

"Great," says Rich. "There's always little adventures in travel."

Or big adventures, I'm thinking, like getting busted on a desert highway and thrown in prison with father rapers. Yah.

"I get a kick out of your car," Rich tells us. "Not what I expected a couple of young guys to be driving."

Alex gives me the "it was his lame idea" look and I want to slap him. "We bought it from an old neighbor," I say, and want to add, "the crustiest old bastard in Orange County," but I hold off out of politeness.

I hadn't thought of Old Man Ching in a while. "He didn't want to sell us the car at first," I explain, and Alex rolls his eyes and makes a weird face, and I want to boing the hot mashed potatoes off my fork right between his eyes. It isn't my fault that Old Man Ching's so damned stubborn.

We'd known he was a mac nut, but it took a while to find out he's also a stubborn old coot. He and his old lady live above their stationer's shop, right across the alley from the ShipShape Bar and the La Casa Grande Mexican restaurant. There's a chain link fence all around his little back yard, the kind with those thin strips of redwood woven into the wire so no one could see in. But there's still cracks and a few pieces missing, and when we were kids we'd look in and try to see what he was up to.

We had all these ideas, like he was an inventor with secret projects and that he hid money in some of the old coffee cans he had laid out on shelves. We'd watch him putter around, trying to see which one he used for the cash. We never did catch him with a money pot, but we figured he somehow knew we were looking and did it at night.

His back yard was all concrete, patched in like he paved it a piece at a time. There was old metal shelving all over the place, and every square inch of it was loaded with junkus maximus, a wingding collection of metal parts, Folger's cans, chunks of wood, glass jars of paint, and all kinds of other oobla-dee.

Tucked in one corner was this car. It was covered by a faded green canvas tarp like you buy in surplus stores. We never got to see the car, but we could tell it was an old one. My sister claimed a bum lived in it when Old Man Ching was asleep, and it made sense to us because there were a few old drunks who hung around the alley entrance to the ShipShape Bar. Of course we never figured out how the bum could get over Old Man Ching's eight-foot high chain link fence, but once we heard some muffled noises coming out of the tarp, and we ran away because we thought the bum had heard us talking and he was mad at us for finding his hideout.

That made sense because even a bum would be scared of Old Man Ching, whose mean streak was eight lanes wide and totally thrombosis. One time the padlock to his chain-link gate was open, and we thought maybe he wasn't home. We snuck around to the front of the stationery store and sure enough only Mrs. Ching was inside. So we ran back to the alley and made sure no bums were watching and then we took off the padlock and creaked open the gate.

We got it open about a foot and were just about to sneak through when we heard this really mean voice yell, "Hey! What you kids doing?" It was Old Man Ching, leaning out his apartment window, and he looked mad enough to melt steel. We hauled derriere, and after that he'd keep an eye out for us. If he spotted us walking by his store window, he'd run out and follow us to make sure we didn't stop in his alley. This made it even more fun to sneak down the alley from the used car lot and spy on him.

When I hit ninth grade I stopped keeping tabs on Old Man Ching, although he was still scary as hell when I saw him because he had this frown and this glint in his eyes and a tough, wiry old body that looked dangerous. He had a dragon tattoo all the way down his forearm, and when we were kids we figured he'd been in World War Two and had probably killed a bunch of guys barehanded. We spotted an old bayonet on his shelving, and we thought he'd kept it after killing all these guys with it. Of course, my sister told me it was still covered with dried blood, and I was pretty impressed with that until somebody else told me it was just rusty. Now I figure he kept it to open paint cans with or something like that.

But as kids, the chains, old generator, coils of rusty wire, steel pipes, and other industrial strength junk all seemed part of Old Man Ching's secret empire, parts that were assembled into weird inventions at night or left over from some previous, totally sinister use. His glare told us we'd be cabbage if he ever caught us inside his yard, and as far as we were concerned that proved we were right—he *did* have something to hide.

49

I hadn't seen Old Man Ching in years, and then I happened to be in the old part of town again dropping off a job app at a hardware store when I saw the used car lot and decided to walk down the alley to see if Old Man Ching was still around. Half the time when you do this there's a new Jank Coffee or Mrs. Wizzy's Cookie Corner right where your favorite old haunt used to be, and I halfway expected to find a four-story building full of dentists or a cheezoid strip mall, but Old Man Ching's yard was still there and still filled with junk.

Not only that, but the gate's open and the tarp is off the car. Old Man Ching is fussing around with something under the dash, so I don't see him right away. I spock the brand of the car—Lancer. It's a tropo name, kind of reminding me of those strat Cervantes beer commercials with Pancho and his windmill.

I've never seen transpo like this in my entire life. It's all fins, chrome bumpers, and weird grills—very katakana. One of the front fenders is light purple, but the rest of the car is a pukey dark green. I guess because he's had it covered all these years, the paint's still pretty shiny.

Old Man Ching must have gripped my presence because he crawls out and stares at me real hard-eyed. "Nice car," I say. "Remember me? The Hernandez kid."

He gives me this laser beam swish-swish drop dead look and then grunts. I ask, "Could I look at your car?" He grunts again and then crawls back under the dash. Alex and I had just started talking about this trip and I'd been looking at every old car I saw that was for sale.

The original idea started with Alex's mom. Right around Easter I'm over at his crib for dinner, and his mom shows us a lame wedding announcement card that has come in the mail. It is from his cousin Tita, who's just married some guy she'd met in graduate school. The card is just folded typing paper with a real amateur-hour red heart drawn on the front and a little off-kilter photo inside of two people you couldn't make out by a row boat on some lake. They're not in the boat, grip, just in the water next to it waving their arms. Printed in some frappy font along the bottom inside is the line, "No gifts—really!!"

If I'd seen a real photo of Tita, and not just two blurry dots in a lake, I would have fallen in love with her right then and not waited to see her in person. But as it was, Alex glances at it for about one second and then hands it back to his mom, who is beaming big about her niece tying the knot. "You haven't seen your cousin in years," she tells Alex. "You should go and visit her this summer."

I'm thinking, yah, talk about a wingding idea, hanging around with lovebirds who send cutesy cards with cripped pictures of themselves.

But then a couple of weeks later we're in my room doing our homework, listening to a DJ string together tunes about cars, when this old Steve Miller song about cruising up and down the road in a Mercury comes on with a big bass sound, and in a flash this complete scene comes into my mind, like a movie, where we're driving across country in this strat old 60s machine. The sun's shining, the highway's smooth and open, the wind's blowing through our hair, the Ray-Bans are on, and we're leaning back, watching all the girls' heads turn when we cruise down Main Street.

"Hey Alex," I blurt out, all excited, "we should get a car like an old Mercury, one with Electroglide and big fins, and drive across country this summer. It would be major. Hell, we could even make your mom happy and stop in New York to see your cuz."

Alex lets me go on for a while, all ramped up like I get, but he doesn't say much so I drop it. Alex is always slow to warm up to the really beach ideas.

While Alex is hammering away on his English Lit paper, I whip out the newspaper and start scanning the help wanted ads. I figure I better start looking now for a full-time summer gig. I can hardly wait to get a job and start piling up the gitas to buy a car. I go to sleep that night thinking about a big old American cruiser with wide seats, lots of chrome, and a gigantia engine purring under the hood.

That weekend I started looking for old cars in the newspaper, online, and even on the bulletin board at Safeway. I figured we could buy a junker for five hun and then fix it up once we started working. I was so naive, thinking maybe a grand would do it. Yah. I went to the library and checked out this thick book on American cars of the 50s and 60s, and pored over that for hours. For a while I was set on a big-fin Cadillac, but then I found out they cost twenty grand.

I got up the courage to make a couple of appointments with guys advertising old cars, and dragged Alex out to see them. I didn't know do-wah-diddly about these old cars, so I could only ask lame questions like, "Does it run?" or "Where'd you get it?" Some days I would get depressed about the whole idea, like it was too much work, too much money, too scary. Guys would be telling me what was wrong with the car and I'd be thinking, Slick, you're talking the m.j.'s here, the mumbo jumbos. I'm not gripping you, Jack, it's all katakana.

I'd wanted to take auto shop but it was always full, so I had to take World History or some other drib class instead. I'd taken apart our lawn mower in my sophomore year, but that was it for my mechanical experience. My dad had a pretty good collection of tools, I guess because he used to work on cars when he was younger, so that was no prob. Alex's dad is an electrical engineer, so I figured he could help us with the wiring. But we couldn't get started on anything until we had a car.

After we graduated I jumped on every job ad I saw. Alex dialed one in right away because of his football connection. The coach got him a summer job as an assistant in some city sports program for kids.

It was perfect for him because all that training and fitness stuff is his main meal. Plus he isn't one of these "do as I say, not as I do" guys. He lives the body-as-temple life every day, and I think the kids spocked that. He'd run alongside them when they were red-lined and all out of breath, saying stuff like, "Come on, only a little farther, you can do it." I gripped that's what he must do for himself every day when he's lifting weights and practicing kung fu, just edging himself along when he gets worn down.

I had a little more trouble getting a job. In fact, if it wasn't for my dream of getting a Cruiser I would have shut down. I was getting rejectomundo uptown, downtown, and crosstown. I even put on a tie, if you can span that, for interviews in stores and restaurants, but I always came up nolo when the wheel stopped spinning.

Finally I got a nibble at a fiberglass shop, and I laid it on thick as soon as I felt the first tug. Start at 7 AM? No prob, Jack. Experience with glass? It's smooth, slick, been doing it since I could walk. Hard worker? Hey, where's the jackhammer? I'd seen the old guy who owned the place in our church a couple of times, and I gooed it up about my altar boy gig when I was eight. His son called me that weekend and told me to show up at 6:30 on Monday.

I went mambo for a few minutes, jumping up and down and doing the humba-humba and then I realized I better learn how to make glass before Monday AM. I ran out to buy some fiberglass to practice with. My first batch went off so fast it nearly fried my hands. The second batch still hasn't popped; it's buried out in the corner of the back yard.

So don't laugh when I tell you the first thing I worked on. Big Madonnas. Yeah, the six-foot ones for churches. We were one of a few places in the country that made them, and we got orders from all over. We made them with these big molds, and we also did the painting. My first job was filling any voids. I was thinking, man, here I am working on a blank statue that somebody is going to be praying to, maybe hoping to get healed or something. How could this thing I'm sanding with emery paper get holy once it's painted and in a church?

I mentioned this to my Mom when I got home and she got a little torqued and said I was missing the point, it wasn't the statue that was holy, it was the spirit that the statue represented. I kept quiet after that, but I still thought it was katakana work.

That's when I gripped that everything, and I mean everything, is made by somebody. Whether it's bottlecaps or the gowns the priest wears or the Academy Award statues, it's all made by some-body in a shop. Somebody's fingerprints are on it, somebody we never see. How many people kneeling in church looking at this big statue of Mary think about me, the guy with the sandpaper and filler who smoothed her all up, ready for painting?

I took my job maximum serious because without it I couldn't get transpo up and running, so I tried real hard to keep my mouth shut and not crimp it with some wise-ass comment. Sometimes it was hard to keep clamped down. When the guys would start talking about the crying Madonnas, you know, the stories about statues that started crying, big miracles, it took all my power not to snap one off.

Most of the guys were religious or at least respectful, otherwise they wouldn't be working for the old man, and I had to phrase things like I was in church. The first time they start talking about the crying Madonnas at break, we have our dust masks off and are drinking sodas from the machine that you kick real hard on the left side and then you don't have to pay, and I say, "I believe in miracles and all that, but what if somebody ran little tubes up through the statue to her eyes?"

Our foreman, Rennie, says, "Nah, you could see the holes right away." So I say, "But you could make them pin holes right in the seam of the eyelid. It'd be hard to see them."

He shakes his head. "Too obvious. They've already checked for tricks. It's real, Daz. How could one of our statues cry? We know better than anybody it can't be faked."

"I saw on TV that some guy said he could make statues cry with some chemical," I say. Jojo, one of the young guys who's really good with the glass, says: "Maybe you could do that once, but these statues in Virginia keep crying for days. How could a chemical do that?"

I say, "I don't know. I'd just like to see it with my own eyes."

Rennie says, "You and a lot of other people. When it happens, the church is jammed, TV crews and everything."

I start to think about running some tubes up through one of the unfinished statues some night just to blow them flat, but it was too complicated, what with glue, tubing, pumps, electrical wires and all that. Then I thought about just putting a plastic bag of water in her head, so water would trickle out without pumps or anything, but then I thought I'd get fired because no one else would do something so defective except me, and I couldn't afford to get spun off just yet.

When I first looked at the classifieds, I thought it was going to be easy to find a car, maybe a week, tops. Dingdong, beep, wrong. They were all too much money or too sad or we'd think about it and then some guy would buy it out from under us or nobody bought it because it was so bow-wow.

Alex and I would go together when we could, which was weekends and after six, but he was leaving the search up to me. He thought this was just another one of my crip ideas that goes nowhere once the heat steams off. But I knew this was different. After a couple of weeks he saw that I was still at it and then he started to take the whole idea more seriously.

We'd struck out so far and he was talking about getting a VW Bug or a muscle car, like a '67 Mustang or a '69 Malibu. I started to go flat when I heard that, and I stopped looking for a week. I mean, sure, a Bug or a 'Stang would be copacetic, but it wouldn't be the same. Lots of guys had Bugs or 'Stangs, and if Alex wasn't as pumped as I was, then maybe the whole idea would melt down.

That was a low point, because I couldn't do this alone and I sure didn't want to just roll off the assembly line: Yeah, I'm going to community college, too, I don't know, something where I can make a lot of bucks, griff griff griff. I decided to stone the whole idea, but then I felt worse so I decided I better talk to Alex.

I guess I got upset as I laid out the scene, maybe because it was like a dream of mine taking the cliff dive if we couldn't get a strat car. He listens to me stone-faced, and after I'm done with the rant, then he pulls a little bank book off his desk, opens it and hands it to me. He's depositing money like clockwork every Friday into his savings. "Daz," he said, "I'm not as picky like you. Any car's okay."

"But isn't this for college?" I say, handing him back the book.

He shook his head. "Later."

So I ask, "What about your folks?"

He takes the bank book back and says, "As long as I go next year, they're okay."

"Where do you want to go?" I ask.

He shrugs and says, "I don't know, what about you?"

I swallow my pride and say, "If we weren't doing this trip, I'd probably just go to the J.C."

"Me too," he says, and I'm blown flat because back around Christmas he'd talked about going to the University of Hawaii in Honolulu. "What about U.H.?" I ask.

He's kind of thoughtful and then he says, "Manoa? I don't know. I already missed the deadline."

I cogitate on this, then ask, "Your parents fragging you about it?"

He shrugs again. "Not yet."

After our talk I got reinspired to look for a car. Okay, I'm picky. The car has to be right. Even my Dad got into the action. He says to me one night, "Daz, are you sure you're not going overboard, trying to find the perfect car?"

"That's not it," I say. "It can be almost any 60s car."

My Mom says, "Wouldn't it be safer to buy a newer, more reliable car?"

"Those things were built like tanks," I tell her. "If they weren't reliable, then how come so many are still on the road?"

"Seems like your mind is already made up," my Dad says.

"Damn right it is," I tell him, and my Mom frowns and says her usual line, "Don't swear at me."

So there I am spocking Old Man Ching's Mystery Car. A Lancer wasn't tops on the list of dream cars. I'd blown right by them in the big book of 60s transpo.

The Lancer looks like a catfish that's wolfed down steroids and heavy metals and gotten huge and ugly. "Does it run?" I ask, and he grunts again. Talkative old fart, I'm thinking to myself. The car is so malignant that I start liking it.

"How much is it worth?" I ask, because for all I know this is some collector's car that pulls down fifty thousand at auctions.

"I don't know," he says from under the dashboard.

"Ever consider selling it?" I ask.

He stops and pulls his head out a little and his short gray hair looks like a bristle brush.

"It's not for sale," he says, and his voice is quiet but angry, like just the question made him mad.

"Just checking," I say. "I'm looking for a 60s car."

"This one's not for sale," he says again, like that's it, end of discussion, and that kicks off the battle between me and Old Man Ching for that car, because it was ugly enough and weird enough for me and I didn't like being told there was no way I could buy it.

"It's been sitting here since I was a kid," I say. "What's the point?"

He pulls his head all the way out and squints real hard at me. "The point is, it's not for sale."

"You'll just let it sit here rotting for another ten years?"

He shoots me one last nasty glare and then his head disappears back under the dash. "Look, if you change your mind, here's my number," I say, putting a piece of paper on the seat. "I really like your car, Mr. Ching. I'd take good care of it."

"I'm not selling it," he says, and there's a weariness in there with the anger.

# CHAPTER SEVEN

Old Man Ching won the first round, but I revved up the scheme machine and figured I could wear him down with common sense and my ingratiating personality. Yah.

So after I got my fiberglass Madonna job, I popped by Old Man Ching's place one afternoon to warm him up and make him see how defective it was to keep hanging onto the Lancer. I figure it might have been the first car he humped Mrs. Ching in or something sentimental like that.

Mrs. Ching smiles real sweetly when I walk into their store, which still seemed to be part of the 60s, too. The curled posters advertising printed envelopes and stuff like that all have Twilight Zone companies and logos, like "Biggs Construction" with a little smiling guy holding a hammer and accounting companies with old-timey lettering.

Old Man Ching comes through the curtain behind the counter like a wiry little bear sniffing out danger, and then he spocks me and puts his hands up. "Don't talk to me about the car," he says, and Mrs. Ching's smile melts away like Frosty the Snowman hitting Phoenix in July.

"It's the only Lancer I've ever seen," I say. "Can't I at least look under the hood?"

Mrs. Ching says, "That wouldn't hurt, would it, Herman?"

He pulls himself up and says, "Young man, I'm not selling the car."

Yeah, I think, you're a stubborn old bastard, but I'm a stubborn young bastard. "I know, I know," I say. "It's just that I've wondered about that car my whole life. All I want to do is see the engine and sit in the driver's seat."

He looks sour like he's just stepped in dog poo and says, "Maybe tomorrow afternoon. I'm busy now."

"Okay, great," I say, and I thought yes! My foot's in the door. So the next afternoon I see that the tarp's been pulled off for only the second time in my whole life and Old Man Ching is puttering around in his junk collection. The steel shelving is so high I only spock him through an empty spot on one of the shelves.

I've studied the big book on old cars, hoping to impress him with my knowledge, but that whiffs three big ones. He doesn't give a damn about the engine size and all that flack. He lifts the hood and says, "See?" and then he slams it down and opens the door. "Go ahead," he says, like I was kryptonite and if I sit there more than ten seconds he'd explode.

I slide into the driver's seat and it feels good. I'm home, man. I like the feel of the big steering wheel and the gigantia dash, which is wide enough to hold a large pizza without even breathing hard.

"How long have you owned this car, Mr. Ching?" I ask.

"A long time," he mutters.

I push one of the radio buttons and ask, "Did you buy it new?"

"Almost new," he answers in a gruff voice.

The old radio dial and the other controls look like they'd been yanked out of a 60s sci-fi comic book. I pull the gear shift lever down into drive.

"Does it run?" I ask.

He's looking more bent at every question. "No battery," he says.

I pin him down with, "So it does run, huh? When's the last time you took it out?"

"The last time my son came home," he says, and that twists me because I'd never seen any young Chings running around and never heard of any, either.

"When was that?" I ask, but he just motions me out of the car and says, "I've got to go inside now."

"Look, Mr. Ching," I say, winding up my altar boy act, "I really appreciate you showing me the car. Don't you think it would be fun to take it out again? Just for old times' sake?"

"No," he says, and his frown pegs the griffometer.

"It looks a little dusty," I say. "I can polish it right up for you."

He throws the Army green tarp over the Lancer and puts bricks along the concrete to hold the cover down. "Young man, I wasn't born yesterday," he tells me. "I know what you're trying to do. I'm not going to sell you the car."

59

I nearly went cats, but I tightened it down. "Mr. Ching, working on your car would be fun for me. I don't have one."

"It's too much trouble," he says.

So I ask him, "Why is it too much trouble? You won't have to do anything."

He just shook his head. "You don't understand," he says. "Sometimes we old people just want to leave things alone."

This old bastard is a tougher nut to crack than I'd originally thought. I decide to go with Plan B From Outer Space and notch the groove with Mrs. Ching.

Since I started work early I had plenty of time to get to their shop in the afternoon. I discovered Old Man Ching made deliveries on Wednesday afternoons so I cruised by then to catch Mrs. Ching alone.

Her smile looks warm so I dive in. "Why is Mr. Ching so fixed on holding on to the car?" I ask.

Her smile sinks like a headstone. "He's very attached to it," she says. "I don't think a young person can understand."

"He says the same thing, Mrs. Ching. Is it a Chinese thing?"

She almost laughs at that one. "No, it's about getting old."

"I sure wish he'd drive me around the block in it," I say.

That night I bounce the mystery off my Mom and Dad at dinner. "What did Mrs. Ching mean?" I say. "That you get real stubborn when you get old?"

"Don't be flippant about Mr. Ching," my Mom says. "It's obvious that he loves that car. You shouldn't pressure him."

"I'd be doing him a favor," I say. "He could take Mrs. Ching on a cruise ship with the gitas."

"You're acting like he's challenged you to a battle of wills," my old man says. "He just doesn't want to sell the car."

"Dad, that's not it," I say, trying not to feel torqued. "I just want that car."

Their Stonewall Jackson bothered me but then I slipped into the fricative mode and came up with Plan C From Planet Rhomboid. The next Wednesday I beam into the Ching's shop with a jar of Turtle Wax and some rags. "Mr. Ching told me I could polish the car today," I tell the Mrs. She looks confused but I push it. "He didn't tell you?" I ask, all innocent sounding. "I kept bugging him

60

and he finally said okay." She still isn't sure, but I just walk past the printing machines to the back door and jump on the job.

I've got Armorall for the tires, chrome polish, regular polish, Windex, the complete menu, and I nectar that car out until I'm sweating like a pig. It's allegro non troppo when I finish, and I tell Mrs. Ching to have Mr. Ching check it out when he gets home. I didn't want to be there when the Old Man hit the stratosphere.

I let a few days go by for him to cool down and then I stop by again. I half-expect him to ream me out right in his store, but he just tells me to come to the back yard.

I follow him out there and he turns to me and says, "Young man, I don't understand why you want my car. There's so many others for sale."

He's really perplexed so I tell him the truth, about Alex and me and the dream trip across country, how I want the right car, how we'd wondered about this car since we were kids, and how much I like it. He listens to me and then he's quiet for a long time. Then he says, "I see," and we go back into the shop.

Alex had given up on me already because he thought I'd never get Old Man Ching's car and by the time I accepted reality I'd be eighty years old myself. But something changed in Old Man Ching's expression after I told him the truth. All my Planet X ideas had blown off, but he seemed impressed with my dream of traveling in his car. And despite what Alex thought, I wasn't giving up on the trip.

I knew Old Man Ching had changed channels the next time I stopped by because there was a brand new Sears Diehard battery sitting next to the front tire of the Lancer. "We close the shop at five," he tells me, and rather than do nothing I help him cut a business card order.

We finish about six and then he nods for me to follow him. We go out the back door and past the shelving to the car. He yanks the old Army tarp off, opens the hood, and then puts the new battery in place.

"Go get the gas can," he says, pointing to one of the metal shelves. I grab the red can and run it back to him. He twists the

61

wing nut off the air cleaner, pulls it off, and sets it carefully on the green tarp. The inside of the carb is clean and shiny. He slops a little gas down the pipe and then climbs in the front seat.

He turns the key and the engine coughs a few times and then catches, a few cylinders at a time. Blue smoke puffs out of the tailpipe, the engine sputters kind of softly, and then it smooths out as all the cylinders fire up. The yard fills with the gray-blue smoke, but the engine is running slow and throaty like Mae West's voice, ka-chunka, ka-chunka, ka-chunka, and the old man seems satisfied.

He sits there for a few minutes listening to the steady rhythm of the pistons, and then he says, "Go open the gate."

I run over and nearly jerk the gate off its hinges. He backs the car out, just that soft ka-chunka ka-chunka, and then he opens the passenger door for me. "Close the gate first," he tells me, and I shut the gate and jump in.

"It's registered as a stored vehicle," he says. "Think the cops will catch us?"

I have to smile a little. "I doubt it."

We ease out the alley past the back entrances to the Shipshape Bar and La Casa Grande Mexican restaurant, and then there's the used car lot and we're on the street. It's like a dream come true. Old Man Ching's foot wasn't even on the gas and we're vectoring about twenty miles per. His hands are high on the wheel and his dragon tattoo ripples every time he makes a turn. He's quiet but neither one of us minds. We cruise around for about a half-hour, the car just gliding down the streets, King Tut of the road, and I'm lighter than air.

# CHAPTER EIGHT

Rich didn't volunteer anything about the war. Alex had to give him the third degree. We're sitting outside his I-state boat in folding lawn chairs, drawing lines through the dried pine needles with crooked little sticks, when Alex asks him if he was in Vietnam. He says, "Yeah. Two tours."

So Alex asks him what it was like. I feel bad because maybe it brings up spiky memories, but Rich just starts talking quietly, his face kind of hard even though he smiles every once in a while. "For most of the guys, it was a one-year hike in the jungle with a full pack."

Alex asks Rich to go on, so he tells us what it's like to be in a helicopter when it's getting shot up.

"You're sitting on your helmet," he says, "so if you catch a few rounds from the jungle you don't lose your balls. You hang on to anything you can because if the pilot slams the stick over you'll slide right out the door. It's noisy as hell. You can barely hear the guy next to you even if he's screaming in your ear. Then wham! wham! wham!"—and he bunches up his fist and slams the side of his motor home really hard and fast—"it's like the Jolly Green Giant is whacking the side of the 'copter with a sledgehammer, and you shit in your pants. Fifty caliber bullets sound just like that."

He pauses for a second, maybe rewinding his internal VCR, and Pauline sticks her head out the door and asks, "Are we taking incoming fire again, dear?" and Rich looks sheepish and says, "The boys were asking about the war."

"So what happened next?" Alex says, and I give him the evil eye, like clamp it down, brah, maybe it's spike to him, but he ignores me.

I expect to see some cloud darken Rich's face, but he just looks at the stick in his hand like it's a million miles away, and he talks so quiet I have to lean forward to hear him.

"If you're lucky, you didn't get hit and the 'copter stays up. If you're not so lucky, your guts are on the floor. Or they hit the rotor or engine and you go down."

We sit there silently for a minute while he sees the whole scene in his head again, maybe for the hundredth time, maybe the thousandth. Then he says, "We had some damn good pilots over there. Real hotshots." He draws a line in the dirt and then scratches it out. "Know what the average life span of scout 'copter pilots was in our sector?"

I look at Alex but he's looking down at Rich's design in the dust.

"Six weeks," Rich says.

Alex is Dumbo the Elephant. He asks Rich: "Were you ever in a 'copter that crashed?"

Rich smiles and shakes his head like he's remembering getting really drunk. "Yeah. One time near Hue we got hit, I didn't think that hard, but we lost power right away and started dropping. The pilot was a kid, maybe your age, but somehow he feathered the rotor so we half-glided down to a road. He was strapped in, but the rest of us had one hell of a ride."

Alex is still looking down at the ground and Rich says, "One of my guys got hit in the arm, and I was trying to find the pressure point in his shoulder like this"—and he grabs me to demonstrate and his fingers are strong like Alex's—"to keep him from bleeding to death. I was trying to hang on to a strap and do this"—he's gripping my shoulder with one hand—"but I wasn't too successful." He smiles a little, and I'm not sure what that means.

"Did he die?" says Alex.

"No, he made it," says Rich, "but he lost most of the use of that arm."

Alex looks up at Rich and asks, "What about you?"

Rich's smile changes and then he answers, "I got tossed around like a rock in a bottle when we hit. The guys thought I was dead, so they didn't even put me on the medivac when it came."

"What happened?" I ask him.

He shrugs and says, "Nothing much. I had a concussion and was out of the hospital in a week."

We didn't say anything, and Rich is drawing circles in the dirt.

"It was a shitty war," he says after a while. "We shouldn't have been there."

I don't know what to say so I say nothing. "There's one good thing about that whole mess, though," Rich tells us. "We won't get into a loser like that one as long as we're still alive—the guys who saw it. We say never again, and we mean it. But after we're gone, look out." He glances up at us. "It might be your sons that get the next dirty one."

Alex asks him, "Weren't you afraid?"

Rich looks at us, grins again and then taps the stick lightly on the ground. "Of course. But it was my job," he says quietly. "You know the score when you take the job. Unless you have a REMF job lined up, you know what might happen. Deep down, you always figure it won't be me. Sometimes you feel that today you'll buy the farm, but you get through it and the feeling passes."

I ask, "What's a REMF?"

He spits out, "Rear-echelon motherfucker. The S.O.B.s who strut around in their uniforms, but who never get near anything more dangerous than a hangover. There were ten REMF's for every guy doing any real fighting."

Alex and I just look at each other.

"As for being afraid," he says, "I had a little trick. I used to keep as busy as possible. I'd never just be sitting there waiting. That was easy because I was an officer, so I had plenty to do. And I always had one goal in mind: keep my men alive. If you have any control over the situation, any control at all, then you feel better. It's only bad if there's not a damn thing you can do except hug the mud."

Then he says, "Let me tell you one thing about leadership, guys. You're young now, but someday you'll have some kind of leadership role, whether you like it or not. The secret is to understand the jobs underneath you. If you've done that guy's job, then you'll know how to provide leadership. If you haven't done every job yourself, you're just another candyass with a title."

I'm thinking, yah, I hope I never have to lead anybody, and then Rich says, "It's like being a good parent. Your guys will follow what you do, not what you say."

That reminded me of the time I met Alex's kung fu master, a dumpy old Filipino guy who says he's eighty, but looks about fifty.

Alex really wanted me to meet him, but to tell the truth, the way Alex raved him up, I was afraid to meet this guy. So one afternoon Alex drags me over to the concrete block church room the guy rents for his classes.

The old man spocks me out and I get this sinking feeling in my stomach. "Come here," he says, and I'm thinking, Oh my God, my worst nightmare, he's going to show everybody some crusty moves on me.

Instead he says, "Try to push your fingers into my shoulders," and he spins around. I look at Alex and he jerks his head like, go ahead, do what he says, dummy, so I tense up my fingers and try to jab them into the meaty part of the old guy's shoulders. "Harder!" he shouts, and I try a little harder, and he says, "Come on, boy, all your strength," and so I figure, okay, old man, here goes, and I really jab my fingers into the spot where his neck hits his shoulders.

Only I can't budge his muscles. They're like granite.

"Now I try you," he says, and I know this is some sort of ritual. So I turn around and he says, "Tighten your shoulders." So I do and then I'm screaming, "Okay! Okay!" because the old man's fingers have sunk through my muscles like they were tapioca pudding and it hurts like hell. I'm a quivering blob, the old man obviously knows all these pressure points, and Alex is looking at me like, see? See? See how great he is? And I'm thinking, yah Alex, thanks for the humiliation.

Then they practice and I am so thankful that I'm not dragged in as a training dummy, like one of those scrawny guys that attacks Bruce Lee and gets dusted in two milliseconds, wheet-chang-whap! Bruce Lee is Alex's big tent hero, but his Master is no slouch either. The guy has these moves which are fluid and abrupt at the same time. I can't really describe it, fast but not jerky.

Alex is his teaching assistant, and he demonstrates stuff on Alex because he knows Alex wants to learn so badly and he can take a little punishment. He asks Alex to try a series of straight punches to his face, and I'm surprised because Alex really tries to nail the old man. I realize that's what the old man wants, to show what it's like for real. He deflects Alex's stabs of brown lightning with these windmill moves and then pushes him away. I think Alex is faking it because he falls over just from this push, but he swears it's the Master's chi, his inner force. He says it makes that little push feel like a wall is falling on you.

"Don't think of yourself or what you're going to do," the Master says after he helps Alex bounce back up from the padding. "Focus on your opponent. Don't look at his eyes, look at his belly," and he slaps his stomach. "Bring your power up from here," and he slaps his round gut again. He repeats the windmill motions slowly. "Now you try it," he tells the class, which is kids, girls, a couple of guys about our age, one older woman, all kinds of people. "Move with your belly," he says, and he corrects a girl's arm swirl to be tighter.

At the end of the class, the Master tells everybody, "Now I'm going to show you what to do if your opponent has a gun." He instructs Alex to point his finger like a gun and stand about six feet in front of him. I'm thinking, okay, here comes some sort of kung fu magic like in the movies, and the old man braces himself in a stance.

He raises one hand, reaches behind his back with the other and slowly removes a thin black wallet. Then he throws it at Alex's feet. The class roars with laughter and Alex looks confused. The Master is laughing too, and he goes to Alex and slaps his back real hard. He reaches up and grabs Alex's chin in the palm of his hand. "Don't get cocky," the Master tells him, and he holds Alex's chin almost like a mother would and squints into his wide eyes.

Alex tries to look down, but the old man makes him look in his eyes. Then the Master lets go of his chin and pats his shoulder. Alex just stands there for a while, and then he starts helping the other students roll up the mats. I want to talk about the class and his Master, but he's silent all the way home.

# CHAPTER NINE

Alex is definitely into this "my body as the temple of the gods" gig because he wants to be like Bruce Lee. One day, right after we became friends, we're standing around the old oak tree in the park after football practice with some of these guys on the team, guys I'm scared blinky of, a gigantia Samoan guy, some tough wiry homeboys, these beefy neckless haoles and bodybuilder Af-Am guys. I'm only there because I'm like a mascot, and they're handing around some herb, and Alex says, "Pass." So they give him a little skag about how Hawaiians can't take it, the Af-Am linebacker Edaniel says something about a natural high, and Alex says, "Bruce Lee doesn't need this crap."

I'm already ozoned so I say, "Who the hell is Bruce Lee?"

There's a couple of laughs because somehow the delivery was funny, or maybe it was the weed. Anyway, Alex whips out a hand and grabs my collar and pulls me like a rag doll up to his face.

"Bruce Lee is my hero," he says.

"Okay," I say, and I wipe the grin off my face even though it's pretty hard to do because Alex is definitely salty. He tosses me back against the tree trunk and launches about twenty quick punches at my face, just boom-boom-boom-boom-boom, stopping just short of my eyebrows.

"Bruce Lee has the moves, bruddah," he says to no one in particular, and there are low whistles and howls, and comments like, "Man, we almost saw cabbage turned into cole slaw," and, "Hernandez, you better watch your mouth." Of course I was humiliated, but at least it was my friend. I mean, what else are friends for? Plus, I knew Alex had just used me to make a point to the other guys.

After that, the guys would make jokes about Bruce Lee before a big game when everyone's nervous and their guts are weak. Some guy would say, "Hey Alex, I heard those assholes from Jefferson say that Bruce Lee's a fake," and he would start looking mean, mean enough to split wood, and then some other guy would say, "Yeah, they say he used doubles for all his fights," and Alex would start growling like a wild animal, and after a few more insults he would get up howling and punch out a locker or just start banging his shoulder pad against a post and grunting.

This would fire up the team a hundred times better than some lame speech by the coach, so he would just let the ritual go on and look busy with the assistant coach. The funny thing is, nine times out of ten after this fire-up Alex would sack the other team's QB within the first series. One time he was so fired up he just tore through their line and sacked the poor clown hard on the first play of the game. He jumped up and ripped off a Klingon victory roar, and the other guys' morale went vertical.

After that, they kept trying sweeps to the other side, but it got so predictable that our linebackers started keying on that side and we just stomped every drive at the line of scrimmage. I think they finally scored on some long desperation bomb, but we won the game.

But grip this. Nobody makes jokes about Bruce Lee except at the pre-game warm-up. When they try, they get the Stare and the Message—shut the hell up about my hero, I'm taking it seriously. So they do.

I had a lot of fun with the football guys after I was accepted as mascot. I always thought water boy and that kind of griff was demeaning, but since I hung out with Alex anyway, I felt I might as well be useful. The coach would say, "Hernandez, as long as you're just standing around, hump this bag of balls up to the upper field," so what am I going to say, no?

After the Bruce Lee incident, the guys would give me a hard time like, "Hey Daz, your nose needs straightening; why not tell Alex that Bruce Lee sucks?" and I would say things like, "Did you read where 98% of all football players are brain-dead?" And then someone would say, usually Alex, "Yeah, but we have big dicks," and I would answer, "It's not the size, it's the frequency," and he would say, "How would you know, cherry?" Sometimes it seems like insults is all anybody ever says anymore, but I guess it's better than nothing. Sometimes they're funny and other times it's yah, ha ha, but you're hurting.

My original point was that Alex doesn't do drugs other than an occasional spliff and maybe a couple of beers once in a while. In fact, he acts like my older brother sometimes, saying, "'Nuff, brah," when I'm reaching for a third beer. So I say, "Who are you, my mother?" and he says, "You're drunk already, brah, and you look sooooo ridiculous when you're ozoned."

So to save face I'll pop it anyway but say, "Okay, I'll split it with you," and then I'll pour off most of it. Of course we had our lapses, like when we drag-raced that VW bug with the Falcon, but hey, all in all he keeps me under control.

Eventually I get to see the old kung fu classics on the big screen. Alex calls me up all excited and tells me there's going to be Bruce Lee flicks playing in Chinatown this weekend. Its a long drive up there, and to tell the truth, I'd never been there except maybe once as a kid.

The scene is strat. Bruce Lee is strat, the Theater is strat, and the girls are totally strat. There are so many cuties with long black hair that I tell Alex, "Spike Orange County, I'm moving up here."

Then he tells me, "You touch these girls and their brothers will cut your left nut off," but he says that everywhere we go, no matter what the ethnic scene or the type of girls.

So this Bruce Lee is amazing after all. I would even say supernova. He moves so quick you can barely follow how many guys he's punched out. We also saw one of Jackie Chan's old Hong Kong flicks, where he does all these loopy stunts, like sliding down three stories on a rickety bamboo ladder.

Alex gets wound up like a clock after seeing Bruce Lee and the young Jackie Chan in action. He jumps up on fire hydrants and then kicks a few imaginary bad guys and leaps off, then demolishes a bad guy/power pole, does some spinning kicks, saying, "Ho, man, did you see that part in the store, when he kicks those guys off the railing? The guy is too much!" Kick leap jab. "And what about when he spits the red pepper sauce in their eyes?" Dragon whips tail, crane beats wings, sweep left sweep right punch punch.

"Yeah, the girls were really cute, too. I wouldn't kick them out of bed," I say.

70

"Yeah yeah, but did you see at the end, when they show the screw-up scenes? Ho, bruddah, it's no act when he fights. It's for real." Spin kick jab punch.

At least I know what hero worship looks like. I mean, Bruce Lee was incredible. He deserves being somebody's hero. Not because he acted like a saint, but because he was just so damned dedicated at ramping up his skill.

\*　\*　\*

After a couple days groving with Rich and Pauline in the campground we're ready to charge the I-states again. Rich gives us their phone number and address in Northern Virginia, and tells us like a command that we have to stop in and see them when we get to the East Coast. Of course we agree, and I'm thinking, yah, we'll be ready for a decent meal by then, guarans ball bearins.

Actually, we planned the second part of our East Coast gig around visiting them. We stayed a lot longer than we thought in New York with Tita and Benny, but that was perfect because Rich and Pauline were still out cruising during that month.

I thought New York was Hell to drive around, but the million little twisty roads in Virginia may be worse. After we gripped that every dinky street was called something like Highway 5237, we found their town without too much map-grabbing and yelling. I'm a little nervous driving up their street, all these big spreads and expensive houses, but they welcome us like we're their favorite nephews. Pauline puts us in their guest room, which has this old-fashioned wallpaper and big thick pillows that feel great after sleeping on rolled-up blue jeans. They show us the photos from their trip, and we show them the few shots we took that aren't too goofy or blurred by Alex's thumb. I swear to God it's him, even though he claims I'm the one who can't keep the camera still. We almost always forget to take pictures anyway, except at the usual places like the Grand Canyon.

The next day Rich offers to show us around the area, and of course we accept. We go in the Lancer because he says he wants to try it. I'm a little worried that it's getting tired, but the engine's been running smooth since we got it fixed in Kansas City and I can't say no. So we let him drive and I sit in the back, which feels really weird since it's the first time one of us isn't driving.

Right away Alex starts asking all these G.I. Joe questions, and it makes me feel mambo. I figure Rich is sick of reliving the war.

Alex asks him, "What's it like to shoot an M-16?"

Rich answers, "It's okay, but I carried an NVA–47 myself. They didn't jam as easy." Later on when we lived for a few days with crazy Elroy in Oakland, that's the only story I ever told that got his respect. This nut Elroy was very interested in what Rich had to say about combat rifles.

After we cruise around town and the countryside for awhile, Rich pointing things out and answering all of Alex's questions about Vietnam, Rich says, "How about we grab some lunch? I'll take you to my favorite place."

It's back in town, down an alley, sort of like the Casa Grande back home, only the alley is the main entrance. It turns out to be nice inside because there's big industrial-size skylights, like it used to be a small factory. It's clean and light and not cluttered up with frew-frew. The burgers and sandwiches are pretty cheap, the waitresses are nectar, and I can see why Rich likes it.

A guy with unkempt shoulder-length blond hair is sitting in the middle of the big bar that runs across the back wall, and when he turns his head to see who just came in he smiles and nods at Rich. I'm surprised that Rich is friends with some old hippie, but he says, "Let's go sit with my buddy Kyle," and we trail behind him as he walks to the bar.

We come up to the guy and I am blown through the floor because the man has no hands. He's wearing two metal arms with mechanical claws on the end, and he's holding a beer mug in one of the claws. The arms have plastic guards that run up almost to his elbows, and I try real hard to keep my eyes on his face. Rich puts his hand on the guy's shoulder and says, "I want you to meet a couple of friends of mine. Daz and Alex." I'm bug-eyed and sweating because I don't know how to meet a guy with no hands. But Kyle just lifts his chin in greeting, and says, "Heard about your car and your trip from the Captain here."

"They've been letting me drive it today," Rich tells him. "Probably let you drive it, too."

"Well, Hell, if they're crazy enough to let you drive it, I guess they might," Kyle says.

"What do you say, boys?" Rich asks us.

Alex is blown flat, too, so I say, "Sure."

Kyle spocks our unspoken question and glances at Rich. "Can't do any brain surgery, but I can drive. Right, Captain?"

"Better than I can," Rich says. "Did you eat yet, Kyle?"

"Haven't decided what to have," he answers. He's got a big weathered face, and he's tan, so I know he's out in the sun a lot. "How about you?"

"The usual," Rich says. "Turkey on French roll with extra mustard."

"Cap, you ought to try something different once in a while," Kyle tells him in a strict way, like he's Rich's teacher. "Think I'll try a BLT. Haven't had one of those in years."

Alex and I order burgers and then we're both silent. It's strange because we don't want it to show that we feel blinky, but we can't help it and they have to act like they don't notice it. So we're all acting like we aren't spocking the obvious.

The waitress brings us our Cokes and Kyle says, "You're from Orange County, huh?"

"Try not to hold it against us," I say.

He laughs and says, "No, I liked it down there. Haven't been there since I was at Pendleton, damn, thirty years ago. Prefer Santa Barbara, though." He sips the beer and says, "Has your car held up pretty good?" So I tell him all about the Lancer and our meltdown in Kansas City, and I try to keep looking in his gray-blue eyes.

"Not too many Lancers or Valiants on the road anymore," he tells us. "It's good you guys are keeping it together."

The food comes and I don't feel like eating because I wonder if Kyle can pick up his sandwich and it doesn't seem right to just chow down in front of him.

"This looks better than I thought it would," says Rich, and he picks up half of Kyle's BLT and nestles it between the pincers of Kyle's steel hand. "Thanks, Cap," Kyle says and he lifts it up to take a bite. "Probably tastes better than you remember, too."

A fat slice of tomato falls out of the sandwich on the way up, and Rich reaches over and puts it on Kyle's plate. There's something

73

about Rich's little matter-of-fact move for his buddy that gets to me, and it's one of those snapshots in my mind I'll never forget.

Rich takes a big bite of his turkey sandwich with oozing mustard and says, "This is what I really missed over there."

"I guess that's why you're never sick of it," Kyle tells him. "What I missed was having a choice." The last bite of his sandwich falls out of the pincers onto the bar and Rich puts it on his plate.

"How's the burgers, guys?" he asks us.

"Good," we say, but I don't think either of us tasted anything.

Rich has been collecting all the parts of the BLT that had fallen out of Kyle's steel hand on the plate, and after Kyle's done with the second half he fixes the plate in the pincers in that easy way people have when they've done something a thousand times. Then he lifts the plate and shovels what's left of the sandwich into his mouth with his other set of pincers.

"The boys have been asking me about the war," Rich says in an off-handed way, like we'd asked about the old Dodgers or some sports gig.

"Guess they asked the right man," Kyle says, and there's no spin on his words; they're flat.

Rich smiles and says, "Yeah, a talkative old son-of-a-bitch," and Kyle chuckles.

"Show them any pictures yet?" Kyle asks him.

"No, I didn't want to bore them too much," Rich says. "Oh, yeah, I almost forgot. I brought you something from D.C." He opens up his wallet and unfolds a piece of heavy paper that has charcoal or pencil rubbed on it. He lays it on the bar while he puts his wallet away and I can see there's a name outlined in white in the middle of the black. He shows it to Kyle, then folds it up and puts it in Kyle's shirt pocket.

"Thanks for remembering," Kyle says. "Did you get any for yourself?"

"Yeah," Rich says. "A guy I lost in '69."

Kyle glances over at him and then takes a sip of his beer. "Was he with you long?"

Rich nods. "Yeah."

They stare at the back wall for a while and then Kyle turns to Alex and says, "Cap says you're from Oahu. I spent a lot of time in the Keys and at Tripler."

74

"The Keys?" I ask him. "I thought they were in Florida."
Kyle chuckles. "Waikiki. Get it? Ki-ki. The keys."

"My treat," Rich says and he grabs the check, and Kyle says, "Thanks, Cap. Might as well put your retirement check to good use."

We go out to the car, and Alex and I sit in the back seat like we're the guests. "Look at this steering wheel," Kyle says after he slides into the drivers' seat. "It's huge." Rich slips the ignition key into his steel claw and Kyle struggles for a moment to get the key in the slot. I'm rigid, trying to relax, and Rich tells us, "Kyle put a British-style starter button in his Pontiac. Just like in the old Austin-Healys."

"Can't be stolen," Kyle says all proudly. "It's hidden real nice."

The keys drop out of his pincers and he takes a deep breath. He exhales and then pounds the dash real hard with his forearm. "Goddammit!" he yells, and his tone of voice scares me, not like I'm scared of getting punched but something worse. "Goddammit," he says again. "Sometimes . . . goddammit, sometimes I just. . . ."

"It's my fault," Rich says flatly and he picks up the keys. "I don't know what the hell I was thinking."

Kyle is still staring out the windshield. Rich puts the keys in the ignition and then sits back silently.

Kyle takes another couple of deep breaths and then says, "Turn it for me, would you, Rich?" Rich leans over, clicks the key and the engine starts right away, thank God. I can barely breath I'm so solid. Kyle just sits there revving the engine for a few minutes and we're all silent. Finally, he pulls the gear shift lever into drive and we leave.

"I like the ride," he says when we turn out into the street. "Smooth." He has both steel hands hooked on the steering wheel at each end of the crossbar. "Steers pretty well, too," he says.

After we've driven around town for awhile Kyle says to Rich, "I want to give you some more green beans," and then he asks us, "Mind if we go out to my place for a minute?"

I say, "Sure," and he drives through town and out into the countryside. Maybe ten minutes later we pull onto a rough gravel driveway and drive back to a tidy saltbox house with white walls and bright green trim. "I see you went with the green," Rich tells

Kyle, who says, "Yeah, it's the compromise color. Looks better than I thought it would."

Rich glances over at his friend and says, "A hell of lot better than that yellow Jackie wanted."

"You got that right," Kyle snorts. "We'll go with the yellow in the kitchen. I figured what the hell, it'll look cheerful in winter."

He shuts off the Cruiser and turns to us. "I want to show you my pride and joy."

I'm thinking it's his Pontiac, but instead he takes us around to the back yard and shows us his garden. There's all kinds of flowers and bushes and a vegetable garden that looks like it's out of a book.

"Look at these beans," he says to us, pointing at the garden with one of his arms. The bean plants are growing thick on poles maybe eight feet high, and they're loaded with long flat green beans. Kyle reaches up, picks one with his claw, and eats it. "They're so sweet you don't even have to cook them. Come here, you guys. Help me pick some for Pauline and Cap."

The beans are hard to spot sometimes because they're about the same color as the leaves, but it's kind of fun to pull the leaves aside and look for them. I've never picked green beans right off the vine before. "Just get the big ones," Kyle says, and we scour each plant, saying, "Look at the size of this one" when we find a gigantia bean.

Kyle throws me a key ring on a fat leather strap and says, "There's plastic bags in the drawer by the sink. Bring us a couple. It's the silver key on its own ring."

I feel weird going into his house alone, but I do it anyway. It's neat inside, too. I see a photo in the dining room of Kyle and his wife or girlfriend, who's a little overweight but still cute, and I want to look in his living room for other pictures. Instead, I rummage through the drawers until I find the recycled plastic bags from the supermarket. They're folded up real carefully. I peel off two and go to the back door.

"Should I lock it?" I yell out, and Kyle nods yes. I bring him the bags and he tells us to divide up the beans evenly. There's enough to fill both bags. "One for you, Cap," Kyle says, "and one for the gals at Jackie's office."

Rich is squatting in front of these huge tomato plants and he says, "You have one hell of a garden here, Kyle."

"Pick me those ripe tomatoes in the center, will you Cap?" Kyle asks.

Rich peers in and gingerly tugs off three nice red tomatoes. "These are beefsteaks," Kyle tells us. "Cap, put one in each bag. The ladies are just going to have to fight over it." He gently pulls the tomato plant leaves aside and says, "There's two things I really miss. Picking vegetables and rubbing my woman's tits."

"At least you can still eat both of them," Rich says, and we all laugh.

"Yeah, thank God for that," Kyle says sheepishly. "Well, let's run back into town and you can drop me off at my car."

After Kyle drives us back to the parking lot and we've all gotten out of the Cruiser, Kyle cradles the bulging bag of green beans in one arm and puts his other arm around Rich's shoulder. "Thanks for the name off the Wall, Cap. I was real tight with Frank. You'd have liked him."

Rich puts his hand on Kyle's shoulder for a few seconds and says, "I'm sure I would have."

Kyle gives Rich the beans and turns to us. "You guys have a good trip," he tells us. "Hope I see California again before too long. I like Santa Barbara a lot."

We nod and he looks over at Rich. "You're lucky to have Rich to talk to about the war. He was really there, weren't you, Cap?"

"Just another grunt taking orders," Rich says, and they both laugh.

After Kyle drives off, Rich sits in the driver's seat, but he doesn't start the Cruiser right away.

"You guys probably guessed Kyle got his hands blown off in Vietnam," he says. "He tried to throw a dead man over a grenade that rolled into his bunker. There were three other guys in there with him. He managed to get the body in front of them before it went off, and that saved four lives. He never told me. I had to check the medals files in Washington to find out."

He shifts around so he can look us both in the eyes. "I consider myself a pretty good soldier, but I can't say I'd have had the guts and quick thinking to do that."

77

He turns the ignition key and the Lancer rumbles to life. "I have a feeling the man he used as a shield was his friend, the one whose name I pulled off the Wall for him."

Neither of us said much on the way back to Rich's house, and I wondered if Rich had planned for us to meet Kyle.

Alex never asked about the war again.

# CHAPTER TEN

We've had enough of Las Vegas already so we stop to gas up and take a leak although you don't need to piss much in that heat. It's mostly habit. The sun's almost down, but it's still blowtorch city. Alex is in full jank mode because he had to call his folks on the pay phone and tell them that the new cell phone they'd given him was now a plastic pancake. Typical Alex; he's under the car that morning, checking the oil pan, and he leaves the phone on the ground while he looks for any leaks. When we leave I hear this crunch, and even though I know him, I'm still blown down that he's already adiosed the phone on the second day of the trip.

I'm at the pump, avoiding him, and this girl wanders over and asks where we're going. "Probably the Grand Canyon," I tell her.

She lifts her shades, spocks us out with these big gray-blue eyes for a minute, and then says, "Mind if I catch a ride with you?"

Alex and I look at each other and figure why not. She's kind of cute, long brown hair, spunky, definitely a 501, you know, tight jeans, tight butt, nice tits under her white tanktop. We say okay, and after Alex gets the Lancer onto some little two-lane highway heading south I turn around and ask her, "What's your name?"

"Tracie," she says, "with an i-e."

I tell her, "There's a town named Tracy in Northern California."

She smiles and says, "It'd be nice to have my own town."

After a while I ask, "Aren't you afraid of hitching alone?" And she whips this automatic pistol out of her backpack, the kind with a clip, and says, "Stop the car."

My heart is beating in full frap mode at the sight of her roscoe, and Alex is spocking her in the rearview mirror. I'm thinking, great. We have to pick up the only girl mass murderer in the country.

"Why?" I ask her, trying not to sound too afraid.

"Just stop," she says very cool. "I want to show you something."

"Is that thing loaded?" I ask.

She snorts and tells me, "Don't worry, I just want to show you something."

So Alex pulls over and gives me The Look, like "What the hell have you got us into this time, numbnuts?" and she pops out, wheels around, and lets two cars go past. Then she braces her arm like lady cops do and just peels off four shots at a speed limit sign maybe eighty or ninety feet away, blam blam blam blam, loud-ass shots.

"Let's go see how I did," she says, and we back up as cars are going past. I'm thinking great, she could have coughed and drilled some poor schmoe through the forehead and I'm up on an accomplice rap. Why me?

She spocks the sign, comes back and says she nailed it three out of four. I don't doubt her. She reloads the clip and shoves it back into the grip and seems real proud of herself. "I also have a knife," she says as she gets in the car. "I'd wait for anyone attacking me to get occupied and then I'd stick it into his kidneys." Great, a medical student mass murderer. Alex gives me the big stink-eye and then gets us back on the highway.

"So what's the point?" I ask her once we get back up to speed.

"To defend myself," she says as if I was stupid.

"No," I tell her, "I mean being out on the road."

"I got tired of Las Vegas," she answers. "I really loved it, but I need to move on. Where are you guys going?"

"Iowa."

"Iowa?" She looks at us like we're wearing Richard Nixon masks. "Most people are trying to get out of places like Iowa."

"Yeah, I know. That's why we want to go there," I tell her. Even though it's not true, it sounds better than the truth about visiting relatives.

"Interesting," she says, kind of nodding. "I like that. Maybe I'll come too." Alex kicks me in the shin to give me the message that he is less than pleased by this prospect.

Alex asks her, "So you got a boyfriend?"

She says, "No, I don't have any boyfriends, I only have friends. I hate that romantic crap. It's slavery for both people."

She takes out a pack of nicspliffs. "Mind if I smoke?"

Alex says, "Yeah. It stinks and it's bad for your body."

"Joe Health Nut, huh," she says in a bent voice.

So I ask, "The tough girl act, right?"

She looks at me like she's deciding whether to laugh or shoot me.

"When a guy smokes it's cool and when a girl does it's phony," she says. "I suppose you're clean."

"Everything but his mouth," says Alex.

She asks, "You guys been friends long?"

I answer, "Long enough."

"Long enough for what?"

"To travel together, I guess," I tell her. "Haven't killed each other yet."

She settles back into the corner with her hands behind her head, and I can see her smooth underarms and bra strap under her top. "Where you guys from?" she asks us. "I saw the California plates."

"L.A."

She sniffs and says, "I guess I shouldn't be prejudiced."

"Yeah, we hate it too but you can't pick where you're from," I tell her. "How about you? Where are you from?"

She answers in that quick way people do when they want to hide something. "All over."

Yeah, uh-huh. The usual evasion. I'm in kind of a booga-booga mood, so I say, "East Do-Wa-Diddly in Kickturd County, right?"

She gives me the "should I laugh or not?" look, and cracks a really small smile. "Yeah, something like that."

I'm looking at her eyes but I can't tell through her dark shades whether her eyes are even open. "Someplace that isn't fashionable enough to openly hate, right?"

She doesn't move, she just says, "Right."

"So you're not going to tell us?" I ask her.

She lowers her arms and looks out the window at the sagebrush. "No."

"Okay, mystery woman. Kansas." No answer. "Minnesota." No answer. "I got it, Arkansas." Moping silence. Well that didn't take long, I say to myself. I got her bent in the first minute of conversation. My fricking mouth. I can't stop it. It's diseased.

After a while Tracie says, "You know what I hate?"

"No, what?" I answer, glad she's not bent at me.

"When guys call me baby or honey," she says. "I feel like kicking them in the nuts."

I try not to smile and ask, "Who calls you that?"

"Strangers. You know, guys who call every girl 'baby' or some bullshit cutie name."

So I tell her, "You know what I hate?"

She says, "No, what."

" DVDs," I tell her. "Camcorders, all that crap."

"DVDs? Why?" she asks.

"Because they're bubble gum for the brain," I say. "I'm not paying the Japanese and Koreans to rot my mind, thank you. I mean they're hard workers and all that, but I'm not buying into their plan to keep us addicted to the latest janky little toy. Big TVs, DVDs, cheezoid little cell phones with all the crappy music ever made, it's all griff."

She shifts around to look at me and asks, "What's griff?"

Alex butts in and says, "Bad. He's got lots of crazy words, but they all mean either 'good' or 'bad.'"

I punch him lightly in the shoulder and say, "Thank you very much, Professor." Then I turn back to Tracie. "Can you even hear the difference between a CD and a tape?" I ask her.

She shrugs. "I don't know. Probably not."

"Nobody can, they just act like they do," I tell her. "People are starving, and rich jerk-offs are buying all this electronic crap that gets adiosed two years later."

"I don't even have a DVD player," she says, kind of caught off-guard.

"Grip this," I tell her. "Someday Joe Kawasaki is going to wake up in his bullet train and think, 'Screw this sacrifice griff; those assholes in San Fernando have huge houses, two cars, a satellite dish, and a houseful of other crap, and I have a hole in my stomach from slaving for some company that should be burned down for the good of the planet.'"

Tracie is silent so I shift into fourth. "You're so down on romance. You know what the guys read in Japan? Porno comics as thick as phone books, that's what. They just can't draw in the crotch."

I can tell she thinks I'm lying. "It's true, I read about it in the *L.A. Times*. Some day maybe Mrs. Kawasaki will torch the porno plant and stop being such a slave, too. Maybe the whole Japanese economy will get like ours, and it'll be great because they'll stop sacrificing themselves to the Sony god just to spread all these stupid toys all over the planet."

Tracie is silent. Then Alex asks, "You know what I hate?"

I'm done with my rant so I say, "No, what?"

Alex is lounging back in the seat, driving with one hand. He says, "Being cold. I hate being cold."

Tracie says, "Then you must be pretty happy here."

"He is," I tell her, "He is."

We keep a small cooler filled with ice on the back seat just for our washcloths. Whenever we get too fried, we soak a towel in ice cold water and slap it on our heads. The ice water drips down your front and juices you; you have to scream it's so cold, but then the heat is bearable for a few minutes. Alex is only wearing swim trunks, but I always wear a T-shirt because I don't like being a wimp-bod laughingstock, especially to 501s like Tracie.

"I like the heat, too," she says, and she looks good in her dark shades and damp tanktop.

"If you get too hot, use one of our cold towels," I tell her.

"Thanks," she says, and she wrings one out and lays it across the back of her neck. Then she slouches down and puts her hands behind her head again, and I can't help noticing her flat belly between her jeans and tanktop.

"You camping out or staying in motels?" Alex asks her. She's got a sleeping bag under her backpack, but it's always a good idea to find out how broke the hitcher is.

"Whatever looks good," she says. I'm thinking copa, she's got some gitas, so we don't have to support her.

"How long were you in Las Vegas?" she asks us.

"Two days," I answer, although it felt like two weeks.

She can't believe it. "Is that all? I was there for three months. I made good money, too."

"Doing what?" I ask.

"Bar hostess," she says. "Old fat guys give you big tips if you just listen to them and smile. What were you guys doing?"

I felt like saying, "Falling into the mouth of Hell," but instead I just told her our story. All we wanted to do was gas the scene, have a few laughs watching people mainline greed, and stuff ourselves on the cheap grinds. Instead Alex immediately drops us into a nice squishy load of griff.

This is our first night, right? Our first night on the road, our first stop. We think we've got lots of money, plus I've got my $300 limit Mastercard, which makes me feel like King Tut. So we decide to stay at the Sands, which is like being beamed to another planet where every excess is considered normal. There's a fake volcano in front which blows up every hour, the whole lobby wall is an aquarium with tropical fish swimming around behind the busboys, and the first floor is a jungle, with palm trees and ferns and vines.

Then there's the people. It's rush hour on the Harbor Freeway without the cars. The place is jammed, even though we didn't get in until 10 at night. There's Asian groups, Hispanic families, Af-Am ladies dressed to the chin, fat white people, gay guys in tight shirts, brats hanging onto Mom, old folks in dayglo clothes, and icy bouncers dressed in blue suits looking bored and carrying walkie-talkies.

The hotel is famous for its white lions, which live behind a glass wall in this white palace with a big pool and a few palm trees. Everybody, including us, is goo-goo-eyed, straining over some fat woman speaking a weird language who's hogging the front for a look at these white lions.

This idea comes to me and I tell Alex, "You know what would be strat? If a big crane came out every once in a while and grabbed one of the tourists and lifted them up and dropped them into the lion's palace. If they could climb this rope ladder, then they could get out. If they couldn't, they'd be Lion Friskies. It would be so Las Vegas."

Alex gives me a "You are weird" look, but I still think it would be great entertainment. It would make looking at the lions a lot more interesting, especially if they picked up the fat lady who's blocking our view. The audience could cheer the victim on, or if he was really ickabod, cheer the lions on.

The casino itself is this dark endless basement with flashing lights that disorient you and make you take your wallet out and remove the big bills and hand them to women in asshugging outfits who give you rolls of quarters out of trays they're carrying around. Then you belly up to one of ten thousand slot machines next to a zombie woman who's sold her soul to the devil for a jackpot of fifty dollars. She's just cranking away on the button because pulling the machine's arm gets tiring after about eight hours or so and she's already on the swing shift of her devil pact. The only thing that breaks her concentration is the jangle of your machine pumping out the quarters, and she gives you this look which says, "That should be my machine!" And if your jackpot was a good one and you get up to take a leak, she'll try to play both yours and hers.

Then there's the nickel players, the people who need to make it last, and the guys who play robot poker with the video screens. You wander around in here for a while and you get lost because it all looks the same, banks of slot machines and flashing lights and an occasional bar that pops up like an oasis for the damned.

Finally, we reach something different, the baccarat and poker tables, which have a bored dealer, man or woman, sitting there waiting to take your money. One dealer is flipping cards to four guys and I want to sit down with them because he's classic, he has a pencil mustache and a black eye patch. But I'm only nineteen so gambling at the tables is out.

Alex goes up to this old Asian guy who he can tell is from Hawaii and asks him to buy us two rolls of quarters, which the guy does and then we sit down to play the machines. I hit a four-quarter jackpot on my third ring and I'm off my seat shouting, "Alex, I won! I'm hot!" but of course the roll is gone about ten minutes later even with a couple of twelve-quarter wins. Alex's roll is vacuumed in five and he's already bored watching me feed the machine. So twenty bucks, four hours work after taxes, is hosed down the gutter in five minutes. That was enough gambling for us, so we take off down the Strip to catch one of those all-you-can-eat grinderias.

85

You have to hand it to these Vegas casino owners. They put the food in the very back of the casino, down by the parking garage, so you have to walk through the entire casino before you can eat. There's all these flashing lights and slot machines so you might drop a fiver just getting to the cafeteria and another fiver trying to get out of the place. Boom, a ten-buck dinner turns a ten dollar profit. But then the low ceilings and the dark and the flashing colored lights and the whole feeling of being in Hell might cause you to fritz out and start ranting about Abe Lincoln or something and then the bouncers would move in like piranhas, grab you, stuff you in a duffel bag, poink you with Valium, and ship you back to L.A. after making sure your room tab is even.

But ten bucks for all the food you can eat is a sure loser when Alex is tromping up to the buffet, so we follow the screaming brats in front of us down these long hallways. We finally get to the eatery which was designed by the same guys who make school cafeterias, only this time they had the room to really stretch out and uglify a whole basement.

Half the people in line should be behind a plow, working off the lard they're already carrying, but no, they're here, picking up a little piece of lettuce and one slice of tomato, and then rushing for the roast beef and turkey and the desserts. What the hell, I didn't even bother with the one chunk of iceberg lettuce, I went straight for the beef and gravy. Alex is a better eater, "my body is a temple of the gods," et cetera, so he takes lettuce, sliced beets, sprouts, lots of carrot and celery sticks, and a few olives, and then he goes for the sliced turkey and some Chinese-style chicken which he pronounces "Okay" after four pieces went gravitational. The desserts look better than they taste, but by then I could only eat two, a cream puff and a cherry tart.

I'm Joe Tuba after one turn, but Alex loads up again and the owners are really losing gitas on this deal. I scan the room for 501s and spot a couple. That keeps me occupied until Alex is done and we can vector.

It's about midnight and the air is finally cooler and, we're walking down the Strip spocking the lights and all the people. It's like the United Nations of Regular People convenes here every day. We're almost back to the Sands when we spock a couple of guys about our age trying to push a big old Chrysler into a parking lot. People are honking at them because they're blocking traffic. Alex nudges me and says, "Let's go help them."

I'm afraid I'm going to hit the vomitorium if I bend over, not to mention push a three-ton car, but Alex and I help the two guys push and I see there's two girls in the front seat. It turns out the transpo just went four paws to the sky for no known reason—it's gassed and charged. The two couples seem nice, so Alex and I, King Widget mechanics, right, pop the hood and see what we can do.

The thing is dead as a can of tuna, it's dark, and there's nothing we can see that's wrong. I look over at Alex and he says, "Maybe we should give them a ride home." I agree it's the least we can do, so he brings the Cruiser around and they pile in the back seat and we're off to their friends' apartment.

We drive up to this concrete block building and I already know which apartment is their friends'. The ground floor unit's door is wide open and people are sitting on the doorstep holding brewkowskis. We can hear the bass thumping and people laughing, and then the guy who owns the old Chrysler invites us to spend the night since it's a two-bedroom apartment and the friend who's renting it works all night anyway.

I'm wary, maybe it's instinct, but Alex says, "Okay," and the gig is launched. We go in and the lanky Chrysler man hands us two brewkowskis, and then we find a spot near the front door and sit down. There's lots of girls at this party, so even though I'm tired it's okay.

There's a raised voice outside, and a sudden hush, so we poke our heads out the front door. Some middle-aged Mexi with a pot belly and a Western-style button-up shirt is standing in front of Chrysler Man and his girlfriend, and Chrysler Man is telling him, "Sorry, man, but you gotta leave," and the guy answers back with with some jank about "We're brothers, man," and it's obvious he is King Tut drunk.

Chrysler Man is hotwired by now, and he grabs his girlfriend and says, "Let's call the cops," and that sets the drunk off on a riff. "So that's how you treat a brother, man. Call the cops on him, huh."

Then the drunk spocks Alex and I get this chill that crawls up my back because I know, uh-oh, the mojo is cranking because Alex is here and the griff is going to hit like a wildfire.

Sure enough, the drunk lurches over to Alex and says, "I know Jose Padrone, man, he's my brother and you're my brother, too."

Alex hates these situations; he doesn't know how to deal with crazies, so he just turns away and acts like he doesn't see the guy. Does this work? Yah, you know the answer. It just winds the guy up more.

"So you don't think I'm a brother, huh?" the guy tells Alex. He's swaying just like a big pine tree in a wind, slowly but creaking so you're not sure if it'll fall over. "I'm Jose Padrone's brother, man, and he shakes my hand." The guy extends his hand to Alex and says, "Shake a brother's hand, man."

Alex still doesn't look at the guy, but he points to me and says, "He's the Mexican."

This also doesn't work, and the drunk insists again on Alex shaking his hand. "Is this how you treat a brother? You won't even shake his hand?"

"I'm not your brother," Alex says, and I'm getting tense because Alex might punch the guy's lights out just to shut him up, and then we'll be in jail with a bunch of drunks and I'll have to get my Dad to bail us out.

Chrysler Man is standing behind me gassing the scene and I ask him, "Who is this guy?" and he answers, "I don't know, he just wandered up."

The drunk says, "Okay, man. I'll leave if you shake my hand." Alex says, "I'm not your brother, pal," and he turns to leave.

This womps the guy's volume to ten and he starts shouting out this same mumbo-jumbo about how his brother won't shake his hand and everyone gets silent. Chrysler Man says, "I called the cops," but my cousin is a cop so I know they might not come if there's deeper action playing somewhere else, which seems likely in Las Vegas. I turn to Alex and tell him, "Just shake the asshole's hand so we can get rid of him."

Alex looks like he'd rather rip my head off than shake this guy's hand, so I say, "You can't whack him, we'll get busted." Everyone is looking at Alex and waiting for him to do something, anything, to adios this drunk.

So Alex caves in, grabs the guy's hand and pushes him back toward the front door. He lets go of the drunk and wipes his hand on his jeans. "Okay," the drunk says. "My brother shook my hand, but he wasn't very friendly. Is that how you treat a brother?"

The guy is teetering on the front door sill so I say, "Bye," and close the door on him. The door pushes him the rest of the way out and he's standing out there, gibbering.

Chrysler Man is at the window and he says, "He's doing something. Cut the lights so we can see outside." The lights click off and we all gather at the window to see what jank Mr. Brother is laying down now.

He gathers up all the beer cans and bottles the party left outside and lines then up in a row on the concrete in front of the door. He's still mumbling some major loco-moco, but he drifts off out of sight and there's a big sigh of relief.

After a minute we go outside; the drunk is gone. His line of empty beers is still standing guard, so I start picking up the cans and bottles and carry them to the kitchen.

This gig has scorched the atmosphere and people are quiet. Talk about a commercial against alcoholism. Nobody feels like drinking anymore after we've seen the zombie you become later. I'm feeling claustrophobic in this little living room with a dozen people, so I tell Alex, "I'm sitting out by the Cruiser for awhile," and he nods and says, "Me, too."

We'd parked the Lancer out on the street because the lot was full. We lean against the hood and watch people drift outside again, and I'm about to say, "I don't know about you, but I've had enough for one night," when a black Jeep squeals into the parking lot and four guys jump out. They scan the people leaning against the wall and go inside.

About five seconds later they come out again pushing a blond guy who's yelling something like, "You started it, Neal," and then one of the Jeep guys punches him full in the gut. The guy doubles over and hits the ground and Neal seems satisfied, but the blond guy rolls over on his knees and springs up at Neal, who screams and I see the sharp glint of a blade, and Neal is holding his face.

Neal's pals start kicking the blond punk and he's swishing the knife, trying to slash their legs. Chrysler Man comes over and tries to pull one of the guys off Blondy and he gets punched in the mouth. Three other guys come out of the room and jump in, and

89

then the cop cars swerve around the corner and they're in the lot, lights flashing, and a voice booms out, "Freeze. Do not move," and two cops jump out and their backup car has a man out behind his car door with his roscoe aimed and ready, and I am solid ice because somebody will get shot right now if they make the wrong move.

Nobody makes a wrong move, they freeze in mid-punch, and the cops move in, frisk everybody, and start cuffing guys and loading everyone into the back seats. An ambulance screams up a few minutes later, and Neal, whose hands and face are all bloody, is helped into the back and the ambulance hauls derriere. A third squad car pulls in and loads up, the cops question the girls and the few guys who stayed out of it, and then all the cop cars vector. The few people left after all this action stand around about a minute, and then they jump into a Toyota and vector.

The apartment is dark, so Alex and I go over to check it out. The front door is closed, but it's not locked, so we go inside. It's silent as a classroom at Christmas. Everyone's gone. My adrenaline has pumped itself out and I feel really tired, so I say, "Why don't we crib here? Nobody's going to mind," and Alex agrees. So we go get our gear and take over the empty bedroom.

I lie awake for just a minute, everything that's happened in just one day rushing through my brain, from packing the Cruiser in the driveway to saying goodbye to Old Man Ching to Hendrix in the desert to slot machines to white lions to cherry tarts to talkative drunks to knife fights and cops to silence.

See what I mean about Alex? He swears it's me, but it's him. This griff never happens when I'm alone.

The next morning I wake up, and Alex is still asleep, so I get up and look around. There's a guy sleeping in the other bedroom and I figure it's Chrysler Man's friend, the one who rents the place. There's no one else around, so I quietly shake Alex out of the dead zone and pack up our stuff, and we tiptoe out the door to the Cruiser. I wonder if the guy even knew we were cribbing in his place. We drive back to the Strip and stumble through the casino again for an "all you can eat" breakfast.

We both drink a lot of coffee with the scrambled eggs and pancakes, and eventually we track out of the robot mode and feel ready to face our second day on the road.

# CHAPTER ELEVEN

Tracie listens to this story and says, "That reminds me of my favorite joke," and I'm thinking uh-oh, cue the fake laughter. "This guy and his eight-year-old daughter are out in the park, and they see two dogs screwing," she says. "The kid asks what the dogs are doing, and the guy doesn't know what to tell her, so he says, 'The dog on top has a hurt paw and the dog underneath is helping it.' Then the kid says, 'Wouldn't you know it. You try to help somebody and you get screwed every time.'"

Tracie cackles and then asks, "So why are you guys going to Iowa?"

I turn around and answer her with, "I'll tell you if you tell us where you're from and where you're going."

"Okay," she finally says, all irritated. "Michigan, and I'm going nowhere."

"No, you're going to the Grand Canyon," I tell her. "Or we can drop you off in Williams."

"No, I'll go with you," she says, and Alex kicks me again. I want to yell at him, "Hey, it's your fault, too."

"So what's with Iowa?" she asks.

"We're visiting Alex's uncle," I tell her. "But it's not just Iowa. We're going wherever we want."

"Got tired of L.A.?" she asks, and I think about it a little before saying, "No, it's more like I've seen the malls and videos and beer commercials and I can't believe that's it, that's all there is, to get a job, and get all this electronic crap, I mean who needs it, and I can't believe that you have to be a monk and meditate ninety hours a day or be a war-zone danger freak to feel alive, or be a rich leech and walk through Borneo because hey, you're rich and you can cruise through and suck off the natives to feel like you're getting it."

"What's 'it'?" she asks, kind of irritated.

"You know, it, nirvana, napalm in the morning, getting born again, Tibetan chants, saving the redwoods, resist the oppressors, all of that," I answer. "Maybe it's having fun, or being an artist and wearing black, or maybe it's losing yourself in a screen like a hacker. I don't know."

"Me neither," she says.

"One thing I do know is that it's more than frats drinking beer," I tell her. "I don't want to get punched out of college, blow through some exotic Asian place, and then jump into a job and a mortgage and screaming brats. Then you go to Bali on your vacation and try to get it for a few weeks. What a joke."

"There's 'it' again," Tracie says. "'It' is the meaning of life, right?"

"No," I say. "More like what's real."

"Everything's real," she says.

"I mean what's really real," I tell her. "I want more than the usual."

"You and me both," she says. "I don't want some dumbshit husband and a bunch of screaming brats, either."

"So is that why you went to Las Vegas?" Alex asks her.

She laughs and says, "I went to Vegas to get a job." She leans forward, rests her arms on the seat back between us, and asks, "What did you guys do to get this car?"

"He watched screaming brats in football uniforms thump on each other and I made fiberglass Madonnas," I tell her.

"Madonnas?" She frowns, like she can't believe I'm not making it up.

"Yeah," I say, "those statues of Mother Mary in Catholic churches. The big ones."

She looks at Alex, who doesn't say anything, so she decides it's true and wrinkles her nose. "Weird job." After a while she asks, "Are you guys camping?"

"Yeah," I answer, and then we're quiet because the sun is going down and the sky is lit up like there's a firestorm over the horizon. Once it's dark, Alex and I load up some tunes and Tracie nods off on her pack. After she looks asleep, Alex points to her and whirls his finger by his ear to show me he thinks she's fifty-one-fifty, you know, orbiting Pluto, and I just hold up my hands, like what I am supposed to do?

We blow through Kingman, and in another couple of hours the air gets cool for the first time since we left the Pacific and I know we're climbing. There's scrawny trees popping up through the sagebrush in the moonlight, and pretty soon we're in a forest of scattered pine trees, and the air gets crispy and smells good.

The moon slowly gets adiosed by clouds, so by the time we roll into the National Park it's pitch black and we can't find the campground. After driving around the loop again we find the entrance just before it closes for the night. Tracie wakes up in time to kick in her share of the camping fee, and then she helps us unload our gear and light the propane lantern and stove. I open some cans of chili and scoop them into the old aluminum pot we have that's about to lose the handle. It hangs on for one more use, and with some big burrito-sized tortillas and a can of fruit cocktail that Tracie pops out of her bag, we do an okay dinner.

The other campsites are dark and still, so we try not to make too much noise with the tent but we can't see do-wah-diddly, and we're starting to swear at it because we've never set it up before. Tracie comes over and whispers, "Forget the tent, it's not cold enough. Just roll your tarp out and sleep on that."

As stupid as it sounds, I've never slept outside with no tent or anything, and I can just see a rattlesnake crawling into my sleeping bag. But we're tired and the tent's a mess, so we throw the tarp and our foam mats down like she says. It's nice to lay on your back and watch the stars break through the clouds and the branches sway a little in the breeze.

The next morning Alex is doing stretching exercises on the pine needles when I wake up, and Tracie is still down under. She's scrunched-up on her side and has a small pillow over her head, so I can only see her brown hair and one arm that's laying outside her sleeping bag. Her skin is smooth and tan, and I see a small red patch like a rash on one of her fingers. She looks small in her sleeping bag, and I think about how much guts she has to travel alone.

I can't wait to see the Canyon, and I don't want to be distracted by any conversation, so I tell Alex I'll see him at the hotel's restaurant in about half an hour. Then I head for the edge.

The sun is up and bright, but it's still cool, and I can't see anything through the trees. I'm kind of trotting because it's so close I can see the stone wall that keeps you from falling over the rim, and as I run to it the Canyon opens up in front of me, like twenty feet away you see nothing and then boom, it's all there.

All I can say is, "Jesus!" The walls across the Canyon are orange-red, maybe fifty different colors of rust, red-brown, tan, layered like a birthday cake for God, hundreds of rock stripes, and it's the biggest, strattest, most tropo thing I've ever seen. I get up on the wall, but I still can't see the bottom, I can only spock the trail zigzagging down the side.

We see a lot of big nature on this trip, but I always remember this first shot of the Grand Canyon the best. No video, no photo, no big screen, nothing looks like the real thing. Nothing makes you feel the size, the colors, the space, like your own eyes and the birds drifting through the updrafts over the rim like pieces of ash from some giant wildfire.

I meet Alex at the restaurant and we grab a couple of seats on the counter because the place is already full of German and Japanese tourists. I'm sitting next to an old scarecrow guy wearing a cowboy hat sipping black coffee and after we order our usual breakfast of eggs, toast, pancakes, juice and coffee, he watches us eat like demons from the Hawaiian Hell, where Alex says there's no food and it's cold. That's hell to the Hawaiians, cold and hunger, and then the guy tells me, "You know, son, that's what I miss. Having an appetite like you boys do. Chemo kills your appetite something fierce."

I don't know what to say so I mumble, "I'm sorry," and he laughs and says, "Don't be. I just enjoy seeing you boys go to town on those hotcakes."

Alex has this look of concentration when he's eating like he's studying for a test. This morning his eyebrows are creased and serious, and I'm thinking how rhomboid it must be not to feel hungry. I pick up a triangle of whole wheat toast off my plate and hand it to the old man. "Can't you at least eat this?" I ask. He waves it off, saying, "No thanks, son. I ate already. You need it. Keep your strength up so you don't get like me."

We go back to our campsite and Tracie is brushing her teeth and a group of kids are hovering like UFOs around the Cruiser. We've gotten used to people staring at the Lancer because there's no other car on the road that looks like a catfish on plutonium. Some brat asks us what it is and I answer, "It's a Dogmeat Seven." It says Lancer right on the side, so it's their own fault. Then the kid asks, "How old is it?" and I tell him, "Fifty years." He and his pals walk around it, read the writing on the gray fender and then run off.

I'm excited about seeing the Canyon again so I run ahead of Alex and Tracie and just stare at the North face until they come alongside. They don't say much and I realize it's hard to say anything about it without sounding stupid. We trot down the trail for a few minutes and Alex wants to go all the way to the bottom, but I'm not in shape like he is, so he and Tracie go on and I just rest at a wide switchback and watch the cliffs change color as the sun shifts.

After awhile I go back up and walk along the Rim trail, listening to German and other weird languages because the place is choked with foreign tourists, and then I go back to our camp and flop out for a while. Alex and Tracie vector in about 5 or so, not do-wopping, they're fragged, but I can see they got along. In fact, I'm thinking, yah, he's going to hump her, but that was just jealousy talking. It's not like that at all between them, and I can't help but feel relieved.

I think she yanks that crazy girl act out early so people leave her alone. We didn't jink her and she helped with the gear and kept up with Alex on the trail, so we all had a mutual respect gig going. Plus she has nice legs and a funny way of looking fake-bent, and doesn't just chatter to hear herself talk. I hate that in anyone, guys or girls.

Alex and I look at the map that night and debate between going south through Phoenix and Tucson and then heading up to Santa Fe or going north to the other National Parks in Utah first and then heading back to Albuquerque and Santa Fe. We both want to see Texas and Colorado as well as New Mexico, and it makes for a lot of routes to choose from. Since it's still May, we decide to head south before it gets really bake-brain city down there. Tracie listens to our route and asks if she can stay with us until we get to Santa Fe, because she has an aunt there who she wants to see. We say okay, and the next morning we tank up and head for I-State 15.

We spend more than a week hitting parks like the Petrified Forest and towns like Tombstone and Silver City, gagging through cities like Albuquerque and goo-gooing tourist traps like Taos. It's pretty strat, camping and hiking and driving, sharing Oreos and apples with Tracie, joking with her, trying to make her a little bent, liking the way she wrinkles her nose at me when I frap her with some fake-critical comment. Even though she's twenty-one, two years older than me, it's easy to be with her.

I especially like watching her pin up her hair. She uses this old steel hairpin that the chrome chipped off of a long time ago, and she piles her loose gold-brown hair up on her head so it doesn't get in her way when it's her turn to make the scrambled eggs or wash our dented old camp plates. I've never seen anybody cook eggs like she does, using a fork to stir them while they're cooking with little swirling movements. I tell her, "You're making them tough," and she wrinkles her nose at me, and actually they're the softest eggs I've ever had.

On a bake-brain night outside Las Cruces we give up on finding a campground and pull into a motel, the kind with one neon light in the sign that flickers on and off, and hand the Pakistani or Indian guy at the counter my Mastercard to pay for the room. He spocks us out and asks if we can pay cash. We've only got a few gitas cash because we've used it all for gas and grinds, so we say "no," and then stand there, shredded after a long day walking around Chochise's Stronghold and Rockhound Park and driving through full–rev sun, while he gimps through making sure my card is still bucks-up.

It's one of those nights that never seems to cool off, and so even though the pool is already closed and the lights around it are off, we all want a swim so bad we can taste the chlorine.

There's only a few other cars in the lot, a rusty Caddie and a few minivans, and it looks like Mom, Dad, and the brats are already asleep, and Willy Loman or whoever owns the Caddie is watching TV and sipping scotch real quietly in his room. It's so late that even the big-rigs have stopped rumbling past, and I see the owner in the office window, watching us head for our room to make sure we don't do anything malignant.

We drop our packs on the bed, and as I make some blinky little comment about the room's weird cooked-cabbage smell, Alex is already stripping down to his boxers. He's tossed his cut-offs on the chair and is about to open the door when I warn him in a whisper that the owner is doing a spy-versus-spy on us. He snaps off the lights, both inside and out, and we all peer through the curtains at the office. The owner sits back down in front of his TV, and a few seconds later Alex creaks the door open and crouches down behind the thirsty little hedge that fronts the parking lot. Then he slips off toward the pool in a bent-over crab-walk shuffle, and Tracie and I watch him until he disappears in the darkness. I hear the chain link gate squeak open, and I can picture how King Tut that cool water must feel.

Tracie must be thinking the same thing, because she closes the door, unzips her jeans, and peels off her top in one quick movement. She pulls down her jeans and I can't believe how beautiful her body is in the dim light seeping through the curtains: the glow of her damp skin, her hair tousled by yanking her top off, her white bra strap crossing her back, the shadowy curves of her legs as she steps out of her crumpled jeans.

Her white panties are below her butt, pulled down by the tight jeans as she took them off, and she catches me staring at her as she pulls the clingy little white triangle back up over her buns. She turns to face me and I eat up her smooth belly and hips with my eyes. She snaps the waistband of her panties and smiles enough for me to see her teeth.

"What, Daz," she says in a soft fake-surprise voice, "haven't you ever seen a girl naked?"

I must have gulped like some idiot in a movie because she giggles when I tell her, "To tell the truth, no."

She glances through the curtains and whispers matter-of-factly, "I don't have a bathing suit."

Without looking at me, she asks real quietly, "You think the creepy owner is looking?"

I join her at the window and look out. I can smell her hair and the warmth of her skin, and I try to act like I'm really looking at the office. I can't help but glance at her, and it's so dim I can't see the freckles on her cheeks. She's still eyeing the office through the curtain crack, and I make a show of spocking the owner.

"No, he's ozoned in front of the tube," I whisper.

She looks outside for a while longer, and I don't want her to ever move away because we're so close I can feel the sweet-smelling electricity of her body. She lets the curtains close and then turns her back to me and lifts her hair. "Here, undo my bra," she whispers.

My heart starts pounding out of my ribs and I figure she must hear it as loud as I do, and I fumble with the clip until I'm afraid she'll get bent that I'm so clumsy, and then it finally snaps open. She turns around and slips the straps off, and her breasts and shoulders are glowing warm with a slight sheen of sweat.

She lets me look at her, and then she puts her arms around my neck and kisses me; she tastes salty and soft. "Is that your first kiss?" she asks me.

"Like that—yes," I croak, and with a little half-smile she pulls my T-shirt up and over my head.

I feel katakana and self-conscious standing in front of her like this, her perfect breasts a few inches from my defective bod, and she seems to be enjoying my dizziness.

She tugs my head down to her nipple and whispers, "Go ahead." She's salty and sugary at the same time, and I am losing my grip on reality, she is so soft and firm, softer than I thought skin could be. She undoes my jeans and touches me, playfully, like she's having fun, and then she pushes my hand under her panties and shows me how she likes to be touched.

I feel like I'm lost somewhere, somewhere dreamy like in the Hanging Gardens of Babylon, because I can't believe how complicated she feels when she moves and breathes and guides me around her. I'm concentrating on her electricity, on the way she presses me with her fingers to show me just how to touch her, and on her little irregular catches of breath. She starts breathing deeper, and I try to tell myself that this isn't a dream, that I am touching her and that she's not like I imagined, she's softer than anything I have ever felt. We stand there, kissing and touching each other for what seems like both seconds and hours.

After all those sex manuals I've read and pictures I've looked at, it's not like I imagined at all. It's a weird mix of things, of noticing it's like she's wet her pants, a wonderful warm okra-slippery juiciness, the concentration it takes not to touch her too hard, the heat of her skin and her breath, and the way her butt tenses the longer we touch, and the most beautiful sight, her face in the half-light, concentrating, her eyes closed, her eyebrows knitted like it hurts while everything else is saying it doesn't hurt at all.

I kiss her like I've dreamed of kissing her since she first set-tled into the back seat of the Lancer and lifted her arms up behind her head, so cool in her shades, and she doesn't seem to mind. I can't believe how good it feels to kiss the mouth I've been looking at and wondering about all these days, watching her, safely hidden behind my shades.

She slips my hand out of her underwear and kisses it and then she pulls me tight to her and makes little adjustments to us with her hand, and I realize with a really stupid surprise that the slippery little front strip of her panties isn't much of an obstruction. Her eyes half-open and I realize we're both in the vines and sweet musky flowers are shading us in the heat, and she's showing me everything wonderful that's growing here.

She kisses me once, quickly, between walking-uphill breaths, and then she nudges me up against the bed and falls on me, the most delicious accident I've ever had.

I'm laying there under her, feeling how incredibly unexpected she is, feeling her breath against my cheek, feeling her move, nat-ural and swaying like fronds in the soft hot wind, and it's like she catches her breath at the sight of something beautiful in the heat waves, like you do when you're caught off-guard, and then she gasps a little at the sheer beauty of it, in that stunned way when you're overwhelmed and you forget yourself.

Then I see it, too, and she hugs me tightly and softly, like I've never been hugged, and she kisses me, suckling sweet, like we just shared a ripe plum on the terrace, and are licking the juice off each others' mouths.

I have never felt a more comforting blanket than her body. After a while she gets up and strips off her panties. Then she pulls me up and holds her hair above her head so I can kiss the back of her neck.

"You're very sweet," she tells me, and for once in my life I have nothing to say. I just hold her, and hope she knows everything I feel. I can't resist touching her some more, and she doesn't seem to mind.

A while later she picks up one of the coarse white motel towels off the dresser and wraps it around her midriff. It's a cheap little towel, and it's so small it can't cover her nipples and butt at the same time. "Here, let me help you," I tell her, and I position the towel so it's under her breasts and just covering her belly button. "Perfect," I say, and she laughs and tosses the towel at me, and pulls her own big striped towel out of her pack.

I pull on my undies—somehow fitting, I think, that they're the purple briefs I bought myself in a moment of daring last summer—and then we creep out the door and head to the pool.

Alex is floating on his back like a sleepy brown dolphin, very easy and quiet, and he doesn't see Tracie slip off her towel and ease into the water with a shiver. She turns to flash me a wow-it's-cold grin, and even though there's almost no light I can see the dark circles of her nipples against the curves of her body. I squeeze her hand and she glides away in a gurgle of cool water and dives under, leaving just a current of swirling silver.

Before I get in, I touch her dampness that's still with me, and lift my fingers to my face and watch her resurface with a small splash, and I promise myself that I will never forget her scent, or her face, or her bare shoulders and dripping wet hair in this midnight pool. The warm sweet smell of damp earth is on my fingertips, and I think I'll never have a more perfect and surprising night in my entire life. I feel a glow like there's a nuclear core inside me, and I know in a weird and happy way that my life has changed forever.

I watch Tracie for a long time before getting into the water. Alex swims over to me, jerks his head toward Tracie and whispers all goo-goo-eyed, "She's skinnydipping." I shrug and whisper, "She says she doesn't have a bathing suit."

She stands up briefly and Alex and I are frozen as she tilts her head back into the water and rises up again, her hair now dripping down her back, and as she smoothes it away from her face we see her smooth underarms and breasts above the silvery flickering water. She turns over and he glances from her magnetic naked body to me.

"What took you so long?" he asks, and my heart races up and I try to shrug again. "She wanted to be sure the owner wasn't watching us."

Alex nods, like he understands, and then he swims away, and I forgive him all the times he made me suffer and all the times he let me know that he'd kissed and touched a girl the night before.

\* \* \*

100

We head toward Santa Fe and Tracie's aunt's place the next morning, and I think about letting Alex go on to New York alone. Tracie is quiet and I hope she isn't regretting what she did, and I wait, all ramped up, for a chance to talk to her alone.

It's her turn to drive, and all morning I sit next to her in front, glancing at her as often as I can get away with, while Alex is slouched in the back seat. Finally, after hours of torture, thinking about what to say to her, it's time to gas up and we get off the highway. I ask Tracie to pull over by the air and water, like I'm going to check the tire pressure, and Alex goes off to take a leak. She's about to follow him to the bathrooms when I touch her elbow to keep her with me. Everything I've been thinking about is tumbling around in my head; I've been trying to figure out how to ask the most important questions, but it's all botched together and I blurt out, "Are you protected?"

I can't see her eyes through her sunglasses, but she half-smiles at my tensed-up worry and dumb way of asking, and she says, "No, but my period's supposed to start tomorrow. I'll be okay." She looks out the windshield and taps the steering wheel, nervously or impatiently I can't tell, and says, "I haven't had a boyfriend in a while. You forget all this stuff when you're alone."

She glances at me, sees I'm still worried, and says, "You don't have to worry about diseases and stuff like that. I'm careful, except with virgins." Her smile widens a little and then fades when she sees that I'm not relieved like she thought I would be.

"I want to stay with you," I tell her. "Your aunt wouldn't mind, would she?" After a few seconds where I can't tell what she's thinking, she reaches over and touches my hand.

"You should finish your trip," she says, and it's a weird moment of something promising fading from view and a feeling of relief at the same time.

"What about later?" I ask her.

She thinks about this like she's surprised I asked. Then she smiles a little and says, "That's what I like about you, Daz," and before I can ask what she means, she looks at me through her shades and says, "You know, I get really hungry before my period." She nods to the jinky little gas station store and says, "Let's go get something, huh?"

She swings open the door and gets out. She's wearing shorts and the white tanktop she was wearing when we first met, and she looks very cool and in charge as she stands in the sun, shading her eyes with her hand as she waits for me. I get out and follow her into the air-conditioned glass box of the minimart. As she strolls around, choosing stuff, I go to the window and watch Alex move the Lancer over to the gas pumps.

All those loopy ideas I had a few minutes before about staying with Tracie seemed so stupid, as stupid and far-fetched as hoping dogs could talk, and I don't know how I can stand being in the car so close to her for another six hours.

I'm thinking, there's nobody I can even talk to, it doesn't seem right to tell Alex, and then Tracie comes alongside and hands me a Milky Way candy bar. "Here," she says, and she smiles as she sees my expression and then takes off her shades. Her eyes are big and gray-blue, and I remember noticing them at the gas station when we first met. "You're sweet," she tells me, and I look at her face and the freckles I couldn't see last night, and I want to say something, something important, but I've forgotten all the words, even my own.

So instead I say the really obvious, dumb thing, which is, "I wish you were coming with us," because I'm realizing the past week with her has been the best week of my whole life.

She grins at me, and for a second or two she's as young as I am again, her eyes are shining like a kid's. It makes me feel good that something I said makes her happy, but it also makes me feel worried. I try to smile back, and then ask her, "Will you be okay?"

She gives me her funny half-bent expression, like it's an insulting question to even ask, and looks away. I know she has her tough-girl act and the nine-shot automatic roscoe in her purse, but I'm still thinking about what might happen to her. I ask, "Are you sure you don't want to come with us?" She's still half-smiling, and she bumps me in a jokey way with her hip and points out the window. I glance outside and Alex is waving at us to get going.

It's his turn to drive, and the whole way north I find some excuse to be turned around, talking with Tracie, looking at her as much as I can. It's not the same as the day before, though, because now I know it's ending, and it will never be the same as when I

102

started out, not thinking about endings and missing her. I get her folk's and her aunt's addresses and e-mail, and give her ours, and I fold the note paper with her writing on it up into a little square and put it in my wallet.

By the time we spin into Santa Fe it's late, and we have some trouble finding her aunt's house. Her aunt invites us in for dinner, but we don't say much, and Alex just stirs his vegetables and mashed potatoes around like he's lost his appetite and his concentration.

# CHAPTER TWELVE

Alex's cousin Tita is a total beauty, just fantastically sexy. I mean goddess face, goddess body. When I first see her at the door to their wingding old apartment in New York, it's sweltering hot and she's wearing tiny blue-jean cutoffs and a faded gold halter top that says "Kauai" on it. When she rushes up to give Alex a hug, I'm hoping the little overworked strap around her neck will break in all the excitement. It doesn't, but the top doesn't hide much anyway, and I can see she's got tits from Planets X and Y, incredible works of art, just like a Renaissance statue. Yeah, I know, it sounds so sexist, but what am I supposed to say, yah, I didn't notice her body? What a lie that would be.

Don't women get hot when they see some guy's tight buns? I never hear about it, but they must. They just don't talk about it, so we look like creeps when we do. Hey, I know it's wrong, but I'm not fake enough to try and hide it.

And it's not just that I'm thinking about being shipwrecked with her on a little turquoise atoll, where the only things not shredded from our bodies by the waves and coral are my jeans— too small for her to fit in, heh-heh—and her bleached-out "Hello Kitty" panties. Of course I start thinking of that as soon as I go in their bathroom and see her undies drying on the shower-rod.

No, it's also that she's so . . . this sounds really loopy, but competent is the only word I think of. I can't even think of a new word to describe the way she looks, but it would have to include making things with a sort of easy, graceful confidence, a kind of long, leggy energy, and smart brown eyes that stay fixed on you when you're talking.

The first night we're there, Alex and I roll out our foam mats and sleeping bags, and as we lay there in the mugwort heat I hear this faint chirping sound, like a weird bird-call clock that chimes every five or ten minutes.

The next morning I ask Tita what it is, and she says it's the smoke alarm; when the battery gets low, it chirps like that. Benny says he would just whack it with a broom, but Tita rolls her eyes and says that she's just been putting off fixing it. She's woven her thick black hair into a braid and pinned it up with a red lacquer chopstick, and she's wearing this ripe-banana-yellow sundress that makes her look incredibly edible. It's sleeveless, so her brown shoulders stand out like smooth chocolate against the yellow straps, and the high waist and thin cotton show off her figure and legs.

But what really fraps me is the way she unfolds their little aluminum ladder, climbs up, torques off the smoke detector, peels the wrapper off a new battery, pops it in, and then twists the round plastic gizmo back in place on just the second try. It's a high ceiling, and she has to reach over a bookcase in the hallway to get to it. I would still be fighting to get the damn wrapping off, and that's if I hadn't broken the gizmo or fallen off the ladder when it popped loose.

I know it sounds loopy to say that you've seen a goddess change a smoke detector battery, but I have.

After she's climbed up to the top step I break out of my trance and go over to hold the ladder. It doesn't need steadying, but it gives me a chance to be close to her. My eyes are about level with her waist, I'm just a few inches from her, and she smells so good. She hands me the dead battery, snaps in the new one, and is stepping off the ladder long before I'm ready. She smiles at me and says thanks, even though we both know she didn't need any help, and I feel weak-kneed, like I just pedaled up Clambake Hill.

Plus Tita is really nice. She doesn't talk down to us, which I really appreciate, even though she's a graduate student in cultural anthropology and eight years older than us. If only I could keep my eyes on her face. It's even worse for Alex because he feels the same way, but it's like incest to want to copa your cousin.

Her boyfriend Benny is a funny guy, a tall, scrawny white guy with a scraggly little beard and a balding head. Why this goddess chose him, I have no idea, but it does give me hope. I mean, this guy is jock-to-the-minus-ten-squared. As soon as I see them with their arms around each other in their little kitchen that first night, I think, "Whatever this guy does, I'm going to copy it."

But I like Benny immediately because he doesn't act superior. He doesn't give us that adult frag about how "you'll learn better, once you're experienced like me."

He's a serious guy, deep into his Ph.D. in developmental psychology, but somehow he's always making Alex and I laugh. As soon as he meets Alex he says very gravely that he's heard about Alex's kung fu.

I think, here we go again, another chunk of macho frap from Alex. But Benny listens politely to Alex's plastic modesty and then he asks Alex to show him some moves.

I'm yawning, like great, it's singing dog time again, and then Benny says, "I'll show you my style: the wimpy cockroach school," and his thin arms flail out in front of him like feelers, and he's weaving around like a drunk and making all these ridiculous kung fu yips and sound effects. Then he moves in on Alex, saying, "Wimpy Cockroach approach strong kung fu Master, but wimpy cockroach is subtle, knows esoteric cockroach way," and he moves around and his legs buckle and pretty soon he's crawling up to Alex and nipping him like a bug, and Alex is starting to laugh, and then Benny motions Tita in and they start tickling Alex.

That night, we get ozoned on a bottle of California Zinfandel they've been saving for some special occasion—like our visit, yah—and I'm defective enough to ask Tita how she ended up with "Hello Kitty" undies. She giggles and doesn't answer, which surprises me. Of course, it's goo-goo to still like "Hello Kitty" stuff when you're twenty-seven, but, hey, it's not that loopy. Benny's smile gets crooked and he says, "In couples, some things are best left secrets to the outside world."

Alex is seven-eighths to the pink himself, so he takes a gulp of the red stuff and says, "What about the weird wedding photo you sent us? Is that a secret, too?"

Benny looks at Tita, all mystified, and she runs her finger around the rim of her wine glass with a small Mona Lisa smile. "Exactly which photo got sent to your relatives, dear one?" Benny asks.

Alex and Tita let Benny's imagination click down to the worst possibility, whatever that is, and then Alex says, "Some lame photo of a lake and two people you can barely see, standing in the water next to a rowboat."

Benny chuckles with relief, like ha-ha, thank God it's not the one of me on the can, and then he shrugs. "It's news to me, Alex. Your cousin will have to do the explaining."

Tita takes a sip of the vino and then gives Benny a look of over-cooked earnestness. "Well," she says, "it's like getting married."

Benny does a fake double-take and then gives her a hammy prosecutor's look. "Do I take that to mean, Lyron dear, that getting married is like falling out of a boat into cold water?"

She widens her eyes at him in phony surprise, and in that moment I am supernova in love with her. Even her weird real name, Lyron, seems high-oxygen to me.

"Maybe it means getting married is all wet," Alex says, and I can feel a hot blush hit my face when both Tita and Benny grin with that embarrassed "heh-heh, sex reference," look that couples still get when they're young. Alex finally catches on and looks down, all dribbled, and Tita fills in the blank by telling us, "We rented that boat for a romantic cruise."

Benny starts to protest and she does a bad job of stifling a laugh. "Benny fell overboard so I had to jump in and save him."

I'm thinking, number one, how could anybody fall out of a rowboat, and number two, the water's only waist deep anyway, but Benny shrugs and says, "And she continues to save me, every day and in every way."

I've never heard such mysterioso storytelling in a couple, and it's obvious there's either no normal answer, or none they want to tell us, so I drop the quirky questions and just look at Lyron or Tita or My Heroine, depending on which guy is talking. Benny calls her Lyron, and Alex calls her Tita in his crunchy Pidgin way, eh, Tee-da, and I'm gutless, as usual, not sure what to call her and afraid that she'll see the Micronesian fantasy in my eyes when I look at her.

*   *   *

It's strat getting to cruise through the Ivy League scam with them. We wander around Columbia, drink coffee in the student hang-outs, check out the library, act intellectual. The only spiked part is that your hair starts falling out as soon as you get into graduate school. All the guys have bald spots, I swear.

I would get into these booga-booga arguments with Benny because we're great motormouths and we both know it. He always tries to reduce my argument down to something that sounded really stupid like, "So you're saying that we ought to enslave all rich people because they're rich, not because they are morally rep-rehensible," and I would have to say, "Yeah, that's right, sell them into slavery, to hell with their morals." I would always try to get him with the "real world" tripwire, you know, "That's fine for the ivory tower scam you're running, Benny, but in the real world your idea is total jank."

He calls this the "you're so naive, simplistic, and idealistic" argument, and it works like this: no matter what anyone says, if there's anything good in it you can shut them down by saying they're naive, simplistic, and idealistic. People like to think they're so hard-nosed. Ever notice how no one accuses the guy who is screaming for the death penalty for drug dealers as being wrong because he's naive? No, it's always the guy who wants to rehabilitate them who's romped on as naive.

So even though I tried the argument on him, I ended up agreeing with Benny that it's a dead-end. People are so afraid of getting torqued because they trusted someone, they'd rather drink piss than get pegged as being too naive or trusting. It's the worst thing about the adult attitude.

Benny is also great at yanking your hidden assumptions. He's a master at this, and I found it hard to beat him at it. It works like this: find the assumptions behind the other guy's case, and then find one flaw in any of the assumptions. Bingo, his house of cards goes gravitational.

These parry-thrust gigs are mostly sport to Benny, but they can be stone-serious to the rest of us. The only time I saw Tita get upset is when Alex and her got into some mambo tiff over Hawaiian giz.

They'd been at the market, picking up some grinds—Alex and I chipped in forty bucks, grip, we're not sponges—and I'm laying on their crappy futon sofa, listening to tunes, when they come in the door very quiet-cranky. Tita looks bent, and so does Alex. At first I figure they just had big-city fun like a parking ticket or an argument with some gorgon over a shopping cart, but the way they plop the full grocery bags down on the counter tells me they're bent at each other. Tita's moving fast, the way you do when you're torqued, and her long batik skirt is going swish-swish as she darts around the kitchen, putting stuff away. There's a trickle of sweat running down her neck into her white blouse, and her face is flushed from climbing the three flights of steps with the heavy grocery bags.

Alex, of course, doesn't even look warm, except in his eyes. Hefting two bags, even in this heat, hardly lights the furnace; his blue tank top is still neatly tucked into his shorts, and his thick arms are just moist with humidity, not from any effort.

He's the opposite of Tita in the way he gets torqued, too. He's moving very deliberately, almost slo-mo, and when I see that, a big knot clinches up in my gut.

I'm not too crazy about the silent treatment, you know, when unsaid stuff is dripping off the walls like gooey thunderstorm sweat, so I go in to help unpack the food and ask Alex, "What's with the salty air in here?"

He has that glazed-steel look in his eyes and he just shrugs. "Guess I'm not Hawaiian enough anymore." Before I can even register how this makes me feel, Tita jumps in and says, "That's not what I said." From her tone and dark eyes, I can tell she's not so much bent as hurt.

Now Alex is proud of being Hawaiian in the same way he's proud of his body and mind, and he's not proud of it the way you're not proud of breathing oxygen.

He opens a bag of apricots and carefully puts them in an old-timey blue ceramic bowl on the counter, one at a time, and I'm thinking, well, that's it, another day shot to hell, when he turns to me and just lets loose.

"So Kamehameha gives his land and women to the haoles for guns. For what? To shoot the fricking haoles? No! To kill some Hawaiians! And I'm supposed to respect that?"

I've never heard his full-rant pidgin before, and I'm amazed at how hot and smooth it is. It's not the sing-songy kind when he's talking to me like I'm three, and it's not the short bursts when he's downright bent, either.

Tita tries to say something, but he just bulldozes ahead.

"And when the ali'i make the maka'ainana cut down all the sandalwood so they can sell it to the Chinese—every frickin' tree, Daz, you know how hard it would be to get every last one out of the Koolaus?—then what, I'm supposed to be proud of that?"

Alex usually ignores what people say—yah, especially me—and just watches what they do, so this hot speech is blowing me down.

"I didn't say that," Tita says. "I agree with you."

He ignores her and says, "Then there's some defective religion where you get adiosed if the fricking ali'i's shadow touches you, and women can't eat bananas, and I'm supposed to preserve that? What the hell for?"

"I didn't say that," Tita says all defensively, and he finally looks at her.

"No, but it's the same thing," he says, and then mimics her. "'Preserve our culture.' Who the hell lost it? The fricking ali'i were so stupid and greedy, anybody could have conquered us."

Tita looks at me and lets out a huge sigh. "All I said was, the language and everything that goes with it will be lost if we don't preserve it."

"Hey, you can preserve whatever you want," Alex tells her. "Just don't tell me how to be Hawaiian."

"That's the last thing I would do," she says, and now she's starting to flame up herself.

"What really fries my ass," he tells her, "is that you crawl out of the crabpot and marry some haole, and then 'cause you study Hawaiian, you get to tell me what for do?"

He frags her off with a disgusted snort, and Tita turns to me and says, "I don't know what set him off, but it's not me."

Alex isn't done yet, and he tells her, "Hey, if Daz or some Japanese guy wants to learn hula, you gonna tell him 'No, because you're not Hawaiian'? What if he's one-thirty-second Hawaiian? Or one-sixty-fourth? Then it's okay for him to be kumu? What the hell difference does it make?"

I know Alex has always racked up big numbers in history, the Boxer Rebellion, World War One, you name it, but I never heard him romp through Hawaiian stuff like this. So I ask Tita, as calmly as I can, "Well then, what did you say?"

She looks at Alex and tells me, "All I was trying to do was encourage him to look into his own culture."

Alex shakes his head, really redlined, and says, "Yeah, *your* idea of what is what. It's like the fricking Thought Control Squad around here. You ever thought that maybe we can make up our own minds?"

"Jesus," she says. "It was just a comment. I didn't expect to unleash a tirade."

He crunches up the paper bag the apricots came in and tosses it into their recycling box. "I'll tell you what's really happening," he tells us. "Making up your own mind always makes you the rebel."

Nobody says anything, and after a few seconds of looking intense he tells me, "I see it, brah. I know. The more people feel lost, the more they grab onto some bogus religion or whatever, and the more they want you to believe the same crap they do."

"Look, Alex," Tita tells him, "I'm all for you thinking and doing whatever you want. I'm sorry if I came across as a know-it-all."

This lets a little of the air out of his bag, and she opens the freezer and takes out some frozen-over lumps wrapped in plastic.

"Maybe this is bad timing, but I thought we could have these lau-laus and poi I've been saving for dinner tonight," she says.

This sounds strat to me since I've never had either, but Alex just kind of shrugs. Tita looks hurt again and I feel like telling Alex, drib, man, she's so beautiful, just forget being bent at her, but he's just standing there, still torqued down tight. After a fricative silence, she gives him a little smile and pats his shoulder.

"Maybe I am still a little lost," she tells him, and this is the first thing she's said that really punches through to him.

I could care less what somebody has to say about my culture—I mean, what does that even mean, seeing as how my family started because the Spanish friars were humping Indian girls like bunnies?—but the political-economic scene can set me off very tropo-electric.

Most of my discussions with Benny are game-boy gigs, parry-thrust, but one time it gets close to my core and isn't just verbal swordplay. It's all economics in the end, grip, and I've done some D-9 brainwork on this. I mean religions, politics, and even anthropology. It's all about who's hitting the jackpots with things the way they are, and who isn't even getting in the casino.

If there's a so-called revolution, is it just a bunch of new guys taking the places of the old guys at the winning slots, or are they really letting everybody belly-up and have a chance to play the machines that pay?

When we first talk economics, Benny says, "So you're presuming that the acquisition of wealth is necessarily an evil process." So I say yes, and then it's easy to shred me with examples of people who made lots of money doing good things. I have to fold my tent. See, this is what graduate students do all day, read books and tear down somebody else's hidden assumptions.

Even if Benny napalms my assumptions, I still think everyone's underwater on this personal property gig. Joe Whitecollar thinks "Gee, the only difference between us and rich guys is that we got a little house, and they got a big house." Wrongo boyo. The rich guys don't just own cribs and transpo—they own jobs, which means they own people. Not all the people, of course, but everyone who doesn't have their own biz.

It doesn't matter if Joe leaves and Fred takes his place—what matters is the jobs. If some rich guy sells the company, he's sold Joe and Fred just like they had a Universal Price Code on their butts.

Stand in this for a while: companies are nothing without the people who run it. Say that a new Hitler owns a biz, and he's so evil that even lawyers won't work for him. Yah, as if that were possible. His biz is totally worthless because no one will work it for him.

People tell you, "No, anyone can quit and go to work for somebody else," but that's not the point. The point is that jobs are markers for people, and whether it's Person A or Person Z doesn't matter.

So if some mutual fund sells a biz to some foreign asshole, and the foreign asshole shuts it down for a tax break, he just torched all those people's lives. Laughing with their friends on break, their work, their pride, all that just got burned down. It's like the master died, and now the slaves have to hope some other master buys them or they'll starve.

That's the difference between regular people and rich people, and no one should have the right to own other people. Yeah, sure, go ahead and own a fancy house and a Mercedes, but you can't burn down people's lives for a tax break.

This is the way it should work. When you hire on, you work your six months or whatever, and then you get a hundred shares of the company. You own those shares just like any rich assbite or mutual fund. When you leave, your shares go back in the pot or to a new hire.

The mutual fund buys into the gig because they think you and your pals are good workers and will make everybody money. But they can't sell you and the company to somebody else and napalm your jobs without you going along with it.

Right now it's no better than the Middle Ages. Rich clowns are the lords and we're the serfs, and because you get to own a camcorder and a Volvo, then you think it's okay for the rich clown to own you.

And another thing. Daddy shouldn't be able to give his fortune to Junior. Junior has to make it like Daddy did. It shouldn't be free. Daddy's pile goes into the pot when he signs off, and Junior gets to keep the stereo, the car and the house, but that's all. What is this, the divine right of kings, that your brats get to rule like you did just because they got born in your family? To hell with that kings and queens jank.

I mean, why would any sane person want a house with 10,000 or 20,000 square feet? Is it their right to rape the earth and everyone on it for their little kingdom? I beg to differ.

Benny thinks this is just another debate until I get good and torqued. I'm serious. If it's a jungle out there, then let everybody feel the fear a little. There shouldn't be a divine right of money. It shouldn't be up to some guy six thousand miles away whether your company disappears or not. It's not right, and nobody can convince me that's the way it should be.

After I get bent Benny looks at me and scratches his wispy chin. Then he says, "Daz, I didn't realize you felt so strongly about it. But it's a difficult problem to solve. If someone else six thousand miles away can make something cheaper than you can, it's the consumer who shuts down your company, not some evil capitalist." So we talk some more about capitalism and socialism and supply and demand, and he doesn't use any debating tricks on me.

Then Tita comes home and drops her backpack on the floor and listens for a while. She starts talking about Trobriand islanders and the cultural contradictions of capitalism, and for once I almost forget what's under her yellow sundress.

# CHAPTER THIRTEEN

One afternoon Alex and I are sitting on Benny and Tita's living room floor reading and listening to the radio when Benny skims in and tells us, "You guys got the parts. First rehearsal is tomorrow afternoon."

We drop jaw and say, "What?" Then he explains that some good friends are putting together a no-budget play, and they need a couple of warm bodies for small parts. He volunteered us because he thought it would add to our trip. We tell him, "You're defective," but he insists. We've decided to stay with them for a while because we're liking the New York scene, so we cave in and agree to try it.

Getting to see Tita more was worth staying with them no matter what else was flipping. If a man doesn't go vertical when he sees her braless then he's in sad shape. Benny has this hokey expression, "It's the greatest thing since the development of frontal sex," and he knows what he's talking about, Jack, because Tita is goddess plus. Front, back, side, up, down, strange, charm, any old way must be heaven with her. Damn.

Sometimes I wonder what it's like to be in love, I mean really in love, not just lust madness. I wondered for a long time if I was in love with Tracie or Leslie, the girl I met in Iowa. I don't think Alex knows about love either, although he was pretty busted up by the rejection he got tagged with in Iowa. But I think that was mostly pride, not love.

Anyway, Benny drags us kicking and screaming to the rehearsal. It's a katakana madhouse in a dirty old brick building with wheat sheaf designs embossed on its rusty sliding door. Benny told us that once upon a time it was a bakery. It's dark inside and smells like stale tortilla chips, and during late rehearsals you can hear rats scurrying around in the attic.

115

The director is this little guy with a close-cropped graying beard and he's wearing this button that says, "That's *Mr*. Fuckhead to You" and it seems to me the gig is out of control, but Mr. Fuckhead has his hand on the wheel, it's in overdrive, and he's got his eyes on the road.

I never went out for the school plays much because I never gripped why it was so much fun. Plus, the type of person who got into pinstripes over it was the art-fart wear-black crowd. So I was geared down into a "show me why I should care" mode.

New York is full of real actors, so even though this was a total amateur gig I figure Benny twisted the director into giving us the slots. Either that or it's because we're free. When I ask Benny why he's so hot on us doing it, he just says he thought we're perfect for the parts. That's his joke, because all our characters did was stumble into scenes, frap everyone out, and then slide off.

So we start walking through the scenes in our jeans and T-shirts, holding these ragged scripts with our parts underlined. There's little penciled-in instructions on the margins next to our lines like, "Enter quickly and come to an abrupt stop," and, "State lines with authority."

The play is a farce, where the main character is always getting caught in compromising situations. People always show up unexpectedly, and he invents really cripped explanations that set up the next scene's jokes.

Alex and I play bumbling private eyes the guy has hired to find out if his partner is ripping him off. The guy is always making up some obviously fake cover for us, and our lines always blow the cover. In the opening scene, we're introduced as his long-lost British relatives, and then, when somebody questions us, we don't know a damn thing about England.

The main plot involves all these notes like "Meet me tonight in the office" that get dropped in the wrong places so everyone shows up unexpectedly. Alex and I arrive first in every scene, get blown down fast, and then leave, so our stage time is pretty short.

In the second scene we stumble into the guy's office just before his wife comes in and discovers him with this lady artist. Nothing is happening, but the guy manages to look guilty as hell. He turns to us and says, "These detectives were just investigating the robbery downstairs," and then he spins off all these lies and we're supposed to support them, but instead everything we say makes him look even more ludicrous. One character comes up to us in every scene and says, "Haven't I met you before?" And of course we say no, even though it's obvious we're the same guys he saw in the last scene.

Alex really gets into this phony English accent we're supposed to use in the first scene. He has the fake Brit pretty tops, "I say, guvnah, quite right, guvnah."

We get into playing around because we're bored in between our bits. We stand backstage when we aren't in the scene, which is most of the time, so we're joking around with the director's instructions, saying stuff like, "I say, guvnah, I state lines with authority," and then the other guy would say, "Do you now, guvnah, that's quite clever, but I state lines with dismay," stuff like that.

Somehow that phrase got to be our standard riff when we're bored, so when one of the real actors is trying to act too big tent one of us would whisper, "He's stating lines with a bit too much authority, guvnah," and the other guy would say, "Quite right. A bit too strong, I say. Cool it off, guvnah."

There's one other complete amateur, this old guy named Gene who said he'd always wanted to try acting. He's thin for an old guy, not much paunch, and he wears his wispy white hair pretty long. He plays the business partner who's suspected of ripping off the main character. He doesn't have much stage time either, but he tries to make the most of it.

Mark, Mr. Fuckhead the director, is very patient with Gene, always telling him something to improve his acting, which is so bad it makes us look good. He overacts every scene, using these big gestures to show he's miffed or whatever, but his voice always makes up for it. He has this great FM voice that carries like summer thunder across the old bakery warehouse, and he'd pause in the middle of each line to make the most of it. It's so theatrical it spins Mark out.

One time Mark is watching him from the side with us and I ask him, "Doesn't Gene know he looks warped when he goes on like that?" and Mark answers, "Daz, just because he's old doesn't

117

mean he knows more about acting than you do. That's why I put up with him."

"Because he's a beginner?" I ask.

"No," he tells me. "Because he's got the guts to try something new."

"Yah," I say, "but what if you're no good?"

Mark looks at me with this frappy little grin and says, "It's not how good you are; it's finding the parts that are right for you."

"And how do you do that?" I ask.

He shrugs and says, "Try as many parts as you can."

Just then Gene is hamming up his key line, which is something like, "You're accusing the senior partner of stealing from his own company?" He says it like, "You dare to accuse . . . the senior partner . . . of stealing . . . from his own company?" Then he tries to look outraged.

Mark yells out, "Gene, have you ever heard anybody talk like that?"

Gene says, "Olivier did it all the time."

Mark rolls up his script for the hundredth time that afternoon and says, "Gene, try to imagine that you really *are* the senior partner of a successful firm, not Lawrence Oliver doing Hamlet."

So then Gene tries it again with only two pauses, and Mark says, "Gene, try emphasizing the words 'senior partner' instead of pausing, and don't raise your arms like that. You have to actually get mad at Martin. He just accused you of stealing from him. Aren't you angry?"

Gene tries it again, and Mark shakes his head. "Gene," he shouts, "the words are somebody else's, but the feelings have to be yours."

I don't mean to make fun of Gene, because I was doing the same thing, thinking about what I was supposed to look like instead of just being a bumbling private eye. I mean, I only had about three lines per scene, but even so I could see what Mark was romping on.

I almost didn't make it through the first night. Mark told us we had two more weeks of rehearsals, but on Wednesday he says we're launching it Friday night because of the theater's scheduling changes. I'd planned to study my lines like a maniac that last week, but now it's compression time.

So on opening night I'm standing backstage sweating, feeling totally unprepared just like this was the physics final and as usual I hadn't studied enough. All the scenes are blending together and I'm not sure which lines follow which anymore. Plus, I can't remember the exact words in each line. They look so clear on the page, but when I put the script down my brain turns to cabbage.

My mind is spinning into panic, there's fifty people out there in folding chairs waiting for the gig to start, and even though they're all friends of Mark and the cast, I'm almost trembling. "Alex," I say, "I can't remember my lines. They're all mixed up in my brain." I'm flipping the pages, hoping I can somehow spark the memory of each scene's lines, and he looks me over and says, "Daz, it's just like a football game. You don't have to make every move right. Just do something that's more or less right."

"I don't think I can, man," I tell him, all frapped, and my tuxedo costume is already soaked with sweat.

"Look," he says. "you know what's supposed to happen in each scene, right? We come in, we say something, Martin says something back and then we say something again. You remember the jokes, right? So don't worry about the lines. Just say the jokes."

"Okay, man, I'll try," I say, and my hands are shaking like those silvery leaves on birch trees.

He looks disgusted and says, "I can't believe this. You've always got some wise-ass thing to say. I'm the one who should be worried."

"No way, man," I tell him. "You're used to pressure."

He peeks out through the curtain and says, "Daz, everybody out there is a friend of Mark's. They don't give a damn about you."

"But if I screw it up then Mark looks defective."

"They already know Mark's defective, but they came anyway," he says and then he punches my shoulder and laughs.

Alex can see I'm still wound too tight, so he says, "Okay. If you screw up and can't remember when to say your lines, just look at me. If I give you a 'shaka' sign"—that's the Hawaiian hand signal where you extend your little finger and your thumb— "then just say anything you can remember of your line."

"What if I can't remember smack?" I ask, and I'm vibrating so much my mouth is dry.

"Then just repeat what the last guy said as a question," he says.

I think about this and then I say, "Alex, you're a genius." This would look pretty natural and the next guy could fake over my mistake.

"Aren't you nervous?" I ask him, and he says, "Stupid, of course I'm nervous."

"You don't look nervous," I say, and he shakes his head.

"Everybody feels it," he says. "Fricking Daz, you got to make an effort."

"Okay, but I don't know what to do," I say.

"Just remember your first line," Alex says. "That's what I do. If I think about what I'm supposed to do in the first play of the game, the rest just happens."

"Okay, man. I'll try." So I whip open my script and try focusing on my first two lines. How could I be so stupid to wait until the last minute? My mind is still whirling with all the different scenes. It's like mashed potatoes in my head, but I make a huge effort and focus on my first line, which is, "No, the Jersey City near London." Then Linda, who plays the wife, says, "I don't remember a Jersey City outside London," and I look dumb and say, "They just built it last year, mum. Veddy big project, mum," and Alex says, "Quite right, it's enormous." I just keep repeating, "No, the Jersey City near London," under my breath while the curtain goes up and the party scene starts.

Then Mark points to us, and I'm hyperventilating and Alex pulls me on stage. I'm like one of those toy robots you control with a joystick, and we go over to Martin like we're supposed to. He gives us our instructions to follow Gene in a stage whisper, and then Linda joins us. Our lines are coming up, but I can't seem to concentrate on what people are saying. I'm circling Jupiter.

I snap back just in time to hear Alex say, "Jersey City, mum," and then Linda says, "Jersey City?," and I yell out, "The Jersey City near London, mum," and there's a few laughs and Linda says, "I don't remember a Jersey City outside London," and I say, "Um, they just built it last year, mum. Veddy big project," and I hear

Alex say in his blinky Brit accent, "Quite right, mum. It's enormous," and there's a few more laughs and Linda says, "I can't imagine why I haven't heard of it. I was just in London last month," and I am incredibly relieved, the biggest relief of my whole life hits me. I've said my lines and didn't botch the whole play.

Gene leaves and Alex has to grab my arm and drag me off after him. That pulls a few laughs, like I'm the dummy partner who has to be reminded of the job, and I'm blown flat that it was funny to somebody out there even though it was really just me orbiting Jupiter and Alex saving my ass. From then on we did that every time, me acting dumb and Alex dragging me off. It always got a few laughs and those were the best laughs I ever heard.

# CHAPTER FOURTEEN

What's strange about acting is how sometimes the switch is toggled on ten and other times it's in the limp mode, even though you're always the same person. There was one night in particular when our gig locked into place and everything we said clicked, and we were like a quarterback and wide receiver who were touched by the gods, every pass was a spiral and an easy catch. Our bodies were just hilarious that night, I don't know why. I knew exactly how to look confused and inspired by a dumb idea and everything else we were supposed to do. Just the way Alex scratched his head launched a lot of laughs. Maybe the audience was spinning, too, I don't know, but they could see we were on, and they clapped their asses off when we came back onstage at the end.

I couldn't sleep that night; I was just so hotwired with that weird energy, like the first night I talked with Leslie. Everything we said was funny or interesting and she was so lapis, her hair and her mouth and her eyes, and it was strange because we'd seen each other for three or four days already, but I never noticed how pretty her eyes were or how her sense of humor was so bongo, just like mine.

I'd gone all through high school admiring girls, but always feeling gumby around them. I concluded I always would, and then it was so beach with Leslie, just palm trees swaying in the breeze, and I wasn't afraid of her. That night Alex started snoring, but I didn't care because I was replaying every minute of my time with Leslie, and stopping on her lips and her eyes and her funny expressions.

The problem was Alex took a cliff dive over Leslie's friend Meg, so we'd left before I could follow through with Leslie. This led to the gig that almost rolled the credits on the whole trip. We were at the beach in North Carolina, sitting in the big dunes, resting and thinking in our own little worlds. We were both tired and a little sick of each other that day. We'd been out eight or nine weeks, we'd reached the East Coast, and I felt lonely for home and just dribbed by the constant moving and spending almost every hour together.

The breeze is cool, the salt spray smells fine, and there's even some lapis lazuli girls half-falling out of their bikini tops drifting by, but none of it lifts either of us off the ground. Sitting on the beach really snaps to the meaning of "coast to coast." Maybe if you're from Nebraska the Pacific and Atlantic beaches might look about the same, but to me the water and waves are so different from SoCal—the water's not so green in Carolina, and there's no steady shore break, it's all chopped up—that you really know you're far from home.

And camping wasn't as fun as it was in the beginning, either. We'd had a pretty tropo time at Rich and Pauline's, and now in comparison canned chili was bow-wow. Plus, gas and grinds were costing more than we'd expected, and we were getting low on gitas.

Alex is sitting maybe fifty feet down the beach so I go over and sit down next to him.

"Are you thinking what I'm thinking?" I ask him.

He shrugs and kind of mutters, "What are you thinking?"

"About heading home," I say. "Not direct, but in that direction."

He looks out at the waves rolling in and says, "I'm ready, too."

I wait a minute and then ask, "Can we go back through Iowa?"

He just looks down and digs his heels into the sand.

"Look," I tell him, "If it was reversed, I'd go with you and just avoid Meg. It won't be that hard."

"Yeah," he snorts. "Easy for you to say."

"I swear it'll only be a few days," I tell him, kind of pleading.

He's quiet for a minute, studying the sand, and then he says, "You always get to say where we're going."

This spins me off and I tell him, "Hey, we went to Iowa because of you, pal, and we went to New York because you wanted to."

"The fricking car broke down, bruddah," he says. "We had to go somewhere."

"Yeah, but it was still your gig," I say. "And what about New York?"

123

"You wanted New York, too," he snaps back. "We stayed 'cause of you."

"Man, it was because Benny wanted us to do the play," I answer, and I'm getting bent. "Don't blame me. You could have said no."

"What about seeing Rich?" he asks, all defensively, and I tell him, "Hey, that was both of us and you know it."

He shakes his head like a bull who's been poked with a stick and says, "You know what I mean."

"No, I don't," I say.

He looks up at the ocean again and says, "Okay, go. I'll drop you off and go home by myself."

"Then how do I get home?" I shout.

"Bus," he says.

"Why don't you take the bus and leave me the car?" I ask.

"See what I mean?" he says. "You always have to control everything."

"That's griff," I say. "I always ask you, 'Where should we go?'"

"But you've already made up your mind," he says.

"What a frag," I say. "Fine. Have it your way. Just don't screw up the car on the way home."

And I get up and head back to the Cruiser.

I go over and sit on the front fender, the one that's still primer-gray. I just sit there and look at it for awhile and think what a jerk Alex is. He's always hated the Lancer, and now he wants to take it. That's what really gets me hearing Griffin Spike and the Funktones.

When we bought the Cruiser, Old Man Ching had put on this purple fender from another junker because the old one had gotten banged up in an accident a long time ago. We planned to repaint the whole car but ended up thinking, let's save the money for the trip, so we had this katakana fender.

We wanted to at least prime it, so we bought a dinkoid spray can of gray primer, and just douched the purple fender, but the primer didn't cover it. Then some guy told us to spray silver paint on first, and then put the primer over that. I thought it was a loon-tune idea, but it worked great. The silver paint covers even a dark color like purple, and then the primer covers the silver.

So we had this gray fender. One day we're sitting around cleaning the car, doing a really good job, you know, Armorall, window cleaner, chrome polish, just a tropo-electric job, and this friend of ours is there with us, breezing.

So she draws a little peace sign in the shape of a heart with a felt pen on the fender. That peace sign in a heart is her insignia, her mark. At first I thought, hey, what's this griff, but she thought we were going to paint it. It wouldn't come off when we tried to wash it, so we just left it and started to like it. Then this other friend draws a little electric guitar and writes, "Les Paul Deluxe forever" on it next to the peace sign. "Get it?" he tells us, "Les Paul on a fender," and I'm thinking what a frap, and then he explains, "There's Fender guitars, you know, Strats and Telecasters, and then there's Gibsons—you know, Les Paul Deluxes and Sunbursts."

Okay, that's clever enough for me, I'm not too picky. Then everyone starts writing little things like "Zimbabwe!" or "Wash Me," just dumb things. So the day before we're leaving, somebody writes a message, "Have fun and stay clean," and I think it's pretty beach. So I even ask my dad, hey, write something on our car, and he writes, "Call me when you need bail." It's a joke because he knows I am by the book.

I knew my parents were worried that we couldn't make it work, but then they were always torturing me with that booga-booga about how some guys my age already had screaming brats at nineteen, and how others were in subs watching over our nuclear arsenal—all these responsible gigs while I was drifting on cruise control, making Madonnas and dribbing.

You know, damned if you do, damned if you don't. You should grow up. Okay, we're going on a trip. What? You're not mature enough. Yah.

So our friends and families wrote these little notes and drawings on the fender with felt pens, like a sketch showing two stick figures behind bars and "Busted!" written below it, a weird face with "Danger! Aliens inside" printed below it, palm trees, a few rhymes like "Save lives, this car doesn't go over 55," cutesy but tolerable.

I started to get worried that the notes would wear off, so I took a few snapshots of the fender in New York. Sitting there in the sun, I just read these little notes and see all the people who wrote them, and I start feeling better. If Alex wants to be totally frapped, I'm

125

thinking, that's up to him. I can't stop him from being a complete asshole.

When Alex comes back about an hour later we don't say jank to each other. If there's one thing I hate it's the silent treatment, but that's Alex's way of not spinning a hurricane, so I have to live with it. But I'll be damned if I'm gonna apologize because he's the one who torqued me.

All the way down the coast we both do a Stonewall Jackson, and I'm thinking, fine, Alex, leave me at Leslie's, I'll have a great time, much better than if I stick it out with you.

I don't want to feel torqued anymore, but I can't help remembering how Alex had spun a total Mr. Jones on me when I first showed him the Lancer. Too old, too ugly, too weird; look, it even has a purple fender, I remember him saying.

He wanted a Firebird or Camaro or some muscle car, and I had to explain without hurting his feelings that we might as well paint "Originality minus" on our foreheads, and just go all the way to fricative and buy a minivan. At least we'd have lots of storage. He didn't grip the main idea, which was to do something a little different, not just ride the bumper cars at Disneyland again.

And it was nark, nark, nark every time something didn't go perfect with the Lancer, instant thrombosis, like this proves my judgment is turdsville. Look, the engine probably needs rebuilding, he says, like it's some surprise, as if even an old Malibu wouldn't need a top end rebuild.

Then when the Cruiser bit the hard one in Kansas City, of course we're both upset, but he goes cattywompus and blames me for buying a crappy car. No, even worse, for making him go along with buying it. He just keeps his mouth shut until it's too late, and then he whips a Mr. Jones and says, you were wrong, griff, griff, griff. Yah, that's so easy, after the other guy catches the jerk by making the call.

I was also spun because Mr. Macho can't bear to face the girl who slagged him off. Mr. Kung Fu is scared of the one girl who saw through his griff and took his edge off. Even King Widget takes a fall sometime, but no, Alex just wants to run away and to hell with what's important to me.

That frap about me taking charge really torques me, too. I always think of his feelings, what he might like to do, but he can't stop one second to think about the fact that this girl could be it for me. I'm not some sports hero or Romeo; this could be my big chance at romance. So will my pal help me out by just breezing for a few days? No.

After an hour of this I am ready to jerk the chain and blow him off right now, to hell with waiting until Iowa to vector on my own. All I have to do, I'm thinking, is survive until Charleston, and then I'll ditti mau on a bus to Iowa; it'll be great, no more of his snoring and farting, and no more worrying about his blinky second-guessing.

We didn't have a map of the Southeast because we'd never had any plans to go there. Old Man Ching had left a thick bundle of maps wrapped with string in the glove compartment, but they were out of date, and so brittle that, when we opened the California one, it split in half. So we just retied the string and put them under the seat. More for something to do than because I really needed a more detailed map, I dig the bundle out and start looking for a map of South Carolina.

There's lots of state maps, but no South Carolina. I was curious how old these maps were, and I found one dated 1960. The California one was dated 1969. All the other maps were 1960 or even earlier. Some were 1957 or '58. I tried to stuff them back under the seat, but something was in the way. I started to feel torqued again, like what the hell is stuck under here? I reached way in, and felt something along the side of the seat frame. I finally got a grip on it, and pulled out a tall thin little book.

It looks like a pocket calendar at first, but it's just plain paper inside, no dates. There's a bunch of entries in small, careful handwriting. I turn to the front and read the first entry dated July 11, 1948. "Kansas City–St. Louis, 254 miles, 5½ hours, 12 gallons–$2.88. Had dinner with Billy Wong (going to Wash U. in SL). He told me to stay with him on the way back."

Firecrackers go off in my head and I realize that this is Old Man Ching's travel notebook from way back when. I flip ahead in the book and find the last entries in August 1969. Half of the little book is empty, just yellowing pages with small blue lines.

I skim through the entries and pick up that Mr. Ching had cruised across country visiting friends and relatives during the summer before his second or third year of college, and gotten married sometime in 1950 because his wife was already pregnant and traveling with him on a trip to Santa Cruz that year. One entry read, "Baby kicked during breakfast." After 1950 there was nothing until '52, like he didn't go anywhere for a few years, and from later entries about visiting his old army buddies, I figure he'd been in the Army during that time, fighting in Korea. After that the family seemed to go somewhere each summer. His son Raymond was mentioned a few times, but mostly it was date, mileage, time, gas purchases, and prices, and one line about where they were and what they did, like, "Camped in Yellowstone, very cold night, snowed a little at dawn."

Alex has been ignoring me this whole time, and I try not to think he's purposely giving me granite. I hold up the little brown book. "Old Man Ching kept a travel diary," I tell him. "He went all over the place back when he was young."

"Oh yeah?" Alex says, all bored, and it's obvious he isn't catching it.

"He did the same thing we're doing," I say, "and at least some of the gigs must have been in this car. Isn't it weird?"

Alex still doesn't look at me. "Kinda."

"Grip this," I say, flipping to the front pages. "'July 30, New York. 5 gallons, $1.80. Hard time finding place to stay. Tracked down my cousin (Aunt May's son Sherman), slept on his couch. He lives above the restaurant, too noisy to sleep.' He went to New York, too, man. It's so winky."

"Yeah," Alex says, and I'm thinking, whiff this griff, Alex isn't gripping the gig, he's so ozoned it's a joke. Too bad our trip has to end with him being so fricking stupid. So I leave him alone and just bury myself in Old Man Ching's careful handwriting and his descriptions of all these trips he made when he and Mrs. Ching were young. Then their kid was born and they traveled around, the perfect little family.

Judging by all the places they went, Old Man Ching must have been pretty curious when he was younger; once he got old he just stayed home and looks mean. It leaves you hoping that won't happen to you.

After reading Mr. Ching's journals for an hour or so I start to soften up a little over Alex's granite mood. Yah, I'm thinking, he was being a complete assholina, but should I let that ruin the whole gig? Maybe his loco-moco mood will blow over tomorrow. After all, I did shove the Lancer down his throat.

Alex pulls off the highway at a gas station, and I pump the gas while he goes in and takes a leak. I'm always a little nervous taking a leak when he's in a bad mood because I'm afraid he'll repeat his driveaway stunt, only this time not come back. Now I figure if he drives away, fine, I've got my Mastercard and I'll vector to Iowa with that. I grab my coat off the back seat so I at least have that if the mojo spins free.

When I come out of the bathroom he's still there, wiping the windshield clean. I head for the passenger door and he says, "You drive a while." After I've pulled back on the highway, he flops down so his head is resting on the top of the seat and then pulls his baseball cap low over his face.

"I'll drop you at Leslie's and then pick you up in a couple days," he says quietly. "If you want to hump her after that, she'll have to come back with us." I can't see his eyes, but his white teeth flash out a sly grin.

I'm blown down and I ask him, "You mean that?"

He says, "Yeah."

I say, "Thanks, man," and that night we buy a six-pack of Cervantes with our fake Hawaiian IDs and make fun of dumb shows on the motel room's blurry color TV.

# CHAPTER FIFTEEN

Alex listens to me rant about how the Masters ought to stand naked in the rain, but he's too practical to get spiked about it. But you have to be careful not to torque his pride.

I found that out in Chicago. It's late afternoon, bake-brain city, and there's more wind in Grandma's oven when she's baking chocolate chip cookies than there is in the Windy City. We fight our way through the thick downtown traffic and Lake Shore Drive, and then vector through some neighborhoods. Parts of Chicago are dirty, man. I don't mean old McDonald's wrappers in the gutter, I mean old brick walls that are greasy and black from a century of God-knows-what.

We're tired of driving all day to get here, tired of the blasting heat, and tired of the stop-and-go bumper car ride through downtown, so when we spock this corner bar, the low, windowless kind with an old martini glass neon sign outside, we decide to stop for a beer. It just looks so hoboken, like the kind of place with a caveman behind the bar, that we think it would be crisp to try it. Plus we want a break to think about where to spend the night.

Sure enough, there's a Neanderthal behind the bar, a squat guy with hairy arms and a patch of black fur poking through his half-opened shirt, and a few dim lights over fake red leather booths. There's big bowls of salted, unshelled peanuts set out on the tables, and the place smells like a peanut butter factory run by drunks.

Two girls in tight dresses, a few years older than us and kind of cute, are sitting alone in one of the booths along the back wall. One is dark-saucy and mixed, like she could be from Hawaii, and her long hair is pulled into a shiny black pony tail that looks nectar against her creamy-lace dress. Her friend is stuffed into a little black party rag that looks about four hours ahead of the clock. There's nobody in the place because it's still afternoon, so we get two horse-piss-on-tap brews at the bar with our frap fake IDs and then sit down at their booth.

We're in our usual uniforms, me in a white T-shirt and blue jeans, so nobody can see my skinny shark-bait legs, and Alex is wearing his "Shaka, brah" tanktop and surfer shorts. I start my "we're new in town" pitch and they look amused. I try the "we're from L.A. and he's from Hawaii" routine and they're almost laughing at us. So in desperation I remember the rule about being interested in them, so I ask them where they work. They're smiling but stone silent. I'm thinking, what, have I got snot running down my face?

I'm on the verge of asking them what the problem is when a greasy-haired big guy wearing a golf shirt and fancy darkened glasses saunters over from the entrance and says, "Okay, fun's over. Get lost." He has an accent I can't place and he smells like room freshener, plus he's wearing all these big-dollar rings. Normally I'd be narking his hoboken Hollywood Hood outfit and delivery, but he means it. I'm not sure who he's talking to, us or the girls, and I get a big splash of fear right on my shoulder blades, like a cold wave hitting you at the beach. Alex isn't moving and I'm still confused until the guy jerks his head at us and says, "Go on, get lost."

I'm suddenly gripping that maybe this guy is their pimp. Yah, I'm that naive. The girls are sitting on one side of the fake red leather booth, and they start looking at their drinks and twiddling the little umbrellas. They aren't smiling any more. I start to stand up and Alex clumps a big hot hand on my shoulder and pushes me back down.

"What, you own them?" Alex asks real belligerently, and he's staring straight ahead at the wall behind the girls. The foreign Joe Cool nods his head and doesn't say anything. He tries to look unworried, and he does a pretty good job of it. Lots of practice, I guess. The girl in the black mini-dress says, "Yeah, go ahead, you guys. We're with him. Sorry."

Alex is just sitting there like some kind of modern statue, the kind that looks like a real guy but isn't—you know, like the bronze businessman with his head in a wall in downtown L.A.

Then another guy shows up behind Joe Cool. He's even bigger, his black suit coat can't even be buttoned, and he says, "Let's go, guys," in a medium soft but definitely threatening voice.

131

I'm thinking, Thank God, we can leave, because it's pretty thick now and I'm scared that this gorgon is with the Mob.

I start to stand up again and the suit makes a big mistake. He puts his hand on Alex's shoulder to pull him out, and Alex explodes like a bomb. He jabs the suit's throat with his elbow, punches his nuts, and then slam-fists his face about twenty times, incredibly fast, just like he demo'd on me once in front of the football guys, only this time he is in a full–rev rage and his fists are just smashing the guy's face again and again, I mean with full force, enough to splinter boards.

Alex kicks the suit in the solar plexus really hard, and he falls backwards like a tree on wheels. Then Alex spins around and grabs the Joe Cool butterball by his greasy hair, reaches in and yanks off this thick gold chain the guy has around his neck. He throws it at one of the girls and says, "Now you don't even have to fuck him."

The guy throws a punch, but Alex wards it off like the guy's fist was a horsefly. Then he rips off the scumbag's glasses and throws them across the room. The guy's eyes are blazing, but there's a trace of the Black Hole in them.

The girls are bug-eyed, flaming out over the chasm they see opening up in front of them. Then Joe Cool makes a terrible decision. He tries to kick Alex in the nuts. Alex blocks the greaseball's knee with one hand and then grabs the guy. In one quick move he pulls him over to the table and beats his head against it like he was cramming a bowling ball into hard dirt, just wham wham wham wham. When he cracks the guy's head back, I see this incredible amount of blood on the guy's face.

The guy waves his arm around, trying to push Alex away, but Alex is so intent and stanced out that the guy's fingers never even get close. Then Alex punches the side of the guy's head and his arm stops waving. He pulls the limp bod up and punches a huge fist right into the guy's nuts, just redlines him. The guy's dick must have been shoved back into his kidneys. Then he tosses the ragdoll pimp on the floor.

The Neanderthal behind the counter has just spotted the action because it's taken all of about three seconds total. He says, "Hey, what the fuck's going on over there?"

I say to Alex, "Come on, let's go." Alex looks like he can't decide whether to wait for someone else to fight or whether to vector. I damn well know I'm not going to touch him, so I just keep pleading, "Come on Alex, the cops will be here any second, let's go!"

He finally turns and starts walking towards the door. He looks like a bull stomping around in the ring, all hot and ready. The tender is out in front of his counter, coming to stop us, and I beg him, "Don't touch him, man, don't touch him," and he looks at me and then at Alex's bloody hands and he hesitates, which saves him a trip to the emergency ward.

When we walk out there's a light green Mercedes parked at the curb that wasn't there when we went in. Alex stops for a second, just long enough to connect the pimp to this car, and then goes over and bends the little antennae over. This doesn't satisfy him, so he reaches in with fingers of death and torques the one big windshield wiper right off, just bending it back and forth until it snaps. Then he starts kicking the side panels, totally grunting and wild. Each thump crumples the sheet metal into recycled steel. In between the kicks he yells, "Assholes!"

I just stare at him beating this vehicle into tin cans until I get the presence of mind to run to the Lancer, get in, start it up, and yell, "I'm leaving!" He's jumping up and down on the roof of the car, and he jumps off onto the hood like he's trying to jump through it. Then he ambles over and gets in, and we roar off in a cloud of blue and black smoke. I'm gripping the wheel real tight because I'm trembling.

They'd asked for it. They just hadn't expected to get it. It's scary to see someone go wild, and I have to admit I was pretty careful with what I said to Alex for a while after that.

It's like this scene we spocked in New York. It's downtown Manhattan, lots of traffic, with maniac cabbies driving down the middle of two lanes so they can switch back from one to the other to dodge triple-parked UPS vans, they're switching back and forth about eighty times a block, their horns are either stuck on or they've got duct tape holding them down, and everyone else is leaning on their horns, too.

We pull up behind some vehicles at a stoplight. There's a hippie VW van with some guy in it, and he's trying to make a right turn from the middle lane. He swerves around a truck in front of him, almost drilling some munchkin on the left, and then he whips back and cuts off some guy trying to make a legal right turn.

So the guy who had to swerve out of the hippie's way flips him off. This giant long-haired hippie, I mean the beefy middle line-backer variety, leaps out of the van and runs over to the guy and starts raving at the top of his lungs, "Come on, you fucker, get out here and fight, you got a problem, come on!" He's raving along, nice and loud, and I'm thinking the weasel he's reaming might just have a roscoe, and maybe he'll get a little hot himself and put a bullet through the wilding hippie. Happens all the time. I mean, this is America.

But the wease, just rolls up his window and stares straight ahead, probably thinking, "Man what the hell did I get my ass into this time? A doped-out middle linebacker wants to rip my face off and throw it do the dogs. Christ, all I did was flip him off. What the hell, this is New York, what does he expect? He must be from Jersey."

The light changes and the killer hippie gets back in the van and hauls chili to the right, finishing his job of cutting off the guy trying to make a legal turn.

So this scene is human life in a nutshell. Some frustration griffs over, you vent a little heat, and all of a sudden the other guy has redlined the whole gig right up to maximum. You thought you were just annoyed at some lame traffic play. Wrongo boyo! Your life is suddenly on the line, and you're in combat to the death.

It's like, "Hey, you owe me ten bucks, I want it back," and the response is, "I'll kill you." Is it worth ten gitas to find out if the guy is loopy? Hell, no. The guy who redlines it and means it will always win. It works exactly the same way with whole countries. Some dictator will invade the small country next door and then tells everyone, "Hey sorry, this used to be our homeland five thousand years ago, so I just reclaimed it and if you don't like it then I'll destroy your army, rape your women, tear down your cities, and salt the earth behind me. Does anyone have a problem?"

Who's got a problem when the maniac has a huge army to back up his madness? Nobody, that's who.

Except there's always the case where the weasel pulls out a gun and blows the maniac to hell, or where the stoned hippie linebacker jerks some guy who turns out to be a kung fu master who promptly whips the linebacker into a pretzel, or where the dictator gets crushed like a bug because the people he attacked didn't cave in.

Or in the case of our gig, where some thirty-weight pimps misjudge the damage they did to Alex's pride when they jerked him around in front of the girls. He felt a loss of face so he smashed theirs to pulp.

# CHAPTER SIXTEEN

The great thing about traveling, especially in the West, is this feeling that you can get up in the morning and leave your problems behind, like they're a chunk of granite that you can just drive away from. Of course that's oobla-dee, the problems always come with you, but the illusion of a fresh start is nice.

And I guess it is a fresh start in the sense that you could wake up, smell the gasoline leaking out of your car, and actually start solving one of your problems. Mostly what people like is the feeling of the problem going away by just pressing on the gas, no work required.

I found out something else about traveling. Now I understand why some people are always going somewhere, like if they stop they'll die. It's because if you run fast enough over a big area, then you can outrun your problems. Not really, grip, but by the time you take care of orienting yourself, finding a cheap place to stay or setting up your camp, getting some grinds, washing the dishes, cleaning some clothes, saying hi to the people you're camped next to, trying to hump some girl you've spocked, looking at a map to see where you're going tomorrow and figuring out how to get there, you're too tired to have any problems. Travel is strat distraction. If I stayed on the road my whole life, I'd never have to decide about college, or worry about Leslie, or have any other problems. That's why people do it.

When you're spinning down an I-State, you feel like all the griff that's torqueing you is a thousand miles away and can't touch you. But all those problems are like little tiny guys living in your ears, they travel with you and talk to you at night when you're asleep and you think you've escaped.

Another good thing about being on the road is that you're King Tut the whole time. People admire you and say how independent and beach you are, and they act interested in you, especially if you've been to Borneo or Siberia or some other exotic place.

136

Even if you're like us and you're just going to places like New York and Iowa, people still give you the King Tut treatment because they wish they could haul derriere from their screaming brats, their buttwipe boss, and waking up at 5:30 in the morning to crawl onto the I-State commute like a hungover iguana.

So instead of feeling the way you normally feel, which is that you're an inferior, malignant troll, you feel like King Tut when you're traveling because everyone treats you like you're special. You can feel that you're all the things you never are in real life but wish you were, which is that you're unique and brave and interesting and in control. And of course lots of people are nice to you because you're giving them money. I always tip fifteen percent unless they treat us like we're aliens from Planet Ick, which is almost never.

Another funny thing about cruising down the I-States is how you miss where you've already been and are ready to broom where you are. One day I'm motating around Columbia University with Benny because Alex and Tita are off sightseeing, and I suddenly feel depressed by all the crap in the streets, by all the beggars and signs and the compression of everything. Buildings, people, even the air feels overloaded.

That made me remember this two-lane road in Kansas and an abandoned farm we saw there. We're blowing east, and I'm getting tired of I-70, so I'd spun off onto a two-laner: we have this rule that whoever's driving chooses the route unless we have to get somewhere by a specific time.

So I'm happy going forty miffs on this two-laner and there's no I-State boats or double-trailer big rigs or highway patrol cars, just a pickup or two and Mrs. Jones in her Delta 88 going to pick up her mail.

On the I-States you're always behind these I-State boats. They look like 747's that landed on the freeway and clipped their wings off going through an overpass. The main RV is gigantia but that's not enough, so they're towing an Accord and motorcycles behind that. If you're as into transpo as these guys, you put together a personal caravan. There's the Titanic on wheels, the Accord, the motorcycle trailer, a bicycle carrier, and then finally a skateboard on the end. You got it covered, slick. Your mobile crib is longer than a eighteen-wheeler big rig; it gets three miles to the gallon, and there's only two people in it, Mr. and Mrs. Jones, mainline members of the American Association of Retired People.

You start passing them and it's a torch-lobe experience. You pass the bikes, then the car, then you get to the ass-end of the RV, you drive about five more minutes and you see the front, you look way up to see the driver and he looks like the pilot in a 747 when you're waiting at the airport, like an ant, and it's always some little skinny guy. Jeez Louise, pal, you need this 747 on wheels to see the sights? Can you imagine driving the damn thing? You have to start turning in Utah to head for L.A.

Talk about rich. These guys are richer than any Topanga Canyon millionaire. They have their satellite dish, cell phone, TV in the cab, full kitchen in the back, transpo for any situation, even nuclear war. They've got the yin and the yang and everything in between.

I'm not saying all these boats are spike. I mean Rich and Pauline's is smaller than a garbage truck, and it's pretty strat inside. There's no rocks jabbing you in the kidneys like when you're camping and no barf-urine-toxic-waste-PineSol-chainsmoker-smell like in gimpy motels. Plus, you can gizmo your frozen burritos in the microwave and save big dollars on food.

But I hate the waste. The wasted space, the wasted gas, the wasted camping spot they take up in the campgrounds. They're just big toys for people with too much time on their hands who don't want to go to any trouble getting somewhere. But what kind of traveling is that?

So I tell Benny about this abandoned farmhouse we saw in Kansas. There's only endless corn fields, a hot sun in the cloudless sky, and the smell of dust raised off a farm road by a pickup. If you turn off the engine, the only sounds are the whine of machinery far away and a few birds singing.

Nothing breaks the line of corn tassels against the blue sky, and then we slide up a gentle rise and suddenly there's this two-story wood house and a big tree, all alone, poking up above the solid gold fields. The house is maybe two or three hundred yards off the road, we can't see it too well, but all the paint's peeled off, and some of the top floor windows are missing glass.

The house hits me with this funny feeling of loneliness, and I pull over to look at it. Alex lifts out of his drift because we've stopped, and I point out the old house. "I'm going to take a look," I say. He comes with me because who can resist an empty old house?

A scraggly barbed wire fence marks out a big square around the house. The corn edges right up to the rusty wire fence, and then inside there's only clumps of dry grass. This giant willow tree shades the house, which was probably great when somebody lived there, but now the tree makes it look dark and spooky.

We stand there for a minute looking at a dead washing machine, the old white round kind on legs with rollers and a handle, and a rusty chunk of farm equipment, one with big curved tines for breaking up the soil.

The strands of barbed wire are loose or broken, so it's easy to lift up the top one and climb in. The front door is locked with a shiny new padlock, but we walk around and notice this old wood cover to the cellar that isn't locked. Back before they had natural gas, these doors opened up and you threw coal down in the basement for the furnace.

I pry the cover open and get a splinter from the cracked old lumber. It's pitch black down there. I don't feel like jumping into blackness so I run back and grab our heavy-duty cop flashlight, the long one that needs six batteries, from under the driver's seat. I shine the light down into the hole and the first thing we see is the red and white of a Budweiser can. Of course the local punks have been here.

Once I see there's no giant rats or razor-sharp spikes or dead bodies, Alex gives me a hand and lowers me into the hole. It's deeper than it looks and I panic when I still can't touch the ground and I'm hanging off Alex's hands. "Man, don't—" I say, and then he drops me.

I fall maybe three inches and hit the dirt.

I spin the light around to make sure some maniac isn't crouching there holding a machete that's dripping blood, and of course there's nothing but some spider webs and trash; it's just that I've seen too many dumb horror movies.

Alex lowers himself down and then jumps the last couple of feet.

"Spooky, bruddah," he says as I pan the flashlight beam over the walls and old newspapers and tin cans. Even though it's hot outside, the cellar is cool and smells musty and damp like the inside of an old trunk. There's a dim light coming from the middle of the house so we shuffle ahead and find the staircase going up. It has these big wood doors in the floor, and I remember that there's tornadoes here, big air funnels that can rip your house off the ground and crumple it into kindling, and whoever lived in this house would run down here and shut the doors and hope they weren't vacuumed out like a loose dustball when the tornado sucked the big doors off their hinges and torqued everything that wasn't cast iron.

There's no furniture in the rooms, but some gauzy curtains are still hanging, and there's old faded flower wallpaper peeling off most of the walls. Some punks have left cigarette butts and some melted candles on the floor, and I'm glad they weren't stupid enough to burn the house down during their secret club meetings.

We climb up the rickety stairs to the second floor, and there's a slight breeze drifting through the open windows. Other than one sagging wooden dresser with a broken mirror and a stained box frame, there's nothing up there. It looks like the secret place you'd take your girlfriend so you could hump her without worrying about her kid brother bursting in on you.

It's not a fancy house—there's only four rooms upstairs—but somebody had put some effort into making it nice—you know, the wallpaper and the curtains. I go over to the window and look over the front yard. The paint's peeled off the window frame, but one frilly curtain is still hanging inside, and the end drifts a little in the breeze.

"This was somebody's dream," I say, and it seems sad that their dream ended like this, all worn out and broken.

Alex comes over and looks out the window, too. "Maybe they moved on to another dream," he says. "Maybe they were done with this one." I like the sound of that, like maybe it wasn't too sad when they stepped off the front porch for the last time and drove out of the yard forever.

I finish telling the story to Benny, and my mind comes back to New York. We pass a group of university students who are laughing at some private joke. They all look like models, so good-looking and confident, and I feel depressed again.

Benny says, "An old friend lives around here. Mind if we stop by?"

I shrug "Okay," so we walk about ten blocks and climb up into an old ashtray building to meet his friend. The guy is tall and skinny, and has a gimpy untrimmed beard, but his apartment is very organized and loaded with Eastern religion stuff: brass incense bowls and posters of gods with blue elephant heads and goddesses with big tits and sixteen hands.

I'm still spocking his spiritual knicknacks when Benny introduces me. I shake the guy's hand and get the h.j.'s because his gray eyes are so steady it's like they're on gyroscopes.

The guy's name is Sadjuruma, even though he's as white as a cream puff, and Benny tells him a little about our trip. The guy smiles and says to me, "So you're a searcher, too."

"We're all searchers," Benny says. "That's the way it is."

The guy was just saying something polite, but for some reason it lights Benny's flame. Sadjuruma glances at him with his even gray eyes and says, "Not all of us."

I can see the red flare fire up behind Benny's eyes and he says, "Oh really? Then why do you keep going back to India?"

The guy still has this little smile. He shakes his head and asks, "Did you come over just to argue?"

"No, I just hate that sanctimonious crap about how you're no longer searching," Benny snaps out. "Other guys have the corner office, you have your rituals. There's no difference."

"Why does my happiness make you angry, Benjamin?" The guys asks, and I'm thinking, yeah, why does this guy's blue-headed elephant and bogus name make you so hot?

"It doesn't," Benny shoots right back. "What makes me mad is, what if some middle-class Indians left Bombay and flew all the way over here to sit at the feet of some cowboy preacher in Texas? Wouldn't that be pretty ridiculous?"

The guy shakes his head and chuckles, "What difference does it make where they come from? If they learn something from the cowboy preacher, then who cares?"

141

"Everybody goes for what's exotic because it seems more wonderful and true than what they already know," Benny says, all disparagingly.

"I'm sorry, Benjamin," the guys says, "but if it makes them happier, what does it matter?"

Benny doesn't have an answer, and he stands there frapped for a moment. Then he shrugs and says, "Well, I'm glad you were home. I wanted Daz to meet you."

"It's good to see you, Benjamin."

Benny puts his fist against the guy's shoulder in a play punch and says, "It's still Benny, Sadj."

Once we're outside I say, "Man, I didn't think anyone could torque you off like that."

Benny looks sheepish and says, "He does. Every time."

"Why?" I ask.

Benny shakes his head, and it's interesting to see him struggling for the first time. "He meditates and visits temples and thinks he's changed," Bennie says. "But that's bullshit. He hasn't changed at all."

"Who cares," I ask, "if that stuff makes him happy?"

Benny shakes his head again and frowns. "It's bullshit," he repeats. "He's still a middle-class New Yorker with a domineering father and a weak mother."

To challenge him a little, I ask, "How would you know?"

"Because I grew up with him," he snaps.

I'm kind of enjoying reversing the roles and having Benny on a hot skewer, so I tell say all innocently, "He looked pretty happy to me."

Benny flares up and says, "If you distract yourself enough, you can fake a happy face because you're not feeling anything."

"So you're perfect and you're friend is dogmeat," I say.

"I don't want to be perfect," he tells me, all wild-eyed. "And I'm not trying to run away from myself. Now let me ask you something. Why did you get all silent after we passed those students?"

I'm surprised he noticed, but I'm also gripping his Psychology 101 way of squirming out of the spotlight by whipping it onto me.

"Nice try, Mister Shrink," I tell him. "I finally get to see you all discombobulated, and you don't like it."

He throws up his hands and says, "Okay, I admit it, I'm just a neurotic wretch who's jealous of Sadj's ability to truly believe in a load of crap. And yes, I wish you didn't see me lose my cool. Now tell me why a dark cloud crossed over you back there."

I decide to answer truthfully, so I think about it for a minute and then say, "I guess because they're going to a hotshot university and I'm just a numbnuts going nowhere."

"You really think that's true?" he asks me, like he can't believe it. I tell him, "Yeah. It's obvious."

He looks over at me and says, "Daz, they're stuck in boring classes while you're cruising around really living. I'm sure they'd admire you."

"That's a joke," I snort.

"Well, I admire you," he says.

I look down at the sidewalk. "That's because you're weird."

"What's weird is that you're telling yourself such a load of crap," he tells me. "What you're doing *is* hotshot, and if they love what they're doing then it's right for them."

"But what if your pal loves meditating?" I ask. "Doesn't that make it right for him, too?"

He waves off my question disgustedly and says, "That's just noble-sounding bullshit to make you feel more righteous than everybody else."

"How do you know that guy isn't right and you're wrong?" I ask.

He looks at me seriously and then laughs and his eyes crinkle up. "We're just mammals, Daz. That's all there is to it. You can dress us up in fancy spiritual clothes, but it doesn't change a damn thing."

"But how can you be so sure?" I ask, just riffing him a little more.

"You'll have to decide for yourself, Daz," he tells me, "but what I've got is science, and what he's got is a bunch of mumbo-jumbo. Once you see how humans need safety and nurturing as kids, and what happens to them if they don't get both of those things, then you can't believe any spiritual crap any more."

"So what happens to them?" I ask.

"They find some happy story that makes them feel better," he says. "A religion, a gang, money, something."

"Nobody gives a damn about happy stories," I say. "Everybody likes stories that are all griff."

"Not that kind of story," he tells me. "I mean the kind of story you believe about yourself, like following my guru makes me a hotshot, or my money makes me a hotshot, or screwing a beautiful woman makes me a hotshot, or helping poor people makes me a hotshot."

"What's your story?" I ask.

"That I don't need a story," he says, and winks.

"I don't know, Benny. Sometimes, your ideas don't make sense."

"Daz, I'd be upset if they did," he says, and then he drags me into one of his favorite delis, which is run by some Korean people, and treats me to a big, thick pastrami sandwich.

# CHAPTER SEVENTEEN

Meg, Leslie and Tracie aren't the only girls we met. One night in Colorado Springs we invited a couple of girls looking for a table to eat with us. Everything seems pretty tropo-electric to me, the glow is on, and so after we say goodbye to them I'm pancaked when Alex says, "Daz, don't you know anything about eating with women? You ate like a pig."

I get bent and say, "You're lipping griff, Jack! I ate like King Tut!"

Alex tells me, "Did King Tut eat with chicken grease running down his chin? Huh? You were disgusting, bruddah. You ground on those chicken bones like a starving dog."

"Hey, slick, I was hungry," I say. "Is that a crime?"

"No, but the way you eat is," he says.

"Well, Mr. Protocol, what do you suggest?" I ask him in my fake Brit accent. "Just sit there drinking water?"

"No, numbnuts," he says. "Don't order chicken when you're with women. Order a steak or something easy to eat. And stop gorging out long enough to look at them sometimes. Man, you acted like they disappeared as soon as that chicken hit the table."

I say, "Thanks for telling me now, pal. Grease on my chin. That's jank. I used my napkin."

"That was disgusting, too, brah," he tells me.

"Who appointed you food critic?" I ask. "And why didn't you tell me before?"

"Hey, no worry," he says. "You weren't that bad."

"Well Jesus, next time tell me before the gig spins down, okay?" I tell him, still bent. "I told you that time snot was running down your face, didn't I? And what about the way you smash the toothpaste in the middle and never put the cap back on?"

"Irrelevant and immaterial," he says, ripping my favorite line from old Perry Mason reruns. "We're talking about eating."

145

Then again I get him occasionally, too. Alex never seems satisfied with the way I start a conversation with girls, so one time in Boston I get frustrated and tell him, "Fine, slick, you go do the intro."

"No problem," he says. So he saunters over to the cafe table where three nice young ladies are eating lunch together, and he says "Hi," like that's all it takes. They look at him like he's the busboy and go back to their gossip and salads.

Then he tries to copy me, but he can't trip the wire. "We just got here, blah blah blah," but they're not buying it, it's wooden but it doesn't float, these girls have already heard every line there is ten times and they hated them the first time. The key is sincerity and spocking clues about what they like and just being friendly, giving them a little time to see you're for real and not some thirty-weight griff.

Alex does his wooden-sailor-in-front-of-the-cheezoid-seafood-restaurant gig for a while longer and then gives up. "Unfriendly women in this town," he says, like Joe Nonchalant, but I'm not letting him suffer in silence.

"Yah," I snort. "You flamed out. Haven't you learned anything from watching me? Take a number, pal, only this time try to learn something instead of just criticizing me."

I've already spocked some katakana jewelry on one of them, it's so airball that it has to be homemade. I go up and say, "Excuse me, I really like your jewelry"—which I did—"and I was wondering if you made it yourself." Compliment—direct hit. Guess that it was handmade—direct hit. Sincere interest plus appropriate amount of standing there relaxed. I am interested in the jewelry, and the deal is done, I know their names, which I instantly memorize with my secret technique, and I'm sitting down with them.

I have this way of talking about our trip that is guaranteed to sound icy, you know, "Yeah, we're from L.A. and we're cruising around the country, going wherever we want to when we want to, yeah, it's not a bad life, we work when we have to, which is as little as possible." The clinch is to ask them what's strat in their town and don't act superior, act interested.

So I motion to the A-Man who is sitting half-bent and half-discombobulated at our table, and I say, "Yeah, my friend is from Hawaii, they're shy over there but he's okay," and he comes over like Mr. Tough Guy and I know his pride is hurt, so I'm careful not to rub it in later. There's no use napalming a good friendship just to lord one moment over somebody.

Like one day back in school I yell out in front of some girls, "Hey Alex! Get your brown Hawaiian ass over here!" They laugh and he doesn't. He shoves the mental gears into synchromesh for a suitable comeback and later on that day he yells at me, "Hey Daz, get your poi dog ass over here!"

I'm thinking, fricking Alex, make your insults intelligible, don't pull this secret Hawaiian language on me, you know, the "Hawaiian good luck sign" or some griff like that.

So after the girls leave I ask him, "Okay, what's a poi dog?," figuring it's obscene, but it turns out it just means a dog with so many breeds in its past it doesn't look like any known animal. I consider this a compliment, but of course I don't tell Alex because then he would think of something worse to call me.

So I say, "That mean I'm poi dogmeat?" and he says, "Yeah, poi dogs make good stew. The black ones taste best."

"You telling me people eat dogs over there?" I ask all incredulously.

"Bruddah, when your favorite poi dog disappears, you look for a luau in the neighborhood," he says. "Maybe the meat in the stew is a little funny, but it tastes pretty good, and then later you think, eh, maybe that was Fluffy."

I guess there's no problem with a dog pound over there, it's more like a fast-food joint. Got anything young and tender today?

Actually, I have to be careful sounding like King Widget when it comes to talking with girls. I'm only good for the first five minutes. After the intros I get wombatitis and don't know what to say. So I never had a girlfriend in high school, just girls I knew. Meanwhile Alex always had girlfriends, even though he just stands there with his thumb up his butt when he meets them for the first time.

The first thing I'm thinking after Alex drags me away from Leslie is, so this is love. But by the time we find Leon in Kansas City and get him to help us fix the Lancer, I'm thinking, let's face it, Jack, I'd fall in love with any girl who was nice to me, and by the time we hit North Carolina and I realize I have to go back and see her, I'm thinking, she's already forgotten me.

147

It's easy to talk yourself into this kind of cliff-dive, especially after you've been traveling for a while and you realize that everybody turns on their best light and tells you all the good things about themselves first, and it's only after you've hung around with them longer than a few days, like we did with Tracie, that you find out if they're okay or you start seeing the green monster oozing through the cracks.

So for all I knew, Leslie was a bitch on boosters most of the time, and she'd just shown me her nice side because I was a new guy. It's also easy to nightmare up all the spliff guys she's been seeing since I saw her, especially when guys like Leon are telling you, "Forget it, Buckwheat. Some other guy is making her wet between the legs by now."

Leon isn't his real name; it's actually Morris. The first time we see him is when he's in the back of his old brick shop wiping the grease off some wrenches because it's about five and he's closing down. We're trying to find somebody to fix the Lancer cheap, and some guy at a towing yard tells us to look up Morris because he's good with old American cars.

His shop is in a rough part of Kansas City, all chain-link gates with big padlocks and "This property patrolled by Ratface Security Company" signs on the warehouses. We snake through the half-assembled engines and the cars under dusty blue plastic tarps until we spot him back at a bench with an open can of de-greaser and some rags.

He lifts his old, brown driftwood face when he hears us shuffle in, gives us a three-count stare and then says, "What's up, Leon?"

I look at Alex, like, you know this guy or what, and he looks as fritzed as I am. "Sorry, neither one of us is Leon," I say. "You expecting him?"

"Don't bullshit me, boy," he says. "You're a Leon if I ever saw one. And your partner is a Mike."

Alex is giving me his you've-done-it-again-asshole look, and as usual I'm giving him my don't-blame-me face.

"I think you've got the wrong guys," I say. "He's Alex and I'm Daz."

He lays down a shiny open-end wrench and picks up one that's dull with black grease and starts wiping it with a soft red cloth. His hands are oily, but his pressed khakis and workshirt are clean. "Alex and Daz, huh," he says, and then he starts shaking his head. "You boys think those handles up before you got here just to see if you could bullshit me?"

"No, man, those are our names," I tell him.

He turns his deep-sunk eyes and big rough face on us and smiles, and I can see his snaggly teeth and a flash of gold. "You're one hell of a pair of actors," he says. He wipes his forefinger clean with a new rag, and then scratches his stubbly white hair right in the middle of his scalp. "Let's drop the bullshit jokes, Leon. Somebody told you I can tell a man's name just by looking at him, and you're trying to throw me off. Now what do you and Mike want?"

"I swear to God my name is Daz," I practically shout at him.

He slams the wrench down on the greasy old counter and says, "Goddammit, Leon, cut the crap and tell me what the hell you want or I'll throw you and Mike right out of here."

This old guy's on full rock-n-roll, he's launched the mojo all the way to Pluto, and I don't know whether to booga-booga or go blind.

Alex kicks in and says, "Some guy told us you work on Lancers."

The crusty old guy puts down the clean wrench and picks up another dirty one. "Thank you, Mike. Now we're getting somewhere. Your dad has a Lancer he wants to sell?"

"No, it's ours," Alex answers. "We want to fix it."

"What's wrong with it?" the old mechanic asks.

Alex says, "Just stopped running. We think it needs a rebuild."

"Most of them do," he says. He's finished with the wrenches so he's moved on to the screwdrivers and other tools, and says to Alex, "Tell me about the car, Mike."

So Alex tells him about the Lancer and Old Man Ching and how we'd changed the gaskets and hoses and all that before the trip.

"California, huh?" he grunts. "Where is it now?"

"On the street," I point, "Just a couple miles over that way."

The old man concentrates on shining up some sockets for a minute and then he says, "Leon, you got money for this rebuild?"

I clear my throat and say, "Well, Mr. Morris—"

149

"Forget that 'Mister' shit, Leon. It's plain Morris. I don't use my last name."

"Well, uh, Morris, that's one thing we wanted to talk about. We were wondering if we could save money by helping you."

"That mean you're broke?" he asks.

"No, I answer, "it means we've got a lot of time and a little money."

He puts the sockets away in a steel tray and says, "You know what they say, boys. It's $25 to do the work, $40 if you watch and $100 if you help."

That flattens it. If we had to spend $700 on a rebuild the trip was over unless we got a job and saved up some more.

We're silent and I nod to Alex, like "let's go," when Morris says, "Leon, go get me that tool kit over there," and he points to a steel Kennedy box on a big old wood table that's black from years of oily parts. Then he nods at Alex and says, "Mike, bring me three beers out of the reefer," and he jerks his head in the direction of an old rounded top white refrigerator in the corner.

The guy's voice doesn't sound like he's making suggestions, so we vector like he says. Alex hands Morris three ice-cold cans of Budweiser, and he gives us each one, pops his, and takes a quick swig.

"Thanks for the beer," I say, and he ignores me.

"Haven't worked on a Lancer in a while," he says. "Pretty goddamned good cars."

We just sip our beer and nod.

"Course, they're better than a Morris," he says, and he loses us again.

"Some guy was looking through the yellow pages and he sees my name, Morris Mechanics," he says, "and he thinks I work on Morris cars." He glances over at us and says, "Well sit down for Christ's sake," and we pull over a couple of folding metal chairs and sit down in front of him, wishing we'd never walked through his roll-up door.

"He got it over in England when he was in the service, and for some reason he brought the damned thing back with him," he says. "He was having a hell of a time keeping it running so he calls me. I'm about to tell him I don't work on foreign crap when I figure,

150

what the hell, my name's Morris, I ought to do Morris cars, so I tell him to bring it in."

I'm trying to think of something to say when he says, "What a pile. No wonder the Brits and the Italians can't sell cars here anymore."

I figure we might as well be straight with this old mac nut and blow him off right now so I say, "Look, Morris, we—"

"Goddammit, Leon, don't get all excited," he says, and he turns to Alex. "Mike, is he always this jumpy?" Alex just shrugs.

"If you got enough scratch for the parts and you do exactly what I tell you to, maybe we can work a deal," he tells us. "I got a dirty old Mopar that needs some serious cleanup. We'll swap labor, four-to-one, and that's a hell of deal."

"Think you can fix our car?" I ask him.

He closes his eyes and nods his head slowly. "Oh yes," he says softly. Then he glances at a big clock on the wall, the kind you see in classrooms, and he says, "Son of a bitch, it's almost six. I got a date to get to." He gets up and extends his hand. "Mike, Leon, you're alright. We'll get your Lancer over here tomorrow and see what we can do. And wear work clothes, not that downtown shit you got on now."

We walk out in the bright sun, and we're both silent for a few blocks. I turn to Alex and say, "This guy Leon is a weird bird, man." Alex laughs, and from then on we call him Leon behind his back.

We talk about going somewhere else to get the Cruiser fixed, but the guy at the towing yard said Morris was a tropo mechanic. Since having some other guy to do it would cost us money we don't have, and the crazy old man was willing to do a trade, we decide to give Morris a chance.

So that first week I make the mistake of telling Morris about Leslie and about how I'm thinking of going back to see her again. From then on he was giving me griff about her, saying I should forget her because some other guy was already humping her, how it was dangerous to fall in love, he knew firsthand, griff griff griff. I'd told Alex how easy it was to talk with her, how I thought she liked me, but he did a Stonewall Jackson, never lipping anything to Morris or making fun of me.

I'd noticed Leslie right away because of her sweet light brown hair and her freckles. She was one of Alex's cousin's best friends, just like Meg, the girl who skagged Alex off. I never got any special feeling off Leslie until the night that a bunch of the cousin's friends came over. It was sort of a party, but without alcohol because the parents were upstairs.

Leslie comes over and asks me about our trip, where we'd been and what's different from what I'd expected. It's an interesting question, and I like her big brown eyes and the way she looks at me without being distracted by everyone else. Plus, she laughs at my lame jokes and makes some of her own in a relaxed way, like she isn't too worried if I laugh or not.

I start realizing how cute she was, her straight eyebrows, her dimples, and her cho-cho lips, which look nectar even with no lipstick.

We wander outside, and I ask her about living on a farm, what they do for fun, what jobs she's had, the regular stuff, and I'm amazed because nothing feels forced. She's almost as tall as me, and it's easy to look into her eyes while we talk.

I guess what really surprised me is how she asks me all these big questions, you know, about the trip and college, and how she's actually interested in my answers. I could tell she's not interested in the usual superficial crap everyone says, and so I tell her the truth. She seems to understand about the trip and the car, and it's the first time I feel like someone understands it the way I feel it.

She'd just graduated, and we talk about college like I've never talked about it before, how I feel so scattered and unsure of what I would major in and what good and bad it might do for me. She lays out her own doubts, and we talk about them for so long I know she's feeling pretty good about me. She seems so thoughtful, and I can't help feeling King Tut that she admires the trip and my reasons for doing it.

I always hide behind a "this trip is an adventure" front because I figure people can understand that and wouldn't jink me. But Leslie tells me she understands exactly what I mean, and I believe her. That's why she can't decide between going to college right away or working for a year or so. She tells me college seems so canned, which is just the way I feel about it, too.

I want to kiss her, but I figure that would look overboard since we're only talking for the first time. I never get a second chance because that night Meg tore Alex down and we hauled derriere the next morning.

I sent both Tracie and Leslie a couple of postcards from New York City, but I didn't expect either one to write back. Then Tita hands me this envelope one afternoon about a week later, I see it's from Leslie, and I am Helium Man, light light light. There's nothing fancy in her letter, but I'm ozoned that she even bothered to write me.

None of this makes it easier to see her again. In fact, it all makes it harder. She writes me and I'm all starred out thinking this might be the real gig, Morris janks me and I'm bow-wow with jealousy, and then we're on the I-State heading north to Iowa and I'm cattiwompus with worry that I'm misreading the fine print that really says, "Hey, slick, you're nothing to me."

By late afternoon we reach the town near where Alex's cousin and Leslie live, and I've dialed in the zombie channel. I'm shaking and sweating like I've been blow-gunned full of a torquomatic poison from the Amazon that turns your insides to orange Jello. I say, "I don't know, man, maybe we should keep going," and Alex just about picks me up and orbits me. "You drag me all this way and you start this?" he yells, and because I'm more afraid of him now than getting blown off by Leslie, I punch in the numbers and wait for the blade to hit my neck.

Her mom answers and I stagger into it. I'd spun off a postcard warning her I was coming back through Iowa, so there's no big surprise. I ask if I can drop by and see Leslie, and her Mom tells me she should be home from work in about a half-hour and, as far as she knows, it'll be okay to come then.

Alex has decided he can stand staying at his uncle's house so long as his cousin doesn't invite Meg over while we're there. This seems a reasonable thing to ask when the girl has napalmed you, so I figure we can stay there a few days and I'm happy.

We find Leslie's place from the name on the mailbox, and it's a white two-story house with a small fenced-in yard of grass in front. I'm hyperventilating, and Alex punches me in the shoulder real hard.

"Alex, is there any snot running down my face or anything?" I ask.

"Pull yourself together, bruddah," he says. "Relax and maintain. You look fine." Then he yawns and tells me, "I'm cribbing in the back seat." He opens the driver door, rolls down the back windows, and lays down with his feet out the window and a *MAD* magazine over his face.

I desperately try to remember how easy it was to be with her, and instead I remember this conversation we had with Morris back in Kansas City: I was getting tired of hearing Morris frap romance all the time, so I ask him, "Hey, Morris. Why are you so down on love? Aren't you getting any?"

He looks at Alex and jerks his head at me. "Mike, has Leon always been such a wise-ass?" he says to Alex, and Alex nods seriously and says, "Always."

"No, really," I say. "What happened? You got crunched, D-9 time?"

Morris doesn't look up; he continues fiddling with the carburetor, and he says, "I'm a patient man, but sometimes I can't figure out why a goddamned car won't run right. Try everything I know, and it's still running ragged."

"Tell us about the woman who dropped you," I say, just to drib him.

Morris drops the screwdriver and looks up at me like Frosty the Snowman just grabbed his nuts. "Godammit, Leon, you're always rushing me. Mike, I don't know how you put up with Leon, I really don't." He picks the screwdriver back up and points it at me. "I have a nice girlfriend now, just for your information, Mr. Wise-Ass," he tells me. "So it ain't because I'm not getting any. You should be so lucky, boy."

Then he starts adjusting one of the screws on the carb. "So it's still running ragged in spite of all your tricks. Now if you don't know the car, then you just give up and let someone else take a shot at it," he says. "It's no big deal to admit defeat and say, 'I can't make it work.' But if you know the car and like it and are used to driving it, then letting go of it just breaks your goddamned heart."

He finishes the adjustment and straightens up. "You boys are too young to be attached to things," he says. "Someday that'll

154

end, and then you'll know what I'm talking about. Women and cars, I've had lots of them, but it don't get any easier to lose them. Gets worse."

He turns to Alex and says, "You probably know what I mean, Mike. Explain it to your pal Leon sometime when he's got his trap shut for a minute or two."

So I knock and Leslie opens the door. She's wearing blue jeans and a white blouse and her hair is as beautiful as I remember, and even though she's wearing a bra, her tits look like they were made by the goddesses on Planet X.

But I know right then something's different. Her smile is friendly, but she seems nervous, too, and that makes me feel even more edgy. She invites me into the living room, and it's so clean and neat I can't even sit down comfortably. She gets me a Coke and asks me where we've been, but it sounds polite and I'm taking on water, sinking a little deeper after every question and answer. I ask about her job, and what's new with her college plans, but her answers don't roll off, they're jitterbuggy, and she can't look me in the eye too long. When she does, then I glance away because her eyes make me feel rhomboid.

I keep thinking, hey, it's daytime, it's her folks' living room, she hasn't seen me in weeks, she's probably tired from work, lots of explanations which could be true. I decide to let her take the ball in the second half. If she wants to see me again in better circumstances, she'll say something. So I tell her that we'll be staying at Alex's uncle's house for a few days, and maybe we could get together some time, catch lunch, something easy.

I can't tell what she's thinking or feeling, and I don't know what to do. Alex always says to just be direct, then everybody's relieved. So I say, "Hey, I know this is kind of sudden, and maybe you weren't sure you wanted to see me again anyway."

She shakes her head and says, "No, it was really nice of you to come over." But that's it.

"Do you have a boyfriend now?" I ask.

She smiles a little and says, "Me have a boyfriend? I don't think anybody's that weird."

So I tell her, "I'm pretty weird."

155

She smiles at me, and for the first time I feel she's relaxed a little. And then she says, "So where are you going next?"

I look out at the Lancer to recover, and I see Alex's brown feet sticking out the window. I try to make my voice cheerful-sounding, and then I just start talking about every place I can think of—San Francisco, Idaho, Seattle, anywhere.

After a while I make up some drib about Alex waiting and she shows me to the door. She looks so nectar I want to grab her and kiss her, but that's a joke.

"I hope you'll send me postcards," she says, and I promise her I will.

I climb into the front seat of the Cruiser, crank the engine over and start driving toward the highway and Alex's uncle's place. Alex is still down under or acting like he is, so I leave him alone and look out the window.

When we first came through Iowa the corn fields were all topped with shiny tassels, but now there are big harvesting machines grinding through the fields, leaving a bare stubble behind that reminds me of Morris's short white hair.

# CHAPTER EIGHTEEN

Leon—I mean Morris—and Old Man Ching would hate each other on sight, just like two big old tomcats facing off in an empty lot. Mr. Ching wouldn't stand for being called Cornelius or whatever weird-ass name Morris would peg him with, and Morris wouldn't swallow Mr. Ching's way of never giving in.

Morris talked so much spike that Old Man Ching would have run him through with his rusty bayonet within the first ten minutes. Maybe the first five. Maybe as soon as Morris opened his mouth. Nobody'd convict him even if he was still holding the bayonet when the cops blew in. Justifiable homicide, aces up, slick.

Mr. Ching might not have agreed with Morris's "Stupid Tax," either. Morris was always saying things like, "That'd cost a hell of a lot more by the time you throw in the Stupid Tax." He first mentioned it when we were sitting outside the shop having a beer after work and a Mercedes drives by, one of the big ones.

"Ought to be a Stupid Tax on a $60,000 car," he says, scratching the white stubble on the top of his head. "Any fool dumb enough to pay that much ought to pay a $25,000 Stupid Tax." He sips his ice cold brewkowski and says, "Cars are cars, boys, and I know. They all got pretty much the same parts, some a little better than others. But there's no way any car's worth $60,000."

He kind of smiles and I brace myself. "Unless, of course, it gives you a blow job every time you tap the horn." Then he gives a laugh that sounds like a diesel engine cranking over and says, "There'd be horns blowing all over town, middle of the night, everywhere."

Morris also wanted to slap a Stupid Tax on those hokey decorative plates advertised in *Parade* magazine on Sunday.

"Look at this," he says, crackling the page in front of us on Monday morning. "Ninety bucks for six goddamn plates of cute dogs. Fifteen bucks a month for six months. It says here, 'Shown actual size.'" He holds the page up to my face. "Leon, look at this plate. This isn't even a good-sized salad plate!"

Then he rattles it at Alex. "Mike, I could buy you six of the cutest dogs ever for sixty bucks and leave you thirty bucks for a shit, shower, and shave." He crumples the sheet up and throws it in his fifty-five gallon trash drum. "It should cost a good hundred and ninety," he says. "A hundred for Stupid Tax, minimum."

I don't know if Mr. Ching was religious or not, but I do know he believes in leaving everybody and their gigs alone unless they're romping on his mojo. So he wouldn't have agreed with Morris's religious opinions either, starting with the picture of a television preacher on his dartboard.

"Every time I get depressed, I just toss a few darts at old Hiney-face and I feel better," he said. "Crooked son-of-a-bitch is going to Hell so fast his pecker'll fall off going through the turnstile."

Morris buys an air filter, but he looks at the box and sees it's made in Mexico so he returns it. "Know why everything turns to shit below the Rio Grande?" he asks us when he gets back. "Because that's where the Catholic Church runs things. Those bastards drain the blood out of every country they take over."

"I'm Catholic," I say, and even though I'm not a good one I still feel a little torqued.

"Nothing personal, Leon," he tells me, "but every Catholic country is poor as a shithouse mouse, and every Protestant country is rich. Christ, don't take my word, look for yourself."

I'm trying to think of a rich Catholic country, and he says, "All these travel posters say Mexico's so romantic, but Leon, what's so goddamn romantic about cardboard shacks and skinny kids? I'll pork my old lady somewhere else, thank you."

"Spain," I blurt out. "That's rich."

He snorts and says, "Spain? It's the poorest damn country over there, Leon. I've seen it for myself. Once the Inca gold ran out they went down the shitter and haven't come up for air since."

"What about Italy?" I ask.

"Italy?" he says, as if it was as stupid as saying Mars. "Go see for yourself, Leon. Up north by the Protestants, they're pretty well off. But down south where it's pure Catholic, hell, the Mafia's the only thing keeping the people from starving."

He starts the wing nut on the new air cleaner and says, "I wouldn't give you a plugged nickel for Mexico. Hell, I'd give you a thousand bucks to take it off my hands. And India, too. Mike, hand me that pair of pliers, would you?"

Alex brings over the big pliers, and Morris asks, "Mike, ever been to India?"

Alex says, "No."

He snorts again and says, "I have. Another goddamn romantic paradise that can't wipe its own ass. They got eight million gods, but the seven million nine-hundred-and-ninety-nine thousand nine-hundred-and-ninety-nine extra ones haven't done them much good. They can't make anything worth a damn, either."

He comes over to the engine stand to see how I'm doing on pulling the heads off the Mopar, and says, "Leon, nothing personal, but the Catholic Church ought to take in every brat that's born because momma couldn't get birth control. Once they use up all their money feeding the kids, we could run 'em off for good."

To get him off the Catholic Church I say, "Morris, have you been any place that isn't a shithole?"

"Not many," he says, "because most of the world is a shithole."

"You just hate every place that isn't Kansas City," I say.

"No," he says. "I just hate shit in the street, and so will you when you smell it."

He hands me a bigger socket handle and says, "For Christ's sake, Leon, use leverage. When you get older you'll want to work smarter."

Morris has one hell of a collection of tools, all U.S. made, and he makes us clean all the ones we use at the end of the day. So I try to use as few as possible.

"Leon, don't say I hate every place," he says, "because I was stationed in Japan for a year and I liked it. They don't shit in the street."

"Glad to hear it," I say.

"Arrogant bastards behind all that polite shit," he says, "but I'll take a polite bastard over a loudmouth any day."

He gets a coffee can of solvent and brings it over to me. "Drop the bolts in here," he tells me. "Course, we kicked their ass in the

159

War and then gave their women the vote." He laughed loudly, and says, "The gals control the money, you know. Papa-san just gets a sake allowance. Same thing in Hawaii, right, Mike?"

Alex says, "Yeah, most of the time."

"Mike, come over here and pull off this trannie," Morris says. "You guys get me jawjacking just so you can sit on your hands."

Old Man Ching wouldn't like Morris's customer service, either. Mrs. Ching has this great smile and her gray bun bobs back and forth when she greets you. If Morris is in a good mood he says, "What can I do you for?" when a customer calls. If he's in a bad mood, he just grunts. At first I couldn't understand why anybody'd give him business, seeing as how he treats them like dogmeat. Then I gripped he's like those waiters who're famous for being maximum rude.

You sure don't want to cross Mr. Ching, but he never yells at you like Morris does. Most of the time Morris would rag on me, but every once in a while he'd break off a piece of Alex. I think he's trying to be fair, in his own way. One time he yells at Alex, "Godammit, Mike, I said 'now,' not next year," and Alex turns this evil eye on him because Alex is a strat worker, he always jumps on whatever you want done, and he doesn't take kindly to getting romped on for no good reason. Morris isn't stupid, but he isn't afraid, either. He looks at Alex's voodoo eyes and says, "I know, you were just remembering your girlfriend's wet panties." And then he tosses him this giant crescent wrench.

Another time Morris says, "Jesus Christ, Mike, I said tighten 'em down a half-turn at a time. You think I was talking just to hear myself jawjack?" and Alex turns to him with the Five Fingers of Death look, and for the first time, I'm afraid for Morris. You don't want to push Alex over the cliff because you're the one who's going to take the smash.

Morris spocks Alex out and then turns back to the engine with a disgusted look and starts tightening the bolts himself. "You can beat me into jelly, Mike, but it won't make you right." Alex just stands there for a minute and then he gets the gaskets that Morris will need next.

I remembered what Morris said when the gig went gravitational in South Dakota.

Despite the fact I know Alex will inevitably get us in griff up to our chins, I am always surprised when we step into it. It always looks so peaceful, like what could go wrong here? That's why I say he creates it. He says, "Brah, it's you. You're always getting us busted and picking up weird girls," but I swear to God it's him. It has to be. This never happens when I'm alone.

It's a warm afternoon, we're cruising west through the farms and we see this Af-Am hitchhiker. We're talking sore thumb city out here. He's in uniform, and after getting to know Rich, I feel some sympathy for all the grunts in uniform so I pull over.

Turns out this guy Rick is trying to get home to Seattle. He's gotten a couple of rides from truckers, usually vets who spotted his skins, and he's ready to get home.

"Nice car," he tells us. He's our age, and I feel the old feeling of being an irresponsible slack-master compared to guys like Rick. You know, learning a trade, defending the country, all that book, and here I am cruising.

We ask him about the Army, where he hopes to be sent next, where he's been. It's a weird life. To think that Alex and I could have joined the Army. It's a strange thought. I'd probably end up in the brig in no time. Alex would just be canned as full–rev jank for the country. He'd probably get us in a war somehow with his triple-shot energy for trouble with major corporate sponsorship.

He nearly started a war right in South Dakota. We were feeling hungry, so we stop in a little town and find the usual homemade cafe. These cafes are the same all over, and they're definitely strat. They're always small, family-run, put out basic food, and have paintings some relative did on the walls and a rack of postcards saying, "Quitcherbellyachin'."

So we go in, and as we sit down, I notice some big corn-fed farm boys are at the counter and I feel a cloud forming, like we just invaded their turf. They're wearing overalls and stained blue jeans, and one of them has a pack of nicspliffs rolled up in the sleeve of his ratty T-shirt, just like some black-and-white movie from the '50s.

They look around at us and hold us in their eyes, and I feel a chill that rips up through my spine and lights a fire when it hits my skull. I have this sinking feeling like, "Here we go again."

161

Sure enough, they spock our car and start making fun of it, guffaws and a few words here and there, just to let us know that they're torqueing us. We order some burgers, and Rick seems oblivious. He and Alex are talking about how hot it is in Texas, and then, all of a sudden, he says to us, "I'm getting a bad feeling about those guys over there. I been on the streets and I know when some bad shit's coming down. Let's get out of here."

So does Alex listen to this common sense? Of course not. His pride is flaring out, and he says, "They're just talking." He'll never look like he's backing down. Rick seems sort of resigned and just looks out the window. I keep hoping the farm boys'll finish eating and leave, but their plates are already gone and they're obviously enjoying riffing off of us. These guys are all D-9s, six-four and beefy. They grow football players out there, believe me. Offensive linemen, linebackers, the big ones.

Finally one of them with scruffy blond hair turns to his friend and says real loud, "Hey look, they're from California. Isn't that where they grow all the fruits?" And they all split out, har har.

This lights Alex's fuse, and he gets this smoky look behind his eyes. He gets real stiff and just disappears into himself. The food comes and he acts like it's not there. Then one with slicked-down black hair says, "Well, there's three of them traveling together, maybe they're from San Francisco," and Blondie tells his buddies, "Yeah, I hear they're letting queers into the Army now."

That's the camel and straw gig for Alex, and he stands up really quick and heads straight for these five guys. Rick says, "Looks like I gotta get ready to kick some farmboy ass," and he gives me this weary look like, "Oh man, why did you clowns have to get me in this ass-breaking fight in the middle of nowhere?"

I just shake my head, like "I don't know, man." So we have to stand up to back Alex and it's just what these assbites are drooling for, a fight five to three on their own turf. Why can't Alex ever pick a gig with odds in our favor? But of course, he'd never fight anyone weaker than himself, so the odds will always be against us.

So these Attilas slide off their stools like, "Oh boy, something to break up the monotony, we get to kick some butt," and the owner comes over.

"There won't be any trouble here, boys," he says. "You just go sit down again, all of you. Your butts will be in the slammer if there's any trouble."

His wife looks out of the kitchen, but she doesn't seem worried. I could just see Alex tearing the place up, tossing these corn dogs into tables, smashing everything like in a Western. This cafe didn't have a big mirror behind the counter, but I could see some major griff being torn down if Alex went bananas in a Hercules-versus-the-Romans gig.

Rick is talking almost to himself: "I am personally going to kick your friend's ass if he gets our asses kicked. Shit, I just spent the last three months kicking ass and now I gotta kick some more. These sumbitches remind me of the big farm boys in my unit. Just protect my back, man. I'm gonna wait until they're on your friend like stink on shit and then peel them off one at a time. Just cover my backside."

We're standing there with our arms folded, and I'm starting to shiver with fright, the first time I ever felt that before. Oh man, I'm thinking, I hope this won't hurt too bad, I guess I'll live, I hope they have a good hospital around here. I cross myself as secretly as I can, like I'm scratching myself, but hey, I need all the help I can get.

Alex is just standing there, no way is he going to back down, and the homeboys are just riffing on empty, not quite sure what to do because they obviously know the owner and don't want to rip his place up, but they'll be damned if they pass up a fight with some salads from California.

"So wanna go outside?" one says, and Alex says, "Yeah, but one at a time—unless you're too lame to fight fair."

So this one big old boy is just anxious as hell to get into it and he says, "Sure, let's go." He looks mean and strong, and I'm worried. His sunburned arms are huge and covered with scratches from some kind of work, and he has these confident little eyes that would fit just fine inside a football helmet.

I'm thinking, maybe Alex isn't invincible; after all, it is their grass. The owner is less than pleased, so he says, "There'll be no fighting here or outside, boys, so just sit down and cool off," and he calls some of the buttwipes by name.

163

Several of them turn around and sit back down, but this one gorgon is just straining at his leash to fight with Alex, like it's the biggest treat of his life, and it's hurting him bad to pass it up. It's strange to see somebody want to either get hurt or hurt somebody so bad. I turn to sit down, but Rick says in a stage whisper, "Stay cool, don't move."

So there's this stand-off. Nobody can move without losing their pride, and then the sheriff walks in, I guess because the wife called him. Thank God, I say to myself. Now we can end this weird gig and get back to the fries, even though by then I had no appetite for anything except to get out of that burg.

I swear to God Alex could be stripped naked in a bare room, and an hour later there'd be some weird griff happening in that room—a fight, a girl, a few holes punched in the walls, some piss pooled in the corner, an empty beer can, the ceiling torn down, and an electrical fire burning out of control. And of course, none of it would be his fault.

The sheriff strolls over like he's in charge. He finally gets something to do in this dirtball town. He's shorter than the big drib who's standing up looking all anxious that maybe there won't be a fight, so he tells him to sit down. The turdhead sits down, and the sheriff is happy because now he can look down on the guy.

"There ain't gonna be a fight today, Matt," he said. "I'd say it's about time to get back to work, wouldn't you?"

"We were gonna take it outside, Sheriff," Dickface said, but the sheriff is damned if he's going to let a giant-ass brawl rip up his town, so he just shakes his head slowly.

"You can fight with the boys from across the county line like usual, Matt, but not here and not with these guys." Maybe it wouldn't look so good; three guys with some dark color in their skin, and three minutes after they blow into town they get their asses kicked by the locals.

Matt is sulking, but he turns back to the counter after giving us this look like a tiger gives an antelope, just "Damn, it would have been great," and I almost wish I could see Alex dismantle this guy. I know Alex takes special pleasure in taking down guys who've never lost before just because they're big and strong.

It's so weird to see the look on their faces when their punches just blow by Alex and he's laid one on a pressure point and their knees are buckling and their expressions say, "What's happening? I punched him, this fight should be all over and instead I'm falling down."

So after the big jerk-off Matt sits down the sheriff comes over to us. "I'd like to recommend that you don't say anything to the boys over there. Just finish your meal and move along. I don't put up with any trouble. Understand?" We all nod like, yup, Mr. Guppy, we hear you loud and clear.

Then the sheriff stands between our table and the counter, and says real loud, "Boys, look here." The clowns at the counter turn to spock him and we're at attention, too. He scans our faces to make sure he's got us, and then he reaches into his mouth and pulls out his lower teeth. He holds his bridge up and swings it around so we can see. One of the numbnuts chuckles, but an iceberg stare from the sheriff nails him shut.

"This is from a stupid fight I got into when I was about your age," he says. "I'm still living with that mistake. Don't you make the same one." He puts the front teeth back in his lower jaw, and nods to Matt and his pack. "Matt, get a move on. Now."

My body's so torqued up I'm still vibrating. "Let's blow this burg," I say. Alex gives me this look which I know means, "And what? Look like we're scared?"

So instead, we dawdle over the cold plates, fingering the stone dead fries around in the catsup. It's some sort of victory to walk out last, and since the sheriff insisted, the jerk-offs leave first, slowly and only after giving us what Alex calls the Big Stink-Eye. After a while we leave and climb in the Cruiser, start it up, and vector toward the nearest I-State.

On the way out of town we're silent. The tension is still dripping off the windows like early morning condensation.

I finally relax a little and try to start a conversation with Rick. "Jimi Hendrix was from Seattle, wasn't he?" I ask, and he nods and then we start chatting up what's worth seeing around Seattle. Alex is driving with one hand, still pumped but slowly deflating.

Just then a dark-blue Camaro on full tach roars past us, cuts in front of us, and hits its brakes. Alex slams on the Cruiser's pads, and these guys pull alongside again, and then speed up and repeat the braking action in front of us.

Alex jerks the wheel over, skids to a stop, and jumps out. He's out of control, and that feeling of doom ramps up and then explodes in my head. The other car spins a U and pulls up on the other side of the two-laner. The big lineman-sized buttwipe Matt is grinning, and he leaps out of the driver's seat.

I'm thinking of what the sheriff said, and then I remember Alex's master and his little demo about the gun.

Rick starts climbing out of the back seat. I grab his shoulder. "Stay here, man," I say.

"And let your pal catch it alone?" he asks.

"They might bring out tire irons," I say. "Maybe it'll cool off."

Rick shakes his head but stays put. "You got one?" he says.

"In the back," I say. Then I yell out, "Hey Alex. Remember your Master." He doesn't even glance back but I know he heard me.

He goes up to the big gorgon Matt, and I'm tensing for the first blow, which is usually the last one for Alex's opponent. The guys have all piled out, and there's five big strong numbnuts standing between their Camaro and Alex. I'm gripping the handle, ready to blow out the door and be cannon fodder.

Alex puts his hands on his hips, so icy and calm, and starts talking to them in a voice so low we can't understand what he's saying. He gestures back to us, kind of lazily, and the poo-eating grins on their faces disappear and they start folding their arms. Then he points to an old shack back in a field and gestures to the big gorgon, like "Come on." The big jerk-off scratches his patch of sweaty dark hair and hesitates, and then follows Alex down a dirt road to the shack, which is maybe a hundred yards away. We all watch them go, and the other four guys are glued in front of the dark-blue Camaro. They don't move and they don't say boo, and neither do we.

Alex and Turdhead go behind the shack, and I expect to see Alex come out alone in a few seconds. But nothing happens, and I start to get scared. "Maybe we should check it out," I say, and Rick says, "He's got it down to one-on-one, man. Let it ride."

Finally Alex comes out, and the dipstick Matt comes out right behind him, walking upright, not staggering or bleeding. No fight? I think to myself, what happened?

They walk to the Camaro and then shake hands kind of formally, and then Alex spins and walks back to us.

"What happened?" I ask.

"Nothing," he says, and he gets in, starts the car and pulls onto the highway.

Rick says, "Whatever you did, you cooled them right off."

Alex keeps his eyes on the road and doesn't say anything.

I'm bug-eyed because when Alex gets shaken loose like this, nothing can stop it. Rick says, "How'd you isolate Big Boy?"

Alex stares at the white line ahead of us and says, "I just told the big one to follow me if he wanted to fight. Once nobody could see us, we talked story, and then I asked him if he still wanted to fight. He said no, so we came back."

I remember Alex's lightning strikes and the way he can whip about fifty fists in your face in two seconds, and I realize he gave the guy air space to come down soft.

"You played that smart," says Rick, and Alex doesn't say anything, but I know he's pleased.

# CHAPTER NINETEEN

I wrote Old Man Ching a few postcards during the trip, usually when we hit one of the places mentioned in his journal. I liked the feeling of bringing the Cruiser full circle, and maybe sparking his memory, like "Hey, I went there, too." I finally wrote him a real letter after we found work and started living in Ron's trailer.

No matter how careful we tried to be, money gushed like a broken hydrant. The Lancer got decent gas mileage, especially when we took the old tropo roads where you don't have to go 75, like on the I-States. But by the time we reached Sacramento our wallets were dead zones—no Jacksons, no Hamiltons, just a few old Georges, and my $300 Mastercard was up to $299 and change.

We saved major dollars in Kansas City, not only because Morris fixed the Cruiser for nothing, but because he let us live in his shop. But after that the gitas disappeared like rain in the desert, even though we camped and ate beans and applesauce as often as we could stand to.

Morris heard us talking about finding a campground close to the city because Motel Six was napalming our gitas major domo, and he says, "Mike, can you keep Leon from shitting on the floor?"

Alex has to smile, and then he says, "Yeah."

"If you promise to keep Leon from shitting on my shop floor, you guys can stay here," he says gruffly. "It's hotter than a bastard, but once you raise the roll-up door, it cools right down. If you take a Bud, replace it with a Bud. Don't buy me cheap-shit beer or any of that fancy foreign horse-piss, either."

"Thanks, Leon, I mean Morris," I say.

He shakes his head and says, "Mike, your pal here's so bad off he can't even remember which name is his. He needs to get some soon."

Not only did Morris fix the Cruiser, he ended up paying us for helping him clear out his backlog. He had more work than he could possibly do, but for some reason he wouldn't turn people away. It was obvious why he didn't hire someone to help him. Nobody'd stay, even somebody who didn't understand English.

We cleaned up a Mopar 383 engine, a Chevy 327, and a Ford 289, and after a week we were starting to wonder if Morris was giving us the oobla-dee about fixing our car.

So I ask him, "Morris, when are we going to get to our car?"

"Leon," he tells me, "you want me to help you, right? Well first you gotta help me. Look at all these damned engines. People are bugging me. You and Mike help me out for another week, and I'll take care of the Lancer. Now quit crying and yank the distributor off that 289."

So after another week of cleaning engine parts and pulling off greasy gaskets and bolts and skinning my knuckles, the blood oozing out of the old black grease covering my hands, Morris pulls the tarp off the Cruiser.

I get in the driver's seat and turn it over. It tries to get off the ground, but it trips after a few cylinders fire. Alex is telling me not to flood it, and I'm getting torqued by his blah-blah, but I finally get it to stay alive, staggering and sputtering on a couple of cylinders.

Morris listens to the ragged pops and chugs real intently, like one of those Chinese doctors who can tell what's wrong with you by feeling your pulse. After listening for a few seconds he signals me, with a hand drawn across his throat, to kill it. I turn off the ignition, and sit there waiting for him to say something.

"What do you boys think is wrong?" he asks us.

"It's a piece of crap, that's what," says Alex, and I want to slap him.

Morris shakes his head slowly. "It ain't that bad, Mike."

"Head gasket's blown," I say.

Morris raises his eyebrows. "Mike?"

Alex is thinking real hard, and then he says, "The rings are shot. Look at all the smoke."

Morris always carries a clean rag in the back pocket of his pressed khaki work trousers, and he takes this out and starts cleaning the top parts of the Cruiser's engine. "So Leon thinks it needs a top-end rebuild and Mike thinks it needs a ring job, is that right?"

We nod, "Yeah."

169

"It's lucky you boys worked the full two weeks," he says, shaking his head. "If you're right, it's gonna cost you." Alex and I look at each other like, "Oh, great."

Morris lets this disaster sink in, and then he goes into his dusty little corner office and pulls a Dodge manual off the shelf. He squints at a few pages, and then slams the thick book shut and comes back to the car. We're following him like we're his medical students: gee Dr. Wizzy, what are you doing now?

"Mike, get me a light," he says, "and Leon, hand me the screwdriver tray." Alex drags over one of the shop lights and sets it up. Morris takes off the air filter, and then he takes a screwdriver and loosens the distributor cap. He pulls the cap off and cleans the points, all the same things we did right after it started running bad.

"We already did that," I say.

He looks at me and shakes his head. "Doesn't hurt to do it again." He pulls out the distributor, checks it over, puts it back in, and rotates it carefully to some spot only he can see.

"Start it again," he tells me, and I'm thinking why bother, but I do it anyway.

I click the ignition on, and not only does it start right up, it's purring like a fat kitten. I'm drop-jaw city, and Alex is blown flat too. Morris gets a timing light and makes a final adjustment, and then gives me the "kill it" signal.

Alex and I are silent because we've just seen a miracle performed. We'd tried cleaning the points, and the distributor was so tight it couldn't possibly have slipped out of adjustment. That's why we were so sure it was something like a blown head gasket.

Morris says, "Might as well change the air filter and the plugs, and check the brakes while we're at it," so we follow him through a minor tuneup and a brake adjustment.

After he slams the hood shut I ask, "How'd you know it was the distributor?"

"I didn't," he says. "But always try the easy stuff first. No advantage in hitting the panic button right off."

I look at Alex and I know he's feeling as lame as I am. We'd been so sure it was major domo. Plus I was thinking that somebody else could have ripped us for seven hundred gitas, but Morris fixed it for nothing.

170

"Hey, Morris, thanks," I say.

He looks at me like I just stepped in dog poo. "Don't thank me for doing my job," he says. "Wish it had been a rebuild. Now I owe you bastards money."

He stands there thinking for a minute, and then asks us, "What would it take for you guys to give me another week? We could finish these last three engines."

"You wouldn't be getting used to us being here, would you?" I say, and I give Alex the sign that I'm going to spin Morris a major mojo.

"Godammit, Leon, you want me to beg, don't you?" he says to me, all exasperated.

"I didn't say that," I tell him. "I just asked if you liked having help."

"Son of a bitch, Mike," he says to Alex, "does he always make you beg like this?"

Alex just shrugs.

"Morris, you got any kids?" I ask.

He wipes his hands on the clean rag and puts it back in his pocket. "No, and it's a lucky thing," he mutters.

"No, I think you'd make a great father," I say.

"Leon, don't talk nonsense," he says, and he fidgets with the screwdrivers. I feel bad because I hit him below the belt without knowing it.

I look at Alex and give him the "Should we stay?" look, and he gives me the "Why not?" shrug, so I say, "Are you going to pay us cash?"

"Leon, do I look like a goddamned downtown accountant to you?" Morris says, and he goes to his office and comes back with time cards he'd been keeping for us and a calculator. I look at the cards and see that he's been keeping the time down to the quarter-hour.

He punches in the numbers on the calculator and then pulls a fat roll of twenties out of his blue jeans. He counts the bills and hands us each a stack. "I rounded it up, not down," he says. "Here, check it yourselves," and he pushes the calculator and time cards across to us. I count the bills and it's more than I expected, especially since Morris has been buying all our lunches and beer.

171

"I'll give you an extra buck an hour for the next week," he says. "But don't try to take advantage, Leon. The extra buck's off if we don't finish these engines."

The cash gitas made us feel mango-mango. We treated Morris to a steak dinner and bought some music. That extra money lasted all the way to Sacramento.

*   *   *

I have to take credit for getting us the jobs outside Sacto. By the time we tanked up in Reno, we had five bucks left, and neither one of us felt like asking for a loan from our parents. We wanted to make enough for gas and food and a few nights in San Francisco before we headed home, not get a real job and find a place to live and all that griff. So I think construction, since I know they hire people just to clean up and we're passing acres of new houses being built.

The first place we stop the guy tells me they don't need any workers, but he is nice enough to tell me to check with small contractors, guys building one or two houses at a time. So we try to find some of these, but we don't see any. Everything is fifty or a hundred houses.

We finally spot a smaller gig, maybe ten houses, out in the middle of nowhere. I find the foreman, a white guy with a gigantia belly flop, and he laughs and says, "One of my Mexicans gets more done than two kids like you, son. Why don't you stick to flipping burgers?" What a diphthong!

That really depresses me, plus it's getting late and we're on the edge of nothing, just barren fields and cars blasting by on I-State 80. Alex thinks we should head back into Sacramento and look for a job washing cars in a dealer's lot. This sounds lame to me and I say so. Then we don't say anything for a while. We split our last can of applesauce and what's left of our Ritz crackers for dinner, and I'm thinking, "This is griffin spike."

We sleep in the Cruiser, and as usual I wake up with leg cramps every couple of hours, and then lie awake, listening to the eighteen-wheelers rumble by.

# CHAPTER TWENTY

The sun rises hot and early around Sacto in summer, so the construction workers show up at 6 AM to start work. We're parked right outside the chain-link gate, so I wake up, and watch them open the gate and drive through with their pickups and vans.

I figure there's no harm in taking a look at the houses since I'm already wide awake and crampy from sleeping in the back seat, and as I walk past an old Volkswagen van a skinny Hispanic guy with a ponytail is pulling his tools out of the side door. "Looking for somebody?" he asks, and since he seems friendly enough I say, "No, just looking. I tried to get a job here yesterday, but the boss said he didn't need any help."

"Doing what?" he asks.

I shrug. "Anything," I say. "Clean up, moving wood, whatever."

He puts on his nail belt, and he's so thin it rides low on his hips. "This guy's an asshole," he says. "A friend of mine just started a job a couple miles from here. Says the supe is okay. You might try there." He draws me a map on a small piece of scrap plywood. "Ask for Ron," he says. "Tell him Lupe sent you."

I help the guy carry his tools into the half-built house and then run back to the car, prop Alex up against the passenger door, start the Cruiser, and then haul chili for this other job.

It's got a chain-link fence like the other one, and a big sign that reads, "Green Valley Estates, Executive Homes." This name is complete booga booga. It's as flat as Kansas, and the only green thing within five miles is an ice chest sitting on some guy's tailgate about halfway down the street. The field beyond the subdivision is brown, the street is brown, the bare dirt between the houses is brown. Green Valley Estates. Yah. The guy who thought that up should be assigned Ray-Bans and a guide dog.

We drive past the white plywood job shack, which looks like it just got painted, and ask the first guy we see where Ron is

173

working. He points up the street and says, "Number 32." There's a stenciled plywood sign on a stake in front of each new house.

I have a good feeling about the Hispanic guy and his pal, but this limps out as soon as I get to 32 and see Ron. He's this big guy with a droopy mustache unloading a huge wooden beam from a new red Ford pickup. His dirt-brown hair is long and snaggle-puss and his face is hard, like it was hacked out of the beam he's hefting on his shoulder. He grunts once, and then his football-player body adjusts to the weight and he carries it toward the house he's working on.

"Want a hand?" I ask him.

"Nah," he tells me. "It's only a four-by-twelve."

"Lupe told me to look you up," I say.

"What for?" he asks, and his voice sinks me.

"I'm looking for work, cleanup, anything, and he said maybe you could help," I answer, trying to sound full of energy.

"You got the wrong man, partner," he says. "I just started here myself. Check with Spence. He's the supe." He lowers the beam, one end at a time, and points to the white job shack by the gate. "He's usually up there." Then he goes off like I just disappeared.

Spike, I'm already here, I tell myself. Might as well give it a shot. I walk up to the shed, and there's a middle-aged Af-Am guy with salt-and-pepper hair talking on the phone. He's wearing a short-sleeve pin-striped dress shirt, and leaning over sun-faded blueprints stained with months of coffee cup rings.

"I ordered rough-sawn and you send me this ess-four-ess shit," he says in a gravelly bent voice. "What the hell is going on?" Then he listens for a minute and says, all disgusted, "I can't wait three days, Tommie. You screwed up my order, now I have to go somewhere else." He cuts the guy off and says, "I keep giving you chances and you keep costing me. Talk to you later." And he slams down the phone.

"Son of a bitch," he says, and starts calling lumberyards looking for this rough-sawn lumber, and there doesn't seem to be much of it around in the sizes he wants. He finally orders some from two different places and makes some notes on a clipboard. Then he sees me.

"What's up?" he asks.

174

"Ron says to ask you about work," I say.

"Know a trade?" he asks.

"No, but my friend and I will do anything. Cleanup, moving wood, you name it."

He looks out the door and down the street, which has about twenty houses on each side. The ones in the back already have roofs, and the ones in front are just concrete slabs. "Your friend here?" he asks me.

"Yeah," I say right away.

"Go get him, and meet me back there where the forklift is unloading the sheetrock."

My heart almost blows out as I run back to the Cruiser. "I got us a job," I yell, and Alex finally wakes up. "What are we doing?" he asks, and I say, "Hell, I don't know, something to do with stone sheet."

So Alex and I get there just as the forklift has finished unloading the last big stack. Spence comes over to us and says, "I'll pay you guys piecework to load this house. Three cents a square foot."

He might as well be speaking Martian, and he sees this. "Come on," he says, and we follow him into the house, which looks almost done from the outside but has nothing on the walls inside, just electrical wires, plumbing pipes, and insulation.

"Stack this number of sheets in the middle of each room," he says, and he writes "25" with the thickest blue crayon I've ever seen on the living room floor, "12" in what looks like the kitchen, and so on in each room except the bathrooms. "Stack it neat and don't break the corners," he says.

"I don't get the money part," I tell him.

He looks me over just like my old boss at the Fiberglas shop did. "Each of the big sheets is four by twelve—48 square feet. The smaller ones are four by eight, 32 feet. We need about 8,000 square feet in this house, which means you get about $240."

Alex's eyes fritz out because this seems like the easiest money ever. "Put ten sheets of green board in the bedroom next to each bathroom," he says. He can see we don't get it again so he points out the window. "See that green pile? It's waterproof board."

We go outside and he says, "Lift with your back, and don't break the corners or it'll cost you."

175

Alex asks, "Which pile of stone sheet do you want us to use first?"

Spence pauses for a long second and then bursts out laughing. "Stone sheet?" He laughs out loud some more, shakes his head and says, "Thank you, Lord." Then he turns to Alex and says, "It's *sheetrock.*" He's still chuckling as he walks off.

Alex is all torqued by this humiliation, and he punches me in the shoulder. "You said stone sheet."

"I don't know what I said," I say, and my shoulder is hurting even though it was just a tap.

"You make me look like an ass," Alex says, and I have to stop smiling or he'll punch my ticket guarans-ball-bearins.

Alex stares at the big piles and says, "Brah, we can't work if we got nothing in the tank. Go get the grinds."

So I run back to the Lancer, and collect the remains of our food supply, which is pretty pathetic: a package of smashed Pop Tarts, a can of chocolate pudding, a couple of slices of molding bread, a can of deviled meat, and the rocky bottom inch of a jar of chunky peanut butter. I'm relieved there's something other than the deviled meat, which looks like it comes out of the Fancy Fiesta cat food factory, while Alex never eats sugar-blitz junk like Pop Tarts.

I bring this back to Alex and he tears off the moldy parts of the bread, pops open the meat tin, digs the stinky glop out with my Swiss Army knife and wolfs down one of the worst deviled ham sandwiches ever made. I tear open the Pop Tart packages and pour the crumbs in my mouth, and we split the chocolate pudding.

Alex takes a minute to do some stretching exercises, and he tells me, "You too, bruddah. I don't want you all jammed up so you can't help me." I roll my eyes and then follow his example, just like when we had to push the Falcon up that hill in Iowa.

So we go over to the first pile of four-by-eight sheetrock and discover this stuff weighs. It looks like compressed chalk covered with thin cardboard, but it's a lot heavier than wood. We decide to get the upstairs over with, and on our first shot up the staircase I drop my end. The corner breaks like I'd dropped it off the roof.

Alex says, "Fricking Daz, you gotta be careful," and I'm staggering around like I'm drunk under the weight of these sheets. They come in pairs, so I say, "Let's break them apart, man."

Alex says, "No way," grabs the second double sheet all by himself, gives a "ki-ai" kung fu yell, and starts running up the stairs by himself. It must weigh 140 pounds, maybe even 150. "Fricking Alex," I yell because even though he's got the whole weight himself, I'm just whipping the front of the sheets around to keep him from smashing into the bare wall studs.

We've just started, but my shirt's already soaked, and Alex strips his soaked tank top off because it's hotter than hell. I'm not about to expose my wimpy body, so I leave mine on. It feels like there's a pipe feeding jet exhaust into the legs of my jeans; you'd be sweating like a maniac even if you weren't running ten tons of stone sheet upstairs.

By the third trip up the stairs, it's obvious this is the hardest damn $240 we're ever going to make. I'm wheezing, of course, but then so is Alex, because he's been carrying most of the weight.

By the third run I'm begging Alex, "Come on, man, please, let's do the downstairs for a while," and he tells me, "You'll thank me when we're pau," which is Hawaiian for "finished." I shake my head and can't say anything else because I don't have the breath.

After we finish two of the bedrooms upstairs it's dehydration city, so we find a spigot and a hose on the house next door. The water tastes bad, I guess from the new pipes, and it's warm, but it's better than nothing. I turn around and look down the street and Alex shoots me in the back with the full spray. I yell and he laughs.

"You gotta keep cool, Brah," he says. That's when I realize he's actually having fun hauling stone sheet. Griffin Spike is laying down the blues, and Alex is hearing light opera.

By the time we finish the upstairs I'm too tired to celebrate, and Alex is on "E," just like the Cruiser. He needs food, and our five bucks aren't going to go far unless we buy refried beans and tortillas. But there's no market around this place; it's all brown meadows growing houses.

There's a big whoop from a house down the street that's still all sticks, so loud we can hear it over the "poomf" of the nail guns and the shrieking banshee sound of the electric saws. A nail gun poomfs real fast, rat-tat-tat-tat, and there's howling like maybe somebody got shot. Then there's silence, and I expect some guy to be carried out and an ambulance to drive up. But a saw winds up and tears into some wood, and everything sounds normal again.

"It's almost eleven," I say. "Maybe Spence will advance us ten bucks for lunch."

Alex says, "Try asking. I'll keep working." I hate asking for money, but there's no way I can complain about Alex busting his eggs carrying stone sheet, so I walk down to the job shack and find Spence.

"My friend and I are down to five bucks," I say. "Think you can advance us ten for lunch?"

"How much rock you stack?" he asks me dubiously.

"The whole upstairs," I say.

"You better be right, because I'll be up there in about ten minutes," he says. He takes a Jackson out of a thin alligator wallet. "Now go get me a quarter-pounder with no cheese and a small fries at McDonald's, and get yourselves something."

I say, "Thanks a lot," and take the gitas, and he tells me, "Long as you're making a run, go see if the Odd Squad wants anything. They're working on 23," and he points to the house where all the whoops came from.

I start walking up the street and he says after me, "And get some extra salt and catsup."

I'm hesitating in front of number 23 because there's nobody working. Then I see four guys behind the house. I wish I didn't have to meet the Odd Squad, but since Spence asked me, I step over the air hoses and power cords and find my way to the back yard, which is littered with two-by-fours and plywood scraps.

One big guy with long black hair, maybe part Indian or black Hispanic, is aiming a nail gun at some empty beer cans that are set up in a row about thirty feet away. Every time he pulls the trigger there's a pop of compressed air and a long nail spits out. He dings three of the cans and a fat guy with a bristly red beard says, "Shit." A rangy cowboy type with a graying ponytail slaps his nail bags and says, "You're buying, Bobo. Herby got three."

Fatso Bobo says, "Wait a minute, Ohzee. Gimpy hasn't shot yet."

"I ain't playing, thank you," says Gimpy, a little thin guy with a droopy blond mustache, and a steely pair of slit eyes which are on me like a hawk on a rabbit.

"Come on, Gimp," says the fat guy, Bobo. "Maybe you'll win for a change." Then he whoops. Bobo's wearing suspenders, and I'm thinking that maybe they're going to snap with the weight of belly on his nail belt.

Gimpy says, "Let's go with hammers tomorrow. No toys."

"Macho Man and his chrome hammer," says the tall cowboy they're calling Ohzee. Then he follows Gimpy's eyes and spots me.

"Well, if it isn't one of the Stone Sheet crew Spence told us about," he says. Then Herby, the big Indian-Hispanic guy, starts singing in a fake Hendrix voice, "Stone sheet, do as I please, stone sheet, ride the breeze." They all have a good laugh and I stand there like a third-grader in front of the sixth-graders.

"Spence is sending me to McDonald's," I say, trying to sound hard. "You guys want anything?"

"I'd like some clouds," says Bobo. "It's too goddamn hot out here. Civilized places aren't this hot."

"This isn't civilization, Bobo," says Ohzee. "This is Sacramento."

They all have another laugh over that and then Herby asks, "Where you from, boy?" in a fake southern-gentleman accent.

"L.A.", I say.

"Do a lot of stone sheet down there?" asks Ohzee.

They all laugh again like this is the world's funniest joke.

"No, this is the first time I've touched the stuff," I say.

"Well, we see your partner's sure going for broke," says Bobo. "If he lives past two o'clock, he'll do okay."

"He's Hawaiian," I say. "Heat doesn't bother him."

"I wish I was Hawaiian," says Bobo. "I may not make it past two. Can't you lazy bastards get the roof on any faster?"

"If you'd get off your fat tush and cut the rafters, we'd be happy to," says Ohzee. "Remember? That's your job."

"You guys want anything or not?" I ask.

Bobo gives me a twenty and writes down the Squad's lunch order on a scrap of plywood. I'm glad to haul chili over to 36 and find out what Alex wants from the local MD. He's finished loading the kitchen, and he orders a D-9 gig: two Big Macs, two fish burgers, a Coke, and a large ice water.

When I get back from Macs, Spence isn't in the shed, so I drive slowly up the street looking for him. When I pass 23 I'm hoping the Odd Squad is busy, but they spot me and hoot and wave and make wise-ass comments about the Lancer.

I spock Spence talking to Ron, who's working with an Af-Am guy putting on siding. I get out and give Spence his burger and his change. He looks inside the bag and says, "Where's the catsup and the extra salt?" and then I remember, damn, I forgot to ask for the extra salt. "They were out of salt," I lie. "Catsup's in the car." When I bring him a fistful of the catsup packets he tries to look mean and says, "Next time, remember the salt."

Ron asks me, "How you like humping sheetrock?"

I say, "Could be worse."

"But not much worse," says Ron, and Spence chuckles.

When I drive up to 36 Alex is carrying a sheet into the living room. As soon as he spocks me he flops the sheet down right in the entry and runs out to the Cruiser, rips open the MD bag and inhales a fish burger. I mean three bites. Then he gulps the ice water dry and vacuums the two burgers. Finally, on the last fish burger he slows down enough to actually taste something.

"I wish some girl could have seen that," I tell him. "'What cho-cho manners you have, big boy.'"

Alex burps and says, "Fricking haole."

Just then Ron and Spence walk up to us and Spence says, "Damn, I forgot about the garage." He spocks each wall and counts invisible sheets. "Stack twenty-four sheets of the twelve-foot Type X here," he says, writing the number on the concrete. "They're in that last stack."

"What's Type X?" I ask.

"Fire-resistant," Spence says. "It's five-eighths, not half-inch."

"You mean it's heavier?"

Spence raises his eyebrows and nods.

"Let's go try a sheet," Alex says, and since I don't want to look humba-humba, I go with him. Spence and Ron are talking about the doors for 36, but they stop for a minute to enjoy us struggling with this gigantia twelve-foot long double-sheet which weighs like two regulars. Sure enough, we break a corner on this first sheet right in front of Spence.

"How much do you think that was worth, Ron?" Spence asks.

180

"I don't know, five bucks?" Ron says, and his granite face looks a lot friendlier when he's smiling.

"At least," says Spence, and he tries to scowl. "A few more like that and you'll be working for free."

Alex insists we carry the Type X first, and I'm stumbling under the weight each time even though Alex is carrying more than half. When we finish that, I flop on the stack and just lay there panting like an old dog. It's like the whole street got moved to Death Valley when I wasn't looking—there's no breeze—and we still have some of the downstairs to load.

"I'm adiosed," I say. "I can't move."

Alex lets me moan for a while and then he hands me the Coke, which is still pretty cold even though all the ice has melted. After I drink some of that I feel better, and he says, "You gotta drink a lot of water, Brah," and he gulps down the rest.

Then he gets up and shadowboxes a little, throws a few punches.

"Quit showing off," I tell him. "There's no girls around."

He whinnies like a horse and says, "Hey man, I feel good," and he throws a few jabs at my face. "Get your poi dog ass up, Brah," he says. "We're almost pau."

"Fricking Alex," I say, trying to mimic him, and he says in that sing-song Hawaiian way I can't quite copy, "Fricking Daz."

Somehow I get a second wind and we finish loading the first floor. We make a careful count of all the sheets, and figure out the square footage, which is 9,942, because there was also all that Type X for the garage. We figure out what we made, which is $298. Cash in pocket, it's more than double what I was making in the fiberglass shop.

We're resting in the garage and I ask, just as a comment, "Do you realize how much gitas we'd make if we did this for a month?"

Alex says, "Think about what good shape we'd be in."

"Yah, one Hawaiian in strat shape and one skinny rich dead guy," I tell him, and he laughs.

Knowing there's no chance for a real shower, we strip to our skivvies and hose off next to the garage. The water's lukewarm, but it feels great after sweating so much, and as I pull on my jeans, I feel a weird pride in the neat piles of sheetrock stacked in each room.

That night we park the Cruiser outside the gate and sleep on a tarp. At first, I'm so tired I can't sleep, but I must have, because then I hear the field birds singing. I open my eyes, and the sun is poking through the new houses and Ron is leaning against the fender of the Cruiser, pouring us some coffee out of a big stainless steel thermos.

# CHAPTER TWENTY-ONE

I sit up and my whole body hurts. Ron hands me a mug. I don't like black coffee much, but it tastes good this morning. "Spence says you guys can stay in my camper," he says.

Alex looks hung over until he splashes some water on his face. "What camper?" he asks.

"It's at the end of the cul-de-sac, by 42," he says. "My old lady and I were living there until last week. Spence likes the security at night."

The gate's already open, and Spence is standing outside the shed, talking on the phone. We follow Ron's red Ford back to 42, and we see his camper is the kind that fits on the back of a pick-up. It's on wood blocks and looks small. Ron opens the door, and it smells like cat food and cat poo combined, which is one of the worst smells ever. Plus it's hot inside, even first thing in the morning.

"Here's the deal," he tells us. "You gotta feed the dog and the cats. Once in the morning, once at night."

A mangy old Labrador wanders over, wagging its tail, and Ron rubs behind its ears. "This apartment we moved into doesn't allow pets," he says. "I don't know what I'm gonna do when this job ends."

He goes inside and shows us the little kitchen. "At least you won't have to eat junk food all the time," he says. "I ran a cord from 42 so you've got a fridge and lights, and there's even a cordless phone we rigged off the one in the job shack."

I'm thinking I'd rather sleep outside than in this mambo crib, but Ron's heart is in the right place so I thank him. The phone was a plus, because we hadn't called home in a long time and our folks were probably worried that we were laying in a ditch somewhere. After he leaves I tell Alex, "If we can air it out, maybe it'll be okay."

He wrinkles his nose and says, "Pilau," which means "dirty" in Hawaiian.

He goes inside and opens the windows, but they're so small it's a joke. "Maybe we can take off the glass," I say.

"We need to string a tarp," Alex says, "like at the beach. We gotta keep the sun off it."

So we borrow a blue Fiberglas tarp from the job shack and rig up some two-by-fours to hold the tarp above the camper, and with our screwdriver we take off the little glass sliding windows. Then we prop the door open, and it already smells and feels better.

I dread lunch because I know I'll have to take the Odd Squad's order again, but they're up on the roof working and they don't give me much griff. I'm sore all over, but by ten o'clock I feel better, and this time I buy a bag of ice from the gas station next to Mickey-D's so Alex and I have lots of cold water in our ice chest. Spence sees me drinking from the hose at 37 and he says, "Don't drink that crud. Get your water from the job shack." The water there does taste a lot better, I guess because everybody uses it so it's lost that new pipe taste.

We finish 37 at about 2:30, and even though I'm dead-zone tired we go back to the camper to see how our plan is working. Somebody has propped a big spray-painted sign against the camper that reads, "The Allreet Stone Sheet Crew of Dry Gulch Executive Mansions."

Alex flops it face down in the dust and we check the interior. It's cooler and not so pilau, and we open the little reefer to see if it's cold yet. There's a six-pack of ice-cold Miller Draft bottles, a can of Coke, and a broken piece of sheetrock inside that reads, "Welcome to Dry Gulch from the Odd Squad." There's a skull-and-crossbones drawing, only instead of bones, there's two-by-fours with nails sticking out.

Alex reads this, pops open two of the brewkowskis, and we drain them. After his second one, he goes outside and sets the "Allreet Stone Sheet" sign up again.

We carry our sleeping bags and a few things into the camper, and about 3:30 we hear voices coming from 42. I glance out and see it's the Odd Squad. When they get closer they start singing that old song "Born Free," only their words are, "Stone sheet, it makes life worth living, and only worth living, if you're stone sheeeeeet."

There's a six-pack swinging from each arm, and big belly Bobo says, "Aren't you even gonna invite us in?"

"I would, but it'd tip over as soon as you sat down," I tell him, and Herby hoots real loud and says, "I like that boy. Stone sheet through and through."

We go through the usual introductions and then get right down to tanking up. It's so hot it's easy to drink three or four beers in a row, and I'm napalmed in about ten minutes. About four o'clock Ron and his partner Wayland drift over, and then about 4:30 Spence walks up and says, "I see the Odd Squad's at it again." Gimpy tosses him a beer and he flips it back. "Anybody got a real drink?" he asks. Bobo tells me, "Get that Coke," and even though I can hardly walk, I go inside the camper, get the Coke, and hand it to Spence.

It turns out all the guys have worked in Hawaii at one time or another, either building hotels or condos during the boom times or after the hurricane, and so Alex and I listen for a couple of hours to stories about crazy people and crazy times and fishing. Spence leaves at six, and Ron says to us, "Why don't you guys give that junk food a rest. My old lady's cooking a roast tonight. With all the fixings, too." I'm too blitzkrieged to talk, but Alex accepts, so we pile into Ron's red Ford pickup and head into the city.

About twenty minutes later we roll into the underground parking lot of a new-looking stucco apartment building, the kind with sliding doors and little patios where everyone puts their bikes and Weber barbecues and dead house plants. Ron's place is on the third floor. I'm still on full rock-and-roll thanks to the brewkowskis, but at least I can stand up straight when we meet his old lady Rosalee. She's a big haole woman with a friendly face, and we relax a little. Her hair is light brown and very fine and straight, and I can see that she was lapis lazuli when she was younger.

"Hope you boys brought your appetites," she says, and I practically have to wipe the drool off Alex's chin because we can smell the roast and there's covered dishes already on the table. The plates and glasses are mismatched, but the silver and everything is laid out real neat, just like my Mom does for guests.

"Sorry about the furniture," Ron tells us, but it looks fine to me, just a little old-fashioned. "We moved in last week and we're still shopping."

185

We plop down on the sofa, and Rosalee brings us a steel tray with different kinds of sodas on it. I pop a Coke and Alex takes an orangeade.

"You've seen the trailer," she says. "So you can understand how thrilled I am with this place. It's got everything, even a hot tub and pool."

It's definitely a step up from the trailer, and I can tell she's mango-mango about it, so I nod and tell her, "Yeah, it's great."

"Think I'll lay down," Ron says. "I don't feel so good."

Rosalee looks worried and asks, "Did you have a drink?"

"One beer," he says, like a kid who ate a candy bar just before dinner.

"Hon, you know better than that," she says softly, and she feels his forehead with the back of her hand.

"Go ahead and start eating," he tells us. "I'll feel better in a few minutes."

She walks with him to the bedroom and I hear her ask, "You didn't take your medication with it, did you?" and he shakes his head no. They go into the bedroom and shut the door, and we're feeling spiky just staring at the bare walls.

I look around and just to break the silence say, "I'd hate to hump sheetrock to the third floor."

"Maybe there's an elevator," Alex says.

"Yeah, but not while they're building it," I snort.

"Maybe there was a crane," he says. "That's what they use in Hawaii."

Rosalee comes out with a strained smile and says, "He says to go ahead."

Alex tells her, "No, we'll wait."

She pulls out the chairs and motions us over, saying, "He'll feel better if he knows you're eating. Besides, sometimes it takes a few hours for him to get over this."

Alex and I look at each other, and she sighs and says, "It'll just get cold," so we go over and sit down at the table.

"Sorry Ron doesn't feel good," I kind of mumble. "It was really nice of you to invite us over."

She smiles again and serves us a fresh salad, baked potatoes, carrots, and thick, juicy slabs of roast beef. "He's not supposed to

186

have any alcohol because of his medication," she tells us in a confidential tone, "but he forgets when everybody else is drinking."

"Spence doesn't drink," I tell her.

"That's what I tell Ron," she says. "'Have a Coke, like Spence.'"

"Is it his heart?" Alex asks her.

She smiles like you do when you're a kid and you're trying to be brave, and says, "No, it's for his moods. He gets real down and real afraid of people. He couldn't work for a long time."

"He's doing good now," I protest.

"Yes," she says, and points to our plates. "Don't be shy, for heaven's sake. I don't want leftovers. Ron won't eat them and Lord knows I don't need it." Her laugh is sweet and I can see that Ron is lucky to have her.

The beef just falls apart when I touch it with my fork, and Alex isn't shy about grinding a second serving.

"Did you get along okay with the Odd Squad?" I ask her.

"Better than you'd expect," she says. "They're the ones who got Ron the job, so I'd put up with a lot before I got pissed off, but they're always very polite. They're vets, too, you know."

I don't know what to say, and she tells us in a low voice, "Ron doesn't talk to me much about the war. The only thing he says is that bullets do terrible things to the human body."

We're silent after that; I remember Kyle and Rich, and I can imagine what Ron saw. "We sure appreciate his helping us get us some work," I tell Rosalee. "We were down to fumes."

"Tell me about it," she says. "I've had to work the dinner shift because tips from breakfast and lunch aren't very big. Plus, we didn't have medical insurance, and the V.A. was a joke."

She pulls her fine hair back over her shoulders and then shakes her head. "Their shrinks wanted to dope Ron up and write him off. Can you believe that? The man's a craftsman, for God's sake."

I fight back a creepy feeling I'm getting about Ron and ask her, "So what happened?"

"I almost didn't make it," she says, and she mixes up the salad again with the two big wooden forks, even though it's already strat. "I borrowed some money from my brother and hired an outside shrink," she tells us. "It's taken a year to pay him off, but it was the best money I ever spent. I believe in natural healing and

187

all that, but I can tell you that these new drugs make miracles happen. They really do."

The door opens and Ron comes out looking haggard and old. He rubs his eyes and squints at the light. "I feel better," he says. Rosalee pats a chair and says, "Come sit down, honey. There's still some left."

"Guess I got up just in time," he says, and she loads a plate for him. After he eats something he looks better, although his features never soften except when he laughs. And he only laughs once, after he repeats the "stone sheet" story to Rosalee.

She shakes her head like a mom and says to us, "They're so hard on the new boys, I don't know why," and Ron looks so much better laughing that even Alex doesn't mind the joke this time.

# CHAPTER TWENTY-TWO

We finished loading sheetrock in the last two Dry Gulch Executive Mansions that were ready, and then we ran out of work. Spence told us another four would be ready in a week, so we couldn't decide between flattening out for a while or heading to San Francisco. Then the Odd Squad offered us cash gitas to help them frame the next house, and that made the decision easy.

Our job was to move all the lumber. "Hell, we're spoiling them," Gimpy says. "After humping these little old two-by-twelves, they won't want to go back to stone sheet."

Turns out these two-by-twelves are soaking wet and heavy as the Cruiser. Plus your hands get covered with sap, you get splinters the size of matches, and your fingers get smashed when you miscalculate the stack or your partner drops his end before you're ready.

Despite the heat and the sap and the splinters, it's interesting watching the Odd Squad work together. They're always joking, but they don't waste motion. One guy measures and cuts the big beams, another guy cuts all the small pieces, and two guys nail it all together. If anyone makes a mistake they get baked by the rest of the Squad, stuff like, "Three-sixteenths, Bobo, that's three little marks," or, "You've been beating off too much, Gimpy, you're going blind. Didn't the preacher tell you about that?"

Gimpy's the smallest man on the Squad but he carries the biggest hammer—a chrome-plated 28-ounce framing hammer with a waffle face. He and Ohzee would whip their air hoses and big Senco nail guns all over the walls they're building on the floor, racing each other, bam-bam, bam-bam, bam-bam, two sixteen-penny nails per stud, and five in each corner.

Gimpy prides himself on his hand nailing, and he has this rhythm on plywood that's something to see. One hit to start the nail, one to sink it, nail after nail. He claims they used to race, a

189

beer per nail, across a whole roof, but the other guys lost so much they gave up the game. Bobo hears this and snorts, "We just got tired of Gimpy moping around when he lost."

Of course "Alex" and "Daz" weren't creative enough for the Odd Squad. They started out calling Alex "Alexander the Great" after they saw how many two-by-fours he could carry, and they shortened it right away to "AG." For me, they twisted "Hernandez" into "Herny-andez" because every time I lift a board, I always grimace like I'm about to have a hernia. Of course "Herny-andez" got shortened to "Herny." I never really gripped how they came up with their own names. The Odd Squad didn't approve of too much explanation, either of nicknames or carpentry or anything else.

We got the camper aired out and after that it was tolerable once the sun went down. Spence, Ron, Wayland and the Odd Squad made it a habit to stop by our crib at "pau hana," which is Hawaiian for "end of work," maybe because the tarp kept the front of the trailer cool and we'd bachelored the place so they felt comfortable: a fifty-five-gallon drum for recycled aluminum cans, a couple of old folding chairs, and a dead sofa we picked up on the side of the highway on the way to McDonald's one day.

Even though Alex and I never ask about it, the wars come up every so often in the Odd Squad's beer-and-bull-sessions: Vietnam for Ron and Bobo, the Desert War for Ohzee, Herby, and Gimpy. After listening to these for a few weeks, I realize that the stories about war that get printed every once in a while in the *New Yorker* are as lame as a three-legged dog because, like all the other stories, they linchpin on some big drama that's not at all like real life. Ones I remember reading have a guy waking up to find some hitch-hiker's blistery hand on his dick, or some sweet young girl getting adiosed across the throat, or some immigrant meeting her store-bought hubby in a sun-dappled garden. Each setting is so dramatic it's bogus because that's not how important things happen, and not how people talk about them afterward.

Take the war gigs that the Odd Squad lived through. If it was some lame-ass short story, then they'd be gathered in some dramatic spot, or pick up a Native American hitchhiker with missing teeth, and he'd tell some perfectly paced story about taking Hill

199-three-dash-A or whatever, and wonder what would have happened to Corporal Grunt if he hadn't gone nuts that day and adiosed that sweet prostitute, ga-ga-ga.

Maybe another vet from some other crew stops by, and he's a little loopy, and he'll start talking about sitting in a foxhole and realizing how the NVA dudes shelling the hell out of them were actually his brothers. Nobody else says anything for a few seconds and then the conversation moves on to fishing or cars.

When somebody does spill you a big drama, then it's no set piece like picking up the hitchhiker with missing teeth, it's just some guy talking while his pals interrupt him to say, oh no, not that story again, and he kind of smiles and keeps on telling it.

During one of Bobo's stories about how he's flying his copter and trying to keep his copter gunner alive until he could land the Loach, he suddenly reaches over and grabs Alex by the neck, right by his collarbone, to show how he stopped the guy's bleeding. When he lets go and Alex asks what happened to the gunner, Gimpy says, "Hell, we only heard this story ten times, Bobo; want me to finish it?"

Bobo ignores Gimpy and he says, he made it, but he was paralyzed because a tiny shell fragment had sliced right through his spine.

Then everybody takes a sip of beer, and then some guy asks when the next rack of two-by-four-by-sixteens is showing up, because if it isn't soon then we're S.O.L. on finishing 24.

During one of these B.S.-and-beer sessions, I can't help noticing that Ron is still accepting beers from the Odd Squad. So the next morning I pull Bobo aside and tell him about Ron's new medication, and how beer hits him the wrong way, and how it worries Rosalee. He listens silently, scratches his thick beard a little and nods.

That afternoon Bobo tosses Ron a Coke like they do to Spence, and Ron acts like it's normal, even though I see the question in his eyes. Spence walks up a little later and notices the red can in Ron's hand right away and says, "So I finally got somebody else to quit drinking horsepiss."

Bobo snorts, holds up his Budweiser, and says, "Yeah, but this here is Clydesdale piss, Spence," and after everybody laughs Spence says, "So that's why they keep those big-ass horses."

191

It takes a week for the Odd Squad to frame up most of the house and then we go back to stacking stone sheet. After three days of that, they finish the roof framing and we helpd them lay the plywood and put in the windows, which have the little panes like French doors. They're heavy, too. Everything's heavy. Fifty-pound boxes of gun nails, three-quarter inch sheets of tongue-and-groove flooring plywood, double French doors, and, of course, stone sheet.

"Don't hurt yourself, Herny," Ohzee tells me whenever he sees me lifting anything real heavy. "We don't have insurance. You bust a nut and there's nothing we can do for you."

Once we pop in the windows the Odd Squad starts putting up the siding and we aren't needed. But then we get a couple of days, work helping Ron and Wayland set kitchen and bath cabinets. Wayland is a tall, dark-skinned Af-Am who always has reggae playing on his tape deck, and his screw gun in his nail bag like a space-cowboy ray gun. I could see why Ron and him are partners. Neither one says much, to each other or anyone else. No jokes, no chatter, maybe just, "Down a hair" or "Make it fifteen and seven-eighths" when they're setting a cabinet. Wayland is serious like Ron, and sometimes looks mean enough to split wood. But when he smiles, his teeth are real white and his laugh comes from deep down, a real "heh-heh-heh" that makes you want to laugh, too.

One time we went out for dinner with Wayland, his old lady, and Ron and Rosalee at the restaurant where Rosalee works. It's a roast-beef-and-mashed-potatoes kind of place, nothing fancy, but they give redwood servings and everybody treats us like King Tut because of Rosalee. Alex and I pay the tab because we're always grinding over at Ron and Rosalee's. I think it's too much, going over there practically every night, but Ron insists and we don't want to hurt his feelings. Plus Alex doesn't want to give up Ros-alee's cooking.

*   *   *

After three weeks of working, we'd accumulated quite a pile of gitas. We liked everybody and the work, but we were starting to get tired of life on the road, and we wanted to push on to San Francisco and then head home. We decided to tell them on Friday night.

Ron always drives us to his apartment because he knows we've been drinking after pau hana, and because he likes to bring us back to the camper so he can see his dog and cats. Just as we turn onto his street, he slows and pulls over.

"What is it?" I say.

"The neighbor's cat got run over back there," he says.

I hadn't seen it so I turn around and watch him take a square-nosed shovel out of the bed of the pickup, go back and gently scoop the dead cat off the pavement and then carry it to some big bushes down the street. He lays it deep inside and then comes back to the truck.

He climbs into the cab and says, "Wouldn't be right for the kids to see their kitten like that tomorrow morning."

After this we don't have the heart to tell him we'll be leaving, so we stay until the work runs out again, and then we tell Ron we're heading home. At the end of that week we go over for dinner one last time. Rosalee gives us each a big hug and Ron shakes our hands, and I promise them, and myself, that I'll write.

I even feel sad saying goodbye to the Odd Squad. "I'm gonna miss you guys," I tell them, and Bobo pats my shoulder. "It's tough losing partners," he says. "That's why we stick together."

Gimpy says, "We're gonna miss you, too, Herny. We haven't laughed so hard since Herby got caught pissing off the roof by that lady architect."

They all laugh and Herby says in a fake British accent, "Madam, I was just checking the wind direction." They laugh again, and Ohzee says, "Bullshit, you didn't say that. You said, 'Oh shit,' and tried to stuff your dong back in your jeans. You pissed all over yourself."

"Look out for Ron, okay?" I tell them.

"Don't worry, partner," Bobo says. "We stick together."

"What about the camper and Ron's dog and cats?" I ask.

Ozee says, "God watches out for the Odd Squad, Herny. Gimpy's girlfriend just threw him out so he'll take over."

Spence was on the phone, as usual, and we had to wait about ten minutes to say goodbye to him. I tell him, "Thanks, man." He shakes our hands and says, "We still got a couple months here, so if you get tired of that candy-ass Frisco life—"

"Who knows," I say. "Thanks again, Spence. For giving us a shot."

"Stone sheet'll never be the same," he says, and breaks out laughing.

# CHAPTER TWENTY-THREE

The stretch of Interstate 80 between Sacramento and San Francisco is dry and hot, and when we get to Vallejo the cool air off the Bay feels good. The map shows that we have to go through Berkeley to get to San Francisco, so I ask Alex if we can stop off there and see what's left of People's Park. He says, "Okay," and that's how we end up in West Oakland.

We get off the I-State at the University Avenue exit, and after a couple of blocks we pull into a Shell station to ask for directions. A skinny redheaded guy in shades and a Hawaiian shirt is there pumping gas into a blue Honda Accord, so I ask him, "Where's People's Park?"

He looks the Cruiser over, spocks the writing on the fender, kind of smiles, and says, "It's off Telegraph Avenue. Just go straight up University to the campus, and then turn right. Go a couple blocks and then turn left. Just ask anybody on Telegraph."

I say, "Thanks," and we roll up to Telegraph Avenue, which is a pain in the butt to drive on because it's one-way. It's all cafés and little shops selling music or clothing, crowds of students, and street people sitting on the sidewalks, holding out their begging cups.

We luck into a parking spot on a side street in front of this Asian girl in a white apron and T-shirt standing outside a bakery smoking a nickspliff. She looks tired and I figure it's her break. Her hair's up in a bandana, her nipples are little bumps in her tight little white T-shirt, and she's kind of cute in a tough way, like Tracie.

Two old guys wearing pants almost up to their armpits walk by, and one admonishes her, "Smoking's bad for you, young lady," and she pulls in a cloud, exhales it, and says, "Cram it."

Just my type. So I go up to her and ask, "Can you tell me where People's Park is?"

195

She sucks in another toxic air dump, checks out me and the Lancer, and nods. "It's a couple of blocks over," she says, gesturing across Telegraph. "Looking for somebody?"

"No," I answer. "It's just for the history."

She taps the ashes off her cig and advises me, "Stay away from the trees in the back. That's where the dealers hang out."

"I can tell already how historic it is," I snort.

She shrugs and stomps the butt out on the sidewalk. Then she adjusts her bandana and I wish I could kiss her, because she's not wearing a bra and she's pushing her shirt out so sweetly in all the right places. Instead I say, "Thanks."

On the way to the park, three different people ask us for spare change. We just shrug and walk by. The park is a full city block, but it doesn't look that big. A few people are sitting on the dirt in the little stand of trees in the back, and another clump of beggars is up in front by a low wooden stage. I read this book about the New Left and all that 60s activism, and I guess I expected some feeling to be hovering overhead. But it's just a bunch of street people camping out.

The best part is this big mural right off the park, which depicts the riots and the dead guy, and then, at the end, a guy holding his hand out for change. I guess somebody thought it's ironic that it's come to beggars, but I don't think so. Some guy got killed, which is no irony, Jack, and for this we get a bunch of bums wanting a free campground close to people to leech off of. They act like they own it, but they can't even keep it clean.

The park and the people are depressing so we go back to the bakery to get something to eat and enjoy another look at "Cram it's" gorgeous bod. She's not as impressive as Tita but she looks good after almost a month of the camper and the Odd Squad.

"Cram it" is behind the counter, and she's pulled off her bandana so her long black hair has fallen down her back. It's very straight and shiny. Alex drifts over to a bulletin board by the door, giving me the big hint, let's haul derriere. The girl still hasn't looked me in the eye, so I go over to look at the board, too. I see a bunch of notices of rooms for rent by the month, and then I notice one hand-drawn sheet for a large room in a Victorian house in Oakland for $50 a week. I wouldn't mind staying a week, so I take

196

off the sheet and go to the counter with it. She asks, "What'll you have?" without smiling, almost cold.

I pick out a couple of pastries and pay for them. Nobody else is in the store, it's the dead-zone part of the afternoon, so I ask her, "Know any place to stay around here?"

Alex kicks me in the shin because he wants to go on to San Francisco, so I say, "I mean either here or in San Francisco."

She doesn't look at me directly, but she says, "Depends on how long you're staying." She looks out the window and says, "Nice car."

"Thanks, " I say. "So where would you recommend we stay?"

She straightens some stuff on the counter and still doesn't look at me. "A lot of people stay at the youth hostel out at Fort Mason in the City," she says. "Over here, everything is more expensive."

I show the hand-drawn poster advertising the Victorian in Oakland to the girl and ask her, "Know where this house is?"

She looks me in the eyes for the first time and there's even a hint of a smile on her lips. "Why do you want to stay there?" she asks.

I tell her the truth. "It's the only place that rents by the week."

Her expression changes and she says, "It's in a bad neighborhood."

"You know the house?" I ask.

She looks away from me again and says, "Yeah. I live there."

"Why, is the house nice?" I ask her.

"No," she says, "but it's cheap and the bedrooms are big."

Alex gives me the Big Stink Eye, but I keep looking at the girl. "Sounds good," I tell her, and I catch her eyes and hold them for a second.

"It's actually Elroy's house," she says. "You'll have to talk to him."

She shoves the phone over the counter to me. "You better call and see if somebody else already got it."

Alex gives me a shin kick, but I ignore him and ask the girl, "What's your name?"

"Nikki," she says.

I call this guy Elroy and he sounds straight enough, asking for a week's deposit and rent in advance, nothing else, and I agree to take a look at the place this afternoon.

Then I ask Nikki, "Want a ride home after your shift? We have to look at the place anyway."

She hesitates for a few seconds and then says, "Okay."

Alex drags me outside and says in a salty voice, "See what I mean? You decide everything by yourself."

"It's cheap," I tell him. "The cheapest. If it's griff, we'll drive over to Ess Eff tomorrow."

Alex cools off, and since Nikki's shift ends at six, we cruise up and down Telegraph for a few hours, looking at all the lapis lazuli women in the coffeehouses and bookstores. So many beautiful girls, it's hang-tongue city. Alex doesn't say anything else about San Francisco, and I'm relieved.

At six we pick up Nikki and she directs us through Berkeley down to West Oakland. The neighborhood starts turning gritty. Dead warehouses with empty parking lots, really old narrow two-story houses with peeling paint, and corner liquor stores with Af-Am guys standing around in front. As the streets begin to look tougher, Alex gives me the Stink Eye again, the "What have you got us into this time?" look.

So we roll up to a tall two-story Victorian with gingerbread trim that could use some paint. From the street it looks okay, no worse than the other houses. The street's a ghetto, but it's not a bunch of stucco boxes. All the houses are narrow gingerbready Victorians, ancient cribs with steep roofs and lots of trim. Half the houses across the street are painted bright yellow and green, and then others are just old. Some have nice flowers in front, and then some look like a stick of dynamite is the only improvement that would work. I see some Asians in the brightly painted houses, and Af-Am and Hispanic people on our side of the street.

We walk up the steps, and I spock that "Oaktown Rules" has been painted really weirdly on the front door, and heavy steel window guards have been bolted over the windows. The steel rods have been welded together during amateur hour, and the rusty bars make the house look like a jail. The bolts attaching the window guards to the walls are the long kind with big, fat heads, and there's two big deadbolt locks on the front door.

198

Nikki fumbles with her keys and then the door suddenly swings open. A tall baby-faced white guy with glasses and a short haircut is standing there, but he doesn't say anything.

"Hi, Elroy," Nikki says.

"Hi, we're Daz and Alex," I say, and we shake hands.

To break the ice with Elroy I ask, "What's with the locks? Is this a high-crime area or something?" and I'm saying this as a joke because this neighborhood is tombstone territory; there are projects close by. It's the kind of place where guys don't make history, they *are* history.

So he says, "These protect *them* from *us*."

Elroy looks straight, but his smile tells me he's a little frittata. He has short neat brown hair, business-major glasses, and a college boy outfit, jeans and sweatshirt. He looks like the kind of boy, and I say boy because he looks our age even though he must be twenty-five, that mothers would trust their daughters to. I find out soon enough that that's a big, big mistake, Mom.

I point to the industrial-strength window guards, the ones that look like they were made by the high school shop class after hours when everyone was totally napalmed, and I ask, "Elroy, you wouldn't be thinking that somebody would try to remove these, would you?"

And he answers, "I don't think so, Daz. I tried to rip them out with a three-quarter ton pick-up and a one-inch chain, and the whole house moved off the foundation an inch-and-a-half. See?" And he points down below the porch to where the house sits on the ground. I figure the guy is torqueing me, but I find out later from Nikki that he really did hook up a truck and try to yank off the weird window guards.

Elroy likes to be specific. Everything is an inch-and-a-half, or three-quarters of a cup, or whatever. I guess its because he's studying for an MBA at Berkeley. I tell him, "Nikki says you're studying business," and he says, "To be a good narc nowadays you gotta have an MBA."

"So you wanna be a narc?" I ask. He smiles and says, "Either that or a dealer. Either way, you need the MBA."

Nikki shows us the house and it's furnished like the standard college crib—torn old couch, cinder block and one-by-twelve shelving, and posters on the walls. But Elroy doesn't let us get too cozy. After he shows us the big bedroom we get to use upstairs, he says, "Do you have any money to chip into the housekeeping pot?" We look at each other and I know we're both thinking about saving our gitas so I say, "Not really."

He says, "No problem. You can do some chores around the place." I'm relieved and say, "Sure."

"Good," he says. "You can take Fido for a walk."

I've got this funny feeling about Fido, and sure enough Fido is an attack German Shepherd, with eyes that tell you he'd prefer ripping your throat out over being patted behind the ears.

"He's a surplus police dog," Elroy explains. "Some criminal sprayed Mace in his eyes so he lost about 75% of his vision. His sense of smell is quite acute, however, so he's very good in the dark." Elroy pats the dog's huge head and says, "He's very well-trained."

No booga-booga, I felt like saying. Trained to rip your face off. "Why do you keep him in the basement?" I ask.

"Too much light hurts his eyes, or so I was told," says Elroy.

"So we just take him around the block?" I ask.

"Yeah, just walk around the neighborhood so he can stretch his legs and relieve himself," Elroy says. "We try to be good neighbors, so take the pooper scooper with you. It's over there in the corner."

"What happened to the guy with the Mace, Elroy?" Alex asks.

He pats Fido's head gently and says, "I don't think he did too well."

Alex's Hawaiian blood gives him a natural affinity with dogs, so he is totally confident about winning this animal's affection and trust. He goes up and reaches out to pat Fido's head when a warning growl makes him think twice.

Elroy tells us to extend our hands so Fido can smell us and get used to our scent. I'm scared that I'll only have one hand after this so I put out my left hand. I'm silently praying, please God, don't let this dog bite my hand off. The dog sniffs us, we survive that encounter, and then Elroy says we should feed him to cement the bond.

This is also typical of Elroy. Everything is a major production. Walk the dog? No problem, right? Wrongo boyo. It requires training in how to command an attack dog, the proper use of the pooper scooper, and a number of other details.

"Just remember to use the command 'heel,'" says Elroy. "Fido will obey a limited number of commands to the death." Great, I think. Kill, maim, and bark are probably the commands.

Elroy leads us to an old fridge in the corner, opens the door, and takes out fresh hamburger meat. "Fido prefers low-fat sirloin," he says, and in answer to the obvious question, "Why feed this expensive food to a damn dog?", he says, "Fido is an important member of our family." I'm thinking, spike, our fifty bucks rent will barely feed this hell-mutt for a week.

So we take the meat out of the package, and put it in Fido's bowl, which is cleaner than most bowls humans eat out of. Elroy instructs us to pet him as he ravenously swallows huge chunks of the raw hamburger, and even though this is contrary to everything I've been told about dogs, I'm beginning to think this will be okay because Fido doesn't growl or jink when we pet him.

Fido finishes the food, laps some water, and is ready for his walk. Elroy fastens the leather collar and leash on the dog, and we proceed upstairs to the afternoon light.

"Have fun," Elroy says and I think, why not? It's just walking a dog. No big deal. Sure, the neighborhood is tough but what the hell, it always turns out okay as long as you don't give other people any griff.

I walk through the little wood gate to the sidewalk, and I turn my head to Alex and say, "Hey, if the dog's eyes are bad maybe we should get little Ray-Bans for him," when the dog barks once and just leaps forward like he's fuel-injected.

The dog's lunge rips the leash out of my hand, and he's running like a panther, low and fast, toward some kids playing on the sidewalk about fifty yards ahead.

"Oh my God," I say, "he's gonna nail the kids!" I start running after him. I am totally, and I mean totally, cattiwompus. The dog is clearly in the attack mode, running like his life depended on it, and Alex says, "Damn!" and takes off ahead of me.

But even as fast as Alex is there's no way he's going to catch the hell-hound before it drills the kids. In a flash, I see the whole scene unfolding. The dog chomps the kids, the mothers scream, the men grab their guns, and we're murdered on the street with this stupid damned dog that should have been shot a long time ago, along with his crazy owner Elroy.

It's like seeing a plane crash in a movie, only this is real, the way the dog is running smooth and lean, the kids looking up with complete terror in their eyes, their little arms frozen by the sight of this attack dog running right at them, and my inability to do a damned thing about it except run after the dog shouting, "Heel, damn you, heel!"

I figure it's all over, the kids will be dusted, and it's my fault because the dog is right up to them. And then the damndest thing happens. The dog just runs right past the kids, screeches to a halt in front of a tree about ten yards beyond the kids, and starts barking and leaping up the tree. We run up huffing and puffing, and the dog ignores us and keeps trying to jump up the tree.

"Must be a cat," says Alex, but there's nothing in the tree. It's empty of everything but leaves. The damn dog has gone nuts over God knows what.

"Maybe a cat was there earlier," I say, and Alex agrees that must be it. The damned dog is so blind it can't tell if the cat is still there or not.

So Alex wraps the leash around his hand about fifty times and tugs on it really hard and says, "Okay, Fido, now you're listening to me." And we proceed with our dog walk.

# CHAPTER TWENTY-FOUR

The next morning is a Saturday, so Nikki offers to be our guide for the day in San Francisco. Alex shrugs and I'm ditti-wom-ditti, just staring all goo-goo eyed at her nectar face and body, and trying not to smile too stupidly. She goes upstairs to get ready and Alex and I grind some corn flakes she shared with us. The other two guys that live here, long-hair computer munchkins, have already gone to work. There's a knock on the door so I get it.

It's two Oakland cops. I'm fricative because I think it's about Fido's blitzkrieg yesterday, but the Af-Am cop with the shades says, "We'd like to speak to Elroy Wilkins."

Elroy told us to use this warning system. If it's somebody we don't know, we're supposed to say, "We got guests." If we know them then we say, "We got visitors." So what do you say about cops? I yell upstairs, "Hey, Elroy, there's some policemen down here for you."

Elroy comes down the steps in his study-hall glasses and pressed shirt, and I see the cops shift just a little. Welcome to the club, I'm thinking. Elroy surprises everybody, one way or another.

"Mr. Wilkins, we're here to ask you about your automatic weapon," the cop with shades says.

Elroy looks mystified and tells him, "I think there's been a mistake, Officer. I don't own any automatic weapons."

"You own the vehicle in the driveway, don't you?" the cop asks. Elroy nods. "Yes, officer. The Crown Victoria is mine."

The cops exchange a quick glance, because this is the same model the cops buy, except they get the big engines.

"We have a report that someone in your car was waving an automatic rifle-type weapon on the freeway last Friday at a Volvo station wagon," the young cop says.

Elroy knits his brows like he's in calculus class and says, "Maybe somebody took my car on a joyride."

The cop in shades, the one who gets to play "bad cop," says, "We have witnesses here in the neighborhood who saw you leaving in the vehicle Friday afternoon."

Elroy nods politely and says, "That's right. I went to pick up my nephew."

The cops are waiting for him to go on, but he just stands there.

"What about the gun, Mr. Wilkins? We have a search warrant."

"Be my guest," he says, waving his arm around the living room. He snaps his fingers and smiles. "Oh my goodness. I think I know what happened. Emmett must have been playing around with his toy gun."

He walks over to the coat closet in the entry and rummages around on the floor. Then he pulls out a plastic M-16 toy gun and hands it to the cops. "I had to take it away from him," Elroy says. "He was getting too wound up playing with it."

The cops examine the toy gun, which looks pretty realistic to me. "They don't make these anymore," Shades says.

"Yeah, I bought it for him some time ago," Elroy says.

"Waving a gun at somebody is a felony," Shades says.

"I'm really sorry," Elroy says. "I wasn't keeping my eye on Emmett. He probably pointed it at someone." He looks pained and says, "I'm extremely upset."

"Mind if we look around?" the young one asks.

"Please do," Elroy says, and then asks, "Can I get you some coffee?"

"No thanks," Shades replies kind of stiffly, and they tour the house. When they come back down the stairs Shades says, "Mr. Wilkins, you're the registered owner of two handguns."

Elroy smiles politely, and I can tell the cops are thinking he's lying about the M-16. I've only seen Elroy in action for a few hours, but I'm thinking he probably enjoys looking like he's lying even when he isn't.

"Yes, Officer. I think you can see why." Then he waves toward the street.

The cops run out of things to ask Elroy and they leave. Elroy watches them drive off and says, "That was exciting," and I'm blown flat that he enjoys getting grilled by cops.

"Alex and Daz, I need to show you something," he says, and he starts up the steps. Alex gives me the "Now what?" look, and I have to shrug. Alex is already salty that we're staying here instead of San Francisco, and it won't take much to put him over the edge.

Elroy leads us into his room, which has art posters on the walls and a big red-and-dark blue Oriental rug on the floor. He pulls the rug away from in front of a big dresser, opens up his Swiss Army knife and pokes the blade in between two of the floor boards. A whole section of planks lifts out and my heart starts pumping fast because there's an M-16 laying in there, all oiled and ready to go.

He takes it out very gently and hands it to Alex. "It's not very heavy, is it?" he says, and his eyes are glowing happy like it's Christmas Eve. Alex hands it to me, but I don't think it's that light. It scares me to even hold it, so I give it back to Elroy. He's kneeling and he lays it flat in his lap. "Here's the safety," he says, pointing to a little catch. "If something bad happens and you need this, don't forget to click off the safety." He turns it off and I'm even more scared because there's a clip in the gun, and if he pulls the trigger, it's live.

"I bought one of those mail-order plates that turns it back into an automatic," he says. "It's amazing on full auto. Just *brrraapp*, and the clip's empty."

He lowers the gun back into the floor like he's putting a baby in a crib, and then puts the cover back on his secret hideaway. He looks up at us with a serious look on his face. "You see, I own this house," he says. "I have to protect my property."

I nod at him, like sure, pal, and he adjusts his glasses. "That Volvo driver was disrespectful," he says. "I notice they often are. I decided to teach the Volvo driver to show some respect." He smiles very slightly. "I believe I did."

I smile and nod at Elroy and then Alex drags me to our room. He stuffs his clothes in his bag and snaps out, "You want to stay here, go ahead, bruddah. I'm going to San Francisco."

I feel instant torque and say, "Fine."

He zips his bag closed real hard and snorts, "You want to get in her pants so bad it's a joke."

"You're lipping griff," I say, but we both know he's right.

He shakes his head and says, "Forget the fake innocent act, man. Stay here and prong her. It's okay with me. But I get the car."

The way he says it doesn't leave me much choice. "This is the ghetto, pal. How do I get around?" I ask.

He shrugs. "All I know is I'm not staying here."

"You're torqued because I like her, is that it?" I ask him, and I'm starting to feel bent myself.

He says, "No, I'm torqued because you didn't even ask me if I liked this place."

I'm stuck because he's right; I didn't ask him. I saw Nikki and she's all I've been thinking about ever since.

I give up and tell him, "Okay, take the car. Just come back in a week and pick me up."

He looks disgusted and says, "A week? Check your tongue, Daz. It's dusty, brah, from one look at her ass."

"She'll probably jink me," I say, shrugging, and I mean it.

He doesn't say anything, just picks up his bag and we leave. Nikki's waiting in the hallway for us, and I figure she's heard the whole conversation even if she doesn't show it. She's dressed in tight black jeans and a loose black blouse with red buttons, and I can't take my eyes off her face. She's wearing eyeliner and red lipstick and her shades are hanging off the front of her blouse.

Alex says, "I want to go to that youth hostel you told us about."

Nikki is as stone-faced as usual and says, "Sure. Let's go."

It's a cloudless sky, nectar Pacific, the salt air on the way across the Bay Bridge is cold and fresh, and normally I'd be all excited about the day. But nobody says anything, so the shiny downtown towers and the orange spider-web Golden Gate Bridge at the mouth of the Bay are all wasted. We pass the downtown and get off the freeway. Nikki gives Alex brief directions every once in a while. I'm thinking, fricking Alex. Why do you have to frag a strat day?

We stop-and-start our way through about fifty stoplights, but the cool air coming off the Pacific takes the pressure off the choked traffic, and I just spock the jimmy-jammy buildings crammed together along every street and up every hill. We drop over a crest and head down toward a slice of green park on the edge of the Bay. The sight of blue water and the Golden Gate Bridge confuse me because I thought we were going toward the ocean, not the Bay, but then San Francisco's streets don't make any sense, and unless you're on a hill, you can't see anything to orient yourself.

The park and the grass turn out to be Fort Mason. It's not really a fort, just a bunch of one-story white buildings scattered around a big lawn. Alex parks the Cruiser and I start to get out to go with him to the youth hostel office, but he waves me off.

Nikki's in the back seat, looking out the window. I turn around, but she doesn't look at me. "Maybe you should stay with him," she says quietly.

"He's just mad because I didn't ask him about your house," I mumble.

"It's a lot nicer over here," she says, but there's no conviction in her voice. I can't see her eyes behind the shades, but her red lips are shaking me loose inside.

"I'm sure it is," I tell her. We sit silently until Alex comes out again. He just leans against the hood and spocks the Bay. We're three statues, all part of some rhomboid sculpture, until Nikki gets out and goes over to Alex. She points to some hills back in the city and says, "It's nice up there. Want to go?"

Alex shrugs, like "Who cares what happens today?" and Nikki gets back in the car. Alex slips behind the wheel, starts the Cruiser, and then eases into the traffic.

The first hill is so steep that I'm worried the Lancer might not make it, but we top out and pull over next to some fancy mansions. Nikki points to a tall round monument on another hill across the city. "That's Coitus Tower," she says flatly.

"No," I protest, but I'm thinking, hey, this is San Francisco.

"See how it looks like a fire hose?" she asks. "It was built by a rich woman who liked to screw firemen."

I'm blown flat and then she laughs, the first time ever. "Not really. The part about the fire hose is true, but she built it to honor the firemen who saved her life when she was a kid. Good old Mrs. Coit." Then she leans over the front seat and I smell her perfume for the first time. "You can climb up inside it," she says. "Want to check it out?"

Alex doesn't say anything but he starts the car and heads down the hill. It's as steep as a ski run, and now I'm worried about the

Lancer's brakes, which are screeching and putting off that chem-ical-hot smell of burning brake pads. Morris had said the shoes were getting thin, but they hold up okay and the mansions disap-pear and we're passing small stucco apartments perched on forty-five-degree angles. We're almost to the bottom of the hill when Nikki suddenly shouts, "Stop!" and I freeze, like Jeez, is it the cops? She points through the windshield and yells, "That parking place! Get it!"

I can't see why she's launching a mojo but Alex spins into a driveway, turns around and pulls into the spot.

God, this is incredible," she says, and I notice her voice is sweet when she's excited. "A parking place near Chinatown on a weekend! I'm *never* this lucky."

I point to Alex. "It's him. He's lucky at everything." I leave out the part about him being mostly lucky at getting us into major griff.

We get out and Nikki leads us into Chinatown. The streets are grooving with people, mostly Asians and a scattering of sunburned Mr. and Mrs. Jones, freezing in their matching shorts. All the narrow little stores have bright red or yellow signs in Chinese and English, and tourist crap or veggies and fruit stacked up outside, so it's even more crowded because these tables take up most of the sidewalk, and half the people have stopped to feel cantaloupes or spock the cheap T-shirts and dribby souvenirs.

The other half are crossing the street between the cars which are semi-permanently parked there, because when the lights change, then a mass of pedestrians pushes into the streets, and the rental cars are stuck in front of the locals' Caddies and Mercedes, which are honking at them to just run over the people like they do.

As soon as Mr. Jones goes loco-moco in the confusion and turns down a one-way street in his rental Taurus, then a delivery truck double-parks, and scrawny guys in dirty undershirts appear out of nowhere and start unloading crates of broccoli. The Caddies and Mercedes folks lean on their horns, but then you have to think, why do these numbnut locals try to drive through Chinatown in the first place? They deserve the aggravation as sort of a Morris's Stupid Tax.

We're walking along, spocking the scenes and the people, and I notice that a smell, a combination of exhaust, sour garbage, and beef-and-tomato-over-rice drifts through every storefront, whether it's a bakery or a hardware store or a restaurant.

Nikki pulls us down a side street and into this little restaurant which is maybe ten feet wide. It's more like a stall because a long counter with warming trays and a stove only leaves about three feet for the customers. If you squeeze past everybody waiting to order, then you see one little dinette table in the back corner. A portable plastic crib takes up the whole table and a boy about ten is half-watching the baby inside wave a yellow plastic ring through the air. The two women working behind the counter look tired, and they're sweating in the hot greasy air coming off the wok and the warmers.

"You guys have got to try the char siu bow here," Nikki says, and she buys these rounded white buns.

"Manapua," Alex tell her.

She hands him one. "That's what they call these in Hawaii, right?" She smiles and for the first time I see her small white teeth. She looks expectantly up at Alex, and he wolfs down the bun and the sticky red pork meat inside with his usual look of concentration and nods grudgingly.

"Good, huh?" she says, and I see the smile in her eyes and I suddenly want to choke Alex to death right here because I don't want Nikki to fall for him. She turns to give me one and her smile doesn't fade.

"You like it?" she asks, and I nod. When the sun catches her eyes just right they're a deep iridescent brown that makes me dizzy. I'm thinking, I'll just go off and die if she goes for Alex, and her expression darkens.

"What's wrong?" she asks me.

"Nothing. It's great, " I say, faking it, and she smiles again.

"Are you Chinese?" I ask, and she says, "Only for the food. Let's go to this other place." She's almost skipping she's so energetic, and I realize that she loves showing us around so much that she's forgotten about her cold tough-girl act.

She leads us through the cute little Chinese girls in pink dresses with ribbons in their hair, the bent-over old Chinese women clutching plastic shopping bags, and the glassy-eyed fat white people with "I'm on Mars" expressions to this narrow alley stuck between rows of old buildings.

There's bright yellow and red balcony railings above some little sewing shops and a fortune cookie factory, and since the alley's not even wide enough for a car, the strip of asphalt is empty except for a middle-aged Chinese woman walking her little terrier. As we're walking underneath these balconies, I'm wishing I had our camera because the colors are so bright against the dingy old bricks and stained concrete of the alley. It reminds me of the Laotian houses in our "Oaktown rules" neighborhood. Plus there's big double doors open behind these balconies, with Chinese characters and tile decorations, and little green and yellow flags are hanging from long poles above the doors. The alley's too narrow for us to step back and look inside, so it's like there's a grimy sweatshop world on the first floor, and a tropo-electric, half-hidden color-world right above the gray, fourteen-hour-workday one.

As we get to the end of the alley, I hear all these little hard slapping sounds coming from one of the balcony doors above us, and I ask Nikki if they're making something up there. She laughs and says, "No, it's just old women playing Mah Jongg." She can see I'm drawing a blank, so she explains, "It's a game sort of like dominos. You slap your tiles down before the other players to win."

"You know how to play?" I ask her.

She shakes her head no and says, "It's boring."

We turn onto a main street and Nikki guides us past a few shops to an open staircase. At first I think it's some sort of basement temple, because the first thing we see is a bright-red lacquer altar with burning incense sticks. Then I spock that the altar's in a big niche off a landing, and the staircase turns to the right. We follow her down and come out in a small restaurant with a bar counter and about a dozen tables. There's no natural light except a dim glow from the stairwell, and the fluorescent tubes hanging off the sagging acoustic tiles make everything look like midnight. But the place is pretty crowded and there's no tourists, so I figure the food makes up for the less-than-tropo look.

Nikki sits us down at a table in the middle by a steel post, and I'm happy because there's a big mirror in front of the counter, so I can look at her without her noticing.

I'm worried about the gitas but Nikki says, "This is my treat," and she orders for us. The waiter speaks Chinese to her, but she

210

shakes her head and says, "Sorry. I only speak English." He takes this in stride, scribbles down the order, and heads into the kitchen. When he comes back out, he stops by the register to talk to the owner or manager. The guy's wearing a black long-sleeve shirt with chunky gold cufflinks that remind me of Vegas. The owner is checking us out, and I guess it's because we're the only non-Chinese guys in the place. Either that, or he's goo-goo eyed over Nikki, because she is incredibly strat with her big-beach eyes and nectar face, and incredibly sexy in her tight black jeans. Her shades are dangling off the second red button of her black blouse because the top one is unbuttoned, and I can't help looking above her shades and noticing the lacey edge of her black bra and her smooth skin.

While we're waiting for the food nobody says much, and so in between staring at Nikki in the mirror I'm spocking the other customers. Right next to us, an old Chinese lady finishes grinding and opens her purse to pay. She gets a crumpled paper bag and pulls out the biggest roll of gitas I've ever seen—even Alex's paw could barely get around it—and slips off the fat rubber band around the roll. She quickly riffs through the bills and peels off a ten from what must be at least a hundred Jacksons, with maybe a few Lincolns mixed in for flavor.

Then the Chinese lady we saw walking her dog comes down the stairs, the pooch tucked under her arm, and sits down with some other ladies at a corner table. The mutt sits quietly in her lap, accepting the occasional treat from her plate, and nobody seems to notice or care.

A few minutes later the waiter brings out huge platters of noodles, a kind of sizzling shrimp, and a veggie dish, and Nikki serves me first and then Alex.

"This is salt-and-pepper shrimp, and this is oyster sauce noodles," she says. "It's *so* good." Alex seems to have forgotten about being griffed because he has that look of total concentration he gets when there's good grinds on the table. I'm relieved that he's not staring at Nikki like I am. Her eyes are sparkling and her lips are so kissable, especially after she wipes her lipstick off on her napkin.

Alex vacuums the noodles, and I can tell that he's impressed. Nikki pays and then buys three incense sticks from Mr. Vegas at the front counter. She hands one to each of us and we stop at the altar on the way out. She shows us how to light them off another stick and then she kneels down, puts hers on the altar, and bows with her hands together. "You don't have to kneel," she whispers, but I try to act respectful by at least bowing a little after I light my incense and put it next to hers. Alex makes a full deep bow like he does to his kung fu master, and I hope he's not trying to impress Nikki.

Then she takes us out of Chinatown and across the street into North Beach, the old Beatnik hangout. The place is gimpy with Italian delis and restaurants and bakeries, and people are groving into all of them to spend big dollars and look cool over double lattes and on-tap Anchor Steam brewkowskis.

A big park next to the main drag spreads out the only grass within a couple of miles, and street people, families, and couples holding hands are sitting on the lawn watching a wedding party come out of a massively ornate Catholic Church that sits right against the park.

It's an epic, like a movie wedding. The bridesmaids all have matching pink dresses, and the groom's pals are all penguins. The bride is wearing this gigantia white Scarlett O'Hara dress with frills and lace, and she looks good enough to eat as she comes down the stone steps on her hubby's arm. She comes down real carefully, and I realize it's because her fluffy parachute dress covers about a quarter acre and she can't see the stairs.

The newlyweds finally make it to the sidewalk, and I'm blown down that people still go to all this trouble to get married. They smile and wave to everybody, climb into a waiting white stretch limo, and haul derriere.

Alex and I walk alongside the park, spocking the weirdbeards throwing a frisbee and the couples making out. Nikki's about a block ahead, motioning us to hurry up. She darts inside a store, which turns out to be an Italian bakery with two grandmotherly types behind a glass counter stuffed with tropo cookies and frew-frew goodies. We vector inside and Nikki's already at the counter buying three huge fluffy pastries dusted with powdered sugar. I'm stuffed already, but it looks so good I eat it anyway.

212

"This is the best," she says. After she takes a big bite of hers, there's powdered sugar all around her mouth and I wish I could kiss her right then.

Coitus Tower is looming right above us and we trudge up the hill to it. It costs a few gitas to get in, but the view and the paintings are worth it. The whole inside is painted with murals from the '30s, in that workingman style where everybody is real muscular and heavy and dressed like they've just joined the Communist Youth Brigade to dig a hundred-mile ditch by hand.

Once we reach the top we stop to cool off in the breeze, which feels like it just came off a glacier. The whole city and bay is spread out below us. We spock the Bay Bridge, Berkeley, and downtown Ess Eff, which looks like they took all the skyscrapers in Manhattan, steam-cleaned them and then crammed them into about eight square blocks. After a few minutes I'm shivering in my T-shirt and we climb down and walk back toward the car.

We're waiting to cross the main drag between North Beach and Chinatown when I hear this bell ringing like crazy and one of those cutesy little cable cars rattles down heading for Fisherman's Wharf. Nikki grabs us and says, "Come on." I'm thinking, this is so hokey, forget it, but she jumps on the cable car and stands in front of the people sitting on the benches, and we take up the spots on either side of her. I'm pushed against her side by the guy standing next to me, and she doesn't try to pull away. It feels so good to touch her, even if it's just our hips.

I look over at Alex and I see that he's trying not to touch Nikki; he's keeping a little space between them, and I forgive him everything in that moment, even that time he drove off and left me in that dogmeat gas station. He doesn't see me looking at him, and Nikki is oblivious, too. I'm holding the cold steel railing, but all I feel is the warmth of her body through our clothes.

# CHAPTER TWENTY-FIVE

My room in the "Oaktown rules" house has a really high ceiling and a fancy molding where the wall and ceiling meet. I'm laying on my sleeping bag, staring up at this molding and the cracks in the plaster, and thinking how mambo it is to have the whole room to myself, to not have Alex around, either ozoned with a wadded-up shirt over his head or studying a map or sprawled out reading. It's like somebody rearranging the stuff in your room while you're away. When you come back everything's still ordinary, but you feel katakana, and I wonder if Alex feels like this, too.

And the Lancer's gone. It should be outside, gassed up and ready to haul chili with the ice chest, comic books, and boxes of crackers in the trunk with Old Man Ching's journal on the dash, the primed fender sticking out like a sore thumb from the puke-green body, but it's not, and that seems alienated, too.

Nikki has to work on Sunday, so I get up early to see if I can go in with her. Elroy and the computer munchkins are still sleeping so the house is quiet; even Fido the nuthouse dog is ozoned. Nikki's got the corner bedroom down the hall, so I go to her door and listen, but I don't hear any rustling inside. I've already spocked her room from the front yard, trying to see inside, but she always keeps her thin white curtains drawn and her door closed tight. Plus, there's a shiny deadbolt lock just to make sure nobody pokes around when she's gone. I knock real quietly, but she doesn't come out, so I creep down the stairs, trying not to make them creak, and then edge through the dining room to peek in the kitchen.

Nikki's sitting at the little pink formica dinette table, dressed for work in a white shirt and black jeans, reading *Parade* maga-zine, and it's the first time I see her wearing glasses. Her hair is pinned up on her head with chopsticks and she looks so studious and cool and gorgeous in her round glasses and red lipstick.

214

The teapot on the big old white stove starts whistling, and she gets up, turns off the burner, and starts making a cup of tea. I can't just keep staring at her secretly so I cough to announce myself and go in.

She looks up from the counter for a second and asks me without smiling, "Want some tea?"

I say, "Sure," and she takes down another mug, tears open a little red foil packet, and pours some brown crystals into the mug.

"What kind of tea is that?" I ask.

She pours hot water into both cups and says, "Ginseng. It's supposed to give you energy."

I take the mug, sip the tea, expecting the worst, but it's not too bad, just sort of an herby flavor. We stand there awkwardly for a minute and I glance over at the *Parade* magazine and remember Morris.

"Ever hear about the Stupid Tax?" I ask her.

She looks at me flatly, no grin, and says, "No."

So I tell her about the dumb plates advertised in *Parade* and Morris's Stupid Tax. She doesn't say anything, and I'm thinking, great, she hates my sense of humor, forget the whole thing.

She puts the corn flakes box, milk, and two glass bowls on the table, and we sit down to breakfast. She pours herself some cereal, shoots me a quick glance, and then sloshes some milk over the flakes. "Why are you staying here instead of with your friend?" she asks, and sweat pops out on my forehead like I'm humping sheetrock because I'm thinking, okay, just lie and say you like Berkeley better than Ess Eff, but I'm a crappy liar so I know that line is going nowhere. In desperation, I tell her the truth.

"Because I like you," I say, and it's unbelievable how hard it is to say these four simple words.

She takes a bite of corn flakes and stares a hole in the cereal box. There's a steel grip on my throat while I wait for her to say something, anything.

"I don't want a boyfriend," she says, and her voice tries to stay flat, but some tension leaks over the top anyway.

"I just said I liked you," I say defensively. "I didn't ask you to get married."

She gives me a funny look and says, "Actually, that might be kind of fun."

I've got no smartass answer to this and I think, why do I always like the ones orbiting Pluto? "You want me to leave?" I ask.

"No," she says. "It's a free country."

Yeah, I'm thinking, we're all free to go la-la for some lapis lazuli girl, and she's free to freeze us off. I have a bad feeling and realize I don't even know what I want with Nikki. I just like looking at her. Real deep, pal, I tell myself. You're just like those jocks you always make fun of.

I sip my tea and think that maybe this is what Morris was talking about when he was riffing on how sometimes nothing seems to work right. Nikki finishes her cereal and goes to her room. I want to kiss her at least once before I leave, but it seems stupid now. I'm thinking, I'm always so gimpy, always thinking some girl likes me just because I like her. What a jank that it never works out like that.

Nikki comes back a few minutes later and leans against the door jamb. She's not wearing glasses anymore, so I figure she put on contacts. She says, of course without really looking at me, "Want to come to Telegraph with me?"

I try not to look too overjoyed and then say, "Sure," and it's better than I thought because I get to ride on her motorscooter, put my arms around her waist, and hold her real tight the whole way. She doesn't complain, and I wish we were going across the whole country instead of a few miles of Oaktown.

She locks her bike behind the bakery and then tells me, "My lunch break starts at one." I nod and watch her walk away and she's got the nicest ass I've ever seen. I realize Alex is right, my tongue is hanging to the ground. This is ridiculous, I say to myself, and try to get on with my business.

I get a large cup of coffee at an empty café and just spock the deserted Twilight Zone avenue outside. It gives me a strange feeling to see nobody around except a few bums curled up in doorways and the first vendors setting up their T-shirt and pottery stands. It's so quiet that it's hard to remember that both sidewalks had been choked with punks begging for spare change and students checking out the jewelry stalls, and every third person was holding a huge slice of pizza on wax paper, trying not to let all the cheese slip off onto the pavement.

I sit there thinking about Nikki until the drug store down the street that's offering a "two for one" print deal opens. I drop off the few rolls of film we took and pay extra to have it done by noon. Then I spend the rest of the morning wandering around the bookstores, trying not to get that crick in your neck that comes from leaning sideways to read titles. People start drifting onto the avenue for coffee and bagels, and by noon it's as crowded as when I first saw it.

At one sharp I pick up Nikki and we go to this place that serves huge salads for a couple of gitas. We get a corner table by the front window, and start grinding a gigantia bowl of salad and the small loaf of whole-wheat bread that comes with it.

I hand her a piece of the bread and ask her, "What's the gig with boyfriends? You have a bad experience with your last one?"

She looks out the window at all the oddbot people passing by, the teenagers trying to be walla-walla, the balding graduate students, and the couples hanging on each other and says, almost as a matter of pride, "I've never had a boyfriend."

"Girlfriend, then?" I ask, because you never know.

She smiles at this and says, "Not the way you mean." Then she gives me a sideways glance and says, "How about you? Some sweet little thing waiting for you in L.A.?"

"No," I say. "I'm like you, nolo contendere."

She lets this pass and I can't tell what she's thinking. Her half-hour lunch break goes by fast and we go back to the bakery. Then I pick up the photos, vector to an upstairs table in a big café across from Moe's used bookstore, and go through them, quickly and then again, slowly. There's not many, and I wish we'd taken some shots of Morris's shop and Tita's apartment and Benny's weird expressions and the old abandoned house we found in Kansas. I wish Alex's digital camera hadn't ended up at the bottom of that canyon in the Rockies, but the goofy pics inside were as lost as the photos we never took at all.

Instead, there's only shots from the few times one of us remembered the camera, stupid photos I took of hokey signs we spocked in old towns and Alex waking up looking really booga-booga, the

217

Cruiser in front of a Midwestern-looking coffee shop on the street in New York and on the beach in North Carolina. There's only two shots of Tracie, one of her stancing "tough girl" with her gun, and another of the three of us that a Japanese guy took at the Grand Canyon.

I feel sad looking at the scattered photos, like the trip is already over, but it's not really over. We're still far from home, and Alex and I aren't even together anymore.

I buy some envelopes, paper, and stamps from a drug store across from the U.C. campus and then go to another café, one with a few white plastic chairs on the sidewalk. I buy a mocha with whipped cream and sit down to write some letters. First, I write Morris, and include the duplicate prints of the Cruiser and Alex looking all gorgon because he's still waking up. I want to send him a photo of the Odd Squad, but we never took any. I tell him the Lancer's holding up fine and that we're heading home, and then I don't know what else to say.

I write more letters sending a couple of the dupe prints to Tita and Benny, to Tracie via her aunt in New Mexico, to Ron and Rosalee, and of course to Old Man Ching. I consider mentioning his travel journal, but decide it's better to talk about it in person. I just tell him the car's held up great and we'll be home pretty soon. By the time I've let our parents know we're okay I've got writer's cramp and it's almost quitting time for Nikki.

The next day when I wake up it still feels rhomboid being alone. The walls are bare except for fat cracks in the plaster and the only things in the big room are my black nylon shoulder bag and my sleeping gear. I'm thinking, what am I even doing here, dreaming some oobla-dee fantasy about a girl who's so stone-faced most of the time it's obvious she could care less if I'm around or not.

I go downstairs and try to call Alex at the youth hostel, but the desk clerk says he's already gone out and that worries me. Maybe he vectored for L.A. and just left me here. I head to the kitchen for a Pop Tart, wondering what I should do, and I'm surprised to see Nikki. I figured she'd already left for work, but she's sitting at the big old black dining room table, holding a bright red mug of tea with both hands.

"I'm going to Oakland Chinatown today," she says. "Want to come?"

"Sure," I say, trying not to look too happy, "but what about work?"

She sips the tea and says, "I told them I started my period." She laughs once, almost like a sneeze, and says, "I'll have to remember that when it really does start."

"Why are you going to Chinatown again?" I ask.

"Grocery shopping," she says. "It's got the best vegetables. Cheap, too."

So we vector down there on her motor scooter and there's no tourists, no trinkets or postcards, no Mr. and Mrs. Jones in the rented Buick. It's Asian women dragging neatly dressed brats around to small stores, old Asian guys with wispy beards sitting at round tables in coffee shops talking and filling out California Lottery tickets, lots of steamy little restaurants with glazed ducks hanging in the front window by the takeout counter, and air that smells like barbecued pork and fish stew.

Since each little market stacks its vegetables and fruit right on the sidewalk, I wonder what's to keep somebody from just grabbing a cabbage and spliffing off. I figure what must happen is one of the clerks runs out, whips a durian around like a slingshot, and bounces it off the thief's skull. That will definitely cure anybody's shoplifting habit.

Ever seen a durian fruit? It's about the size of a fat melon, but it's covered with giant thick spikes like a medieval weapon. They're so sharp that you can't even touch the fruit, much less grab one. They come in plastic webbing bags so you can pick them up without your hands getting adiosed. If you got thumped upside the head by one you wouldn't forget it.

Nikki doesn't buy a durian, but she goes into practically every one of these little markets to buy something—vegetables or a bottle of weird black sauce. The aisles are so narrow that I have to hover right behind her to let other people squeeze past. She doesn't seem to notice I'm with her, and that's fine with me because I get to just stare at her while she decides which bundle of green beans she's going to buy.

She's loading me up with plastic bags of veggies and I ask her, "Who's going to eat all this? I never see you grind anything but corn flakes."

Her eyes widen at this challenge and she can't resist a superior little smile. "Tonight I'll cook like my grandmother taught me."

"Oh, you mean corn flakes and vegetables," I say. "Sounds great."

She tries not to smile, but either she can't suppress it or she doesn't really want to. She pokes me lightly in the chest and says, "And you're going to be my prep chef."

"Me and a sharp knife? Better get the paramedics ready," I tell her, and her laugh surprises me because she's been making so sure it doesn't look like she's having fun with me.

We buy the stuff at the counter and then go into the next little market. I'm checking out all the katakana candy, little chewy things made with stuff I've never heard of, like jackfruit, and rectangles of sesame seed candy, and when I turn around Nikki's gone.

At first I figure she's in the back of the store by the cooler, but she isn't. When I go out on the sidewalk, I can't see her, and she's not in the stores on either side. I get this panicky feeling of complete disorientation, like I don't know where I am, I don't know how to get back to the Oaktown Rules house, I don't even have transpo.

It's already one of the worst feelings I've ever had, and then it gets worse because I start wondering if this is Nikki's idea of fun, and that maybe she's left me hanging just for laughs. I'm looking around, realizing I can't remember the first thing about getting home because all I was concentrating on was holding tight to Nikki, and it hits me that I'm really alone here. I'm stuck, brah, really stuck, as Alex would put it, and I try not to let my mind get ahead of reality.

I'm thinking, the stupidest move would be to wander around and get really lost, so I just hang around the front of the market, scanning the sidewalks for Nikki. Suddenly, someone bumps into my back and I spin around to apologize. It's Nikki, and it's obvious my expression surprises the hell out of her because her little grin drops off the planet.

"Thought I left you?" she asks as she takes my arm.

"It did occur to me," I say, and then I tell her the story of Alex leaving me at the gas station for a half-hour just to frap me. She listens and then says, "It's just that I couldn't decide between some things, so I ran back to that store across the street. Sorry."

I'm massively relieved, but I just shrug. We walk a few more blocks and then Nikki drags me down a narrow stairway between two restaurants. The steps are wet and I act like my feet slip so I can grab her shoulder. She grips my arm tight and says, "Don't kill yourself." She holds onto me the rest of the way down and I'm thinking, ha, you're brilliant, Daz.

A fishy smell gets stronger the farther down we go and I see big tanks of lobsters in the dim light at the foot of the stairs. We get to the bottom and the whole narrow little shop is humming and gurgling with circulation pumps and splashing water because gigantia tanks of fish and crabs and even turtles take up almost all the floor space. The strip of floor between the counter and the tanks is covered with water, so they've laid wood planks to walk on so customers don't adios themselves on the slick concrete. I look at the turtles and feel sorry for them in their dark tanks. Nikki goes up to the Asian guy in a stained white apron behind the counter. She takes out her little yellow and red purse, points to the prawns laid out on crushed ice alongside whole catfish, and buys a few handfuls of the most expensive ones. I'm getting dizzy from the smell and the claustrophobia and I'm massively grateful I don't have to work here.

We leave the fish shop and Nikki buys us Vietnamese sandwiches. They're good, crunchy French rolls hollowed out and filled with veggies and meat, but I torch my mouth on the Jalapeno peppers hidden inside the barbecued chicken and have to buy a Coke to kill the burn. Then we walk back to her scooter, and a few minutes later we're buzzing past the Laotians' green-and-yellow Victorians and pulling into our crib's cracked and broken concrete driveway.

While Nikki locks her scooter I look up at her room and wish I could see inside. The corner of the house is pooched out a few feet to make a little square tower with its own cutesy peaked-cap roof, and one of these corner windows is open and the thin curtain is fluttering in the breeze.

221

She sees me spocking her room, but she doesn't say anything. We go up the rickety front steps and stow the food in the kitchen, and then Nikki helps me take Fido for his walk. This time I tie the leash around my waist, figuring worst case, my body rolling and dragging on the concrete will slow him down if he goes into another red-zone attack mode. But the dog doesn't jink us and we get home okay. Since Elroy and the munchkins aren't around, we get the kitchen to ourselves.

The kitchen window has so many layers of paint on it that it doesn't open much, and with the work and the heat of the stove, pretty soon we're both sweating. Nikki shows me how to to peel off a prawn's shell and slice the back to clean out the little thread of sandy black guts, and I'm blown flat that I don't know any of this cooking stuff. She makes a pan of brownies loaded with white chocolate chips and walnuts while I slice up onions, green beans, and a red bell pepper.

We don't talk much during the prep. I'm just trying to mince the garlic and grate the chunk of fresh ginger with this little bamboo grater the way she showed me so I won't embarrass myself. While she strips the strings off of the Chinese peas, I steal glances at her. We're working side by side at the old cracked ceramic tile counter, and I'm glad she set me up right next to her. I finish the prep, she starts the rice cooker, and we sit down at the pink dinette table to rest.

She cuts a lemon in two and squeezes one half into two tall glasses of ice water and then hands me one. I watch her drink it, her brown face flushed with heat and glistening with sweat, her hair half-falling out of the chopstick hairpins, and it takes all my willpower not to leap up and kiss her. I've never wanted to kiss a girl so much, and I suddenly feel afraid, like maybe this is it, maybe I'm orbiting Venus for real.

"Is this not having a boyfriend gig like being a vegetarian?" I ask her, "Or is it just that you haven't liked anybody that much?"

"You mean do I eat my boyfriends like those spiders do?" she says, and I laugh and feel embarrassed at the connotation. "No, really," I say.

She tilts her head, squints, and says, "Both."

"So yes, it's a principle and yes, you haven't met anyone," I say.

She shifts uncomfortably on the chair and says, "Yeah."

"Well, what's the principle?" I ask. "I don't mean to be Perry Mason. I'm just curious."

She stares at the glass and thinks for a while. Then she tells me, "I've always envied the way that guys meet somebody, sleep with them, and then just walk away."

"What's so wonderful about that?" I ask her.

"There's no suffering," she answers.

"You mean for the guy," I snort.

"No, for the girl, too," she says coldly. "She knows the guy's going to bang her and leave. It keeps things simple."

I spock her hard expression and say, "It doesn't sound so great to me."

She gives me a quick glance and looks down again. "Why? Have you tried it?"

My face is hot with shame, and I tell her, "No, I've always hated that scorecard griff."

She looks all skeptical and asks, "Why?"

"It doesn't go anywhere," I tell her. "It's just like the beer ads and the malls and the rest of the ickabod jank they try to sell you."

She looks puzzled and says, "I don't get it."

"It's the plan," I tell her. I'm kind of torqued by her bogus just-don't-feel-anything attitude. "You're supposed to buy into that 'sex is all there is' griff along with the ads and all the worthless toys they want you to buy. They don't want you to feel anything except sex, because that's what they use to sell you all this crap. If you don't feel anything, you stop hoping. You'll put up with being a gumby, and wasting your whole life paying for all the horsepoo you bought into."

She kind of smirks and says, "So you're a romantic."

I shrug her off. "I don't know what I am," I say. "I just know bullshit when I see it."

This shuts her up and she spins her glass around in the water that's condensed on the glass and dripped down to the pink formica. I'm thinking, okay, you launched that mojo to Pluto, now try to repair the damage.

"I'm sorry I got bent about it," I say.

She pulls the chopsticks out of her hair and lets it fall down the front of her white T-shirt in a shiny black cascade. She divides it into two parts, twists each into thick rough black rope and starts weaving the two pieces into a thick braid. "That's okay," she says without looking at me. "I like what you said." She pulls a gold rubber band out of her pocket and puts it on the end of the braid. Then she looks up at me and asks, "Want to eat?"

I nod, and she goes to the stove and turns the burner on under the greasy black wok pan. Once it's hot she pours a big dollop of corn oil in it. She scrapes the grated garlic and ginger into the sizzling oil, stirring them around with a curved spatula. After a minute or so she empties all the sliced veggies into the wok and mixes them up with quick strokes, just like they do on cooking shows.

When the veggies are all jumbled together, she sprinkles on some of the sauces she bought, throws in some salt and pepper, and mixes it up. When the veggies are done she moves them onto one side of the wok and throws the prawns into the other side. They cook in no time, and she hands me the curved spatula. "Stir while I add this, but not too fast, okay?" She splashes in a corn starch-and-water mixture, and I crank the whole thing around and hope I'm not botching it.

I guess I do okay because she turns off the gas a minute later and says, "Okay, let's eat." Then she scoops the prawns and vegetables off onto a white oval platter with dark-blue Chinese dragons along the edges. I serve us each some rice and then we sit down to eat the way her grandmother taught her.

# CHAPTER TWENTY-SIX

She asks me, "You like it?" and tries to look like she doesn't care one way or the other, but I can tell she does.

"It's the best," I tell her, and she relaxes a little.

"It's not as good as my grandmother's," she says.

For some reason I remember Mrs. Ching and her gray bun of hair and I say, "I'm sure she'd say it is."

Nikki kind of snorts and says, "I doubt it."

"Why, is she a real dragon lady?"

"No," she says, but she doesn't go on, and I figure she doesn't want to lip any griff about her grandma, even if it's true.

After we finish eating I hope there's no ickabod pieces of food stuck between my teeth, and I wonder how I can keep the gig going. I wish I could ask Alex for advice, and then Nikki gives me a sly little grin.

"There's a secret place in this house," she says, and I immediately think of Elroy's oiled M-16 under the floorboards.

"I know," I say, and she frowns at my hoboken expression.

"Why, did Elroy take you up there?" she asks, and I grip that I don't know what she's talking about.

"You mean Elroy's gun, right?" I ask her, and she rolls her eyes. "No, this is a good secret," she says, and stands up. "Come on."

We go up the stairs to the second floor and down to a short door by the bathroom. She opens it, ducks under the low jamb, and clicks on a pull-chain light bulb. Inside is a narrow set of super-steep dark brown steps leading up into the darkness. She disappears up these stairs, using her hands like she's climbing a rock wall. There's a creaking sound, light pours down, and I can see her standing halfway out of a trap door at the top of the stairs.

I follow her through the opening and there's a small deck made of unpainted two-by-fours perched over the old steep-pitched tar paper roof. The last of the day's sun is lighting the hills behind Berkeley and Oakland, and with no railing or tall buildings around to block the view we can see the whole range from north to south.

I don't mind heights as long as there's something to hold onto, but this setup makes me feel a little oojie. I crouch down and sit cross-legged on the deck and she points to a thin tower way over by the hills. "See? That's the Campanile and the U.C. campus," and then she sees me squatting on the two-by-fours, trying not to look too scared. She giggles and says, "A little scary up here, huh?" and I have to say, "A little," because we're three stories up and it's a real quick ride down the steep roof to the rotted gutter. You'd get a second or two there, hoping it will hold, and of course it doesn't, and then you scream and *thump*, you're laying adiosed on the rockhard dirt in the front yard.

She sits down next to me and I say, "But I like it. Great views."

I'm wondering if she's a little nervous, too, because she's never giggled before, and as she gazes out at the hills, I sneak a glance at her. She looks good enough to eat in her white shirt and black jeans, and I want to undo her thick braid and kiss her real hard. But I'm a coward in more ways than one, so I just watch her eyebrows knit up like she's thinking hard. She turns to me and I look away real fast, as if I wasn't staring all goo-goo eyed at her.

"So tell me about your trip," she says, and I come back to her with, "Okay, but first you have to tell me about your grandmother."

She wraps her arms around her knees and sighs, "It's just the usual boring stuff."

I nudge her. "No, come on, tell me. Is she always criticizing you?"

Nikki is quiet and then she says, "Something like that. But she doesn't mean to."

"Yeah, I know how that goes," I say. She opens up some and tells me about her grandmother, her mom, and a little about her dad and her older sister. I tell her about Mr. and Mrs. Ching and how we got the Cruiser and our time in New York with Benny and Tita.

It doesn't seem like we talk that long, but the sky gets dark, Venus shows up above the horizon, and lights in the houses scattered across the hills come on. I can't see her expression, only her

226

black glossy braid against her white shirt. She seems more comfortable in the dark, and the light from the unbroken streetlamps reflects off her eyes when she looks at me.

"Are you already out of college?" I ask her.

"I wish. No, I've got three more years, and that's if I stay in art. If I switch majors, then it'll be even more."

I try not to sound insulting and say, "Art, huh?"

"Yeah. Pretty worthless, huh?"

"Hey, the more worthless the better," I tell her, and she laughs. "What's your main artistic gig?"

"Painting," she says, and her voice is flat and protective.

"I'd like to see your stuff," I tell her, and I mean it. "Do you have any here?"

"Yeah," and I can tell she can't decide whether to show me or not.

"Don't worry, I won't be critical," I tell her. "I only jink stuff I know about."

Nikki hesitates and then says, "Okay."

We climb down the steep steps and go to her room. She pulls out a key and unlocks the door, and my heart speeds up because I'm actually getting to see her inner sanctum.

Nikki clicks on the light and we go in. It smells faintly of cigarette smoke, and I'd just about forgotten that she smokes because she never does when we're together. The room is larger than mine, kind of bare, and I finally get to see the big windows in the corner and the white gauzy curtains from inside. Her half-made futon is in one corner, next to a concrete block-and-pine board shelf unit that's filled with neatly folded socks and T-shirts. The only other furniture is a narrow little pine bookcase jammed with paperbacks. Her unframed paintings are propped on either side of the bookcase, and like most art-student stuff I've seen, they're big and dark and filled with distorted human faces and weird symbolic shapes. Some crumpled T-shirts and underwear have been tossed in the corner, and I notice that the panties are all black.

I walk over to her closet and pull back the Indian print curtain. "What are you looking for, skeletons?" she asks.

I laugh and say, "No, I'm seeing if you own anything that isn't black." She doesn't have many clothes, and other than a long silvery skirt, a red blouse, and some white work shirts, everything is black. There's a furry black sweater with sequins, a black silk robe, a faded black cotton dress and an almost new black leather jacket.

"It's some law, right?" I ask her. "Artists have to wear black."

"God, is it that cliché?" she snorts.

"I'm afraid so, my dear," I say in a fake British accent, and turn to her paintings. One is obviously a self-portrait. A sad-looking Asian woman in a dark purple dress is looking down so you can't see her eyes. Her arms are hanging by her sides, and the hands look small and stiff.

"This is how you look in the morning, you know," I tell her, and she punches me in the shoulder.

"I thought you weren't going to criticize," she says.

I'm laughing and I say, "I'm not. It's a great painting. That's exactly how you look before the ginseng kicks in."

She punches me again, only harder, and I ask her, "Is there some rule in art school that if you paint somebody smiling then you get adiosed?"

She puts on a fake pout and says, "And that's not critical, either, right?"

"Right," I say. "It's just a general comment." She gives me a funny look and I hope I haven't insulted her. She reaches up and pulls my head down a little and kisses me. Her lips are soft and moist and suddenly the room is crackling like the air under thunderclouds when lightning is about to strike. My mind is fuzzy with shock for a few seconds and then I kiss her like I've wanted to kiss her.

She puts her arms around me and I'm blown flat to find the eyes I've admired so many times suddenly right in front of me. While we're kissing she pulls me backwards toward her bed, and I'm hoping I don't trip over the concrete blocks and pine boards and crash us both to the hardwood floor. We manage to edge over to the bed and she pulls me down with her. Then she takes my hand and puts it under her shirt.

She's softer than I thought possible and my heart is pounding—I am actually touching her perfect breast after all my fantasies—but what's funny is that what I really want to touch is her face. I

228

pull my hand out and stop kissing her so I can look into her iridescent brown eyes and touch her cheek and her hair.

For the first time ever she doesn't glance away as soon as our eyes meet. In those long seconds I can see her softness and her hurt and her brightness; a strange feeling rushes up my spine and explodes in my head, and I have never wanted anything in my whole life as much as I want to look at her and touch her.

Her eyes are so warm and full that I suddenly know we're sharing the same feelings. Then a flicker of doubt darkens her expression, and she puts her hand on mine and we squeeze each others' fingers hard.

She closes her eyes and we start touching each other. She is sweet about letting me know what she likes, and I like everything. I've got no illusions, it's no secret she's done this a lot more times than I have. She's not embarrassed about the logistics like I am, but I've got a dreamy floating feeling because I am actually with her and she is more beautiful than any fantasy I ever imagined.

It's funny how it's easier for people to share sex than it is to just say what their feelings are for each other. It's like they're ashamed to admit that they truly like somebody, or that somebody truly likes them. Even me, I'm thinking, how could she like me this much? It didn't seem possible. What's there to like about a skinny smartass?

I've read that people are often disappointed by their first sex gigs, and it's no wonder. What's interesting is not all the monitoring and the mechanics, which is all you hear about, the sweaty-palm test approach, how am I doing, I've got to reach point A while she reaches point B, tally your points up, but the little things you've wanted to touch, like those fine hairs that girls have instead of sideburns, the things you've wanted to feel like the muscles in her legs when she squeezes you and her eyebrows and her nose, all the dumb-sounding things you want to know about that aren't the ropes-and-pulleys stuff.

I think I'm going to have a heart attack when I slip her lacy red panties off. I can't help thinking, is this her only red pair, did she wear them on purpose? And when she sighs a little I'm about to crash onto Venus in a fireball because it's the first time her feelings aren't totally controlled.

229

But what really sinks in is not how much I want her, but how close I want to be to her, how I want to know everything about her and share everything with her. I want to see how she gets dressed, not just how she undresses, the way she wakes up, how she looks when she knows I like her a lot, even the way she looks when she's torqued at me.

Nobody says anything about tasting the person for the first time, finding out how good they smell, burying your face in her hair and smelling it up close instead of a whiff that drifts through the kitchen. Nobody says how wonderful that is. The way it's sold is hot dogs and knotholes, conquests and losses and keeping track of the pleasurometer readings. Somewhere inside my head I'm thinking, man, it's what I've always thought, that all the mechanical-engineering scorecards and fake passion are total jank, and there is something real behind all the movie and ad crap.

So when we're laying there and I'm enjoying her warm breath on my cheek, I'm thinking, I know this feeling can't last, the sense that everything is perfect and she's perfect and the world is actually whole, that it's still a dead-battery-in-the-morning and why-are-you-so-griffy world, but I'm so grateful that I get to feel this way with Nikki.

All of a sudden she pulls away from me, walks to the closet, and puts on her thin black silk robe. She sits on the bed and leans against the wall and doesn't look at me. I heave a big sigh because her shields are back up, and I know, in a funny hollow way, how bad women feel when the guy doesn't care about them and he's done with their knothole, he's whistling while he dresses, it's another one in the win column, seven-point-eight on the pleasurometer, orgasm in five-point-four minutes, another day, another dollar.

"What's wrong?" I ask her.

She tries to smile and says, "Nothing."

I try to keep my voice as flat as hers and ask, "Then why did you jump up?"

Her smile disappears and she looks at her paintings. "I decided a long time ago to always be the first one to get up," she says, and her voice is cold.

"I think I know why," I say. "But can't it be different this time?"

230

She doesn't say anything and I sit up. "Don't worry," I tell her, and I'm a little griffed. "I can see you're not mushy."

She's still silent and I flop back down on the bed. I'm thinking, what a gimpy way for it to end. Without looking at her I say, "I'd rather be mushy than dead."

Nikki is quiet, and I turn over and look at her room and console myself with the thought that at least we were close for those few seconds when she didn't look away from my eyes. Plus, I got to see her room, her paintings, and her pile of undies in the corner, and that's as close as anybody can get to her.

It doesn't really work, though, and I feel sad until the bed spread rustles and she lays down next to me and I can smell her again. She puts her hand on my forehead, almost like she's checking me for a fever. When I reach up and hold her hand, she squeezes my fingers hard, and I feel hopeful again.

# CHAPTER TWENTY-SEVEN

When I call the youth hostel early the next morning the guy tells me Alex is still there, he'll go get him, and I'm relieved Alex hasn't vectored yet. When he comes on the line his voice sounds miffed, but he promises to give me at least a day's notice before he hauls derriere. He doesn't even ask me how long I'm planning to stay, so I know he can tell it's already a semi-permanent gig with Nikki.

The whole conversation leaves me feeling fragged, but there's nothing I can do about it. I spend the rest of the week with Nikki, and while they're some of the best days of my life, I keep snagging on this worry about the future. Should I stay here with her and get a job and go to community college in the fall? Or should I ask her to come south with me? And then what? We'd have to get an apartment, she'd have to transfer to UCLA, and maybe it's too much too soon. Or maybe we should leave both gigs behind and live somewhere new.

I know it's wrong to spin all this out so soon, we've just met each other, but fall is coming and I feel an urgency to lock in something serious. Nikki is her usual shields-up self—she doesn't mention the future and I worry about the worst possibility, that maybe she sees this as summer fun, and she'll adios me when her classes start. I don't want her to get the idea that I'm planning out our life together already, but then she's the one who's got her job, her school, and her crib all set, while I've got nothing laid out. I keep telling myself, today is the day I'll talk it all out with her, but I don't want to bring it up and maybe spoil the fun we're having.

On Friday we grab Thai takeout after Nikki gets off work and go to the Berkeley Marina to eat an early dinner by the bay. The late afternoon breeze is cool, the sun is still warm, and the thick grass we're sitting on smells good. Kids are trying to get kites off the ground, people are walking their Fidos, and old guys are sitting on the rocks nursing their fishing poles, even though I never see one catch anything.

After we finish eating, we lay down together, look up at the few puffball clouds in the sky, and just enjoy the warmth of each other. I think, maybe now is a good time, and then I tell myself, no, do it tonight in her room. This is too strat to weigh down with all the heavy decisions about the future. So I'm silent and I can tell she's happy, maybe for the first time in a long time, or maybe ever, and that makes me happy.

We vector home at dusk and find Elroy's blue Crown Victoria in the driveway, and I'm hoping he's in his room studying so we don't have to deal with him. Since the computer munchkins aren't hogging the living room to play lame video games, Nikki and I toss their magazines and old Cracker Jack boxes on the floor and sprawl out on the lumpy plaid sofa to watch dumb TV shows. I start my usual wise-ass commentary, Nikki joins in, and it's fun to rip every show we spock and make each other laugh.

There's a knock at the front door, and I figure the munchkins forgot one of the fourteen keys you need to open all the locks. So I disentangle myself from Nikki, unlock the door, and swing it open.

The joke line I'm about to spring disappears because it's not the munchkins. It's a haole couple I've never seen before, and the guy is pointing a black automatic pistol at me.

"Hi," he says like it's a normal conversation. "Mind if we come in?"

My mind and body freeze for a few seconds as a massive shock wave rolls over me. I've seen this a million times on TV, but it hasn't prepared me to look down that little black hole of the gun barrel. I step back and the hoods come in, locking the door behind them.

The guy scratches his neat little black beard and looks around warily. The woman is a little younger than him, maybe in her early twenties, and she's dressed in a low-cut clingy top, tight red skirt, and black nylons. Nikki looks up from the couch and then freezes, just like I did, and the guy motions me with the gun to go sit down with her. I walk over and sit down real slowly. The lady hood reaches into her big handbag and pulls out a little handgun, maybe a .25 caliber, and points it kind of lazily at us.

I take Nikki's hand, and it's cold and sweaty at the same time, just like mine. I suddenly remember I was supposed to yell out Elroy's warning, we have visitors or guests, I can't remember which, but I'm glad I didn't because the guy might have shot me.

The hood is dressed like an artist, black leather jacket over a T-shirt tucked into gray jeans, and his eyes look us over calmly, soaking up our fear. "Anybody else home?" he whispers, and I nod.

"How many?" he asks, and I hold up one finger and point upstairs.

"Where do you keep the stuff?" he asks, and I'm thinking, what stuff, and then I realize he thinks we're hiding drugs in the crib. I shake my head and shrug, and he looks me over to see if I'm lying. He decides I'm not, and then points his gun at my chest and says real quietly, "Give me your wallet."

I ease my wallet out and think, fine, Jack, the Mastercard's got $299 on a $300 limit and the seven bucks cash is yours. He takes the fake leather billfold and flips it open with one hand. He can tell it's no dealer's wallet, I mean seven bucks, come on, but he pulls out the seven dollars and tosses the wallet back to me. Then he nods at his ladyfriend and creeps up the staircase.

Now I'm more scared than before, if that's possible, because Elroy is not the type to let some guy wander around his house with a gun. Either Elroy is going to get drilled or he'll drill Beardman, and then his girlfriend might go off the tracks and shoot us or try to pull a hostage gig with us and then Elroy will shoot her and maybe us, too, if we're in the way.

The seconds go by like minutes because we don't hear anything but the TV sitcom's lame jokes and laugh tracks, and I can imagine Beardman trying each doorknob and getting suspicious when he gets to Nikki's locked door. The lady hood is getting more nervous, too, half-looking at the entry for her man and half-spocking us, as if we're going to jump her. I stage-whisper to her, "Lady, we're cool, okay?"

She doesn't say anything, but she relaxes a little bit and that's all I want.

A door clicks open upstairs and we all stop breathing. I squeeze Nikki's hand, hoping to give her some reassurance, and the hooker-hood looks up at the ceiling, as if she can sense her pal

234

from underneath. We're all waiting for some follow-up sound, a voice or a gunshot or a thud, but the only sound is the tinny voices and the laugh track's fake guffaws from the TV.

Then the floorboards in the hallway creak under somebody's weight, and a few seconds later the steps at the top of the stairs groan and we all look to see who's coming down. I'm afraid my heart is going to explode, I'm thinking about what to do if the gun-moll panics and tries to shoot us, but my mind is spinning so fast I can't pin anything down except that I want this sweatflop-seizure-light-speed fear to end.

"Daz and Nikki, where are you?" Elroy asks in a strange sing-song tone, and we all three jump at the sound of his voice.

The lady hood is wild-eyed, and I don't know whether to say anything or not because I don't want her to orbit Mars and pull the trigger.

We're all quiet, and after a few seconds Elroy says, in the same sing-song voice, "This man is going to have a very unpleasant experience if I don't hear your voices in three seconds."

The gun-lady's eyes bulge out in a cornered-wildebeest panic and she aims the gun at the empty entry and then back at us. "They're down here," she yells, and her voice is buckling like a sidewalk in an earthquake.

"Daz and Nikki, are you alright?" Elroy asks.

We both shout, "Yeah!" and our voices sound weirdly loud.

"Good," he says. "Now turn off the TV."

I click off the set and the room is silent. After a few seconds Elroy says, "Now I'm sure we'd all like to avoid any surprises, so whoever else is down there, don't try anything foolish. If you have a gun, drop it on the floor in the next three seconds, or very bad things will happen to your friend."

The lady stares frantically at the empty entry again, and then bends down and drops the gun on the hardwood. It clunks hard, and Elroy says, real slow and nice, like he's talking to a naughty five-year-old, "Good. Now lay down and put your hands on the floor. If I come down and your hands aren't on the floor, then a very bad thing will happen to your friend."

For the first time Beardman says something, and his voice tells us he's on the edge. "Honey, do like he says."

The lady gets on her hands and knees and her tiny skirt hikes up and I can see her white panties. Then she lays down facing the door, arms and legs spreadeagled out, and says, "Okay, I'm down. Just don't hurt him."

"Everything's fine," says Elroy, and a creepy feeling, not like being saved at all, goes up my back because I realize that he's actually enjoying this.

"Now we're coming down," he says in that same careful singsong voice. "Just stay right where you are, don't try to be John Wayne, and everything will be alright."

Suddenly Beardman stumbles into the doorway with his hands on his head. His eyes have that out-of-breath game-animal glaze. He glances up the stairs, Elroy says, "Go on," and then Beardman walks slowly into the room.

"Is everything as it should be?" Elroy asks him.

"Yeah," Beardman answers, and Elroy pops into the doorway, his M-16 at the ready. He's wearing a dull-black flak jacket, and it makes him look like a baseball umpire. He motions with the rifle barrel for Beardman to lay down next to his girlfriend, which he does. The lady takes one look at Elroy's gun and his excited expression and then she pisses in her pants. The stream flows down between her legs and then trickles under the sofa, and I'm thinking, hey, the floor's not very level. I don't look at Beardman's crotch, but I figure he pissed in his pants as soon as Elroy surprised him with the M-16.

"It's funny," Elroy says to Nikki and me, like we're all sharing a brewkowski. "Silence can be the best warning. When I heard the front door open and there's no conversation, I knew something was wrong."

He points the thin little gun barrel down at the two hoods and says, "Now, what did you expect to find here?"

Neither of them answers, and Elroy says, all reassuringly, "I'm sure you can understand why I'm curious."

"We were told this was a dealer's house," Beardman says.

"You should double-check your sources of information next time," Elroy tells him.

"Can we go now?" the woman asks, and she sounds salty, maybe from the humiliation of pissing in her pants.

236

"No," Elroy says. "Not yet." He looks up at me and says, "Daz, remove their wallets and put the money on the sofa."

Beardman turns his head to look up at Elroy and says, "Come on, man!"

Elroy points the gun at the guy's face and asks me, "Daz, they seem to think I won't use this. Can you reassure them I will?"

I say, "Don't mess with him, he'll use it, I'm serious," and my voice sounds edgy and weird.

"Daz, please get the money," he says, so I take out their wallets and lay out their Jacksons and Lincolns on the sofa next to Nikki. There's quite a pile of twenties, and a couple of hundred dollars, and I figure maybe they're low-rent dealers themselves. Then I sit down again and Elroy says very politely, "Thank you."

Then he looks down at the hoods and says, "Gunfire is pretty unexceptional in this neighborhood. I could pull the trigger and bury you both in the backyard tonight, and no one would know or care. I think the criminal justice system is overloaded enough, don't you?"

Elroy's enjoying his I-am-your-master routine, and I'm hoping he'll get his fill and just let these assholes get out of our lives.

He lowers the gun barrel to the floor in front of the hoods and then bang, he pumps a bullet through the floor. We all jump, even though it isn't that loud. It's actually kind of a flat pop, but there's a splintery hole in the floor about six inches from Beardman's face and he starts mumbling, "Oh, shit," again and again like it's a mantra that might save his life. The lady blurts out, "Oh man, please don't kill us," and I'm ozoned, thinking, oh my God, he's going to adios them, he's really going to do it.

"Elroy," I say, but he cuts me off. "Shut up, Daz."

Everyone's quiet, even Beardman.

"Don't you think it's ironic, white people trying to rob the only white people in the neighborhood?" Elroy asks. He doesn't expect an answer, and nobody gives him one.

"White people only come down here to buy drugs," Elroy says. "Except us. We don't use drugs." I'm wishing Elroy did use drugs, that he was on something massive like lithium, but he doesn't even drink beer.

I say, "Elroy, I think—" but he cuts me off again. "Daz, you're starting to irritate me," he says. Everyone can hear the mojo vibration in his voice, and right then I know that if we can just get through this alright, then I'm leaving tomorrow no matter what.

Nikki is silent, but then she usually is, so I'm not surprised. She puts her hand over mine and squeezes it, and I think she's telling me to just leave it alone, it'll all be okay. So I slump back against Nikki, like this is all just a typical evening's fun in the "Oaktown Rules" household. Elroy's expression changes and I suddenly grip that he's afraid of losing his audience, that our fear is part of the gig's spin for him.

A car pulls up in the driveway and we all look out the window. The headlights shut off, the car door slams shut, and footsteps clump up the creaky wood steps to the front porch. Elroy says, "Shhhhh," and we're all very still.

Keys jangle and then the three deadbolt locks are turned, click, pause, click, pause, click. Fido the hellmutt suddenly starts barking down in the basement and I think, great timing, Fido. The door is pushed open and the computer munchkins come in. They spock the scene and freeze like guys hit with some alien space beam.

Elroy looks at their dropjaw expressions and decides he's had enough fun for one night. "Our guests were just leaving," he says, and he raises the rifle and clicks the safety switch on. The two hoods look up, see they won't get shot, and trade stares with the computer munchkins for a few seconds. Then they get shakily to their feet and head for the door.

"I don't think it would be a good idea to come around our neighborhood anymore," Elroy tells them, and they both nod, still glazed over. Elroy picks up the lady's gun and their money, and tosses their empty wallets into the entry. They grab them, shuffle out to the porch, and then close the door very slowly behind them.

Elroy counts the hoods' money and then slips the bills in his pocket. "Fido's happy," he says to no one. "This is twenty-point-five weeks of sirloin."

He trots lightly up the stairs with his gun, and I start breathing again.

# CHAPTER TWENTY-EIGHT

The munchkins run off to their rooms, and Nikki and I just sit there for a few minutes, staring at the splintery bullet hole in the oak flooring. "Too bad it didn't put Fido out of his misery," I say, because you never knew where in the basement you'd find the hellmutt, but Nikki doesn't grin. She gives me a quick glance and I know I can't wait any longer to talk with her.

"Would you come up to the roof with me?" I ask her, and she nods. I stand up and my legs feel weak, like I just ran a mile as fast as I could. We climb up the steep staircase to the spooky deck with no railings and sit down. The moon is out this night, a fat crescent shining above a few thin clouds gripping the hilltops. There's a soft cool breeze, and I'm glad I've got my denim jacket. Nikki's still wearing her white blouse and black jeans from work, and she hugs her knees and shivers. "Want my jacket?" I ask her.

She shakes her head and says, "No, thanks."

She's staring out at the lights speckling the hills, and I can't tell what she's thinking. I figure she must be vibrating off the craziness we just spocked like I am, but as usual she doesn't say anything.

Without really planning it, I slide over and put my arm around her. At first she's still, but then she puts her arm around my waist and I feel like it's okay to just blurt out what's been filling my mind for days. So I take a deep breath and say, "Nikki, you're it for me."

She does the Sphinx gig, doesn't move and stares straight ahead, but it's too late so I rush into the rest.

"This sounds cliché," I say, trying too hard to sound light, "but you make me think of you all the time."

"I don't," she says kind of disparagingly. "That would be telepathy or something." She turns her head to glance at me and

239

the moonlight glitters off her eyes. "Besides, isn't the cliché just, 'I think of you all the time?'"

"I guess so," I say, "but I wasn't trying to get goo-goo-eyed. So it's got to be you."

She doesn't smile or make a joke and a lead ball forms in my stomach. She's quiet for a while and I'm breathing shallow, waiting for the axe to fall. "I have my own cliché," she says, and her voice sounds tired. "I don't know what to say."

"Then I'll just say what's on my mind," I tell her, and I lay out everything I've been thinking, that I can't just act like nothing's happened, that I want to be with her, and my ideas about us getting an apartment together, either down south or up here. Before she can answer I say that even though she doesn't seem that happy here, if she wants to stay, then I'll come back up and find a job and start community college.

I feel a great relief, like to hell with it, if she skags me off, so be it, at least I finally told the truth. She lets go of my waist and shivers again, so I struggle out of my jacket and put it over her shoulders, the Sir Walter Raleigh gig, guvnah, and she huddles under the coat without looking at me. The cool air feels good on my arms and face, and I look at the moon and think, I don't care, I told her how I feel, and a sadness mixes in with the relief; I feel far away from everything, as far as the moon is from the Earth.

The one reaction that spins me into overload is her silence, so after a long pause I say, "Don't worry, I can take it. Just tell me what you're thinking."

"I don't know what I'm thinking," she says.

"Then tell me what you're feeling," I say, almost desperately.

She's silent again and I'm starting to feel griffed. "I can't wait until you make it all clean and pretty," I tell her. "I'm leaving tomorrow, so just spit it out."

A car with booming speakers rolls up the street, and the deck starts vibrating with its woofers. It slowly cruises past, the oom-pocka-pocka dopplers down and then the street is calm again.

"Here's another cliché," she says. "It's hard for me to know what I feel because most of the time I'm trying not to feel anything."

I don't know what to say to this, so I keep quiet. She lowers her head and stares at the deck. "It seems so easy for you."

"It's not," I tell her. "I've been thinking about it for days. Maybe I only did it because of the craziness tonight."

I reach over and stroke her shiny black hair. She squeezes my hand and pulls her long mane from under the jacket and starts twisting it into thick braids again. The light from the streetlamps and the moon is pretty dim, so she's twisting and weaving the two halves of her hair together almost automatically while she stares out at the night.

"I have fun with you, Daz," she says, and my heart leaps at these simple words, which I know are so hard for her to say. She pauses, and then says, "You're so full of—"

"Yeah, I know, crap," I say, and she laughs, and it's wonderful, a laugh she can't bury.

"No, more like sparks," she says. "Things are fresh to you; I like that."

I'm blown down because I don't know how to respond to compliments, especially from her.

"I like the way you care about me," she says, very simply and flatly, and a tingling sensation runs up my backbone. She lets go of the braid and I reach over and take her hand. Her fingers feel cold, and I hold them tight.

"I know it sounds dumb, but no one's been interested in actually knowing me," she says in the same flat voice. "I don't mean just guys, I mean anyone."

She glances over at me. "I know I look like a zombie most of the time, but that's not the way I feel inside." She makes a sound that's part sigh and part laugh and says, "Here's another cliché. I haven't said anything because—I know, it sounds so stupid and dramatic—I don't want a revolution in my life."

My brain numbs out and I ask her, "So does that mean no?"

She says, "No. It just means I'm afraid."

"I'm scared, too," I tell her, and I can feel her relax.

"So you don't mind me not saying yes until I've thought about it some more?" she asks me.

I squeeze her hand to reassure her, even though I feel worried, and say, "I just hope it's yes and not no."

"Why do you have to leave tomorrow?" she asks, and even though she tries to keep it flat, her feelings still light up the edges of the words.

At first I think of saying, why else, nutso Elroy, but that's only because the real reason sounds so mushy. The real reason is that Alex and I both want to finish the trip like we started it. But instead of trying to explain this I blurt out the whole story of Old Man Ching, of fighting him for the Lancer and his travel diaries and his son.

"What happened to the son?" Nikki asks.

"I don't know," I say. "Old Man Ching never mentioned him. Maybe he's a hippie and Old Man Ching disowned him."

Nikki turns to me and says, half-joking, "I think he's kind of adopted you."

"Nah," I say, and I'm embarrassed by the whole topic. "He's mean enough to be my old man, though."

Nikki laughs and says, "I can see why you want to go back." She hesitates, then asks, "Who's going to keep the car? You or your friend?"

I'm not sure what this means. Is she saying that Alex and I can't share the car because she wants me to come back up here?

"He's always hated it," I say. "So I guess it'll be mine."

This seems to satisfy her, and we look out at the lights. After a while I start shivering so we go back down to her room and climb into bed.

After we touch each other, a lot and for a long time, she falls asleep and starts breathing very rhythmically and deeply. I can't sleep so I turn over and look up at her ceiling. I've never looked above her bed, I've always been focused on her, and I spock some faint glowing spots way up in the darkness. At first, I think it's probably just streetlight glare leaking through the curtains and bouncing off something shiny in the room, but after staring at them a few seconds I realize they're little iridescent stars Nikki pasted up there.

I look at the stars in her handmade constellation for a long time and feel her warmth against me. When I think that maybe this is the last night I'll ever sleep next to her, it's the worst feeling of my whole life.

# CHAPTER TWENTY-NINE

The next morning I almost change my mind and decide to stay a while longer, but I know nothing will change, that I can't help bugging Nikki for an answer about us, yes or no, and it will just annoy her. So I call the youth hostel in San Francisco and tell Alex I want to go home.

He's quiet for a few seconds and then asks, "What about Nikki?" His voice is guarded, and I know he's trying to find out if it's over without hurting my feelings.

"We still like each other," I say, "but I'm ready to head out. What about you?"

"I don't know," he says, and I can almost feel his shrug. "There's some nice girls here. I'm having pretty good fun."

I can't hide my surprise, and suddenly I feel very stupid, because I've been acting as if I'm the only one who's interested in a girl. "Sure, I understand," I say, as if I'm not surprised at all. "But can I stay with you for a few days?"

He's quiet and I get this hollow feeling, like turnabout is fair play, and now he's blowing me off to be with a girl he met.

"I'll see you in an hour," he says, and I'm wondering if I can stand seeing him goo-goo-eyed with a girl while I'm all alone thinking of Nikki. It's too bad we can't end the trip together, I tell myself, but I can't hang around San Francisco feeling like this. I'd rather take the bus home.

Nikki comes down, ready to go to work, and she's got her usual unemotional face on. We say goodbye and agree to call and write each other, and I don't know if she wants me to hug her or not. I decide, what the hell, I want to, so we hug each other one last time and it feels so awkward.

I go with her out to the driveway and watch while she puts on her helmet and starts the scooter. She looks at me, and her face

243

looks so small inside the helmet. She gives me a little smile and wave, and hauls derriere.

She turns the corner a few blocks down and I lose sight of her. The street is empty, but I think I can still hear the buzzing of her bumblebee engine, and then even that's gone. I suddenly wish there was a cliff nearby, so I could jump off it. I feel as down as I ever have.

Maybe because I don't see how things could get any worse, I decide to give Fido one more walk. I go down to the basement and he hears me coming. He sits up and starts wagging his tail, like he can tell it's me from my footsteps. I put my hand out so he can smell me, and I pet him and put the thick leather leash on his collar.

"Fido, I feel like hell," I say, and he just wags his tail and nuzzles my hand. For the first time I'm not afraid of him; I actually feel sorry for him, being half-blind and living in this crappy basement most of the time. I stop begrudging Fido his top sirloin, and even feel that Elroy has one good spot in him for buying Fido and trying to give him a good life. I rub Fido's ears and think, even the basement isn't too bad. It's easy on his eyes, it's cool in summer, and there's lots of places to nod out in.

I wrap the leash around my waist to make a human anchor, and then we climb up the stairs and go out onto the street for one last morning walk down the cracked sidewalks and past the dead weeds in the empty lots.

When we come back from our jaunt I see the puke-green Cruiser parked in the driveway, and Alex is rearranging some junk in the back seat.

We walk up to the car and Alex pats the dog's head. "Hey, Fido," he says, and then he looks up and squints at me for a few seconds.

"So what, bruddah, you ready?" he asks, and I nod. He can tell I feel blown down about Nikki, and I think he knows there's nothing he can say to make me feel better. I take Fido down into the basement and then go get my sleeping stuff and nylon clothes bag from my room. I tear off a sheet of paper from my notebook and draw a heart, write our names inside it, and slip the paper under Nikki's door on my way out.

I throw my gear on the back seat and get in the passenger seat. "I tanked up," Alex says. "Thanks, man," I tell him, and I put on my shades and slump back. Alex starts the Lancer and drives slowly past the green-and-yellow Laotian Victorians and Mrs. Jones's neat little flower beds and the guys standing by the corner liquor store. In a few minutes we're on an I-State heading south, and my mind is whirling just like the Cruiser's tires, around and around the same things.

I suddenly realize we're not crossing the bay and that snaps me back. "Aren't we going to the youth hostel?" I ask, and Alex just shakes his head.

"What about the girls?" I ask, and I'm wondering if he just invented them to yank me around a bit, to show me what it felt like to wait around while your buddy works a romance.

He kind of smiles, almost to himself, and says, "There were two really nice girls staying there, a Puerto Rican girl from New York and this Danish girl. We had a lot of fun, but they're leaving in a few days."

I'm relieved Alex had a strat time because I knew he'd been waiting for me, but I'm even more relieved that we're heading home. I feel like I owe Alex an explanation, but I don't feel like talking and he doesn't, either. We're silent all the way from Oakland to San Jose. Even though it'll add a few hours to our trip, we both want to go down 101 instead of 5, to avoid the worst of the heat and to catch a little of the Pacific on the way.

He pulls off in Salinas to take a leak and then offers me the wheel. I feel better once I start driving, and after a while I ask him about the University of Hawaii and whether he still wants to go there. He says yeah, and we start talking about what it would take to go in January instead of waiting until next September. An idea suddenly hits me and I feel hopeful again for the first time since last night. I turn to tell it to Alex and then stop. What if he doesn't like it? There's only one way to find out, and I try to sound casual.

I stare real hard at the I-State lanes stretching through the farmland ahead of us and then ask, "Would you mind if I invite Nikki along?"

He doesn't say anything right away and I think, to hell with it, you can't have everything, and then he says, "No worry, brah. We gotta have girlfriends. The main thing is, no one tells us what for do. Right?"

"Yeah, that's right," I say, and a big chunk of granite lifts off my chest. I know he means that as long as nobody, not even a girl-friend, can tell us we can't be together whenever we feel like it, then everything's okay.

Alex takes over driving again and we reach King City in early afternoon. Suddenly I remember that the James Dean Memorial is somewhere just to the east. I yank out the map and my notebook to confirm this, and getting all excited, ask Alex if he minds going there. He just shrugs and a few minutes later we're on Highway 46, heading into low hills of golden grass. We drop into a blistering hot valley of drying hay with a dusty haze that hangs above the fields after pickup trucks have hauled derriere along the bake-brain dirt roads that crisscross the valley floor.

The town turns out to be just a wide spot in the road with a small store and a gravel parking area around Dean's memorial, which is under the only tree within fifty miles. Some rich Japanese guy popped the gitas, and whatever it cost, it was worth it. It's simple, just a couple of big shiny chrome ells stuck in the ground, but it's the most tropo-electric sculpture I've ever seen. I dig our camera out of the trunk and get Alex to take some pictures of me posing, Joe Cool, shades and all, in front of the memorial. I spock the dates and realize he was only twenty-four when he went down. I think, griff, that's just four more years for me. Right then it really hits me that I can't afford to just cruise through fantasyland any-more, I've got to make it happen just like I did with the Lancer, and I make up my mind to get Nikki to come with us to Hawaii, even if she's as stubborn as Old Man Ching.

I go in the store to buy us two overpriced sodas and then we vector back toward King City. For the first time in days I feel like my old self. I'm riffing on what we can do in Hawaii, about what it would cost to ship the Cruiser there, asking Alex what places he thinks are the most strat on Oahu, and everything else that's spin-ning through my mind.

In no time at all we're in Pismo Beach by the deep blue Pacific, the cool breeze blowing that tangy smell of rotting kelp and salt air over the pink stucco motels. It all makes me I feel like I'm finally getting close to home.

We leave the Pacific behind and I feel sleepy once we hit all that hot farmland between Pismo and Santa Barbara in the late afternoon. I ozone in the back seat with a shirt over my head until Alex wakes me up in Ventura to take the last stretch through the smoggy sunsets of L.A. to Costa Mesa. The city seems even more endless than I remember, and the red taillights of a million people pumping their brakes go all the way to the horizon and way beyond.

About halfway through L.A. I get a major domo for a tamale, and we get off in Buena Park and stop at one of my mom's favorite places, a narrow dump with three little tables inside that makes fat little tamales in corn leaves and huge burritos with about half a chicken inside. We call our parents from there so they won't have heart attacks when we show up, and then we hit the I-State one more time. I guess we're supposed to feel something momentous, but we're so tired all we want to do is get home and go to sleep.

I drop Alex off at his house and it looks so katakana now, more like a house I've seen on TV a million times than a place where Alex lives. We're so fragged we don't say anything but "bye" and I vector the few blocks to my house. The front porch light is on, the garage door is open, and my folks' cars are there so I know they're both home.

I almost forget which key is the one to our front door and then I remember handing the three keys to the "Oaktown Rules" house to Nikki that morning, and I feel a sharp pain in my chest. I think about Nikki coming home, the way she climbs the stairs without making the steps creak, and her unlocking her door and flopping down on her bed. Her unsmiling mouth looked like a small flower decoration on a fancy cake, and I remember kissing her until she went mmmmm and then lifting off her white shirt and touching her creamy brown skin.

The keys are in my hand and I realize I'm standing on my front porch, but I don't feel like I'm home. It's all very familiar, but it doesn't make me feel comfortable anymore. I take a deep breath, unlock the door and get a hug from my mom and dad, and we sit down at the dining room table. My mom serves an ice cream cake she had in the freezer for a special occasion and I ramble on about the trip, thinking all the time, no, that's not how it actually was, nobody can describe how Alex's face looked after he got dumped by Meg, or that gleam in Morris's eyes when he's telling you to get your ass in gear, or the way my body shakes when five huge farm boys are hoping they can put me in a hospital because it's so damn fun to fight, or the sickening feeling you get when your car stutters on a hot Kansas City freeway and then dies.

They ask a lot of questions and listen politely and say they're glad I'm home safely, but somehow none of it is connecting to me; I'm orbiting Pluto and hurting even though I'm glad to be back. I yawn and excuse myself, and as I'm walking down the hall to my room my mom calls out, "Don't forget, tomorrow's trash day," and something breaks down inside me, that after all this, the thing to remember is that tomorrow is trash day and it's my little chore to haul the trash cans out to the curb, just like it's been my little chore since I was eight years old.

Right then I know I can't stay here until we leave for Hawaii in January. That's four months away, and I won't be able to stand it. I wonder if Alex is feeling the same griff, and it doesn't take long to figure that he is.

Even though I'm so very tired I can't fall asleep. I stare up at my ceiling and wish with all my might that I was next to Nikki's hot sleeping body and that I was looking up at the little iridescent stars above her bed. I think what I've been thinking all day: that I can't go back until she makes up her mind one way or the other, and I feel miserable again.

# CHAPTER THIRTY

After I take the trash cans out the next morning, I get in the Lancer and go straight to the Ching's stationery shop. I want to see Old Man Ching before they open the shop, so we can talk without getting interrupted by customers.

I park the Cruiser in front of the shop and then hesitate by the door to their apartment. It's right next to the shop entrance, and a long straight staircase leads up to their crib. They've never asked me up there, and I'm afraid I'm being rude inviting myself, especially this early. But then I think, what the hell, there isn't going to be a better time, so I take a deep breath and ring the bell.

A few seconds later an upstairs window opens and Mrs. Ching sticks her head out to see who it is. I smile and wave at her, and her gray bun bobs up and down as she nods and smiles back. She disappears and then a lock release buzzes. I push the door open and start up the stairs.

I know this sounds mambo, but the first thing I notice is the old-people smell. Old people's houses always smell sort of musty, like they never open the windows wide and let the wind blow through the place. Maybe it's because they feel cold a lot, I don't know. And then there's this perfumy clean smell, from all the bleach and Pine Sol they use.

The other musty air gig is old furniture and old books. Old people always have shelves of old books, hardbound novels by Steinbeck from when he was still alive, paperbacks with brown pages that are falling apart, faded *Life* magazines from when it was a weekly.

There's some photos hanging on the wall at the top of the staircase, and I scan them real quick for any shots of the Chings with their son, but I don't see any. Then Mrs. Ching bustles out of a door, takes my hand, and leads me into their living room.

249

It's small but cozy, a plaid sofa and chair and a black lacquer coffee table and sure enough, a tall shelf of books and knicknacks, all very tidy.

A hollow metallic clank makes me look over and down, and I see Old Man Ching kneeling on the floor, peering into an old gas wall furnace. The cover is leaning against the wall next to an open toolbox, and he's fussing inside the furnace with a small crescent wrench. I've never seen him wear anything but tan slacks and long-sleeve shirts, but he's wearing almost-new blue jeans and an ironed short-sleeve shirt.

He shifts around and looks up at me. His hands are smudged with black soot, and the dragon tattoos on his thin forearms ripple as he sets the crescent wrench down with a *thunk* next to him.

"Damn thing doesn't work right," he says, all disgusted. "Gotta fix it now before winter starts."

"What's wrong with it?" I ask him.

"The pilot light won't stay on," he says, and then he peers back into the innards again. "Don't know why."

"Have you had breakfast?" Mrs. Ching asks me.

"Well, no, but I just stopped over to say hi," I tell her.

"Please, eat with us," she says. "I'm just making breakfast now. Do you drink coffee?"

I remember waking up and smelling the strong black coffee that Ron handed me outside Dry Gulch our second day there, and I say, "Yeah, I do."

"I'll get you a cup," she says, and I follow her through the dining room with its square black table and cabinet filled with china and crystal to her narrow little kitchen. I look around at the shiny white tile counters and the hanging bamboo baskets, and then I am blown down by their cork bulletin board next to their wall phone. Every postcard I sent them is tacked there with red push pins, and there's a small map of the U.S. at the bottom, with stars inked on every city or place I'd written from or even mentioned in the postcards.

"Do you take milk or sugar?" Mrs. Ching asks. I turn around and my face must look as spun out as I feel, because her smile gets almost embarrassed and she says, "It was so nice to get your cards."

"I wish I'd sent more," I mumble. Then she hands me a hefty white coffee cup and saucer, a little clear glass tray with a sugar bowl and a small pitcher of milk, and says, "I'll let you fix it the way you like it." The tray is the old-fashioned kind that's edged with nubby round glass balls. I set it down and ask, "Do you mind if I go keep Mr. Ching company?"

She puts a black cast-iron pan on the stove and smiles at me. "Just watch out for his mood. Do you like scrambled eggs?"

"Yeah, sounds great," I say, and I remember the soft scrambled eggs Tracie made for breakfast at the Grand Canyon campground.

I go back to the living room and squat down next to Old Man Ching. He's cleaning the grimy black pilot fitting with a soft rag and some solvent, and he doesn't say anything. I don't know how to start, so I put my coffee cup on the hardwood floor and take his travel diary out of my jacket pocket. I say, "I found this in your car. I thought you might want it back."

His expression changes from pure jank to surprise. His eyebrows knit and he puts down his rag and takes the thin little notebook out of my hand. He opens it and reads an entry, turns to another page and reads another one. He does this a few times and then Mrs. Ching calls out, "Come and eat." I grab my coffee and stand up. Mr. Ching gets up slowly like he's dizzy, and we go into the dining room.

Mrs. Ching smiles at me and says, "I hope you brought your appetite," and I nod, trying to smile back. She serves the scrambled eggs and white-bread toast, and then she sees Mr. Ching's face and her smile disappears. He takes the chair at the head of the table and hands her the travel diary. "Look what Daz found," he tells her. She looks puzzled and asks, "What is it?" She opens the book, reads for a few seconds and says, "Oh, my."

Mrs. Ching looks nervously at her husband and then turns to me. "Please eat while it's hot." She sits down and glances over at Mr. Ching again. I take a bite of egg. It's good, but I don't feel hungry.

"I hope you don't mind me asking," I say, "but where's your son now?"

Mrs. Ching's face turns to ashes and Mr. Ching's hardens into a frozen mask. He looks just like he did when he yelled at us for sneaking into his yard, and I wish I hadn't asked.

"He's dead," Mr. Ching says gruffly, and he takes a big bite of toast.

Mr. Ching noisily chews his dry toast and stares straight ahead and I feel like I just saw a car crash; my head is spinning and my chest feels heavy. I swallow hard and say, "I'm sorry. I didn't mean to bring up any bad memories. It's just that I never heard you mention him."

"It's okay," Old Man Ching says, but I know it's not okay.

Mrs. Ching gives me a quick look. "He was killed in Vietnam," she says. "Very early in the war."

I hate this situation because everything I say sounds so cripped. "I'm sorry, I didn't know," I tell them.

"How could you?" Mr. Ching says gruffly. "It was a long time ago."

Mrs. Ching forces herself to eat a bite of egg, and I feel real bad that they have to act like everything's fine. "Could I see some pictures of him?" I ask.

"What for?" Mr. Ching says real meanly, and sips his coffee like, forget it, end of subject.

"I don't see any harm in it," Mrs. Ching says cautiously, and looks at Old Man Ching with a worried expression.

He glances at me, not her. "It's a private matter," he tells me.

"Yeah, of course," I say, all embarrassed. Mrs. Ching starts to say something, but Mr. Ching's rockhard old face makes her think twice, and we all choke down a few mouthfuls of egg and cold toast.

Then this idea hits me, I don't know where it came from, and I see instantly that that's it's totally right. I clear my throat and say, "I've been thinking that you should take the Lancer back."

This spins Old Man Ching out and he looks up at me.

"It's still your car," I tell him.

He puts his fork down with an exasperated look and shakes his head. "You mean after all that trouble to get the car, you want me to take it back?" he yells. "Why on earth would I do that?"

"It still runs great," I tell him. "I think you guys should take a trip in it, just like you used to."

Mrs. Ching gives me a puzzled look and Mr. Ching squints at me like I just beamed down from Pluto. "Young man, I don't know where you get these notions." he says, but when he sips his coffee again his eyes are looking into the distance, and I know the wheels are turning inside his mind. Then he shakes his head again and says, "We don't need another car," he says. "You're the one who needs it."

"You can borrow it from me for a while," I say, and this torques him loose again.

"Now why in hell would I want to borrow your car?" he yells at me.

"To take a trip," I say.

He snorts and tells me, "First, you fight me for the car, and now you fight me to give it back. Do you just like fighting me?"

"No," I tell him real flatly, "I just think you'll have fun."

Old Man Ching mutters something irritably and goes back to his toast. I figure that's it, nice try, Daz, now leave the old bastard alone.

"Daz, I'll show you our photo albums after breakfast," Mrs. Ching says, and when Mr. Ching looks up all outraged she gives him a Mount Rushmore gaze, like don't waste your breath. So he doesn't. He takes his plate into the kitchen and goes back to his toolbox and his dead furnace.

After Mrs. Ching stacks the dishes in the sink she takes me into the living room and sits me down on the plaid sofa. Then she pulls several big leather-bound photo albums out of a cabinet and sits down next to me. She's close to me so I can smell her perfume, which is nice but faint, almost not there. She opens the book and the first page is of their wedding, and I am blown down to see that Mrs. Ching was totally lapis lazuli when she was young, skinny and cute with nice tits.

There's a black-and-white photo of her at a beach in one of those one-piece 1950s bathing suits. Her short hair is damp and her skin is gleaming with the water dripping off her, like she just stepped out of the surf. She's got this big, shy grin, like she knows she looks lapis and it embarrasses her. With the angle of the sun just right and her wet dacron swimsuit skintight against her little waist and nectar breasts, I can see her nipples are pointing up like new buds turning to face the sun.

She's right next to me, and I suddenly get this strange feeling that Mrs. Ching is still a woman, and that she still wants Mr. Ching to hump her, and maybe hump her long and hard.

A few pages later their son's birth certificate from the Santa Monica Hospital shows up, and then there's tons of photos of him as a kid, first in diapers, and pretty soon in a cowboy outfit, and then in front of the Matterhorn in Disneyland. Old Man Ching is hunched down in front of the furnace, mumbling every once in a while as his frustration builds up and vents, and Mrs. Ching occasionally points to a photo and fills in the blanks of who the adults are and where the photo was taken.

One page is pictures of the Grand Canyon, Mr. and Mrs. Ching and their son, who's about ten, looking seriously over the steel railing at the North Rim. "After the Grand Canyon, we went to Tucson," Mrs. Ching says, and I nod and say, "Uh-huh."

Mr. Ching turns to us and says all irritably, "Not Tucson. Santa Fe."

"The pictures are Tucson," she tells him, and he creakily stands up and comes over to the couch to spock the photos.

"I guess you're right," he says kind of reluctantly. "But we went to Santa Fe right after that."

After a few minutes of leaning over and looking at the album upside down, he sits down next to Mrs. Ching and puts in his own comments as she turns the pages and identifies this cousin and that auntie, and this vacation to Yellowstone and that drive to the redwoods.

Halfway into the third book I glance at them and see how totally immersed they are in these photographs. I figure they haven't looked at them together in years, and it's almost like Mr. Ching has forgotten that he's all busted up about his son and that he has to stay griffed forever.

I can see the son's entire life in these albums: a church choir, a shot of the track team, a skinny kid running real fast, ahead of the pack, a photo of him with his senior prom date, a cute Chinese girl in a frilly pink dress, a report card from his senior year, all A's except for one B, and him smiling in his crisp Army uniform, with polished black boots and his Special Forces beret.

When Mrs. Ching closes the last book, Old Man Ching looks up sort of disoriented, like he's caught off-guard by reality, and the broken furnace is less real than the photos of the past. Then his sour mask clicks back into place and he goes back to his toolbox and the stubborn pilot light. Mrs. Ching walks me out to the stairs and I tell her, "I mean it about the car. I think you guys would have fun." She says, "Thank you. And also for asking to see the pictures of my son." Without thinking about it I give her a hug and she puts her arms around my waist and squeezes me harder than I thought she could.

I let go of her, suddenly awkward about it all, and I say, "Let me know if you need any help around the shop. I don't have a job yet."

She says "Thank you, we'll keep it in mind," and I clump down the steps to the Lancer and drive home. I park in the driveway and spend the rest of the morning cleaning out all the junk and washing it, so it will be ready for the Chings if they ask for it.

I see Alex that afternoon, but we don't do much; we're both still ozoned from the trip and trying not to go loco-moco from being home again. He says he's looking for a job, but I can tell by his voice it's a pretty half-baked search at this point. That's why when Mrs. Ching calls me a few days later and says they got a couple of big jobs, could I come in and help, I ask her if there's enough work for Alex, too. She says she's sure there is, and I feel a spark of energy for the first time in days.

So we start working half-days for the Chings, and it's great because all we have to do is assemble orders, fold and staple brochures, easy, repetitive stuff, and Mr. Ching keeps his eye on our quality, but otherwise he lets us just do the work. Mrs. Ching brings us homemade coffeecake and feeds us lunch, which, of course, puts her right with Alex from the first day.

Old Man Ching can see that we're good workers, and he starts relaxing a little around us. One morning I'm standing by the high-speed copier while it pumps out a thick community college reader, making sure it doesn't jam and waiting to add some more paper, when Mr. Ching comes over and watches the copier for a while. Then he turns to me and says, over the whoosh-whoosh-whoosh of the copier, "So the car runs good, huh?"

This is so out-of-the-ozone that it takes me a few seconds to come up with an answer. "Yeah, real good," I say, figuring the bad timing adjustment that stranded us in Kansas City was probably our fault anyway. He nods and goes back to the big press, and I'm wondering why he asks me about the Lancer all of a sudden.

The next week he starts showing Alex how to set up the press. At first I'm bent that he's not showing me, but then I figure he wants Alex to show me later, rather than have both of us standing around with our thumbs up our butt while he explains it.

Old Man Ching usually lets you just do your work, but for some reason he starts watching me work more than usual. At first, I expect him to ream me out for some flaw, but he doesn't say anything about the job. He's either silent, which makes me nervous, or he'll blurt out a question about our trip like, "What did you think of New York?" So I tell him some of my impressions and he nods and goes back to the press.

Eventually, I catch on that he wants to tell me something, but he can't quite work it up to the surface. I consider asking him, but I know that's the wrong approach with Old Man Ching. He's stubborn and you have to let him get to whatever it is on his own speed.

Finally, after another week of coming around a few times a day and silently watching me work, making me gatta-gatta each time, he drifts over just before quitting time on Friday and watches me assemble a customer's sales packets. As usual I think, what, I'm not doing it neat enough, but also as usual he doesn't say anything. I finish the batch and am about to get another stack of brochures and cards when all of a sudden Mr. Ching says, "Daz, I need to ask you something."

He's nervous, like his usual gruff manner got beamed to another galaxy. I've never seen him so rhomboid, so I try to make it easy for him to spit it out. "Sure, Mr. Ching. What is it?"

He hesitates, and I wonder what's making him so futless. Finally, he gets torqued off that it's so damn hard to say, and then he can say it. "Mrs. Ching would like to take a drive in the old car."

I make damned sure that no hint of victory touches my expression and I answer, "Sure. When?"

Old Man Ching scratches his head, and it kind of reminds me of the way Morris would scratch behind his ear, and then he asks, "Think you boys can run the shop without us for a few days?"

My mind is clicking, clicking, I don't see these two wires connecting, and then I say, "Sure. So you'd like the car next week?"

He looks around the shop like he's hoping to escape, and I think, is this the same guy we were sure bayoneted guys in the war and made secret inventions in his shop out of junk?

He turns back to me and a small grin twitches over his lips. "Mrs. Ching would like to leave this afternoon."

This blows me flat, but I do a pretty good job of acting like this is all normal. "Yeah, sure," I tell him.

He looks relieved and says, in his usual gruff voice, "Any gas in the car?"

"It's full," I say.

He nods and tells me, "We'll drop you boys off at home."

"No, that's okay," I say. "We'll finish up here and just walk." He nods again and leaves the shop. As soon as he turns to go up to his apartment, I dash over to the press and repeat it all to Alex. He looks at me all seriously, but he can't figure out why this is so exciting. I can't explain so I run out to the alley and bring the Lancer around to the front. I make sure there's no soda cans or burger wrappers under the front seat, and then I go back in and start assembling packets again.

A few minutes later Mrs. Ching comes into the shop and I just stare at her. She's wearing a simple peach-colored dress and a pearl necklace, and she looks strat. She smiles at my expression and walks over to me. "Thank you for taking care of the shop," she says, and she squeezes my hand. Then she goes over to Alex and tells him the same thing. He shrugs it off, but I know he's happy to do it for them.

Old Man Ching comes in. He's wearing a suit jacket, carrying two old suitcases, and he looks embarrassed. He waits for Mrs. Ching at the door, and when she joins him, they walk out to the Lancer and he loads the suitcases in the trunk. He opens the door for Mrs. Ching, like he's on a date, and then he gets in and starts the engine. They sit there for a little while, getting used to it again, and then they drive off.

I go out to the sidewalk to watch them leave, and Alex comes out with me. They're waiting at the stoplight, and Alex looks at the Lancer with the same concentration he has when he's eating. The light changes and Old Man Ching heads down the street toward the I-State on-ramp.

Alex watches the car for a few more seconds and then he looks over at me. He has a sly smile on his face, and he punches my shoulder with a soft straight jab. Even though it hurts, I'm happy because he understands.

# AFTERWORD

Given that the meanings of a novel are necessarily a pact between author and reader, it is always hazardous for an author to comment on his own work. Despite these misgivings, I sketch the themes of this "small" story in the hopes of enriching the reader's enjoyment.

Perhaps the most profound historical change taking place in the United States is the intermingling of races. By this I mean not the integration of various ethnicities within communities but the mixing of bloodlines within individuals. In Hawaii, people of mixed heritage are often called "hapas," which means "half" in Hawaiian. Over the course of a very few generations, ethnicities have become so melded that many in Hawaii possess four, five, or even six different lineages. My own family has mixed Anglo, Asian, and African-American bloodlines in a single generation.

This book stems from a belief that the single greatest strength of our nation is the independence of American identity from any racial, religious, or ideological profile. The immigrant experience, so integral to the nation's history and identity, has long been a well of inspiration to writers; the frictions between the first generation and its fantasies of returning to the the Old Country, and their children, to whom the Old Country will forever be alien, resonate with each new wave of Americans.

This is a story not of immigrants coming to a new American identity, but of two mixed-blood Americans forging their identity within a New America of blended ethnicities.

A nuanced but debilitating trap awaits those of multiple bloodlines. Traditional ethnic groups feel compelled to maintain triplines of identity, and failure to meet these standards introduces an "either-or" dilemma: since you are not quite one of "us," you have forfeited your "authentic" heritage for a false one. Alex vociferously rejects his cousin's attempt to judge his state of grace,

259

for in simply being himself he is Hawaiian; there is no Otherness in being Hawaiian which requires approval by others.

While circumstances may make Daz aware of his skin, his identity is entirely a question of exploring the boundaries of his unconventionality. If, along with Wittgenstein, we see language and thought as one, then it is clear that Daz thinks along entirely unique pathways; as a result he will never fit anyone's conception of identity. Like Alex, his identity is always that of an individual, never of a group; it is this unflagging independence of spirit which binds the two despite their very different characters.

Being neither here nor there within the various ethnic triplines, the two are bound by the liberty and burden of not fitting in—not just ethnically, but in the broader reaches of conventionality.

The refuge of tradition offers a deep, enduring comfort to humanity; follow these rules, and the peace of a ready-made identity is yours for the taking. All human societies provide expansive refuges of tradition, but America also proffers up a more unique refuge: freedom from tradition.

This alternative refuge is rooted in our nation's history of religious freedom and the barricade between church and state which protects that freedom; but it is also rooted in the country's vast geography. The other national bastions of personal freedom can be crossed in a day's drive; the diversity of their landscapes and societies is, in comparison with the United States, rather poor.

The American landscape—an unspoken but omnipresent protagonist in any story of continental wandering—offers a place to leave histories behind and, somewhere, to start fresh; its open skies provide space to ask the big questions and elbow room for unlimited possibility. While other cultures are shackled to the past, we are all young in America; breaking free of the demands for conformity requires little more than a tank of gas or a bus ticket to some place a hundred zip codes away, where the one element you are sure to find is surprise—at what you come across in the landscape and in yourself.

Great journeys are inevitably stories of transformation or discovery—of territory or self, or perhaps both. The cliché is that there are only two stories: a stranger comes to town or a journey is undertaken. Daz and Alex are both strangers who come to town

260

and seekers. Their aim is not the recovery of riches or vine-choked exotica, nor is it the stretching of license in some exploration of excess. With nowhere else to go at home, their response is quintessentially American: get moving.

This movement is not metaphorical; responsibilities and even entire identities can be abandoned, re-invented, or discovered in another place. In this sense the American love of cars is entirely practical, for the ability to transport oneself is integral to American optimism.

Physical labor has fallen into disfavor in what passes for popular culture in the United States. The most coveted careers require clean fingernails, multiple gadgets, an office cleaned after hours by persons unseen and unknown, and the cutting of a wide swath through either entrepreneurial derring-do or media exposure. Although Daz suffers bouts of doubt over his inability to pursue this hectic blandness with the expected gusto, both he and Alex are naturally drawn to the authenticities of handwork.

Like the Odd Squad, they are unable to squeeze themselves into a world of cubicles and staff meetings. The world of tools and dirt offers a satisfaction which is inexplicable to those content to stare at glowing screens all day, and it is the last and best refuge for all who rebel at chains of authority and fluorescent-lit interiors.

You would be justified in suspecting an authorial prejudice here, but it is less than you might expect of someone who pursued a degree in philosophy and a career in carpentry with equal enthusiasm. One well-tilled element of the American character is self-reliance; we are a nation of do-it-yourselfers and tinkerers, and there is yet a latent respect for those who actually make as opposed to those who create pointers to that made or nurtured by others. Thus we find Daz as enthralled with Nikki's cooking—from scratch, with real ingredients—as he is with her paintings.

I have found that many of the people pursuing tradecraft for their livelihood are as intellectually gifted as any in corner offices; but they, like Morris and the Odd Squad, have no heart for more regimented work, regardless of its higher pay or status.

The inauthenticity of a status-driven skin fuels Daz's spontaneous rancor, as it should; for as the cliché has it, if you are not a socialist at twenty, you have no heart, but if you are still a socialist at thirty, you have no brains. But beyond this cliché of youthful idealism lies Emerson's understanding of American identity: there is no authenticity but that which resides within oneself. The process of teasing out an understanding of oneself is inexact, and there is no substitute for trying things on for size, be they jeans or jobs or even roles in a play.

Young men are by nature drawn to testing themselves through the rigors of danger. The selective underpinnings of this drive are obvious; the timid have been left to die at the evaporating watering holes for too many millennia for those genes to dominate the ones encoding adventure and daring. Although it is not popular to acknowledge that the highest pinnacle of danger is combat, this accounts for Alex's fascination with the Vietnam veterans' stories. It is only when Alex is viscerally confronted with the terrible physical legacy of combat that he gains a realistic appreciation for its cost.

Military service has long been the highest proof of citizenship; like the young Japanese-American men who formed Hawaii's 442nd Combat Team in World War II and made it the most decorated unit of the war, the Chings' son served the nation most dutifully. This sacrifice haunts the father in ways Daz and Alex cannot yet understand, for the death of the son is not just a crushing loss of an only child but the extinguishing of a family lineage—and thus of the future itself.

The battle to break Mr. Ching's grip on the mothballed Lancer, and the subsequent return of the car at the story's end, is a measure of Mr. Ching's burden and Daz's growth; in the end, the life force of his matured optimism shakes the foundations of the older man's bitterness. This is the most personal promise of America: there is always a future and a hope, no matter how painful the sacrifices of the past.

A simple line divides child from adult; the latter gives in full measure while the former thoughtlessly receives. Maturity can be defined as a generosity of spirit unknown to the self-absorbed. What Daz and Alex offer up to the Chings at journey's end is beyond easy distillation; but it is certainly tenderness, kindness, curiosity, and the rare exhilaration of an unexpected gift.

Of the conditions for happiness, Freud identified but two: work and love. He would have been wise to add friendship, that most mysterious kinship of opposites and likenesses. For this is also a story of friendship, of being on your own and relying on another, of the truths and tolerances of a journey's confined intimacy, of shared adventures experienced in unique ways, and of that ineffable essential, trust.